i

The Captive Within

What does it take
to free the soul
of a defiled woman?

A Prairie Heritage, Book 4

VIKKI KESTELL

*Faith-Filled
Fiction*™

www.faith-filledfiction.com | www.vikkikestell.com

A Prairie Heritage, Book 4
©2013 Vikki Kestell
All Rights Reserved
Also Available in eBook Format

BOOKS BY VIKKI KESTELL

A PRAIRIE HERITAGE
  Book 1: *A Rose Blooms Twice*, **free eBook, most online retailers**
  Book 3: *Joy on This Mountain*
  Book 4: *The Captive Within*
  Book 5: *Stolen*
  Book 6: *Lost Are Found*
  Book 7: *All God's Promises*

GIRLS FROM THE MOUNTAIN
  Book 1: *Tabitha*

NANOSTEALTH
  Book 1: *Stealthy Steps*
  Book 2: *Stealth Power*, **fall 2016**

A Prairie Heritage, Book 4
by Vikki Kestell
Also Available in eBook Format from Most Online Retailers

The Captive Within opens the day after Joy on This Mountain ends. The two infamous houses of Corinth, Colorado, are closed and the young women who had been imprisoned there have been released. Soon after, Rose and Joy leave Corinth to establish a home and a haven for "their" girls in Denver.

Before long, Rose and Joy face a heartrending challenge: What does it take to unlock and free the soul of a defiled woman? And as they wrestle for a foothold in Denver, Rose discovers that the long abandoned house given to them hides a dark secret of its own.

COVER DESIGN
Vikki Kestell

Cover background photo courtesy of
Lenny DiBrango.
http://www.flickr.com/photos/7185088@N07/

PRONUNCIATION GUIDE

Bao Shin Xang	Ba´-oh Shin Jang
Fang Hua	Fahng Hwah
Jan	Yahn
Jinhai	Gin-high
Mei-Xing Li	May´-Jing Lee
Søren	Soor´-ren
Thoresen	Tor´-eh-sen
Wei Lin	Way Lin
Yaochuan Min Liáng	Yow´-chew-ahn Min Lee-ang

DEDICATION

Dedicated to my husband, Conrad Smith.
You give me courage.

ACKNOWLEDGEMENTS

Many thanks to my esteemed proofreaders,
Cheryl Adkins and **Greg McCann**.
I could not do this without you!
The Lord reward and bless you.

TO MY READERS

This book is a work of fiction,
what I term "Faith-Filled Fiction™,"
intended to demonstrate how
people of God should and can respond
to difficult and dangerous situations
with courage and conviction.
The characters and events that appear in this book
are not based on any known persons or historical facts;
the challenges described are, however,
very real, both historically and contemporarily.
I give God all the glory.

CHAPTER 1

*Come unto me, all ye that labour
and are heavy laden, and I will give you rest.
Take my yoke upon you, and learn of me;
for I am meek and lowly in heart:
and ye shall find rest unto your souls.
(Matthew 11:28, 29)*

April 24, 1909

Edmund O'Dell, Pinkerton agent, squinted in the early light as he studied the remains of Corinth Mountain Lodge. At his feet embers steamed under the morning sun. He gingerly toed what might have been a silver tea tray, now a twisted and blackened lump.

His brow furrowed. He'd seen a tea service on the lodge's ornate side board, hadn't he? The sideboard itself had been massive, constructed from solid wood, intricately carved, oiled, and polished to a fare-thee-well.

No doubt it had burned splendidly, he snarled to himself. He whipped off his bowler and ran a hand through his dark hair, stopping to rub at the dull headache throbbing at the back of his neck.

He'd been a "guest" at the lodge a little more than four months. Yes, he had been working an active case, but in that short time he had begun to feel . . . at home. More at home than anywhere he'd laid his head since he'd left childhood behind. At one point he'd allowed himself to wonder, to almost hope that somehow, someway, he might have a future connected with—

He pulled himself up short, stopped himself from following that thought further. It could only lead to a dark hole, one with no bottom.

It was clear to him now that he had deceived himself. He had allowed himself to forget his real role in Corinth. And what he had witnessed in the first light of this new day had stamped "paid" to the dream and jerked him back to harsh reality.

He rubbed his weary, smoke-stung eyes. Like the others who had lived at the lodge, O'Dell had been up most of the night. He clenched an unlit cigar between his teeth as he again relived the events of a few hours past.

The lodge's residents had awakened when Banner's men had thrown their fiery brands through the lodge's front windows to force them out. Once the household members had safely escaped the burning building, they had been backed up against its blazing timbers, outnumbered and outgunned.

Banner's gang had nearly won last night. Sheriff Wyndom and his deputies had arrived scarcely in time to stop what would have been sure disaster.

Worse than disaster. A slaughter, O'Dell mused with a grimace.

Wyndom had marched both the gang and the lodge's residents through the dark to Corinth's little town plaza. A crowd of disquieted town residents, wakened by bells tolling news of the fire, had gathered there.

O'Dell mentally replayed the confrontation in the plaza: Joy Thoresen—no, Joy *Michaels*—had delivered a stunning indictment against Dean Morgan, Banner's boss and the figurehead who owned the two houses of unspeakable evil in little Corinth.

O'Dell had watched and listened, mouth open, as spellbound as the crowd had been. Joy had been magnificent; even, perhaps, *inspired*.

By torchlight, the impact of the butt of Banner's shotgun stamped on her face, her long, blonde hair tumbling down around her shoulders, Joy Michaels had bested Morgan. She had publicly laid bare his secrets and plots. And, doing so, she had turned the people of Corinth against him.

O'Dell shuddered and turned to let the sunlight warm his face. Things had been dicey for a few minutes after that. Morgan's thugs had overcome Wyndom and his men and had nearly taken Joy by force. But then federal marshals and O'Dell's fellow Pinkerton agents had stormed the plaza, surrounding Morgan and his men.

In a desperate move, Morgan and his bodyguard had used Joy's mother, Rose, as a shield for their escape—and had almost succeeded. Almost. The men were safely in custody now, headed down the mountain on a train that would take them to the county jail.

When Morgan's bodyguard, Su-Chong, had released Rose, O'Dell had seen Joy sag and nearly collapse. She had taken a beating that night. He had seen her pain and exhaustion and had wanted to go to her, but her cousins and friends had come to her aid first.

So he had backed away and done his duty, assisting in the identification of those being arrested and the charges to be laid against them.

O'Dell slapped his derby against his thigh. He could still see her, could not get the image to leave his mind. Her hair had hung about her slender shoulders like a cloud filled with moonlight.

After he had finished with the marshals, he had returned to the plaza, hoping to speak to her. O'Dell shook his head and ground his teeth. He didn't want to remember what he had witnessed then, but he was powerless *not* to.

Night was slowly giving way as morning crept over the mountains. Out of the waning shadows had stepped a man, a man O'Dell knew well, an honorable man he considered a friend. *A man he had promised he would help.*

As the shadowed figure approached Joy and her cousin Arnie, O'Dell had seen the hesitant, unbelieving recognition. He'd witnessed the sweet, gentle touching and tearful embraces of a husband and wife reunited.

He shuddered. So then it was over. For him, in any case.

It wouldn't have worked anyway, he told himself, and not for the first time. He swore aloud in frustration. He and Joy were far too different, she with her living, breathing faith and he set in his cynical, pragmatic ways.

And yet it hadn't seemed to matter that they were so very different. His heart had just kept hoping.

Yer a fool, O'Dell, he charged himself. He seethed with self-recrimination.

He released a laugh, harsh and discordant, and crushed the stogie between his teeth. He needed to get out of Corinth and away from the people here. Quickly.

Get out? It won't be hard and shouldn't take long, he fumed. *It's not as though I have bags to pack.*

In fact, he had nothing left in this place but the clothes on his back. Everything he'd had—hopes and dreams included—swirled around him in the ashes and smoke.

I only need a little cash to get down the mountain to the Denver Pinkerton office and a nearby bank, he planned. Groman, head of the Omaha Pinkerton office, was still in Corinth helping with the investigation. *Groman will stake me for my train fare.*

Yes. He needed to be on the next train, away from Corinth. He had his investigations to complete and young women to, hopefully, locate and reunite with their families.

His next step would be to question Gretl Plüff, one of those missing girls. She had been found in one of Corinth's two "elite" houses of ill-repute. With her help he hoped to track down a few more of the girls whose disappearances had brought him to Colorado in the first place.

If Morgan's crew had sold the missing girls to other brothels, they were likely in nearby Denver. He would find them, wind up the investigations as quickly possible, and leave Denver to return to his Chicago home office. He couldn't be done here in Colorado fast enough.

O'Dell spit pieces of tobacco. He had ground through the cigar until it had fallen apart in his mouth. Throwing the remaining stub down and grinding it with his boot, O'Dell turned his back on the cooling embers of the lodge.

He turned resolutely from a hope that could never be realized.

———

Joy slept fitfully through the day and into the late afternoon, when her aching bruises and cracked ribs finally overcame her exhaustion. It took her a few moments to remember that she was in David and Uli's home, tucked into their daughter Ruth's bed.

Something stirred and wriggled near her feet. As she lifted her head—cautiously, given the throbbing of her face and chest—the wriggling bundle licked the fingers of her hand.

"Blackie!" she exclaimed softly. The half-grown black-and-white puppy scrambled up and over her body in a frenzy to wash her face with his tongue. Before Joy could feel his full weight on her bruised chest, the pup was deftly scooped up and off the bed.

Looking up, Joy saw Blackie held by . . . her husband.

Still unbelieving, she stared at him, taking slow inventory . . . his brown hair, prematurely shot with silver, but curling about his face as she'd remembered; the roughened, scarred patch on one cheek; the many unfamiliar lines about his mouth.

And his hazel eyes . . . She would know those eyes anywhere!

"I know I must look different than you remember me," he said hesitantly. He offered a tentative half smile.

His voice was also rough and damaged, but Joy could still tell it was Grant. She longed for him to come nearer and lifted her hand to him. Grant gently deposited Blackie on the floor, pulled his chair close to the bed, and touched her outstretched fingers. All this he did with his left hand. His right arm hung motionless at his side.

"You look just as I saw you in my dreams, again and again," he whispered, gazing hungrily at her blue eyes and the shimmer of blonde hair spread across her pillow. "Even though I couldn't remember your name," here he looked down, shamefaced, "or even how I knew you."

Tears sprang to Joy's eyes. "It *is* you," she breathed. She closed her fingers around his and drew him to her. Nothing mattered at that moment but to feel his breath on her face, his lips upon hers.

Gently, tenderly, their faces drew closer until their lips touched. Joy sighed and wrapped her arms about his neck, pulling him closer.

A few minutes later a discreet knock sounded on the door and they drew apart. Uli, Joy's cousin, peeked in. "Are you awake then? I thought I heard you talking." She smiled and, staring at Grant, shook her head in happy amazement. "We still can't—it's entirely *too* wonderful."

Grant ducked his head, that half smile still curving his lips. "I'm sorry I don't remember you yet."

"It's all right, Grant," Uli told him sincerely. "Things will come right eventually. We are just so glad to see you."

Joy had not relinquished his hand. "Will you help me to sit up?" she asked him.

He bent over the bed and slid his left arm behind her. "You may take my other arm and hold on to it," he instructed. "It won't hurt me." He nodded at his right arm.

Joy did as he suggested, and he gently lifted her up. The arm she grasped felt thin, slack. Uli helped Grant turn Joy until she was sitting on the bed's edge gasping a little in pain. Uli knelt down and placed slippers on Joy's bare feet. Together, Grant and Uli helped Joy into the chair Grant had been using.

"I will bring you some broth, Joy," Uli stated. She smiled again and slipped out of the room.

Joy's eyes never left Grant's face, but her expression had become solemn. "How did it happen? Do you know? Do you remember?"

He knew what she meant and hesitated before pulling the covers up on the bed and taking a seat on its edge. Their knees touching, he replied. "I don't remember, but the kind men who pulled me from the water told me my arm was tangled in a line wrapped about a life preserver. The type of preserver that they tell me is usually lashed to the rails of a ship."

He gestured with his chin toward his motionless arm. "A doctor told me that the rope cut into my arm and kept blood from the nerves too long. I can't move it anymore."

He looked at the floor. "I'm sorry."

Joy was quiet for a moment, thinking through what he had told her. "So the rope was twined around the life preserver and your arm was twined within the rope. And when the ship went down and took you with it . . . the preserver pulled you back to the surface." She spoke it as a statement, searching his face.

"Yes, I suppose that's right," Grant replied, still staring at the floor.

"So the very thing that took the strength from your arm also saved your life, allowing you to come back to me?"

His head jerked up; his eyes found hers.

"Oh Grant," she said, emotion clogging her voice. "Without that rope and that life preserver, we would not, at this moment, be looking at each other. This was God's great grace and mercy to you, to *us*. Please don't be sorry. Not ever again."

She held out both her arms and he leaned into her, nestling his face in the warm crook of her neck, both of them weeping tears of gratitude.

CHAPTER 2

Rose Thoresen, her nephew Arnie Thoresen, and Pastor David Kalbørg arrived at the Kalbørg parsonage shortly before dinner. Arnie insisted that Rose step away and rest; he was concerned about how worn she was looking.

Of course he had not noticed until Breona had pulled him aside—pulled him aside and chided him soundly—insisting he take Rose away before she collapsed. Indeed, none of them had slept the larger part of the night, and the day's affairs had been difficult, both physically and emotionally.

After the marshals had rounded up Morgan, Banner, and their gang, Sheriff Wyndom had pointed the marshals to the "houses"— Corinth's fashionable and expensive bordellos. Within their walls horrible acts of perversion and sadism were said to take place. Many of the working girls were young, involuntary participants, kidnapped and forced into prostitution through rape, repeated beatings, and starvation.

The marshals had entered the larger, more exclusive of the two houses, the "Corinth Gentlemen's Club," with David, Arnie, Rose, Breona, and Mei-Xing on their heels. They had accompanied the marshals as they searched the first floor and then up the stairs to the second floor. There they witnessed them search the bedrooms, taking two guards and the club's madam, Roxanne Cleary, into custody.

Miss Cleary had apparently retired only a few hours before. Rousted from her bed, disheveled and disoriented, she was clearly unprepared for the humiliation of her arrest. Mei-Xing had softly but clearly identified her to Pounder, the head marshal. At Roxanne's indignant shrieks, Mei-Xing had cringed and retreated hastily behind the wide, sheltering back of Arnie Thoresen.

Rose was saddened by Roxanne's distress, but she could spare no compassion for her at present. All her concern was for the girls of the club, girls like fifteen-year-old Mei-Xing, who had been kidnapped and bound over to a life of depravity. Roxanne would have to answer for her role in their degradation.

With a few whispered directions from Mei-Xing, Rose continued up the stairs to the next floor. Breona kept close to Rose, her eyes wide at the over-blown luxury of the house and its furnishings.

The women of the club, exhausted from their night's labor but awakened by the noisy entrance of the marshals, were beginning to mill about the hallways of the third floor. They were nervous and confused, until Rose spoke to them with Mei-Xing near her side.

"My name is Rose Thoresen." Rose spoke calmly and gently. "I'm sorry to have awakened you so abruptly, but we have some important news for you." She took a deep breath and prayed for inspiration.

Just then, from down the stairs, the sounds of a scuffle reached them. All of them could clearly hear Roxanne's shrieking curses as her distress gave way to rage and resistance. The women in the hallway became more agitated, one sobbing noisily. Rose looked around as two more women—girls, really—peeped from doorways along the hall.

Rose raised her voice a little more to be heard over the commotion. "As I said, we have some important news for you. Good news! But why don't we do this? Why don't you ladies take a moment to dress? Please join me downstairs in the, er, parlor, as soon as you are able."

The women stared at Rose and began to whisper among themselves. One of them pointed at Mei-Xing.

"Yes, it is I, Mei-Xing," the tiny Chinese girl with almond-shaped eyes said softly. "*Little Plum Blossom*. Please dress and come downstairs. We have something . . . wonderful to tell you."

Rose asked the women, "Ten minutes?"

A tall brunette spoke to the other women. "Let's go, girls. Dress quickly so we can hear what she has to say."

By the time the women had assembled downstairs, the marshals had gone, taking the house guards and Roxanne Cleary with them. The marshals were going directly from the club to the second house, a somewhat less discriminating, less exotic, but still quite "exclusive" brothel, to arrest the guards they found there. Arnie and David accompanied them, promising to ask the women they found there to dress and come to the club and meet with Rose.

When Rose stood to address her audience, perhaps fifteen sets of eyes stared back at her silently, some with anxiety, some with guarded hostility. What they saw was a slight, older woman with ash blonde hair lightly streaked with gray. Her face held a sweetly composed mouth and two steady, gray eyes.

14

As Rose looked back at them, she found it difficult, in her mind, to call the girls *women*. They were all so young! She had to remind herself that, while these girls were young in years, what they had endured had to have aged them years beyond counting. The women assembled in the great room of the house finally quieted and waited for Rose to speak.

Dear Lord, please help me. Help me to say just the right thing to speak hope into their hearts, Rose prayed silently.

"Ladies, in case you did not hear me introduce myself, my name is Rose Thoresen. Some of you already know Miss Li." Rose opened her hand gracefully in Mei-Xing's direction. Mei-Xing acknowledged the introduction self-consciously but then sat up straighter and frankly met the questioning eyes from around the room.

"I would also like you to meet our dear friend, Miss Byrne," Rose nodded at Breona who stood against the wall, her arms tightly crossed, warily observing from outside the circle of chairs.

Rose continued. "My daughter, Joy Thoresen Michaels, owns Corinth Mountain Lodge, near the train siding on the edge of town." Several heads nodded and eyes turned again toward Mei-Xing. Apparently they knew of the lodge, had heard rumors concerning Mei-Xing's escape and disappearance.

"Yes. Mei-Xing came to us when she escaped several months ago now. We have kept her hidden in the lodge all this time." Rose took a deep breath. "Last night, Mr. Banner and his men burned the lodge."

Gasps sounded around the room and fearful eyes darted toward the doors. Rose raised her hands in what she hoped was a reassuring gesture. "We are grateful to the Lord that no one was hurt in the fire. All of us escaped from the lodge without injury."

The eyes in the room fixed on Rose again. "But we told you that we had good news." Rose tried to smile, but she couldn't. The moment was too charged, her news too momentous.

Through trembling lips she said, "What we would like you to know is that, just over two hours ago, federal marshals took Mr. Banner and all his men—Darrow, too—into custody."

She looked around, making eye contact with each woman. "They have also removed Miss Cleary and the guards from this house. Most important, they have arrested Mr. Morgan, the owner of this house and its neighbor just to our east." She nodded in the general direction of the second brothel.

In the silence of the room, Rose drew another deep breath. "We came here to tell you that you are—*all of you*—free."

The eyes staring at Rose blinked, and she could see the uncertainty, the questions, as her words sank in. The tall, dark-haired woman who had spoken upstairs, voice shaking now, asked, "Do you mean we can leave? No one will stop us? No one will come after us and chase us down?"

Rose nodded. She did not trust herself to speak and had to bite her bottom lip. Around the room, the silence was only interrupted by sniffling and then sobs as each woman opened her heart to the possibilities before her.

By noon Rose had informally met with each of the nine women from the club, including little Gretl Plüff, the club's cook, while Breona and Mei-Xing were arranging individual meetings in the afternoon with the girls of the second house.

The questions she heard again and again were, "Are you sure they are in jail? Are we really safe?" and, the more difficult question, "What will we do now?"

Arnie and David Kalbørg returned to the house and stayed close by, reassuring the women that they had witnessed the marshals take away Morgan, Roxanne, Banner, and all his men in handcuffs, loading them on the train to Denver.

Repeatedly Rose reassured every girl that she was safe. Individually and in knots of two or three Rose explained that each of them was free to go home, if she had a home, or free to go wherever she liked. They would help them travel to where they decided to go.

She saw the indecision and fear writ plainly on each face. *Could they go home? Was there a place for them back home after . . . this?*

Of course, some of them admitted they had no homes to return to. That was when Rose began to talk about the lodge and the vision that had inspired Joy to buy it, a vision of helping young women—in the same situation they found themselves—to learn honest skills to support themselves.

"But you said the lodge burnt down last night," a plump girl of about sixteen years reminded Rose.

"Yes," Rose responded, still dazed by the certainty of her words. "Banner and his men burned it. It is gone, but we were already making plans to buy a house in Denver and begin our work in earnest. Denver, being a large city, has more opportunities for good employment." A few more of the young women gathered near as Rose explained.

It was nearly four-thirty in the afternoon, and Rose's voice was failing her. That was when Breona had insisted Arnie take Rose away to eat and rest.

Mei-Xing and Breona looked at each other then. Breona squared her shoulders and called to the women still milling in the great room. "Aye, so 'tis bein' up t' us now t' be makin' some plans for th' evenin', I'm thinkin'."

The women looked to her, clearly accustomed to being told what to do. Curbing her natural tendency to take charge, Breona put forward a few suggestions about dinner and sleeping arrangements for herself and Mei-Xing. Soon the girls were offering suggestions and, by consensus, making some simple decisions.

"Well, I am going bake pies." Gretl announced abruptly and overly loud. "*Lots* of pies!" she added defiantly.

All eyes turned to her and she blushed. "Miss Cleary never let us eat pie," she explained, breathing hard. "Nor cakes nor tarts nor cookies! I had to make every sort of tempting treat for the *club members*," she sneered those words, "but *we* were never allowed to eat them ourselves!"

Suddenly all the girls were clamoring for desserts, excited at the prospect of exercising their freedom.

Breona grinned, her black eyes snapping in delight. "Miss Gretl, I be fancyin' a fat slice o' cherry pie, me sel'!"

She put her hands on her hips. "Let us be bakin' pies!"

$\mathcal{C}$HAPTER 3

(Journal Entry, April 25, 1909)

Dear Lord, as I arose this morning I felt led to chronicle this new endeavor upon which we have embarked. I confess though, that as this new day begins, I also need to pour out my heart to you.

We have been so pressed in the past 48 hours. It was not until this morning I realized what I had lost in the fire: The only likenesses of Jan I possessed and the few photographs I owned of Joy as a baby and as she grew up. All of them burned in the lodge with everything else. Oh, Lord! Grief, heavy as a great rock, struck my heart at this realization.

So I pick up pen and ink and pour my sorrow onto this page. Father, please help me to bear the loss. I recall with gratitude that Søren and Meg still have a few photographs of Jan and one in particular of Søren and Joy together when she was a toddler. Thank you, Lord, for reminding me. I will ask them to have reproductions made for me, no matter how costly.

I must also acknowledge a great truth, if only to you. I acknowledge that had I been given a choice between keeping my precious mementoes or gaining the freedom of these even more valuable treasures—I speak of these young women, Lord!—I must have chosen these women.

For on those whom you have poured your Son's lifeblood, you have also placed the most value. Can any earthly treasures be worth more? No, Lord, they cannot.

So I commit today, Lord, to honor these young women with the care I would have given my precious photographs. Strengthen me to care with all my heart, I pray, Lord God!

—

Edmund O'Dell had spent an uncomfortable night in a run-down Corinth hostel. It was the only place in town to board, now that the lodge was gone. The mattress had been lumpy, the pillow thin and threadbare, the bedbugs plenty. He rubbed his neck where the muscles were knotted still.

As much as he'd wanted to leave by yesterday's afternoon train, his plans had been thwarted. First, Groman, his superior at the moment, had insisted that he remain in Corinth the entire day.

"We may need your direction in this case, and I don't want to have to track you down. Besides, Gretl Plüff, having been in Corinth the longest, is our best lead to other kidnapped girls who may have been here. If they were moved elsewhere, I want you to find them."

But Gretl Plüff had put him off, quite firmly, telling him that she was "otherwise engaged" for the day "so's I can hear all what Miss Rose has to say and be cooking good hot meals for the girls," she'd said, adding, "I'm plannin' to go with her and Miss Joy soon as they buys a house down mountain in Denver City. You and I can talk tomorrow."

She had shut the door in his face, and with the sound of the latch his plan to leave later in the day was soundly scotched!

Mrs. Thoresen and her daughter have the knack of engendering that kind of loyalty, O'Dell reflected with a snarl and tried again to un-kink his neck. *Just look what it did to me!*

He frowned and pounded on the front door of the house. He'd dallied about until he felt he could call on the girl the next day. It was now half-past seven in the morning, and he was determined to be on the morning train.

He was mildly nonplussed when Breona opened the door for him. "Good morn, Mr. O'Dell, sir!" She was in good spirits and pleased to see him.

"Fancy meeting you here, Miss Byrne," he grinned, glad in spite of his sour mood to see her looking rosy and well. "I've come to interview Gretl Plüff. Is she about?"

Breona answered with a sardonic snort. "'Tis still abed these girls air, Mr. O'Dell, sir. 'Twas loik t' herdin' cats las' eve'n t' be gettin' 'em t' bed! Why, they's days 'n' nights be so mixed, come bedtime, you'd hev thought th' cock be a-crowin'! Could hardly catch a wink, what with th' goin's on mos' th' night!"

She leaned toward him conspiratorially. "Miss Rose is sayin' we'll be gettin' th'm up a wee bit earlier each day an' t' bed a wee bit earlier each night, s' as t' put th'm right again!"

O'Dell frowned. "When do you think Miss Plüff will be up?"

Breona shrugged. "Sure an' Miss Rose is jist arrived. Would ye come t' th' kitchen an' be havin' a cup? An' a great slice o' pie, too, if'n ye hev an appetite!"

O'Dell didn't want to go to the kitchen to "be havin' a cup" or a slice of pie! It meant seeing some of the people he had purposed to be quickly shut of. He shuffled his feet in indecision but found himself being pulled into the house and down a long hall to where he presumed the kitchen would be found.

He sighed and drew out his watch along the way. He would miss his train—again.

Sure enough, Rose and Mei-Xing were seated at a kitchen table talking quietly, their hands wrapped about cups of coffee.

"Mr. O'Dell!" Rose's happy greeting pricked him. He had hoped to slip away without goodbyes. Her pleasure at seeing him only made him feel even more of a cad.

"Good morning, Mrs. Thoresen, Miss Li," he replied stiffly. Breona had already placed a filled cup at the table for him, so he reluctantly seated himself.

"We were just talking over the wonder of the past two days," Rose explained. "Who would have thought that in one night, so much could have changed? Not just the arrest of Darrow and his men, but the return of my son-in-law, Grant Michaels!"

Why, she is positively gushing, O'Dell observed with a sneer. Then she reached across the table and clasped his hand earnestly.

"We have *you* to thank for Grant's return, Mr. O'Dell." Her eyes were brimming with tears. "He told us how hard you have been looking for most of the past year, trying to find where he belonged. We are more grateful than we can possibly express."

O'Dell looked away in embarrassment and caught Mei-Xing watching him. Her wide, almond-shaped eyes were soft and compassionate.

She knows, O'Dell thought, and swore under his breath. *Of course she does. They probably all do.*

He sat back abruptly and assumed a more formal tone. "I would like to see Gretl Plüff as soon as possible. Would you kindly rouse her?"

"I, well yes, I suppose I can," Rose replied softly. She withdrew her hand. "Let me see what I can do. Mei-Xing, would you please help me? We should try to rouse all the girls. It will be a difficult transition, but we should begin today."

O'Dell finished his interview with Gretl and scanned the single name she had recognized. She knew of only one of the missing women he had tracked to Colorado.

It is better than none, he admitted. She had, in addition, been able to suggest a house in Denver where she may have been taken.

"Darrow and his men always talk big an' loud," she explained. "We girls listen good an' try t' warn each other when something bad is afoot."

"Are you certain you don't want to go home? Your aunt and uncle have been looking for you for nearly two years." He had been surprised when she had flatly turned down his offer of a train ticket.

Gretl, a plump, soft girl, pleasant but perhaps not overly bright, looked away for a long moment. "No sir, don't b'lieve I do. See, bein' a whore changes you. I'm not like how they 'member me."

She gave O'Dell a penetrating look. "I'll write 'em a nice letter, sir, but I b'lieve I'll stay with Miss Rose and Miss Joy. They understand how it is. And I'm a good cook, y' see. Miss Rose tells me that after a bit I can get a good job somewheres an' take care of m'self. That's probably better."

O'Dell saw the reality of Gretl's choice in her honest eyes. She was, perhaps, brighter than he gave her credit for.

At last O'Dell had completed his tasks in Corinth. "All right. Head down to Denver," Groman ordered. "Take two of my men. I trust 'em. I know they aren't part of Beau Bickle's corrupt bunch. We don't want to take any chances that they would find out you're coming."

"What about the law?" O'Dell asked.

"You can find Marshal Pounder at this address." Groman scribbled on a scrap of paper. "I 'spect he'll go along with you or send a few of his men. Hates these whorehouses and what they do to young women, he does."

He pointed his finger at O'Dell. "You find that girl, O'Dell and wrap up these disappearances, and I'm guessing you can write your own ticket. Maybe McParland will even set you up to run the Denver office. God knows he needs someone honest to clean out that den o' thieves.

Not a chance, O'Dell thought wryly, but he nodded and kept that thought to himself.

He had an hour to kill before the afternoon train, and found himself back where he'd been yesterday morning. He stared for several moments at the now-cold ashes of the lodge. Then he turned and sauntered down the winding trail to the overlook.

So much had happened in the past 48 hours, so much gone forever. But the mountains, unchanging, full of inviolate splendor, beckoned to him. He stood with his hands deep in his pockets and stared. He would miss this daily feast of beauty.

He didn't know how long he'd stood there in solitude but eventually the sound of someone shuffling down the trail toward him broke through. He turned and raised his hand in greeting to Flinty. The old man, grizzled and worn looking, nodded back.

"Saw ya walk down this a-way. Knowed ya got a ticket on th' next train. Jest wanted t' wish ya well."

O'Dell held out his hand and they shook. The experiences they shared in Corinth would bind them for life.

"Guess yer gittin' shut o' this place, heh?" Flinty asked, probing gently.

"Well, the job here is finished, but I have leads to follow down in Denver." O'Dell did not rise to the bait.

"Uh-huh." He paused. "Kinder a miracle, what, Joy's husband a-comin' back from th' dead an' all."

"Yeah. Kinda that."

They did not speak further but stood together in companionable silence, allowing the purple and white majesty to speak all they needed to hear until the distant whistle of the coming train roused them.

—

That evening O'Dell, the two Pinkerton agents Groman had assigned to him, Marshal Pounder, and two of his men planned their raid on the *Silver Spurs Bawdy Hall*. "We are looking for a young woman by the name of Monika Vogel. I've been told she may be known as Monique. She is five feet, two inches, light blonde hair, fifteen years old."

"Fifteen?" Pounder swore under his breath.

"She was barely fourteen when they snatched her. She and her brother emigrated from Germany to New York a year and a half ago. She answered an employment advertisement to work here in Denver and instead ended up in Corinth—you know where. She was there for a short while before we believe they brought her down mountain."

He glanced at Pounder. "When her brother did not hear from her after she left for Denver, he asked us to find her."

22

O'Dell pushed his hat back on his head, put his hands on his hips, and looked at each man in the room. "I want two men inside playing the role of customers, two men out front with the motor car, and Pounder with me." He hesitated. "Any questions?"

"I 'spect Cal Judd, the *Spurs'* owner, will not take kindly to our honorable intentions," one of Pounder's marshals drawled. The man was holding up a wall with his backside, arms folded across his chest.

"I don't intend to start a war," O'Dell replied, "and we aren't going in to close the place down—seeing as how Denver has more crooked elected officials and cops on the take than a stray dog has fleas. It's unfortunate, but the present political climate will not support shutting him down.

"But this is kidnapping. So Pounder and I will locate the girl and take her out. Anybody gets in our way, and we'll deal with them."

He nodded to the two men who would be posing as customers inside the saloon. "Watch our backs. Be discreet, but pay attention. Keep your side arms out of sight unless you need them. Don't drink too much."

Pounder hefted a double-barreled shot gun. "And me?"

"You? Oh, I want you right out in front, Marshal. Out in plain sight with your badge on your chest and that hog leg of yours at the ready. I'll be right behind you with my little beauty." O'Dell tucked his revolver into his pocket.

O'Dell and Pounder shoved past the two thugs at the front door. O'Dell could see the guards were itching to take them on, but the marshal's star and shotgun gave them pause.

The hall was hot and smoke-filled, the crowd boisterous. O'Dell headed directly for the stairway that led to the cribs on the second floor. A burly guard put a hand on O'Dell's chest and quickly removed it when the marshal leveled his shotgun.

"We don't want any trouble," Pounder growled. "You just stay out of our way, right?"

The burly guard nodded, but his eyes slanted around the crowded hall, looking for help.

O'Dell and the marshal hit the top of the stairs. A hall opened up in both directions.

"Go left. I'll go right. Start at the end and work your way back."

Pounder jogged down the hall until he hit the end. He threw open the door of a room and strode inside. "Monika Vogel!" he yelled.

The girl inside was not her. He withdrew and threw open the next door.

O'Dell was doing the same at his end of the hall. On his fifth room, he called out the girl's name and saw a terrified dish-water blonde raise her head. The man in the bed with her scowled at O'Dell.

"You." O'Dell pointed his gun at the man. "Get up. Over there."

Slowly the man complied, his face suffused with rage. "I don't know who you are, but you are making a big mistake."

O'Dell looked at him now. He was a bull of a man, ruddy, with a hard, chiseled face, obviously a man accustomed getting what he wanted.

"Cal Judd?" O'Dell asked. He was guessing, but something about the man's manner told him he was not wrong.

"You got a problem with that?" the man spat back.

O'Dell tipped his head toward the girl. "She's fifteen. I have a *big* problem with that." Keeping his gun trained on Judd, O'Dell asked again, "You Monika Vogel?"

The girl trembled in fear and cut her eyes to Judd and back. She did not answer.

"Your brother Ernst sent me to find you," O'Dell added, his eyes not leaving Judd. "I'm a Pinkerton man. We're taking you out of here."

The girl moaned and looked at Judd. The man stared hard at her, and O'Dell could feel the fear radiating from the girl.

"Get up. Get some clothes on," he ordered. When she still did not move, O'Dell stepped back until she and Judd were both in his view. Her eyes shifted to him and he snarled, "Get dressed. *Now!*"

She scrambled to obey him. O'Dell backed into the hall and yelled, "Pounder!" A few seconds later the marshal joined him.

"This her?"

"Yup. And this here's Cal Judd."

"I know who he is." Pounder lifted his shotgun and Judd flinched. "O'Dell, we don't have much time."

The girl had slipped on a faded cotton dress and was lacing up her boots. O'Dell grabbed her by the arm and dragged her to her feet. Keeping his gun on Judd, O'Dell rasped, "Move out, Pounder."

The marshal stuck the barrel of his shotgun into the hallway and heard bodies hit the floor in panic. He jumped out of the doorway and leveled the gun down the hall.

24

"You men throw your guns out on the floor!"

The two men who'd panicked and thrown themselves on the floor reluctantly complied.

"Get up and back slowly down those stairs. Just four steps, then stop. If anybody down the stairs starts shooting, you'll be the first to die," Pounder shouted.

He headed down the hallway. O'Dell, who was dragging the girl, stopped before he left the room and issued Judd a warning. "Open this door, Judd, and you'll catch a bullet."

Judd stared with hatred at O'Dell. "This isn't over," he promised.

The girl shuddered in O'Dell's grasp but he kept her moving. A door behind him opened and he swung around. A woman, a frizzled redhead, held out her hands. "I'm alone! Please! Please take me with you!"

O'Dell cursed. He gestured to the woman to fall in behind them. Barefoot and clad in nothing more than a diaphanous wrapper, the woman obeyed.

Seconds later Pounder and O'Dell were on the bottom stairs. Judd's two men, their hands up, shielded them from gunfire. The hall had gone eerily quiet. The two Pinkerton agents they had sent in before them were standing back-to back, their guns out, covering the guards around the room. As Pounder, O'Dell, and the two women moved toward the door, the Pinkerton men retreated with them.

The six of them slammed through the front door and out onto the street. Pounder's marshal driving the car pulled up and threw open a door. And then they were away.

CHAPTER 4

O'Dell, Pounder, and the girls spent a miserable night at the Pinkerton office. While the girls slept, the men took turns watching the street until the sun rose in the morning. Grimy and grizzled, Pounder and O'Dell planned their next steps.

"I'm catching the early train to Chicago," O'Dell stated. He nodded at Monika Vogel. "Taking her with me."

"What do I do with *her*," Pounder demanded. He pointed at the other woman. In the stark morning light she looked older than Monika, street-savvy, and worn.

"What's your name?" O'Dell asked her.

"I go by Red," she replied carefully.

O'Dell snorted. "That's original. Where are you from?"

"Kansas City."

"You want to go back there?"

"No," she answered quickly and shivered. She was still barefoot and wearing the thin wrapper she had left the *Silver Spurs* in, but O'Dell had given her a coat he'd found hanging in what had been Bickle's office.

"Where do you want to go?" he pressed.

She opened her mouth and then closed it. Finally, she answered, "I don't know. I just don't want to—I *can't*—go back . . . there."

O'Dell put an unlit cigar in his mouth and rolled it around for a moment. "Pounder?"

"Yeah?"

"Do me a favor. Take Red here up to Corinth. Make sure she gets to Rose Thoresen."

"That I will."

"Thanks."

—

Marshal Pounder knocked on the door of the former Corinth Gentlemen's Club. It was midmorning and he could hear bustling activity within the doors of the house. Beside him, Red, as she called herself, shivered in uncertainty.

One of the girls from the house opened the door. "Yes? May I help you?"

She was wearing a simple dress and, without the garish makeup so many of the girls had been wearing the other night, he did not recognize her. She looked curiously at Red, who stared daggers in return.

"Good morning, miss. I'm Marshal Jake Pounder. Is Mrs. Thoresen in?"

"Yes sir. Would you come this way, please?" Sarah opened the door and gestured. She showed them into a small room that looked as if it were being used as an office.

A few minutes later Rose Thoresen greeted him. "Marshal! It is a pleasure to see you." She shook his hand. Somehow, instinctively perhaps, she knew why he was there.

She extended her hand to Red. "I'm Rose."

"Red . . ." she mumbled in return.

"I can see why." Rose replied. "Your hair is a lovely color."

Red stared hard at Rose, searching for condescension or sarcasm. When she didn't find it, she relaxed a little.

"Have you come to try us out, then?" Rose asked her gently.

Red looked nervous and unsure and cut her eyes at the marshal. Suddenly he realized he needed to explain why they were there.

"Mr. O'Dell figured, er, suggested, that Miss Red here . . . uh, he asked me to bring her to you."

"Mr. O'Dell! Have you seen him then?" Rose asked eagerly. "He left abruptly and we did not have an opportunity to wish him God Speed."

"Well, he, uh, found the girl he was looking for," Marshal Pounder offered. "Monika Vogel, I think her name was. Three nights back. Took her off to Chicago next morning."

Rose clasped her hands together. "What an answer to prayer! I believe that she and Gretl are the only two girls on his list he found after all this time."

She turned to Red. "And did he also find you, my dear?"

Red, as prickly as a cactus and looking for a reason to be offended, fired back tartly, "I wasn't lost and I'm not your *dear*."

Marshal Pounder, standing behind Red, raised his eyebrows to Rose and shrugged his shoulders.

Rose smiled. "I apologize. It was presumptuous of me. Can you tell me why you are here?"

Red huffed and pursed her lips. "I just asked that other man, O'Dell it was, to . . . take me outta that place. I didn't ask to be taken to *another* whorehouse."

Rose nodded sagely. "It still looks that way, doesn't it? We are working on that. I can assure you, though, that it is no longer a, er, *whorehouse*. The marshal here, his men, plus Mr. O'Dell, and others arrested the men who ran this house. Less than a week ago, in fact. So the girls here are no longer in that, er, line of work."

She gestured for them to sit down. "Red, my daughter Joy and I and a few of our friends plan to secure a house in Denver and move there. We intend to help the girls who come with us to learn new skills and find honest employment so that they may become independent." She looked at Red. "Does that sound like something that interests you?"

Red frowned. "I can't be in Denver if it's gonna be too close to the *Silver Spurs*." She threw a worried look at Pounder. "That Cal Judd holds a grudge, I can tell you. If he finds out I'm in Denver and where I am, he'll come for me."

"Cal Judd?" Rose directed this to the Marshal.

"Man who runs the *Silver Spurs*, Mrs. Thoresen," he explained.

Rose nodded and thought. "We will need to be far enough from that part of town that our girls are not in danger yet close enough that perhaps others will find their way to us. But you raise a valid point, my d—I mean, Miss Red. We will need to take precautions such as solid doors with good locks and not advertising our location."

She looked at Red again. "If you are interested in staying with us for a bit, you are welcome. For the time being we can feed you, probably find you some clothing, and give you a place to stay. If you choose not to move with us to Denver, we can offer you a train ticket away from the city. That is about all we have."

Red stared at Rose a little longer and then answered, "I reckon I can stay a while."

"All right then. Marshal, would you care to stay for dinner?"

Blushing furiously, Marshal Pounder declined. "Thank you, no. I, uh, will just catch the afternoon train back down the mountain. The little missus will be expecting me."

———

(Journal Entry, May 1, 1909)

We already have a new girl, or I should say young woman. She is a little older than the rest, perhaps Joy's age. She is, as I heard Breona phrase it, "a wee bit crusty," which is to say she is touchy and easily offended.

This morning I asked if she had a given name. She replied with some heat that "Red" had been given to her—she hadn't stolen it. I calmly asked if she had another name she preferred that we use. After a few minutes she mumbled that her mother had called her Tabitha.

Careful not to step on her toes again, I asked if she would like us to call her Tabitha or was it too special, since her mother had given it to her. (Thank you, Lord, for helping me to think on my feet!) Apparently asking was the right thing. She thought it over and decided we could call her Tabitha.

I told her it was a good name, one that is found in the Bible. She was curious about that, so I opened my Bible to the Book of Acts and read to her about the woman named Tabitha, a woman known for her good works, and how she sickened and died but the Apostle Peter prayed for her and she came back to life.

This account impressed our Tabitha. She was actually quite smitten with the idea that her namesake had been raised from the dead. A few minutes later she was back asking what Tabitha meant. When I told her it meant "deer" or "gazelle," she was highly disappointed, I might even say disgusted, so I had to chuckle. To myself, of course!

I know she has been deeply hurt in her life, for she looks for the bad in every situation. It will take time, patience, and love. And of course, you, *my Jesus!*

—

Two mornings after the raid on the *Silver Spurs*, O'Dell showed up in his home office in Chicago. He'd taken Monika Vogel to a hotel not far from the office and paid for her room, a bath, several meals, and some second-hand clothes.

He spent the day writing an extensive report for Parsons, his boss and the head of the Chicago office, then sent a wire to the New York Pinkerton office:

Have located M. Vogel. Sending NY with Chicago agent. Notify brother. Report following.

Parsons spent an hour reading O'Dell's report. He saw his boss shaking his head several times. Finally, he waved O'Dell into his office.

"You embellished this, right?" The frown lines between Parsons' eyes were deep and permanent.

O'Dell shrugged. "What do you think? You can't make this stuff up."

"To be frank, after four months of sitting on your backside in that little mountain village with no results, Pinkerton was on the verge of cutting you loose. Nobody here thought you were actually working the case."

"I get that."

"But you pulled it off. And to think that Branch . . . and that Thoresen woman—"

"Michaels. Joy Michaels."

"—That she was tied into our kidnapping case *and* was married to Branch?"

"Grant Michaels."

"Yeah, OK. And this guy, Dean Morgan. He'd burned her out in Omaha? This gets stranger by the minute. Unbelievable." Parsons rocked back in his chair and looked O'Dell over. "So now what?"

O'Dell shrugged. "I'm ready for another case."

"You know, McParland is looking for a new head of the Denver office. It would mean a promotion for you, a chance to clean up that town."

"No thanks. Let someone else have it."

Parsons studied him. "All right. I'll have someone escort Miss Vogel to New York. You be back here in the morning. I've got a few things for you."

———

(Journal Entry, May 9, 1909)

We celebrated a wedding this morning, right after Sunday service! I'm sure Billy and Marit would have liked to have had more time to prepare, but now that we are all starting "from scratch," so to speak, it made no sense to put their wedding off, and they surely did not wish to wait longer.

Our wonderful little church family has already been so good to us providing clothing, food, and all the ordinary, everyday things we take for granted. Today they gave Billy and Marit bedding and kitchen items and the use of a little cabin until we relocate to Denver.

I am so glad for them to have a place of respite where they can go to learn of each other and just be a family. Will is five months old now, and he will never know any father other than Billy. How good you are, Lord!

CHAPTER 5

Rose and Joy studied the list of names on the table before them. Little Blackie slept curled in a contented heap at Joy's feet. Nearly seven weeks had passed since the lodge had burned; almost seven weeks had gone by since the marshals had arrested Morgan, Banner, Darrow, and the rest.

O'Dell had left Corinth without saying good bye, and Joy still felt the sting of his abrupt departure. At the same time, she recognized how awkward it would have been for him to remain.

She was not the only one who felt his absence keenly—those who had lived at the lodge felt strangely abandoned by the man who had been steadfastly with them through so many difficulties. One or two remarked how unlike him it was but most kept their own counsel.

Arnie had remained in Corinth until Joy was on her way to recovery. He and Grant had spent a great deal of time together. Joy realized Grant had needed someone to talk to, a male friend and family member who had known him before, someone other than Joy who could reassure him as he attempted to stitch together the many blank places in his memories.

Grant. Joy's heart soared each time she thought of him. Their reunion was sweet but tentative as they learned each other all over again. They spent hours talking, rehearsing their courtship, wedding, and married life. Grant knew nothing of those years but was gaining the particulars from their conversations.

Occasionally he would experience a moment of clarity, just as, that night in the plaza, he had recalled his own dog, Blackie, when he had picked up Joy's puppy and Arnie had called out reminders to him. Those rare occurrences assured him that he *was* "home again," home with Joy, her family, and their new mission.

When Joy had explained to Grant all the events leading her to Corinth and he fully understood the cruel depravity the girls had been subjected to, he embraced their endeavor with grim determination.

"Even with one arm, I'm strong and can do many things. I can run a business. I can serve customers. Whatever you need me to do, I will do it," he'd vowed.

Now, more than six weeks after the climax of events in Corinth, it was time for them to push ahead with their plans. Blackie yawned, circled, and lay down again while Rose and Joy studied the list before them. Of the original fifteen girls that the marshals had liberated from the two houses, nine remained.

Two girls, Dotty and Crystal, had contacted their families immediately and had left within days. Rose and Joy had not spoken of it much, but they both wondered how they were doing, wondered how difficult it was proving to be for the girls, ages sixteen and seventeen, to reenter and adjust to their former lives. Wondered if they would find help for their wounded souls.

And then ten days ago, four more had unexpectedly announced their plan to open their own "house" in Denver.

"We are whores and good ones," Esther, their self-appointed leader, proclaimed. "We'll rent our own place, decorate it tastefully, and take care of each other. We intend to make excellent money and never allow abuse from our customers. No man will ever mistreat us again. No; this time, *we'll* be in control."

Esther was possibly the most beautiful woman either Rose or Joy had ever seen—they did not wonder why she had been "assigned" to the Corinth Gentlemen's Club. She was slender and graceful with exquisite bone structure, creamy skin, and large, midnight blue eyes framed with thick, inky lashes. More than that, she possessed a fine mind and a charming, appealing way.

The girls had produced trunks they had already packed and politely demanded train tickets to Denver. "We thank you for helping us get shut of this place, but you promised you would give us tickets to wherever we wanted to go," Esther stated matter-of-factly. "We have decided we don't want to stay here. It's not like we have families waiting for us with open arms. No, we're going to make our own way."

"You could wait and go to Denver with us when we buy our house there," Rose offered again, silently chiding herself for sounding desperate. "We can train you to work and give you jobs or help you find positions. You don't have to live like . . . that."

"Like 'that'?" Esther's laugh was brittle. "You mean as 'soiled doves'? Whores? The fact is, we *are* whores. 'Once a whore, always a whore,' like they say. Anyway, I'm not going to slave away waiting tables or sewing for wealthy society ladies for mere pennies a day."

She tossed her lovely head and smiled that winsome, 'come hither' look she knew was to her advantage. "This is *our* golden opportunity. We're young and well-trained, and we're going to make a lot of money. And when I have money then I'll do whatever *I* want."

Joy's mouth had dropped open at Esther's defiant speech, and Rose had stared sadly. She wondered how they would finance their endeavor.

Later Breona, always the shrewd, observant one, pointed out that many of the costly knick-knacks around both houses had quietly disappeared as well as Roxanne's jewelry. And Roxanne had been the only woman in the house to have had near-respectable street clothes. Those were gone, also.

Then the tall brunette, whom Rose and Joy now knew as Sarah, mentioned that someone had gone through her clothes and taken the best she had. "Only the best whoring garments," she added wryly. "But it's not as though I'd be wearing them again if I'm not going to be a 'dove' anymore."

Sarah's cynical smile went straight to Rose's heart. She felt as though she spent every free moment praying for these young women—all of them. The burden she felt for them was barely short of crushing.

Lord, she grieved, *I am so out of my depth. I don't know how to help them. I cannot even relate to their lives! If you don't lead and guide, we are lost. I trust you, Lord. I do! Please help me—help us— today.*

Joy prayed in a similar but more practical manner, *O Lord, please guide us to the house you have for us in Denver—and quickly. Help us to take these girls down the mountain, away from this place of nightmares, and begin the process of training them in work that will give them dignity and self-reliance. And Father God, Grant and I need to find and open our store . . . yesterday!* She alternately planned and fretted over both undertakings.

Rose and Joy stared again at the list of names, six crossed off, nine remaining. At least three more girls would be leaving, going to distant relatives who had agreed to take them.

It had been difficult work. The three girls were very young— ages fourteen and younger—without known parents and siblings. They were only vaguely acquainted with these far-away relatives. Nevertheless, all involved, including the girls, agreed that they would be better off going to their families and finishing school.

It had taken the exchange of several letters, letters from Pastor Kalbørg with enclosures from Rose and Joy, to explain in clear terms what their young niece, grandniece, or second cousin (as the relations turned out) had gone through, and then to receive assurances from their relations in return. Those assurances needed to express to David, Rose, and Joy's satisfaction that the home each girl would be going to would be safe and nurturing.

When these three girls departed, the list would stand at six names. Six young women, ages fifteen to eighteen, who had agreed to stay with them, move to Denver, and be trained to support themselves. Counting Tabitha, who was older than the others, the number was seven.

Joy looked at her mother. "Seven. Can we manage?"

"We *will* manage," Rose replied firmly. "We must. I don't know precisely how, but I am willing to place my confidence in the Lord to show us how."

Emily Van der Pol and her small band of supporters were scouting the city below Corinth, looking for a house that would suit their needs. Rose would buy the house with her own money, and Emily's group of women had pledged to match her contribution. The women's group was making progress on their promise to help furnish the house and get the household on its feet.

In two days Rose and Joy would address them and other women they had invited to hear about the project. While Joy struggled to list the many practical aspects of their plans and what she would need to recount to the ladies, Rose prepared her heart to convey the great spiritual needs they would be addressing. Together, they prayed the Lord would move on compassionate hearts to help them.

———

Esther critically appraised the parlor of their new home and place of business. She and the girls had sold the most expensive knick-knacks and jewelry they had pilfered from the two houses in Corinth. The money they gained from the sales had been scarcely enough to rent this house and decorate it in the manner necessary.

But Esther was shrewd. Yes, she and her girls had sold nearly all they had, *but not all*. She had kept back a few select pieces, knowing that certain touches were essential to attracting and retaining the wealthy clients she desired.

She repositioned the ornate Ansonia mantle clock to display its floral porcelain box most effectively. Two small Tiffany lamps graced the end tables, their glow illuminating the brightly colored panes of glass.

They had papered the parlor themselves with expensive ivory watermarked damask. Their furniture was used but of excellent quality. She and Ava had spent hours mending flaws in the upholstery and disguising worn spots with cleverly placed antimacassars while Molly and Jess rubbed dark oil into the woods to cover scratches.

With the last of their monies, excepting a small emergency fund, they had purchased wine and liqueurs. Jess had secreted two empty liqueur decanters and a dozen crystal tumblers in one of Roxanne's carpet bags when they left Corinth.

Esther chuckled. She, herself, had wrapped a heavy silver tea service in clothing and packed it at the bottom of her trunk. It now graced a prominent table in the corner of the parlor. A few other costly items—statuettes, ashtrays, lighters—added to the overall welcoming effect of the room.

And their calling cards. Esther had visited a printer and selected a fine quality stock. This morning she and the girls had dressed in Roxanne's elegant street clothes, made over to fit themselves, of course. Bedecked in the finest day styles, their eyes discreetly shaded by plumed and veiled hats, they were indistinguishable from any other fashionable ladies on the street.

All day, two-by-two, they had casually traversed the streets of the upper-class red light district. When they encountered well-dressed gentlemen, they would politely hand them one of their cards and continue their walk. The cards read simply

Cultured Conversation and Companionship
Monday–Saturday Evenings, Eight O'clock

In discreet lettering across the bottom of each card was printed their address. Esther smiled. With luck, they would be receiving their first clients within the hour.

$\mathcal{C}$HAPTER 6

Rose and Joy stood together before the sizable group of women gathered in the fellowship hall of a Denver church. The audience was comprised of obviously upper-class ladies. Elegant hats and spotless gloves bedecked the women seated in the hall, and Rose rejoiced for it.

Lord, do not think me crass in this observation, she prayed. *But these women have the wherewithal to do much good for your Kingdom. I thank you in advance for their generosity.*

Their dear friend Emily Van der Pol finished her introduction and nodded to Joy. Rose seated herself and waited her turn to speak.

Joy, her thick hair bound into a heavy braided chignon, smiled cordially and began, "Thank you for allowing us to speak before you today. For the last two months my mother and I have been living in what was one of the most notorious brothels in Colorado." Her first words shocked their audience, but she had intended to do so. Even her mother shot her a nervous glance.

"I say it 'was' a notorious brothel. It no longer is. We and others have been ministering to the women there who, through brute force, were obliged to work in this brothel. The souls and needs of these young women, if they are to leave their past behind, are why we are here today."

"Before we talk about their needs, I would like to recount how we came to be involved." Joy, in her straightforward manner, walked the gathered women through the last year. She began with the challenging letter she had received from her cousin Uli describing the situation in Corinth and begging her to come and secretly help enslaved girls to escape.

She told of the ads that scheming, deceitful men—and women— placed in newspapers in eastern cities. Ads designed to lure unsuspecting young women to employment opportunities in Denver.

"These women would arrive in Denver expecting to be met by honest employers. Instead, they were taken against their will to the houses we speak of in Corinth. There they were drugged and had their innocence forcibly taken by debauched men. Afterwards, the young women would be beaten, starved, and," Joy swallowed, "raped . . . repeatedly until they submitted to a life of prostitution."

"I know Denver has its share of bordellos and streetwalkers. You must know the areas of town where these activities are conducted every night. However, the house we presently live in and its next door neighbor were especially evil. They pandered to men who paid high prices to take the innocence of girls—girls as young as eleven and twelve. And they provided unwilling participants to men who demanded acts of cruelty and perversion I dare not speak of."

The women in the room sat stunned. Some were openly weeping.

"Although I will not speak of them, my mother and I have heard these horrible acts described in detail. We have heard them from the mouths of young women as they cry out their pain on our shoulders and sob themselves to sleep under our praying hands. We, my mother and I, can scarcely bear to hear that of which these wounded hearts must unburden themselves."

Joy held up a year-old newspaper from Boston. "May I read this advertisement to you?" she asked. Her audience stirred and some nodded. Joy read aloud,

> *Help Wanted*
> *Young woman for light domestic work. Must be able to relocate, Denver, Colorado. Travel paid; good wage. Children allowed with prior approval. Send letter of inquiry to . . .*

She left off reading and set the paper down. "This advertisement sounded like an answer to prayer to a young woman in Boston all alone in the world, a woman who only wanted a good job so that she could make her own way in the world. I know, because I met her while she was on her way to Denver."

Joy recounted her train ride from RiverBend to Denver, and how she met two such girls, Breona and Marit, both traveling to new "jobs" in Denver.

"When we met, I showed them five different advertisements from five different newspapers. Then they showed me the advertisements they had answered. The advertisements were nearly identical.

When we arrived in Denver, hard, harsh men were waiting for these two girls. They were waiting to take them, not to honest jobs in Denver, but to one of the two brothels in Corinth of which I have spoken. It was a narrow escape."

Not a sound in the room interrupted Joy. She then described buying an old house in Corinth and renovating it, naming it 'Corinth Mountain Lodge.'

"We hoped that we would somehow be able to get word to the girls in the brothels and that they would be able to escape to us, one at a time. From there, we would pass them to others who could spirit them away.

"Breona, Marit, and I, along with two of my previous employees from Omaha, made that lodge beautiful and inviting. We hoped to support our efforts by attracting guests from Denver and beyond, guests who would appreciate the beauty of the mountains around Corinth."

Joy smiled fondly at Emily Van der Pol. "And that is how we met our dear friend Emily. She came to spend the first week of this past December with us and fell in love with the lodge and its views, just as we had." Joy paused and took a small sip of water.

"Then one night during her stay, we received our first escapee."

Women sat forward on their chairs, spellbound, as Joy recounted Mei-Xing's escape from the 'Corinth Gentlemen's Club.' "Mei-Xing had been horribly abused. She had attempted to run away the night before and had been caught and punished.

"When she came to us she was beaten, broken, and violated in ways I cannot name. Instead of giving up, she used her last bit of strength to, even in her broken condition, attempt escape again."

"Mrs. Van der Pol overheard the goings-on during the night as we ministered to Mei-Xing's broken body and heart. It was the following day that Emily and I had a frank conversation about the horrible secret Corinth harbored." Joy nodded to Emily. "And she confessed that God had placed the burden of helping us on her heart."

"That is how we have come to you now to speak of the great needs we have." Joy, feeling the power of the Holy Spirit in the room, pushed on. "Denver is a dark stronghold of vice. We are now preparing to move from Corinth to Denver. We are moving, first of all, because the men behind the evil in Corinth burned our beautiful Corinth Mountain Lodge to the ground.

"And we say, *so be it, Lord*. We will not be deterred. We are moving to Denver, secondly, because the city offers opportunities for training and work for the seven women who live with us at this time. But we do not expect only these seven women."

She looked around, meeting the eyes of many women in the room. "Yes, Corinth was a particularly vile stronghold, but that evil has now been stamped out. Those who perpetuated this evil are in jail, facing trial. Prostitution will not be able to raise its head in Corinth again. The people of Corinth, soundly chastised of the Lord, have pledged to never again allow such wickedness within their town."

A smattering of applause interrupted Joy, and she smiled. "Yes, God has done something wondrous in Corinth. We are so grateful to him."

She became serious again. "Denver, however, is rife with this evil. Once we are established and stable here, we hope to reach out and receive other women who wish to leave a life of prostitution.

"We must have a house that allows us to grow in this manner. A house, here in Denver, in a good neighborhood but not too far from honest work opportunities. This house must also not be so far from the area of town where prostitution is practiced that they cannot run to us.

"You know the area I speak of—Market Street and its surrounds. We must be near enough for those women who would flee to us for refuge. This house is our first need.

"After we find the house and make our move here, my husband and I will open a fine furnishings store. We own considerable inventory already, and we will take on two of the seven women we have as employees. We will train them and give them jobs. But that leaves five young women who will require employment."

Joy stopped, nearly empty of words. "We covet your prayers, for it is not only honest work these women need. They have been damaged beyond description. Only the saving, restoring power of God can heal such damage."

Joy's voice cracked and her eyes filled with tears. "Will you not pray with us? More than anything, these young women need Jesus. It will take time for him to heal them. My mother, Mrs. Rose Thoresen," Joy nodded to Rose, "will lead the house in Bible study and prayer, in counseling and encouragement. Restoration will not be easy, and it will not be fast. Will you pray with us? Will you help us?"

She was done. Spent. Her head bowed, Joy simply stopped. Rose stood and walked to her side.

Addressing the women, she said, "I believe you have heard all that we have to say and all you need to make decisions today. If you are led of the Lord to help us, please address yourselves to Mrs. Van der Pol and our dear Grace Minton." Rose nodded to those ladies.

"Joy and I will be available to speak with you during the refreshment hour. Please feel free to ask us any questions you may have." With that, Rose turned the meeting back to Emily.

"Mrs. Thoresen, might I have a word with you?" The question came from near Rose's elbow. She turned, looked down, and found a thin, elderly woman with a wizened face and a shock of white hair. She stooped heavily, bent nearly double, over a cane.

"How do you do?" Rose extended her hand. The elderly woman trembled as she leaned her left side more heavily on her cane so that she could reach Rose's outstretched grasp. Her skin was soft but dry and fragile, like raw spun silk.

"Mrs. Chester Palmer. Please call me Martha. P'rhaps we could set in that corner for a moment?"

Rose felt it important to remain available to all of the women still gathered in the hall, but she graciously nodded. A few moments later Mrs. Palmer sank into an armchair with an appreciative sigh. Even seated, she remained bent over and had to turn her head and look up to meet Rose's eyes. Rose wondered how badly it discomforted the woman to be bowed so.

"I won't take much of your time, Mrs. Thoresen, but I felt so impressed by the Spirit to speak to you . . . and I didn't want to let the moment pass by."

"Of course," Rose agreed. She waited attentively.

"The thing of it is," Mrs. Palmer began slowly, "I b'lieve I have your house."

Rose's eyebrows rose sharply.

"I must warn you," Mrs. Palmer continued, "the house is in poor shape. Once it was a beautiful place, but it's been empty and has not been maintained for nigh on ten years."

She turned her head down and fidgeted with a hanky up her sleeve. "It's large, though. Very large. Has a sizable spot of prop'ty with servant quarters and a carriage house in the back."

She turned her head and looked up at Rose again. "I want to give it to you."

Rose's mouth dropped open.

"That house has quite a story, I assure you," Mrs. Palmer continued in her thin voice, "and half of Denver would be happy to regale you with its history. But today is not the time. It was only important for me to follow the Spirit's prompting and tell you I will give you this house. D'ye have paper and pencil?"

Rose snapped to attention. "Yes—that is, no—but I will find some immediately." She spied Joy across the room holding a tea cup and saucer, conversing with a knot of ladies. "Please excuse me. I will be back straight away."

A few moments later Rose returned with paper and pencil and wrote the address Mrs. Palmer dictated to her. "Take a look, if you will," the old woman told her, "and if it seems suitable from the outside, I'll have my great-nephew give you a key to get inside."

Mrs. Palmer struggled to get out of the chair. "Will you give me your arm, Mrs. Thoresen?"

"Gladly," Rose answered. She helped the elderly woman to her feet and held her arm until she was steady.

"That's fine, then," Mrs. Palmer assured her. "My servant is just there by the door. He will help me to my motor car."

When Grant arrived to escort them back to the hotel, Rose could hardly contain herself. She read the address aloud to Joy and Grant, but neither could place its location.

"Surely Emily will know," Joy suggested. They called to their friend, who joined them near the door.

"Why, this is Chester and Martha Palmer's old house," Emily realized in wonder.

"Yes; Mrs. Palmer has said she will give it to us! I still cannot believe it," Rose replied.

Emily nodded thoughtfully. "I confess I am surprised, but Martha is a great woman of God. She would do what the Lord directed her to do, no matter what it cost her." She looked pensive. "I do not refer to money when I say 'cost.'"

She added directions to the address. "The house is west of the river and south of Colfax, a respectable distance from Larimer and Market. It is in deplorable condition. Really, if Martha did not have the connections and influence she has, her neighbors would have prevailed on the city to do something about it."

She saw them out. "Sometime I will tell you of this house and its history. I do not wish to do so now. Instead, please go and see it. The Lord himself will speak to you about its suitability."

The corner lot was wide and deep, and the house was set far back from the street. Pines and junipers, thorny climbing roses and pyracantha were once shaped and well cared for; now their thick and tangled boughs and branches clogged the yard.

However, neither the untrimmed trees and shrubs smothering the grounds nor the vines thick upon the walls could conceal the size of the house. It was massive, an aging Victorian splendor, rising three stories and more into the crisp evening air.

The overgrowth in the yard shrouded much of the house's shape, but its asymmetrical profile—pediment-topped dormer windows, impressive gables, and octagonal turrets—reached into the sky. Stained glass and gingerbread eaves, only glimpsed through a morass of woody Virginia creeper, tantalized the trio standing outside the gates.

The covered porch, which appeared to wrap the length of the front, terminated somewhere near the corner of the house in the sizable gazebo peeping through the overgrowth.

They stared at the estate before them awed by its size and grandeur and half cowed by the evident decay and neglect. The day's last rays glanced off cracked windows, peeling paint, and towers with missing shingles.

"It is . . . gargantuan," Grant exclaimed. "It isn't a house—it's a *mansion!*"

"It's perfect," Rose and Joy answered together. They had clasped hands at first sight of the house.

"It must be three times the size of the lodge," Joy added. "Why, how deep it must be for those turrets to belong to it!" She gestured at the pointed towers peeping through the angles of the roof line.

Grant soberly commented, "It will take a great deal of cash to make repairs. I daresay the plumbing and gas lines will need work. Look at the roof! Billy and I can do the work, but we'll still need materials."

"I imagine all the rooms will need paint and paper," Joy mused. "Not to mention carpets."

Rose shushed both of them. "I had intended to buy us a house, remember? That money can now be used to make the repairs." She suddenly giggled. "But can you imagine what Breona is going to say?"

Suddenly Joy and Rose were laughing and hugging each other. Still laughing, Joy threw her arms around Grant.

"We must obtain the keys as quickly as we can!" Joy said breathlessly between chuckles.

CHAPTER 7

(Journal Entry, June 17, 1909)

O Lord, how I thank you. We have a house!

You have provided a house for our ministry, and what a house! It must have been magnificent once, but it has been closed up for many years. We must now open it to the light and bring to bear all of our care and efforts to restore it.

Lord, you do that with us, too, don't you? You bring your light to our lives but still it takes care, effort, and time to restore us so that we reflect your image, the glory for which you designed us.

Joy and I will call on Mrs. Palmer first thing in the morning to thank her and arrange for the keys. Grant is hesitant and wants to ensure that all of the legal issues are settled before we begin work on the house. We will leave those matters in his hands.

Dear Lord, I miss Jan tonight. I miss his strength, his wisdom, and his arms around me. I miss the warmth of his breath on my neck as we sleep. Good night, Father God. I am so glad Jan is with you. I know we will see each other again, someday.

———

Up until now, moving to Denver had been their dream, a shining hope and vision Rose and Joy often spoke of but not in concrete terms. Now it was time for the dream to assume shape and substance. Rose and Joy called a meeting with Breona, Mei-Xing, and the rest of the girls and told them about the house Martha Palmer was giving to them.

"It was once a beautiful house," Joy said as she described it. "And it is far larger than this one. It has three stories, several turrets and towers, and a large attic. We don't even know yet how many bedrooms it has, but we are guessing ten to twelve, with room for more in the attic. It sits on a large lot and has several out-buildings in the back."

"It *was* beautiful once," Rose cautioned, "but it has been closed up for more than twelve years and, unfortunately, looks to have sustained some serious damage. What we should be clear about is that whatever work needs to be done, will fall mostly to us."

She gestured to all of them gathered in the parlor. "Of course this includes Grant, Billy, and Mr. Wheatley. Some repairs we must hire out to be done. However, just cleaning the house so that we can move in will be a colossal undertaking."

The women began chattering and asking questions, their voices rising in excitement. Rose held up a hand.

"Before we go any further, I think we should also describe our vision for the house and clarify our expectations of you if you embark with us on this journey. You see, just as we did at the lodge, we will manage our home in a way that honors God."

Some of the girls looked confused; a few looked at each other nervously.

Joy spoke up. "Our goal is to help you learn a skill or trade and then help you find employment so that you can support yourselves in an honorable, independent manner. But that is not all we will teach you."

"Yes, that is not all," Rose agreed. "We understand that you come from different backgrounds and have had different experiences. We will show you how to dress, speak, and conduct yourself so that you are comfortable and confident in whatever social situation you find yourself."

Her voice softened. "A few of you were left on the street as children and have never known what it is to have a family. Even as you prepare to go out into the world and take care of yourself, we want you to become part of *our* family. When the time comes for you to fly our little nest, wherever you go and whatever you do, you will always be part of our family and be welcome to visit."

Mei-Xing timidly raised her hand. Rose smiled. "Mei-Xing, did you wish to say something?"

"Er, yes. I only wished to say that at first, at the lodge, the things we did together—the Bible studies, praying for God to meet our needs and needs we saw in the community—were all strange and sometimes difficult for me to understand."

"But after a little while, I began to love our time together and love the way we worked together like a family." She stopped, a little embarrassed. "I, well, I never had a family like that, a family that shared every aspect of living. It, that is, I began to see what being part of a family is supposed to be like."

She looked at Rose. "I began to know what it was like to have a mother who loved me and knew how to nurture me," she looked from Joy to Breona, "and sisters who cared for me and wanted God's best for me."

Tears sprang to Rose's eyes. "That is what we are speaking of. When we move to Denver, it is our hope that we will grow together and experience those family bonds."

She continued. "Everything we do in our home, we will do together with care for each other. We will clean and cook together. We will study and pray together. We will support each other through illness and difficulties."

"We will treat each other with respect and civility, even when we disagree. Yes, we will not always agree or like what others do. We will sometimes have little spats. But we will make up and never give up on each other."

As the girls were thinking over what Rose had said, Joy added, "Miss Rose will live in the house with you while Mr. Grant and I will, as soon as it can be readied, live in the caretaker's cottage and Billy and Marit in the carriage house. Miss Rose will be in charge of the house, particularly its spiritual tone."

"Breona will be the housekeeper," Rose said. "She will assign chores and manage the household."

"All of us," she added, "including me, will work. No one will be exempt as long as they live in the house. All of us will take meals together morning and evening and participate in Bible study and prayer at those meals. I assure you, those times will not be arduous. Just as we have already been doing the past few weeks, I intend to make them encouraging and engaging."

She looked around at each girl. "This is what our expectations are and what you must prayerfully consider. If you cannot agree to abide by our expectations, then you must, in good conscience, decline our offer. We will think no less of you and will still provide you with a train ticket if you choose to go elsewhere."

"I will go," Mei-Xing volunteered first. "Of course, I think you must have known my answer?" She smiled shyly, and Rose nodded and smiled back.

"I will go, too!" Gretl proclaimed eagerly.

Then the table lapsed into silence. The remainder of the girls considered Rose's proposition soberly.

"We ask that you give us your answer no later than this Friday," Rose concluded.

—

(*Journal Entry, June 21, 1909*)

So many things to do! Our remaining six Corinth girls, Sarah, Gretl, Corrine, Flora, Nancy, and Maria, have accepted our proposal. Tabitha will come, too, making seven. I had my doubts about her, our rough little cob, but Friday she made a decision and will also accompany us.

My concern with Tabitha is that she is older than the other girls, although exactly what age, she has not said. She may be Joy's age, but the life she has lived has worn her considerably, both inside and out. I have been praying for the Lord to win her heart, for we can sense how hard and empty of hope it is at present.

I do not forget Mei-Xing! Truthfully, Lord, I hardly think of Mei-Xing as one of the girls, because you have done such a work in her heart already and have knit her to me as a daughter. Breona, Mei-Xing, dear Mr. Wheatley, and I will live in the house as we did in the lodge. I am so happy Mr. Wheatley will be with us!

Marit and Billy and Joy and Grant will share the third floor at first. It may be several months before the cottages out back are ready. We realized, too, that we cannot have a baby with us at first; the house is entirely too dirty. David and Uli will keep little Will until the house is clean enough for him. As I said, Lord, so much to do!

Marit and Gretl will share the cooking initially, for we will be feeding an army while we work on the house. Gretl aspires to become a great cook for a wealthy family. Father, I thank you for the hope and vision you have placed in her precious heart.

The house itself possesses more than enough space for our needs at present. The problem, initially, will be readying it enough for us to move from Corinth to it.

The dust is thick everywhere, and mice have made it their home. A few rooms have cracked or broken windows and have sustained water damage. Our little family will surely be "roughing it," as I've heard someone call it, sleeping on the floors before we are far enough along to bring in furniture. My old bones do not relish the prospect, Lord!

After that will come a period of true renovation that may well test our souls, for we must, of necessity, be shifting our bedrooms and living space from room to room as the work goes on.

I can't help but believe, though, that the sooner we leave the houses in Corinth for good, the better. They are a constant reminder to the girls of the evil done within their walls.

Although some have suggested it, we do not wish to appropriate any of the furniture from these houses nor should we. Until a court decides what is to be done with the houses, they will remain unoccupied and their furnishings unused.

Lord, I trust you. Perhaps working together to make our house in Denver livable will help these young women to feel that it is their home. As we begin this great endeavor, I am still humbled that you chose us to minister to their wounds. Oh Lord, give us your wisdom, for we have none of our own.

———

The doorbell had chimed four times so far this evening, and it was still quite early. Esther splashed whiskey into a short tumbler for the portly gentleman seated across from her and then added a generous portion of water.

Henry, already a regular customer, had spoken nonstop for the last hour on the history of the monarchy in France and Britain. He was content just to have a lovely, attentive ear. Esther was more than happy to listen, smile, and nod at whatever dear Henry said. Oh, and refill his glass with her overpriced, watered-down drinks.

Money was still very tight, but Esther was pleased so far with the progress of their business. As their clientele grew, she would be looking for fresh girls to add to the house.

The doorbell chimed again and she rose gracefully, murmuring her excuses to Henry. Tom, the only muscle she could afford at present, answered the door.

His job was to screen potential clients. Only well-dressed, well-groomed gentlemen were admitted. And only sober ones. Intoxicated men were often unruly and were less likely to purchase drinks. Esther wanted only an upscale, *thirsty* clientele.

Esther was ready to greet her customer after Tom cleared him to pass through the large entryway. "Good evening," she said pleasantly, eyeing the tall, powerfully built man. He wore a charcoal three-piece suit and wore it well.

"Good evening," he replied. The man's face was ruddy; his eyes a strikingly pale blue.

Many men stared at Esther, some agape at her startling beauty, some boldly or suggestively. Others avoided her eyes while taking inventory of the rest of her assets. But this man looked directly into her eyes . . . deeply, almost intimately. Esther felt a pull she had not experienced in a long time.

"Would you care to join us in the parlor?" Esther smiled again and hooked her arm through his to show him the way. "Please call me Esther. Would you care for a glass of wine? Something stronger?"

"You're a lovely woman, Esther," the man replied, placing his hand lightly on hers.

Heat shot down Esther's spine. She looked from his hand resting on hers into his eyes again. *I could get lost in those eyes*, she thought. It was uncharacteristic of her to be moved by a client but . . .

He squeezed her hand gently. "My name is Cal. Cal Judd. What a pleasant establishment you have."

CHAPTER 8

The group that gathered in front of the house studied it with wide eyes. Rose Brownlee Thoresen, however, was studying *them*, the courageous band (crazy or misguided, some might insist!) as they sized up the job ahead.

They all wore old and worn clothing, appropriate for embarking on an arduous task. They were ready to unpack a wagon load of bedding, cleaning supplies, cookware and kitchen utensils, and yard and carpentry tools. But the sight before them gave them pause.

A tall iron fence surrounded the property. Between the wrought iron gate and the front door lay an obstacle course of downed branches, dense shrubs, and tangled weeds and bushes. Tree roots lifted the stone walkway here and there; out-of-control vines covered windows and twined upon the porch.

"Eh!" was Breona's first remark.

Rose smiled, looked for, and found the gleam in the tough young woman's eye. "Breona, you are in charge of the cleaning of this house; you are our official housekeeper! The men will begin by clearing a path to the door and making a list of essential repairs and then getting to them. We ladies, however, are at *your* disposal." Rose handed her a key.

Breona smiled broadly, her black eyes flashing. "Well then!"

The women of the group—Rose, Joy, Breona, Marit, Mei-Xing, Gretl, Sarah, Corrine, Maria, Nancy, Flora, and Tabitha—chuckled. The men—Mr. Wheatley, Billy, and Grant—smiled. No one in their band underestimated the determination of Breona Byrne once she set her mind to a task.

Breona pushed through the gate, jumped handily over several branches lying on the walk, dodged the thorny arms of a few bushes, and trotted victoriously up the wisteria-clogged steps to the front door. On the enormous covered porch she turned and held up the key triumphantly.

"Fer God an' 'is glory!" she called loudly to them.

"Hear, hear!" Grant shouted back.

"For God and his glory!" Rose and Joy echoed, catching her excitement.

The women grinned and forged ahead. As Rose had directed, the men stayed behind to clear a wide path from the street to the house.

Inside, the women's excitement and banter tapered off to silence. The interior of the house was dim and dank. Although it was June, the skies over Denver were overcast this early morning, providing little natural light for them to work by. They gathered in the house's great room and stared about them in awe and something else, what Rose could only characterize as *trepidation*.

Wallpaper hung in faded tatters from the walls. Heavy drapes sagged under the weight of thick dust. Fragments of carpets littered the floors.

Breona asked Marit and Corrine to pull back the draperies from the windows. "Hev a care," she warned, but the sound of rending fabric interrupted her.

"Rotten," Marit stated flatly.

Breona nodded and gestured at the remaining window hangings. "We mus' be takin' th'm doon."

The women covered their hair with kerchiefs and then removed tattered drapes from three windows and piled them in the center of the room. They coughed and choked as dust filled the air.

"We can't clean all of this," Flora blurted. Her words were tinged with panic. No one responded.

Breona ignored her and pursed her lips. "Aye then. Miss Joy, will ye please t' be foindin' us a burnin' pit in th' back?"

Joy nodded. She and Sarah wandered down the dark halls in search of a door to the back of the house.

Throughout the morning the women removed and burned dozens of rotted drapes, mildewed curtains, and ragged carpets. Breona set Marit and Gretl to clean the kitchen and its pantries and assigned Joy and Rose to the great room and dining room.

Corrine and Nancy tackled the parlor, library, and the butler's pantry and office. The rest of the women she assigned to the first three bedrooms on the second floor.

"'Tis here we'll be a-sleepin' t'night," Breona decided before they began. Shudders ran down several spines as they viewed the condition of the rooms and the work before them.

Marit and Gretl found two stoves in the massive kitchen, one wood-burning, the other gas fueled. Grant had firmly instructed all of them not to attempt to light any gas appliance until the gas company had inspected the house's gas lines and approved each fixture.

After asking the men to supply them with some fire wood, the two women bent their efforts on cleaning the wood-burning stove and its pipe so they could get a fire going. An hour later they announced that they had hot water for cleaning.

Rose and Joy set about their task by sweeping dust and cobwebs from the ceilings, walls, floors, windows, and two fireplaces. After repeated passes, they still had full dustpans to empty. The tall ceilings were hardest—Joy stood on a sturdy box and swept the ceiling in sections, the dust falling on her kerchiefed head and into her eyes. After two full passes, her arms and shoulders burned and ached.

"We cannot even think to wash the windows until this dust is tamed," Rose lamented.

"Perhaps we should wash them and the walls and floors regardless," Joy suggested. "It is the only way to tame this dust. No doubt we'll have to do so at least twice or three times." *And again tomorrow*, she thought with dogged determination.

"You are right. We may as well wash the windows even if they run with grime," Rose replied. "We need the light to work by." She studied the walls, frowning. "This wallpaper will dissolve when we wash it."

Joy nodded, her mouth set in a grim line. "I will ask the men to empty our rubbish bin into the burning pit and keep the fire going."

The men were not without their challenges. Billy and Grant chopped and sawed their way through wildly overgrown climber roses and pyracantha until their arms bled from the thorny branches.

"Marit will not be pleased with the tears in my shirt," Billy remarked with a reckless grin. Grant, not having considered Joy's reaction to a torn shirt, looked askance when he realized his shirt was shredded beyond repair.

Mr. Wheatley pulled up his suspenders and went to work hacking Virginia creeper from the porch posts and wild trumpet vines from the window casings. His hair stood wildly on end, but he worked with a determined set to his jaw. What the others cut up and discarded, he doggedly loaded onto a cart and hauled to the burning pit.

Breona called a break at half past noon. Hot, grimy, and bedraggled, they washed in the kitchen and then gathered in what had been the dining room. Gretl and Marit passed out sandwiches, apple slices, and cups of water. They sat upon blankets and ate in weary silence.

At the end of 30 minutes, Breona took charge again. "Aye, 'tis a mote o' work we've doon this morn, boot we're nae doon this day." She glanced at Rose. "Kin we b' doin' a wee bit o' dreamin' afore we begin agin, Miss Rose, Miss Joy?"

At first Rose didn't understand what she meant, but Joy thought she did. "You mean . . . shall we walk through the house with eyes of faith, Breona? Imagining what it will be when we are done?

"Aye, tha's th' ticket!" Breona exclaimed, her eyes alight.

Groaning and rubbing sore muscles, the party arose from the floor. Joy clapped her hands then opened her arms grandly and walked about the room. "Ladies and gentlemen, your attention, please! I give you *our dining room.*"

"I would like our dining table to be large enough to seat our entire family here. On special occasions we will lay a lace cloth, indulge in dozens of candles, and use our best china." She giggled. "We don't have a table *or* china yet, but I'm using my eyes of faith!" Joy curtsied prettily and several of the girls giggled.

"This way, please!" Rose ushered them toward the great room. As they traipsed into it, Joy and Rose were rewarded by appreciative murmurs of "It is so different!" and "Wonderful!" and "Oh, look at the windows and all the light they allow in!"

Rose curtsied also and gestured graciously toward the fireplaces, one at each end of the room. "Ladies and gentlemen, kindly envision many soft, deep chairs with pillows and footstools for all. Here we will sit of an evening, warm and cozy by a fire, sipping our tea, and telling of all our day's adventures."

"Oh," asked Maria softly. "Will someone read wonderful books to us here?"

"Of course," Rose replied. She wrapped an arm about Maria's waist. "It would be my pleasure to do so. For hours, if you like."

"What color wallpaper will we have?" Flora asked, utterly caught up. "Please say it will be pink and cream, with rosebuds and ivy!"

The empty room echoed with laughter and chatter. "Not *pink,*" someone objected. Flora flushed and started to retort, but Joy laid a calming hand on her arm.

"Flora, I love the sound of pink rosebuds and ivy. Perhaps we can find them in the perfect paper for your bedroom."

Flora brightened at that and the group trooped across the entry into the parlor to admire the progress there and to speculate on how the room would look when repainted and papered. The library, however, was a different story.

Nancy, her strawberry hair and translucent skin covered in fine dust, gestured toward the book shelves—two walls of them, floor to ceiling. "Breona, all these books are ruined."

She then pointed to the several stacks of books sitting on the floor, their edges furred in fine mold. The stench of mildew permeated the room. Where the carpets had been pulled, the wood floors bore evidence to water damage.

Missing window panes were boarded over, but the damage was evident. The group grew serious at the prospect of burning so many books—books that would cost a small fortune to ever replace!

"Sunlight, strong sunlight moight be th' savin' o' th'm," Breona muttered. But to all of them, the reek of mold was overpowering and the likelihood of saving the hundreds—perhaps a thousand!—volumes seemed remote.

"What should we do?" Nancy asked. Rose was pleased that she looked to Breona for her guidance.

"I'll be askin' Billy t' open t' room t' th' air an' then fittin' new glass," Breona replied, a little distracted by the enormity of the problem.

Next they toured the butler's pantry with its wine case and walls of empty shelves, slots, drawers. Adjacent was a modest room with a single, high window, the former butler's quarters. The room was snug and dry, and Nancy and Corrine had cleaned it thoroughly.

"Why, this is a perfect bedroom for our Mr. Wheatley, is it not?" Joy asked. They unanimously echoed Joy's sentiments. Mr. Wheatley, with a happy air of possession, examined the built-in drawers and small wardrobe.

Up the wide staircase they trudged. They explored the second floor, counting the bedrooms, bathrooms, linen closets, staircases, and passages. They admired rounded rooms, odd angled rooms, and projecting windows with wide views of the grounds. They did so while studiously ignoring water stains, mold, crumbling plaster, and mouse droppings.

Up the next flight of stairs they wandered onto the third floor where they discovered three unique turret rooms, each with high ceilings and three other rooms more regular in size. Through a passage to the back of the house they encountered a row of small servant quarters.

The tiny rooms were built into the angled pitch of one of the house's roofs. Their dormer windows protruded from the roof, each window with its own peaked roof.

Finally, they discovered a quaint set of wooden steps, only six of them, leading to a locked door.

"This must lead to the attic," Grant suggested. "Odd that the door is locked. I will see about finding a key."

They spent an hour touring the house and "dreaming" as Breona had put it. Rose and Joy agreed that it had been well worth the time as the happy possibilities they envisioned grew larger—at least for a few minutes—than the tasks ahead of them.

At the bottom of the wide staircase, Joy hugged Breona tightly. The men were already heading outside and the women returning to their chores. "You are brilliant, my dear friend," she said sincerely.

"Nay," she replied softly. "Did no' th' Lord say t' Abraham, 'lift up yer eyes an' *look*'? An' what e're Abraham was seein', th' Lord was givin' t' him."

She cast an eye up the staircase to the floors above. "These bairns mus' b' *lookin'* t' what th' Lord will be givin' th'm, I'm thinkin'."

At half past five the mingled scents of baking bread and beef simmering in thick gravy began to waft through the house. At six the household gathered in the dining room again.

Grant and Billy brought in a pair of sawhorses and placed three long planks across them. Then they carried in several benches Billy and Mr. Wheatley had knocked together from scraps they found in the carriage house.

Tabitha and Nancy washed down the planks and laid clean sheets upon them. Marit placed two kerosene lamps on their makeshift dining table as they gathered gratefully for a hot meal.

They ate voraciously, but made little conversation. No one had the energy. Rose found herself nodding off over her plate and jerked awake in chagrin, but no one had noticed. They were, all of them, exhausted beyond measure.

Breona set them to cleaning up and arranging bedrolls soon after. The girls followed Breona's instructions mechanically; no one objected when she suggested they turn in as soon as the beds were ready.

Breona split the girls between three bedrooms and Rose joined them, their few blankets poor padding against the hardwood floors. Mr. Wheatley chose the butler's quarters, Grant and Joy the parlor, and Billy and Marit bedded down in the great room.

The night was difficult for most of them, and the next morning was brutal. Aching, short on sleep, and cranky, many tempers were short, and the day began badly.

Rose could scarcely lead devotions nor did anyone at the breakfast table seem to care. She asked Grant to read to them while they ate and slowly woke up. He managed a chapter in Matthew and then, with no objections, closed the Bible she'd handed him and yawned. Breona, herself looking worn, finally got them moving for the day.

Mid morning, Rose passed by the staircase and heard voices from the hallway above.

"But washing floors and windows is *ruining* my hands," Rose heard a girl whine. "Miss Cleary always demanded that we keep our hands soft and smooth! She never allowed us to put them in hot water."

Breona's no-nonsense lilt echoed down the stairwell. "Ach! Ye poor bairn! And where ist precious Miss Cleary a-settin' at this ver' minute? D' ye think her hands will be stayin' soft and smooth in th' jailhouse? Eh? Loikley 'tis scrubbin' th' toilets and washin' th' laundry she is this minute!"

Rose heard an unintelligible reply from the girl, Flora, she believed, followed again by the final word from Breona. "Th' winders all doon th' hall air yers t' be cleanin'. I giv ye sixtry minutes, lass."

Rose could plainly visualize Breona's thin hands, red and rough from years of cleaning, although she was not yet twenty years of age. One more sentence sounded faintly down the stairs. "An' 'tis no more excuses from ye, little miss."

Dear Lord, we need your grace! Rose pleaded as she hurried away,

❧ ✸ ☙

CHAPTER 9

(Journal Entry, July 13, 1909)

Moving day is upon us. We are all, without exception, weary. Breona, with the wisdom of Solomon, called a holiday yesterday, although we have more than enough work to keep us employed for months. She assigned us to two groups and we set out to walk the neighborhood and picnic at the river.

I admit we are hardening to this work. I have slept well several nights now although I believe I have grown a permanent callous upon each hip.

I noticed, too, that we seemed to have energy to play and enjoy ourselves yesterday. Everyone, excepting perhaps, myself and our Mr. Wheatley. He and I were content to sit upon a blanket in the cool shade, nodding off with our backs against a tree, much of the morning.

The dear man has overextended himself, I fear. Grant took him aside and begged him not to try to keep up with him and Billy. If this approach fails, we will fall back on a stronger force, and have Breona speak with him. We simply cannot do without this sweet, gentle man.

In his own quiet way, he seems to impart a stability to our new home that our youthful, unruly, and sometimes wild girls crave. They will listen, spellbound, as he tells of his experiences in the war, although I am sure he frequently embellishes his tales. I only say so as I have heard at least three differing renderings of a certain Southern Army incursion against whom his company defended a vital armory.

Every evening he begins a game of checkers with whomever he can cajole into playing. The girls are quickly learning his moves and are making his wins a bit more hard-bought. He can also be a great tease with the girls, which they now receive with laughter and giggles.

It is something to behold, his charming, doting ways with them, for they know, quite intuitively, that he is a safe and sheltering harbor in a world where the men they have known have been only selfish and cruel.

—

The long, arduous process of making the house livable enough for them to move into was over. They had painted and papered the dining room, great room, parlor, and three bedrooms. The remaining repairs and refurbishments would be done a room at a time, shifting furniture from room to room as they went.

The task had taken longer than any of them had anticipated, and Rose had never been more exhausted. As she dressed in the dim light of early morning she realized with a start that the waistband of her skirt was loose.

Oh Jan! I can hear you chiding me right now, and I can see your blue eyes, so filled with love and strength. You would insist that I eat more, wouldn't you? she thought fondly. *How I wish you were here.*

She brushed her hair thoroughly, braided it, and twisted the braid into the coil she wore pinned at the back of her head. Cleaning the hair from her brush she sighed. More and more silver strands seemed to find their way into her hairbrush to mix with dark blonde ones.

The rest of the household was also up early that morning. They were anxious to receive the furniture that the women from Emily's Bible study group had collected for them.

"I have never appreciated a real bed as much as I will this evening," Rose confessed at breakfast. Her comments elicited a generous chorus of agreement.

David, Uli, their children, and Flinty arrived first, coming down the mountain on the morning train. They brought the household's remaining personal belongings and more donations from their Corinth church family.

They also brought young Will back to his mama and Blackie to Joy. Once in Marit's arms, Will refused to let her set him down or anyone else to take him. He clung to her neck refusing even Billy's outstretched arms, although he peeped at Billy long enough to exchange happy grins.

Blackie ran ecstatic circles about Joy. Although not puppy sized any longer, Grant picked Blackie up and held him between himself and Joy while Joy rubbed Blackie's ears and under his chin. Rose greeted them all with heartfelt embraces, and Mr. Wheatley grinned unabashedly when he saw his old checkers partner.

Flinty, too was delighted to see them all and kept repeating, "Yep. Sight fer sore eyes, fer certain!" and "Jest what th' doctor ordered, I'm thinkin'!"

Breona, however, looked him over, her sharp eyes missing nothing. She sidled up to Uli and, out of the side of her mouth, asked, "Whist? 'Tis off his feed he's lookin' t' me eyes!"

Uli, still smiling and watching everyone hugging and talking, whispered back, "We're a little concerned. I don't think he's taking very good care of himself. He misses all of you terribly."

David and Uli walked over every inch of the house, praising God for the space and the progress they had made. Flinty, eyes bright, slowly followed Mr. Wheatley around, commenting and grinning the entire time.

Before the real work of the day began, the household and their guests, still chattering happily, gathered in the great room.

Grant smiled at their swelled ranks and asked for their attention. "Before we truly make this house our home, and while we have many more family and friends gathered here with us, let us take time to thank God for his provision and ask him to bless this house and all we will do here in his name."

He turned to David Kalbørg. "Pastor, will you lead us in prayer?"

"What will you name this house?" David asked first.

Rose, Joy, and Grant looked at each other and then at the others. "We have been so busy cleaning and repairing, I don't believe we even considered giving the house a name," Joy confessed. "Does anyone have a suggestion?"

All were quiet, thinking on Joy's question. Finally, Marit offered softly, "Mrs. Palmer gave us this vonderful house. Could ve not call it Palmer House?"

Her suggestion drew several thoughtful nods. Finally, Breona replied, "Aye. 'Tis fittin', I'm thinkin'."

As simply as that, the name Palmer House was adopted.

Every head bowed as David prayed, "Lord, we consecrate this house, Palmer House, to your service. Every room, every hall, every nook and cranny, we dedicate to your purposes. We ask your Holy Spirit to be present and active in this place. We ask that you lead in every decision made here. And especially, Mighty God, we purpose to glorify you with every word spoken and deed accomplished within these walls. We pledge these things in Jesus' name."

Amens sounded across the circle, and then the work began.

The women from Emily's Bible study group, true to their word, had arranged for two wagons and a few strong young men to haul the donated furnishings to the house. The first loads arrived midday, and chaos reigned as everyone from the house swarmed out to the street, chattering and laughing, to unload the bounty.

"Mama, don't look now," Joy said quietly, "But we have an audience."

Rose, of course, looked around immediately. Several neighbors stared askance from their front gates or the upper windows of nearby houses.

"Oh dear," she murmured. "Perhaps we should ask everyone to talk softly."

"They are only enjoying themselves, Mama," Joy pointed out.

Joy stepped to the edge of the street and, with a wide smile plastered on her face, waved in a friendly manner to each person she saw watching. Reluctantly, several returned her neighborly greeting.

One woman, though, frowned and appeared to stomp back down the walkway to her front door. Joy gazed after her, hand still upraised.

With everyone helping to bring the furnishings into the house, the wagons emptied quickly. As the men offloaded the cargo, they placed the heavy pieces to the side but handed boxes and lighter items to the women to carry in.

Breona stood on the front porch and directed where the things would go. Blackie raced in and out of the house, following Joy or Grant and generally getting underfoot.

As soon as they emptied the two wagons, the drivers left to refill them. Inside the house, the great room was cluttered with bedroom furniture. Breona was sorting out the different bedsteads and chest of drawers.

"If ye be wishin' t' hev a certain bed, will ye be lettin' me know?" she asked.

Immediately the girls were examining the headboards and dressers and calling their preferences. Some beds and dressers were obvious matching sets, well worn but serviceable; others pieces were one-of-a-kind, and the girls were compelled to mix and match.

It didn't take long before a squabble broke out. Nancy asked for a small cherry bedstead with a tiny matching nightstand and chest of drawers. Tabitha, setting her jaw, insisted she had already asked for it.

"Why, of course you didn't," Nancy exclaimed. "Billy and Mr. Wheatley only just now brought it in!"

In a matter of seconds, their quarrel turned ugly and their jabs became personal and hurtful. Rose walked into the great room just as Tabitha loosed a string of colorful curse words at Nancy and Nancy, in response, slapped Tabitha in the face. Tabitha clenched her fist and raised it.

"Nancy! Tabitha!" Rose's tone was sharp, and both girls drew themselves up abruptly. Nancy had a guilty look on her face, but Tabitha was seething. Most of the household was standing about gawking and amazed at how quickly the confrontation had escalated.

Rose had not yet had to deal with an all-out fight, and she was not about to permit one now. "Nancy and Tabitha, the two of you will be the *last* to select beds," she decreed. "In fact, I am inclined to say you should both continue to sleep on the floor until such time as I say otherwise."

Eyes around the room widened. None of them had seen Rose in a righteous anger before. She looked around gravely and reminded all of them, "Was it only a few hours ago we committed our actions *and our words* to the glory of God? Therefore, rudeness, quarreling, and cursing are *not* acceptable under this roof. Nancy and Tabitha, you will apologize to each other and to everyone here, immediately."

Nancy, already sorry for her part, quickly responded. "I am sorry, Tabitha. And I apologize for my bad behavior, everyone."

Tabitha scowled and fixed her mouth in a straight line. Rose raised an eyebrow and said firmly, "You had best get it over quickly, Tabitha. I will not tolerate strife in this house."

Tabitha stared at her, weighing her options. Finally, she shrugged. "I apologize."

"You will please apologize first to Nancy and then to the rest of the house," Rose insisted.

Tabitha gave a short laugh under her breath. "All right." She turned to Nancy. "I apologize, *Nancy*. And I apologize to everyone else."

"Thank you," Rose said watching her closely. Tabitha nodded, then turned to Breona. "Where would you like this bedding?" She held up a stack of blankets tied together with twine.

"Second bedroom on th' left will do foine," Breona replied evenly. Tabitha nodded and headed upstairs. With that the rest of the household shook themselves and picked up where they'd left off.

Rose watched Tabitha go thoughtfully. The woman's heart was harder than the rest of the girls' in the house. Rose wondered again if Tabitha was going to develop into a serious problem.

By that evening many of the rooms in the house were comfortably furnished. The great room held an eclectic collection of overstuffed chairs, ottomans, and sofas. The dining room had a real table, long enough to seat them all, and a variety of dining chairs. Joy counted chairs from four different dining sets but, arranged artfully, they did not seem to clash too terribly.

Billy, with Grant's assistance, moved a bed, a large chest of drawers, and Will's baby bed into the tower room they had been using on the third floor; Joy and Grant added furniture, a few personal items, and a basket for Blackie to another room on that floor. Both couples would eventually be moving to what were now the carriage house and the caretaker's cottage, but that day seemed a long ways off today.

Mr. Wheatley settled into the butler's quarters with a small bed and lamp stand, sighing as he settled his old bones into the mattress. They had made up a bed for Flinty in the Butler's pantry close by.

David, Uli, and their children departed for a nearby hotel. They would come by in the morning to collect Flinty and catch the train back up the mountain.

———

Esther had known Cal for little more than four weeks, but she had found him to be smart, kind, and a terrific lover. As the house's madam, she didn't service clients herself, but Cal was no longer a client in her eyes.

She only saw him once or twice a week and, lately, it hadn't been enough for her. He looked at her with such admiration and spoke such sweet praise into her ears. She found herself longing to hear his voice and to feel his hands, more and more often.

When she asked him what he did for a living, though, he simply replied that he was in business for himself. The details he provided were vague, except that the demands of his work kept him too busy to see her as often as she would like.

One evening he offered a few suggestions regarding her house, and Esther, to her surprise, found them constructive. *Here is a man I could depend on*, she thought one late night after the customers had gone.

ℰHAPTER 10

(Journal Entry, July 16, 1909)

We had unexpected visitors just before dinner today, a party of four of our neighbors, two men and two women. They were stony faced and I knew we were going to be tested.

Breona showed them into the parlor (our nicest room at present) where Joy, Grant, and I received them. I am grateful for your wisdom, Lord, for it took all we had.

Mr. and Mrs. Brewster were solemn and mostly quiet. A Mr. Haney and Miss DeWitt did most of the speaking: "We represent the interests and concerns of the neighborhood," "It is rumored that you have opened an establishment for 'soiled doves'," and lastly, "This neighborhood is not zoned for boarding houses" were their main points, as I recall.

Joy was simple and direct, explaining that the girls had been forced into prostitution but, by God's grace, were no longer so engaged. They were, at present, either working at or seeking honest employment.

I may be exaggerating when I say that Miss DeWitt's eyes nearly fell out of her head when Joy calmly used the word "prostitution."

Of course, dear Lord, I remember how difficult it was at first for us to use words such as brothel and prostitute. I suppose I am not as sheltered from the harsh realities of the world as I once was.

Grant clarified that we do not operate a boarding house but rather a small vocational school. He showed them our charter and proceeded to tell them of our training in fine household furnishings and the culinary arts. God bless Arnie for applying for such a variance from the city! Of course Mrs. Palmer's influence was instrumental in its approval.

Lastly, we took the group on a tour and introduced them to our little family. Everyone in our household dresses so practically and the house itself already has such a sweet, homey atmosphere. Marit and Gretl were in the kitchen preparing dinner and all the while Will was laughing and banging his little cup on his highchair when we passed through the kitchen.

We invited them to stay for dinner, but they declined very graciously, I must say, so we sent them on their way bearing plates of Marit's Swedish ginger cookies. Perhaps they will become regular customers!

Oh, I know I am being glib, Lord. We only hope that they will not stir up trouble against us. Mr. Wheatley handed the ladies down the porch steps in true gentlemanly fashion.

He reported that Miss DeWitt wasn't quite won over and began complaining almost immediately that Mr. Haney had not been forceful enough. That is until Mrs. Brewster responded (quite firmly, Mr. Wheatley insisted), "Cora, do hush up. I declare you have the compassion and intelligence of a fruit fly."

———

"Now that we are settled in, shouldn't we ask the Lord to direct us to a church?" Grant asked at breakfast Sunday morning. "It has been weeks since we left Corinth and our little church there."

No one responded at first. A few of the girls looked nervous at the proposition, and it wasn't hard for Rose or Joy to understand why. It had been less than three months since some of them had left their past profession. How would a new church receive them?

Rose spoke carefully. "Perhaps we should ask Emily's pastor to pay us a visit. He does know of our work here, of course. We could discuss how to best approach finding a church home."

Grant nodded, and the tension at the table relaxed.

———

"Rose, may I introduce Pastor Jamison? Pastor, this is Mrs. Thoresen," Emily said formally the following Wednesday.

"Mrs. Thoresen, so pleased to finally meet you," Pastor Jamison said while holding her hand and smiling kindly. He was tall, gray haired, and a bit stooped. He may have been older than Rose, but his eyes, even while over shadowed by bushy, white brows, were young and lively.

"Thank you for calling on us," Rose replied. She immediately liked the man's steady voice and clear eyes. "Would you care to take tea or would you like to see the house first?"

"Oh, I enjoy my tea very much, ma'am, but I confess I have been looking forward to seeing your progress! It has been many years since I have been here."

"Then we will see the house first," Rose answered, smiling at both him and Emily. "This is our parlor," she said, showing them to the left side of the house. "We will take tea here when we are done."

Rose escorted them through the downstairs, taking them next to the great room, dining room, and kitchen. On the second floor she showed them the empty rooms but only one of the girls' bedrooms before advancing to the third floor.

"We respect each other's privacy," Rose explained. "Sarah and Corrine granted permission for me to show you their room today."

She did not mention the small row she'd had with Tabitha earlier in the day. "I don't want some stranger looking at and touching my things!" Tabitha had raised her voice to Rose and attached a descriptive curse word to the word "stranger" before Rose had even had the opportunity to assure the girls that she would guard their privacy.

"Please tell the young ladies for me that I appreciate their kind regard," Pastor Jamison replied.

On the third floor she showed them Billy and Marit's tower room, the unoccupied bedrooms, and the old servant quarters. Eventually they ended at the six steps leading to the attic.

"The attic door is locked," Rose murmured. "We have not yet opened it."

Pastor Jamison's brows drew together and he replied softly, "I do understand. Perfectly."

Rose did *not* understand, but tucked his comment away, determined to ask Emily about it later. She escorted her guests back to the parlor and Breona appeared straight away with their donated tea service. The tray also held Marit's ginger cookies and a plate of steaming scones.

"Wonderful!" Pastor Jamison exclaimed, observing the goodies with gusto.

After Rose had served the tea, she broached her subject. "Pastor Jamison, I confess I had a purpose in mind when I asked Mrs. Van der Pol to bring you to meet us."

"Yes? Please do feel at ease to ask me anything." The gentle old man took another bite of ginger cookie, obviously enjoying himself.

"Well, we, as a household, are in need of a home church," Rose answered. "Since we are a company of fifteen, sixteen if we include Mr. and Mrs. Evans' little one, our arrival would surely not be overlooked and would, I believe, engender questions . . ."

She cleared her throat and took a sip of tea herself. "I suppose I am asking if we would be welcomed at your church, given the, shall we say, unorthodox history of some of our household."

Rose looked to Emily who nodded encouragement to continue. "While curiosity is perfectly normal, we would not wish to . . . offend any of your parishioners, nor would we wish our girls to be the recipients of any . . . judgmental comments or harshness."

Pastor Jamison set his cup down and folded his hands on his knee, and he nodded that he understood.

"I pray I am not being too forward," Rose pressed on, "but frankly, several of our girls are not yet Christians and have never been to church. We would not wish them to experience . . . a cool reception . . . rather than the presence and power of Christ."

Pastor Jamison continued to nod, but his brows pulled together in serious contemplation. "Mrs. Thoresen, please do not fret yourself; I perfectly understand your concerns. I wish I had better tidings regarding our church—but perhaps I am getting somewhat ahead of myself.

"You see, I had a sense that you might approach me on this very topic, and I brought you something I read but lately. Read and wept over, I am afraid. Have you heard of the *Soiled Dove Plea*?"

Rose and Emily both shook their heads.

"May I be permitted to read a portion of it to you? Sadly, I believe it sums up perfectly the decidedly unwelcome culture we find in many of our churches."

This time Rose and Emily nodded. Both were curious.

"Before I read this passage I will tell you that it is the true closing argument of an attorney who represented a young woman accused of prostitution." He paused and looked earnestly at Rose and Emily.

"I pray you do not fault me for using such a word? I must be so careful not to offend the sensibilities of many, even in my own church!" He huffed a little. "How we speak of bringing the gospel *to* the lost but cannot abide speaking *of* the lost is beyond me!"

He stopped again. "Dear me. Off on a tangent. Please do forgive me. I will read but several lines and leave the copy with you to read in full later[1]." He read quietly,

---

[1] See full text on page 277.

"Gentlemen of the jury: You heard with what cold cruelty the prosecution referred to the sins of this woman, as if her condition were of her own preference. The evidence has painted you a picture of her life and surroundings.

Do you think that they were embraced of her own choosing? Do you think that she willingly embraced a life so revolting and horrible? Ah, no! Gentlemen, one of our own sex was the author of her ruin, more to blame than she.

Then let us judge her gently. What could be more pathetic than the spectacle she presents? An immortal soul in ruin! Where the star of purity once glittered on her girlish brow, burning shame has set its seal and forever.

And only a moment ago, they reproached her for the depths to which she had sunk, the company she kept, the life she led. Now, what else is left her? Where can she go and her sin not pursue her?

Gentlemen, the very promises of God are denied her. He said: "Come unto me all ye that labor and are heavy laden and I will give you rest." She has indeed labored, and is heavily laden, but if, at this instant she were to kneel before us all and confess to her Redeemer and beseech His tender mercies, where is the church that would receive her?

And even if they accepted her, when she passed the portals to worship and to claim her rest, scorn and mockery would greet her; those she met would gather around them their spirits the more closely to avoid the pollution of her touch."

His voice trembled at the last. Rose and Emily had clasped hands as he read, their eyes filling with tears.

"You see, dear Mrs. Thoresen, I am in a quandary, for this reading so aptly describes many of my own congregation—and I, their shepherd, am so deeply grieved to tell you so."

Rose murmured quietly. "Thank you. Thank you for being candid. I appreciate you coming to visit today."

"I hope I did not discourage you too severely," he said, straightening. "For while your girls would likely receive a cold welcome from my congregation, I can direct you to where they will be warmly received."

Rose looked up. "Indeed? Please do tell where, Pastor Jamison."

"Near to the infamous houses of Denver, a fine young man has begun a good work. He reaches out to the lost—those bound in chains of alcohol and opium, as well as those described in this reading." Pastor Jamison took a card from his breast pocket and scrawled on it.

Smiling again, he handed the card to Rose. "This pastor's church is young but thriving. He will welcome you and your young ladies. I have heard him speak the truth of the Gospel in love and with hope for the lost. You need not fear receiving a cold hand of fellowship from him."

Rose grasped the card eagerly. "Thank you! I thank you truly, Pastor."

CHAPTER 11

(Journal Entry, July 26, 1909)

Lord, thank you! Yesterday Joy and Grant visited the little church, Calvary Temple, recommended so highly by Pastor Jamison. They shared their report at dinner last evening. How pleased and enthused they were!

Grant, in particular, spoke highly of the young minister. His name is Mr. Isaac Carmichael. As he described Pastor Carmichael's ministry he certainly had the attention of all of us. The pastor preached from Luke 19:10, "For the Son of man is come to seek and save that which was lost," and had a good crowd of lost souls who came to listen.

During the service a man gave his testimony, sharing how the Lord had set him free from drink after thirteen years of bondage. An older woman, too, shared how Jesus forgave her shameful past and removed her guilt. Grant described her so clearly, and I believe I saw hope flicker in the eyes of some of our lost girls! Thank you, Father, for giving us these young women to love and to share Jesus with.

I posed the question after Joy and Grant finished their report, should we attend this church on Sunday? Of course a few, Tabitha being the most vocal, do not wish to go at all; however, I reminded everyone that we will attend church as a family—we have only to decide in which church the Lord wishes us to plant us.

And so we will attend Calvary Temple this Sunday! I am eager to see this work in action. And although we have some hard, hurt hearts in our family, I am trusting you, Lord, to heal those hearts! I believe you have led us this far and will guide us forward.

——

The remainder of the week passed slowly for Rose. She was impatient for Sunday to arrive so the household could attend this new church. She was eager to see this work with her own eyes.

During the week the Lord reminded Rose of her early days in RiverBend, how he had called her and won her heart, and how important her church had been to her. After she had surrendered to Jesus, Rose had longed to share her new faith with other women in their little town—women who were as hungry for the Savior as she had been.

She and Vera Medford had started a home Bible study that led many of these women into a relationship with the Lord. Recalling this time, Rose was again fired with seeing "her girls," as she now thought of the young women in Palmer House, find Jesus in the same powerful way she had so many years ago.

When Sunday at last arrived, nerves were taut, particularly in the girls who had never attended church before. Several had preconceptions of the expected fashion standards and worried their clothing would not measure up.

Rose and Joy downplayed dressing "up" for church and set an example by appearing at breakfast in good quality but moderately trimmed outfits.

"We may all feel a bit of trepidation this morning," Rose suggested gently. "I don't know, any more than you, what to expect. As this is a new church located near the, ah, red light area of town, I have a sense that it will be different from what I am accustomed to."

She added, "And, since it is located in that area of town, I do wish our mode of dress to distinguish us from the 'working girls,' so that none of you risk being, ah, approached as such."

She colored a little. "To be clear, we must be careful for each other's safety. Please, let us keep together at all times. Agreed?"

She received a chorus of 'yeses' and nods in response.

———

The church was housed in a brick warehouse, high and cavernous, but already filled near capacity. The seating was the most eclectic hodge-podge of seats Rose, Joy, or Grant had ever seen in a church. Whatever could be sat upon was put to use including dining chairs, sofas, boxes, benches, and cast-off church pews.

An usher wearing a checkered shirt and suspenders found them seating in three rows, five to six of their group in each row, so that they were seated together. Crowded around them, all standing and singing, was a crowd comprised of every segment of society: Caucasian, Negro, Chinese, Mexican, poor, middle-class, wealthy.

And the singing! The singing struck them all. A large organ on a platform at the front of the room played song after song and the voices raised with it were loud, filled with unrestrained joy and uninhibited praise.

No one led the singing; the organ played and the congregants sang, and sang with all their being. Rose could hardly bear the sweetness of the worship. Her thirsty soul opened wide to receive as the presence of God came down in that hall.

Praise ye the Lord,
the Almighty, the King of creation!
O my soul, praise Him,
for He is thy health and salvation!
All ye who hear,
Now to His temple draw near
Join me in glad adoration!

and

Blessed assurance, Jesus is mine!
Oh, what a foretaste of glory divine!
Heir of salvation, purchase of God
Born of His Spirit, washed in His blood!

This is my story, this is my song
Praising my Saviour, all the day long
This is my story, this is my song
Praising my Saviour, all the day long

and

What a fellowship, what a joy Divine
Leaning on the Everlasting Arms
What a blessedness, what a peace is mine
Leaning on the Everlasting Arms!

After thirty minutes or so, a young man walked onto the stage. He was ordinary looking, slender but not tall, with light brown hair and a strong chin. The singing tapered off and the crowd hushed and settled in their seats as he prepared to speak. The man's voice, unaided, carried to every corner of the lofty warehouse.

"And, behold, a woman in the city, which was a sinner,
when she knew that Jesus sat at meat
in the Pharisee's house,
brought an alabaster box of ointment,
And stood at his feet behind him weeping,
and began to wash his feet with tears,

and did wipe them with the hairs of her head,
and kissed his feet,
and anointed them with the ointment.
Now when the Pharisee
which had bidden him saw it,
he spake within himself, saying,
This man, if he were a prophet,
would have known who and
what manner of woman this is
that toucheth him: for she is a sinner."

He laid his Bible down. "The Pharisee of Jesus' day is like unto a religious man of today. He was willing to welcome Jesus into his house, but he did not understand Jesus or his calling," the preacher said. "In his private thoughts, the religious man wondered why Jesus would allow a sinful woman to touch him."

Isaac Carmichael looked earnestly at the congregation. "Friends, let us be clear. The sinful woman of this passage was what we call a soiled dove, a prostitute. And the religious man truly believed that Jesus should have known better than to let a fallen woman touch his holy feet."

He strode across the platform and gazed out at the crowd again. "Are any of you here today willing to say, 'I am like that woman. I am a sinful, fallen woman?'"

A murmur rippled across the room, and Rose saw some of her girls go quiet and still with shock.

Pastor Carmichael continued. "I have good news for you. Jesus heard the religious man's thoughts. He turned to the man, whose name was Simon, and answered his question!" In a clear voice he read,

"And Jesus answering said unto him,
Simon, I have somewhat to say unto thee.
And he saith, Master, say on.

"And Jesus told Simon this parable:

"There was a certain creditor
which had two debtors:
the one owed five hundred pence,
and the other fifty.
And when they had nothing to pay,
he frankly forgave them both.

Tell me therefore,
which of them will love him most?

"Simon answered and said,
I suppose that he, to whom he forgave most.
And he said unto him, Thou hast rightly judged.

"And he turned to the woman,
and said unto Simon, Seest thou this woman?
I entered into thine house,
thou gavest me no water for my feet:
but she hath washed my feet with tears,
and wiped them with the hairs of her head.

"Thou gavest me no kiss:
but this woman since the time I came in
hath not ceased to kiss my feet.
My head with oil thou didst not anoint:
but this woman hath anointed my feet with ointment."

His voice softened. "You see, Simon, the religious man, did not see himself as a debtor to God, a sinner. He did not feel he owed God anything! Because he had led a *respectable* life, he did not feel sinful! And because 'he owed little,' he had never experienced the strength and power of forgiveness. You see, he had never acknowledged his own need to be forgiven! Dear ones, to not recognize one's own sinfulness is a dangerous place to be."

The preacher paused. "But the sinful woman? She knew. Oh, yes, she *knew* she was a sinner. And she loved Jesus because he knew her for what she was *and still* he forgave her.

"Are you a sinner? Do you know how far you have fallen from God and what you owe him? Be sure of this: You cannot repay what you owe. No effort on your part can repay the debt you owe. No effort on my part can repay the debt I owe! Only Jesus can pay the debts we owe. And here is good news, dear friends. Jesus said,

"Wherefore I say unto thee,
'Her sins, which are many, are forgiven;
for she loved much:
but to whom little is forgiven, the same loveth little.'
And he said unto her, 'Thy sins are forgiven.'

"Your sins are forgiven! Do you want to be like this woman, forgiven and received by Jesus? Do not wait another day. No matter what your sins, no matter what you owe, come to Jesus today. Come right now."

Repentant souls, wealthy and poor, streamed to the altar to confess their sins and receive forgiveness. The power of that moment was beyond anything Rose had ever experienced, beyond what Joy or Grant or any of Palmer House had ever witnessed. Around them, people fell to their knees to pray. Rose joined them and poured out her heart to God.

The organ played softly and gentle singing accompanied it. No one closed the service. Pastor Carmichael and others prayed with those at the altar and eventually the congregation began to disperse.

The walk back to Palmer House was quiet. Rose could not speak; her heart was still too overwhelmed by what she had seen, had experienced.

—

The shop was modest in size but the location was all Joy could have hoped for. She and Grant paused before following the landlord inside. The narrow brick building faced a bustling street. Quality shops of many types lined the avenue, and motor car and foot traffic were plenteous.

Inside the shop it was plain to Joy and Grant that the previous tenant had been a dressmaker and that her taste in interior design had run to the decidedly feminine—overly fussy and froufrou in Joy's opinion, but that could be remedied.

They followed the landlord through the shop, which included a small showroom in the front, two fitting rooms in the rear, a tiny parlor, and an office. A sewing room ran the length of the side of the building.

"The folks as live upstairs are gone during the day," the gentleman explained, "and I never heard no complaints of disturbances from the last folks as let this place."

Joy and Grant nodded, both engrossed in envisioning how—or if—the shop would fit their needs. Grant pointed out that the fitting room walls were new additions and could be removed. However, even if they knocked the walls out and joined the fitting rooms with the showroom it would not be as large as what they had discussed and determined they needed.

Their warehouse in Omaha still held a large amount of fine household articles and furnishings. Grant did not remember selecting and purchasing them during his fateful trip to Boston. He did not recall having them shipped to Omaha, just before he boarded the *Richmond* on his way to England. He was obliged to take Joy's word for it.

"Mr. Benson, I'm afraid we need a larger showroom than what this shop affords," Joy admitted, considerably disappointed.

She sighed and walked to the front windows. It was such a perfect location. Across the way and down the street she glimpsed a park, its lawn beckoning with a pleasant emerald glint. Couples strolled by and knots of shoppers chattered as they paused to stare into neighboring windows. Fine carriages and motor cars passed back and forth in front of the store.

"Joy," Grant offered hesitantly, "What if we were to also open up the sewing studio? Not knock down the walls, of course," he hastened to assure the owner, "but perhaps construct two graceful arches where the existing doors are."

He gestured with his arms where he had the locations of the archways in mind "By doing so, our customers would feel invited into the room and could pass through and out the other archway into the rear of the showroom."

He rubbed his face, something Joy noticed he did when thinking hard, as though the effort tired him. "Perhaps . . . Joy, could you envision the front of the shop as parlor furnishings, the rear as dining, and the side area through the arches as bedroom suites?"

Joy walked into the long sewing room and immediately grasped his idea. "Yes. Yes!" She turned to the owner. "Would you have any objections to us opening up the doorways as my husband described?"

An hour later Joy and Grant left the building with a signed lease and a set of keys. Joy stopped on the sidewalk and turned to stare at the shop windows. They were tall, wide, and framed the door on either side. She was already planning how to dress the windows.

"It's not at all like our store in Omaha," she mused. "Do you remember it even a bit? Rough planked floors that creaked and 'clunked' with a lovely hollow sound; long, wooden counters that gleamed with the wax Mr. Wheatley rubbed into them?"

Grant shook his head. "I don't know. The one thing I do seem to recall is the old Blackie curled up near . . . a stove? Did he have a basket near the stove?"

"Yes, he did," Joy replied, smiling softly. "You loved your Blackie so much. He was a great comfort to me after you . . . you were gone. We both missed you so."

Grant tipped her chin toward him and kissed her. "What do we need to do next?"

"Well . . . the shop must be ready to receive the merchandise before it arrives. So we must complete—or nearly complete—the refurbishment before we send Billy to Omaha to empty the warehouse and ship the furnishings."

"Besides taking down the fitting room walls and making the arched doorways, what other refurbishments did you have in mind?" Grant asked.

They chatted enthusiastically back and forth, exchanging ideas, until they reached the trolley stop. Joy was scribbling a list when they stepped onto the trolley for the ride home.

———

Esther was in love. She felt it in her heart, in its deep longing. The more she saw of Cal, the more she craved him. His presence made her feel safe; his thoughtfulness made her feel valued.

He was becoming more and more helpful with the house's business, too. Their clientele had picked up quite a bit. When she mentioned that she was looking for another man to work the door with Tom, he said he knew someone who would be perfect.

The next afternoon a large, soft-spoken man appeared at her door. "I'm Jack, ma'am. Mr. Judd mentioned you might have a position open," the man said quietly. On the strength of Cal's recommendation, she hired him right away.

And it was a good thing she had. She introduced Jack to Tom and asked Tom to show him the ropes, but just two nights later, Tom quit without notice. Refusing to meet her eyes and mumbling that he'd found something better, he was gone.

Esther was surprised and disappointed. Tom had seemed happy with his job and she'd never had any problems with him. Cal, however, came to her aid again and sent around another man to replace Tom. Donovan started the next evening.

Against her better judgment, she began daydreaming of a future with Cal. *He is so kind, so helpful,* she mused. *He treats me with such respect! We could be happy together . . .*

CHAPTER 12

(Journal Entry, August 30, 1909)
Attendance at Calvary Temple is now a regular part of our week.
What wonderful messages Pastor Carmichael brings us! I am fed,
comforted, encouraged, and spurred to serve you more, dear Lord.

I have overheard Breona, Mei-Xing, and Marit talking
enthusiastically about Pastor's messages, so I know they are
learning, too. The other girls will sometimes join in or ask questions.
I am hopeful that soon they will hear the Savior calling them and
will answer.

———

Martha Palmer arrived unexpectedly one afternoon. Hearing the
knock at the front door, Mr. Wheatley peered through door's
peephole but saw only the departing back of a uniformed chauffeur.
Puzzled, he cracked the door, looked around, and finally looked
down to spy the slight figure of Mrs. Palmer stooped over her cane.

"Well, are you going to ask me in?" she demanded.

Mr. Wheatley backed away from the door with alacrity and
waited for the bent little lady to thump her way into the entry.
Breona, catching a glimpse of their surprise guest, alerted Rose and
then ran to the kitchen to prepare a tea tray. She bade the rest of the
girls to continue with their chores.

"Mrs. Palmer! What a delightful surprise." Rose swept into the
entryway and allowed the woman to lean on her arm until they
reached a comfortable chair in the parlor.

"No, no; not yet," Mrs. Palmer said testily. "I came to see what
you have done to the place. I can sit after."

"Really, we have scarcely begun," Rose remonstrated gently. "It
is livable, but only just."

From her bent over position Mrs. Palmer craned her neck sideways
and peered about the parlor with interest. "I'd like to see the great room,
kitchen, and dining room, if you don't mind," she stated.

Rose walked her out of the parlor, across the entry, into the
spacious great room, and then through the dining room and into the
kitchen. Marit, who curtsied and reddened, was baking bread.
Breona and Mei-Xing were preparing the tea tray.

Will, bouncing up and down in his high chair, went still and stared with large eyes at the frail little stranger with white hair. He sucked in his lower lip and looked to his mama.

"Very nice, very nice," the old woman muttered and fumbled for Rose's arm. "I'll sit now and take a cup of tea."

Rose helped Mrs. Palmer into a comfortable chair where she sat, bent over, hands clasped upon the silver head of her cane, but tipping her head and looking about, missing nothing. Almost immediately Mei-Xing entered the parlor with a laden tray. She set the tray on the low table near Mrs. Palmer's chair, seated herself in front of it, and began to gracefully serve the tea.

"How do you care for your tea, Mrs. Palmer?" she inquired.

"Eh? Oh. One lump, just a scant spoonful of cream. Not milk, mind you."

"Of course." In short order, she placed a tiny side table within Mrs. Palmer's reach and set her cup of tea on it.

Mrs. Palmer ignored the tea and studied Mei-Xing closely. Mei-Xing, flushing slightly under Mrs. Palmer's scrutiny, finished serving Rose's tea and gently inclined her head toward both of them. "Will you take cake?"

"You are a tiny thing, ain't you?"

"Yes, ma'am," Mei-Xing responded, unperturbed, slicing the lemon cake on the tray.

"None for me. What is your name, girl?"

"Yes, ma'am. Mei-Xing Li, ma'am." Mei-Xing poured herself a cup of tea and cradled it on her knee.

Martha Palmer's gnarled fingers reached for her cup. The cup quivered in her tentative grip as she sipped from it. "Are you one of the girls who came down the mountain?"

Rose winced at her bluntness, but Mei-Xing returned Mrs. Palmer's question calmly.

"Yes, ma'am. However, I was fortunate to escape to Miss Thoresen's lodge several months before . . . before the marshals freed the other girls."

"You did, did you? And how'd you do that?"

Mei-Xing smiled a small smile. "I tied together all the clothes I could find to make a rope and climbed out a third-floor window. Unfortunately, the rope only went to the bottom of the second floor, so I had to drop the rest of the way."

Mrs. Palmer's mouth fell open and her cup rattled as she set it on the saucer. "Land sakes! You don't say. Were you hurt?"

Rose cleared her throat in distress. She vividly recalled how damaged and broken Mei-Xing had been and how terrified she had been to sleep for fear she would be discovered and dragged back.

Mei-Xing, however, answered simply and calmly again. "I landed in the shrubbery and suffered a few scratches. I did also sprain my ankle when I dropped, but it was preferable to what would have become of me if I had not attempted to escape again."

"Again? Escape again? Had you tried before?" The woman craned her neck to stare at Mei-Xing.

"Yes, ma'am. The night before, but . . . they caught me."

Mrs. Palmer's voice dropped to a soft whisper. "They caught you! They . . . what did they do when they caught you, my dear?"

Despite her calm, Mei-Xing had begun to tremble, and her voice shook a little. "Three men took me to a room at the top of the house and . . . had their way with me for several hours."

"They . . . they . . ." Mrs. Palmer's sharpness abandoned her.

"Mei-Xing, perhaps a little slice of that cake?" Rose asked, anxious to turn the conversation.

Mei-Xing, though shaking, maintained her composure. "Yes, Mrs. Palmer, they violated and beat me."

Martha Palmer was silent and unmoving for several moments. Finally, she beckoned to Mei-Xing.

"Would ye come here, Miss Li, where I may see your face better? Just kneel down here next to me on the carpet where I can look at you."

For a moment Mei-Xing did not move and then, sighing softly, she set her cup on the tea tray and knelt before Mrs. Palmer's chair. The woman reached out a gnarled hand and, with great tenderness, cupped Mei-Xing's chin and, in her peculiar manner, cocked her head to the side so she could look Mei-Xing in the eye.

For a long moment she stared at Mei-Xing before she spoke. "I am sorry, child, that these things happened to you. So very sorry. I see, however, that you have great strength within you. Tell me, is that strength from the Lord?"

Mei-Xing seemed transfixed by the old woman's scrutiny and by the unexpected kindness that seeped like healing oil from her touch and her words. "Yes, ma'am. I have come to love the Lord Jesus and to know he loves me. I do not believe I could face life without the strength his love gives me each day."

Martha Palmer patted Mei-Xing's cheek gently and nodded. "I am so glad to hear this. I, too, have faced great loss in my life. I know this is hard, my dear. Be strong and grow in your faith. I will remember to pray for you diligently."

Clearing her throat and placing her hands once again on the top of her cane, Mrs. Palmer signaled the end of the unexpectedly tender moment. "Tell me a bit more about yourself, Miss Li. Do ye have an education?"

Mei-Xing returned to her chair and composed herself. "Yes, Mrs. Palmer. I was very well educated."

"Oh? Read and write, do you?"

"In English, French, German, and Mandarin, ma'am."

"Eh? You don't say." Mrs. Palmer stared at her hands a moment. "You don't say. Accomplishments? Music? Art?"

Mei-Xing's smile was wan. "I sketch a little. I also play piano and violin. Or I did."

Rose's eyebrows went up. She'd had no idea. And what was the purpose of Mrs. Palmer's many questions?

"Indeed! How did you come by such accomplishments, if I may ask?"

Here Mei-Xing's manner shifted subtly although her response retained its gracious tone. "Mrs. Palmer, do you mean to ask how a whore received such a fine education?"

Mrs. Palmer stared at her. "Don't be cheeky, miss. Besides, I was under the impression that you were *not* a whore, Miss Li."

Rose choked on her tea and fumbled with her napkin, while Mei-Xing reddened, whether in embarrassment or anger, Rose could not know which.

"Well, speak up, child. Are you a whore or are you not?"

"Really! Mrs. Palmer!" Rose uttered sharply, rising from her seat.

"Hush, Mrs. Thoresen. Let the girl answer for herself."

Mei-Xing straightened in her chair and faced Mrs. Palmer. For several moments she struggled within herself, staring at the old woman and breathing hard.

"No, Mrs. Palmer, I am not a whore," she finally answered.

"I'm sorry, my dear. My old ears are somewhat hard of hearing. Would you mind speaking up?"

Rose, now perplexed, shot looks back and forth between the two women. She knew for a fact that Martha Palmer's hearing was untouched by age.

Suddenly Mei-Xing smiled. It was a tiny smile, but she nodded at the same time. Quite clearly and firmly she repeated to herself, "No, Mrs. Palmer, I am not a whore. I am a child of the living God. I am a new creation in him."

Mrs. Palmer nodded in satisfaction over her cane and then gave it one good thump on the carpeted floor. "Very good. Yes, *well done.*"

She struggled to stand and complained to Rose, "Mrs. Thoresen, this chair is entirely too deep!" She then gestured imperiously to Mei-Xing. "Miss Li, give this interfering old woman your arm, if you please."

The old lady grasped Mei-Xing's arm and managed to extricate herself from the chair. Side-by-side, the two women stood nearly eye-to-eye, Mrs. Palmer from her bent over position, Mei-Xing from her tiny height.

"You have a lovely quality about you, my dear. Your parents must have cared for you very much to have given you such an upbringing," Mrs. Palmer said softly.

If she were looking for something to finally prick Mei-Xing's heart, Mrs. Palmer had found it. The girl, just turned sixteen years old, suddenly had tears in her eyes.

"There, there," Mrs. Palmer whispered, again in that tender tone. "Forgive this old woman."

She turned toward Rose to include her in what she was about to say. "I am in need of a personal companion and social secretary. As much as I fight it, I am unable to manage many things by myself these days. And I do detest getting behind.

"The woman I engage must be gracious, educated, and socially adept. I carry considerable influence in this town; nevertheless, some of my acquaintances have the tact of a cactus and the discretion of a jay bird."

She nodded at Mei-Xing. "I needed to know how you would conduct yourself should someone as direct as I question you regarding your background. Miss Li, we can talk more on this later, but today I would like to ask if you would be interested in such a position?"

Mei-Xing shot a glance at Rose, dumbfounded. "I, that is, I . . ."

Rose stepped in. "Thank you for such an honor, Mrs. Palmer. Perhaps we can prayerfully consider your offer before Mei-Xing gives you her answer?"

"Yes, yes. Of course. I will pay $10 a week. You may live with me during the week and return here on your night off or my chauffeur, Benton, can bring you daily to my home and back. It will be your choice. The hours will, occasionally, be long, but I do not go out of an evening as much as before. Generally I am abed by eight o'clock in the evening.

"Oh, and I will require that you install a telephone in this house. I will not send Benton across town simply to deliver a message when a telephone call will suffice."

Mei-Xing's eyes grew large. The salary was generous—not overly so, but still . . . much more than she would ever earn clerking or sewing in a shop. And the work would be engaging and varied.

"By the by, I understand that some of your neighbors paid a visit," Mrs. Palmer remarked with a raised eyebrow.

Rose nodded. "Yes, Mrs. Palmer."

"I think you can rest easy regarding Mr. Haney and the Brewsters. Cora DeWitt, however, may provide you with additional opportunities to grow in grace." She smiled shrewdly at Rose.

———

"She did not!" Joy expostulated. "She asked Mei-Xing if she were a whore?"

"Shhh, Joy. The whole house will hear you," Rose cautioned her, looking around. News spread faster in Palmer House than ants on sugar!

"I just cannot envision Mrs. Palmer using such a word," Joy returned in a quieter voice.

"It was truly amazing, though. Something happened inside Mei-Xing at that moment. She no longer sees herself in the same way and confidently said so! I tell you, you should have heard her: 'No, Mrs. Palmer, I am not a whore. I am a child of the living God.' It was beautiful, Joy. It was powerful."

Somehow Mei-Xing's encounter with Mrs. Palmer percolated through the house, with many opinions as to "what *I* would have told that old lady" passing among the girls. Tabitha, predictably, had choice and colorful words on the matter.

Once the novelty wore away, however, the girls seemed to ponder Mei-Xing's response more deeply. And Rose wondered what was going on in their young minds and hearts.

❧ ✻ ❧

$\mathcal{C}$HAPTER 13

September 1909

Joy kept one eye on the young man painting the signage on the windows and door while she arranged the items in the window display. Today those signs would announce their business to all of Denver.

Already the steady stream of foot traffic along the walkway paused and looked with interest at the gold and black curlicues emerging from the boy's brushes. Potential customers studied both the items in the window and the slender woman with the heavy chignon the color of ripe wheat organizing the display. Joy was arranging a dining hutch and table with eye-catching table settings in a manner she hoped would tempt them to step into the shop.

Grant, Billy, Sarah, Corrine, and Joy had worked tirelessly to redecorate the shop. The men had torn down walls and built arches and shelves, had scraped wallpaper and sanded and polished wood floors. Joy and the girls had come behind them to clean, paint, re-paper walls, and hang tasteful draperies. Instead of a fussy, feminine-only dress shop, the store's decor was now simple, elegant, and welcoming to both feminine and masculine sensibilities.

They discussed at length the need for a telephone. Joy had not grown up with one and felt it an unnecessary expense. Grant suggested that customers were more likely to expect one on the cusp of 1910. He also pointed out that Rose could call them from Palmer House if an emergency arose. Joy reluctantly gave her assent.

As they came close to finishing the repairs and decorating, Joy and Grant sent Billy to Omaha to empty Joy's warehouse. At three-quarters full, it still contained enough furniture, linens, fine house wares, and dishes to stock the Denver store.

Joy glanced again at the boy and smiled in satisfaction at what she saw emerging from his brushes: *Michaels' Fine Furnishings.* The lettering was a shimmering gold edged in glossy black. She stepped out of the window display and scratched Blackie behind the ears. "Looks wonderful, doesn't it, Little Blackie?"

How long had it been now since *Michaels' Tools, Hardware, and Farm Implements* had burned down and all of their dreams with it? The Lord had given them a new dream now.

Still, it did her heart good to see *their* name, *Michaels*, on the door and along the bottom of one tall window. Soon it would be seen along the bottom of the opposing tall window, too.

Her heart was full of late. For a moment she drifted into thoughts of the love and intimacy she and Grant were reviving. At first they had been so careful, even scared. She knew Grant had been terrified that he would, in some unknowing manner, spoil the relationship they were forming.

Yes, in many ways it was a new relationship. Without his memories, they were beginning all over. And yet, the sweetness of their love was the same to Joy as it had been when it was first born, when she was only nineteen years old.

———

(Journal Entry, September 12, 1909)

We attended Calvary Temple again this morning. Thank you, Lord! I have been so nourished and strengthened by the worship and the pastor's messages. This morning he spoke on eternal life using John 6:67-69:

> *Then said Jesus unto the twelve,*
> *Will ye also go away?*
> *Then Simon Peter answered him,*
> *Lord, to whom shall we go?*
> *Thou hast the words of eternal life.*
> *And we believe and are sure*
> *that thou art that Christ,*
> *the Son of the living God.*

How your words thrilled me, Lord Jesus! I felt the Holy Spirit begin to move among the people and saw hope and belief begin to bloom on many faces! Then the pastor turned to John 10:27-29 and read

> *My sheep hear my voice,*
> *and I know them, and they follow me:*
> *And I give unto them eternal life;*
> *and they shall never perish,*
> *neither shall any man pluck them out of my hand.*
> *My Father, which gave them me,*
> *is greater than all;*
> *and no man is able to pluck them*
> *out of my Father's hand.*

Pastor explained that when Jesus redeems us, buys us out of sin, nothing and no one can ever steal us away from him. We are safe! We are free!

He called those who wished to surrender to Jesus to the altar to pray. Thank you, Lord! Gretl and Maria, nervous and scared, walked together to the altar and gave their lives to you. I could tell the Spirit was moving on our other girls—it may take a little longer, Lord, but I am greatly encouraged.

Oh yes. Tomorrow is an eventful day. Palmer House will be receiving a telephone. Mei-Xing accepted the position with Mrs. Palmer, and the dear lady insists on being able to call Mei-Xing when she is needed. I have never had a telephone so close at hand. Jan and I certainly never had one in our little prairie home.

———

Customers flocked to the store's opening, and the six staff members spent the day on their feet greeting shoppers and serving their new clientele. Sarah, Corrine, and Billy took turns at the shiny new cash register. Throughout the day, the store resounded with the jingling of the bell hanging from the front door, the muted conversations of their customers, and the chiming of the register.

Joy was most in demand, as Sarah, Corrine, Billy, and Grant regularly requested her advice and deferred to her suggestions or direction. At closing time, the exhausted but elated staff gathered to recap the day's events and issues.

"We have had a good day, Joy," Grant smiled as he completed the bank deposit. "But I must say I never realized there was so much to know about laundering linens before today—or that I should even be versed on this subject!"

They all laughed. Grant was right. Customers not only perused their stock but asked myriads of questions—many that did not pertain to the sale of fine household furnishings but rather their care. In fact, their clientele assumed the shop's staff should possess expertise on all aspects of household management!

Sarah grinned. "I was lectured today on the difference between pine and heart pine!"

Corrine laughed and agreed. "I can converse at length on art, history, and literature with the most knowledgeable individuals—but do I know anything of the care of fine china? No, I do not!"

"If you think that is bad, my background is in tools and hardware!" Billy interjected. "What do I know about cut glass versus leaded crystal?"

"Working here will certainly be a learning experience," Joy assured them, "but all of you did well today. Just remember, whenever your customer has a question you cannot answer, you are free to call on me to assist, just as you did today. If you listen carefully to my answers to their questions, you will soon be able to field those situations yourself. The most important thing is to remain gracious and helpful at all times. Even if we cannot provide an answer, a genuinely solicitous response will suffice."

"And how did you fare today, my dear?" Joy asked Grant. He had been mostly silent as they chattered and shared the day's experiences.

He took a moment to answer. "I confess that I am out of my element at present, but if the others can learn, so can I."

He looked searchingly at Joy before continuing. "I also had an interesting moment today. I was guiding a customer to the register when I had a . . . memory, I guess. Suddenly I felt that I done so before, but somewhere else. In this other place I remembered a large room, much larger than this store, with aisles and aisles of bins and shelves and a large stove of some sort in the center of the room."

He grinned. "I think it had to be our store in Omaha. Does my description sound right? Do you think it was?"

"It does sound like our store! Oh, Grant, how wonderful!"

———

(Journal Entry, October 4, 1909)

I woke this morning with a heart filled with song. Our church sings so many wonderful songs of praise each service, not just two or three as some churches do.

Their joyous worship takes me back to those many years ago when I first arrived in RiverBend. The singing in our old church stirred my soul and the presence of the Lord gripped my very being, just as I am feeling him again.

The chorus of this song came to me as I awoke this morning. It is a new one for me, but my feet want to dance as I sing it!

It is joy unspeakable and full of glory,
Full of glory, full of glory;
It is joy unspeakable and full of glory,
Oh, the half has never yet been told.

And how my heart overflowed when we sang My Jesus, I Love
Thee. *O, yes! I love thee, Lord!*

I love Thee because Thou hast first loved me,
And purchased my pardon on Calvary's tree;
I love Thee for wearing the thorns on Thy brow;
If ever I loved Thee, my Jesus, 'tis now.

In mansions of glory and endless delight,
I'll ever adore Thee in heaven so bright;
I'll sing with the glittering crown on my brow,
If ever I loved Thee, my Jesus, 'tis now.

———

Three weeks after the shop's opening, the staff had settled into a routine. Sarah and Corrine were feeling more confident of themselves, and Billy was learning to distinguish between silk and satin, china and bisque. More importantly, Joy and Grant were growing more assured of the store's success. They were even discussing how to restock since merchandise was moving nicely.

Grant sent an unspoken question at Joy who responded immediately and firmly, "You are never going *anywhere* without me again, Grant Michaels. Never." The set of her jaw told Grant more than her words did.

"I only wanted to see your reaction," he teased. They shared a chuckle but it did not last. It touched too near the heart.

Joy could not help herself when her eyes filled. "I cannot lose you again, Grant." He did not answer right away, but gently took her hand and pressed it to his lips and held it there for a long moment.

When he did speak, his voice was rough. "We *can* do all things through Christ, Joy. When hard times come . . . we can bear what comes." He searched her face. "God's grace is sufficient for today—not tomorrow, but *today*, my lovely Joy. Would it not be wrong to look ahead and decide today that his grace for tomorrow will not be able to carry us?"

Joy nodded but said nothing. She laid her head on Grant's shoulder and they held each other.

———

One night Cal commented that Esther's house seemed a great investment opportunity. "You excel as a madam, Esther," he complimented her. "The house's ambiance and your girls are first-rate. Why with a little cash infusion, my dear, you could move to a larger house I know of and hire a few more girls. I would be happy to loan you the money."

Esther was a little unsettled by his offer, but promised to bring it up to the other girls. "We all own this place," she explained almost apologetically.

Cal just smiled and nodded, but Esther thought she saw something flicker in his eyes, something that disturbed her.

When she did tell the girls, their sullen looks said plainly that they weren't pleased. "This is our house, Esther, all of us. We're doing fine just like this. And we don't need a man to help us."

Ava added, "You are getting too chummy with Cal, Esther. We don't do that, remember?"

Esther flushed a little. "I will tell him we don't need the loan," she answered, secretly relieved. She didn't want to give control of her business to anyone, even if just a little, even if it was just a loan. Even from Cal.

CHAPTER 14

Dean Morgan, AKA Shelby Franklin, sat gingerly on the jail cell's single bunk. He was impeccably dressed and shaved, his hair oiled, combed, and recently trimmed. He took a fastidious pride in his appearance—even in *this* place—and he was not without his resources, both people and money.

Yes, he still had money, discreetly tucked away but accessible, and people to do his bidding. For the right price.

Denver was rife with those who wielded political power and judicial influence—and who were serious about lining their pockets with easy cash. In the five months Morgan had been in this *hole* awaiting trial, he had made several beneficial connections, connections that supplied food, drink, clothing, and other necessities to his liking. All for a price, but a price he was willing to pay.

Morgan sat upright, careful not to lean against the dank bricks of the jail wall, and he delicately pinched the crease of his trousers. All the while he kept his face impassive—calm, even—but inside his mind churned, and his considerable intellect chewed away on his present problem.

They intended to hang him, his attorneys told him, but he did not intend to oblige *them*. "They," firstly, was the State of Colorado. However, his lawyers, the best money could afford, were delaying a trial as long as possible. They were as busy as bees in Nebraska, stirring up rivalries and competition between the bureaucracies of the two states.

Yes, apparently Nebraska would like to hang him also. Oh, how his popularity had grown! His attorneys were spreading enough cash around in Lincoln and Omaha to ensure that every corrupt politician and bureaucrat in those fair cities would protest Colorado's right to try—*and hang*—him first.

He hadn't anticipated *quite* the backlash from Omaha. He was rather amazed at the intensity of their sentiment, actually.

Apparently the people of that town truly disliked how he had framed Joy Michaels for arson, arranged for her property to be auctioned out from under her, and had left a certain insurance company in dire straits. And somehow the deaths of Percher and Robertson had been mixed into their complaints.

Posh! They would be hard pressed to lay those deaths at his door. Su-Chong, on the other hand . . .

Unfortunately, a number of other states east of Nebraska (thanks to the work of those *infernal* Pinkertons!) had entered the fray, each sure he had committed atrocities in their fair states and all most anxious to extradite him and host their own highly publicized necktie party—using *his* neck. This, of course, was unacceptable.

The problem at hand was that his over-compensated attorneys could not delay the inevitable forever. Even as he considered, discarded, or filed away ideas, options, and possibilities, other thoughts and questions intruded. Three individuals figured prominently in those *infernally* intrusive questions.

How had that woman—that interfering Michaels *woman—ended up in the very place he had decided to stake his future? How had she managed to ferret out his dealings in Corinth? Had she somehow tracked him there? Impossible! And how had she met and become acquainted with that blasted Pinkerton man?* O'Dell.

Morgan's stare was directed no farther than the opposite wall, but the coldness of his look would have chilled the blood of many a strong man, had it been aimed their way. He continued to sift facts and examine potential plans, but the disquieting questions intruded once more.

He had left no trail in Omaha. Certainly nothing to link Shelby Franklin with Dean Morgan. How had they teased out and connected so many distinct and discrete threads, ultimately finding their way to him? And the edgy gambit she had played before the throng in the plaza?

Nicely done, he was forced to admit with a sneer.

The final scene in the small Corinth plaza played out before him: Joy Thoresen—*Joy Michaels*—with the polish of a veteran orator, demolishing his carefully crafted identity, exposing his business dealings, and in such a manner as to turn the Corinth peons against him.

He would have defeated her regardless—*and made her disappear forever that night*—except for the phalanx of armed federal and Pinkerton officers that had, *at that very moment*, rushed from out of the darkness. All avenues of escape were blocked until, led by his bodyguard, Su-Chong, a way of egress seemed certain.

And then the appearance of a tiny Asian girl—*his Little Plum Blossom!*—flummoxed Su-Chong and incited his disloyalty. Toward *him*!

It was out-and-out treachery. And he never allowed treachery to go unanswered.

Morgan sniffed nonchalantly and looked critically at his immaculate hands, his long fingers, and their well-shaped and buffed nails. But within, the slow rage he kept tamped down by sheer will was building.

Joy Thoresen Michaels.

Edmund O'Dell.

Su-Chong Chen.

Su-Chong Chen. No doubt languishing in a cell not far from here. *May he rot there*, Morgan raged silently. *No; not good enough.* Those three had figured prominently in his undoing. For that they would figure prominently in his future plans.

He had paid his lawyers to represent Su-Chong also. He could not afford the possibility of his bodyguard telling tales—hence, Morgan made sure one of *his* attorneys was always present when the prosecutors were questioning him.

His lead attorney, Kent Jergins, reported that Su-Chong remained uncommunicative and sullen during official interviews. In fact, according to Jergins, Morgan's bodyguard had said not one word while being interrogated. Not then, not during Jergins' initial meeting with him, nor after the questioning. Su-Chong had withdrawn into himself and would speak to no one.

Morgan was no fool—he knew the Chinaman's thoughts and feelings ran deep, dangerously so, perhaps to an irrational level. More importantly, he was the only individual alive who could speak directly to Morgan's activities in Omaha and Denver.

To do so would assuredly implicate himself, Morgan mused. The man was a heartless killer who had murdered on Morgan's behalf several times. *Yet if his rage against me were hot enough, he would sing like a bird.*

And so he needed to exercise caution with his former bodyguard. He had seen the look Su-Chong turned on him when he realized the *Little Plum Blossom* was his long, lost love.

Morgan sneered as he relived that moment. *Not everything, my trusted minion*, he raged. *You don't know all. I have resources hidden even from you.*

His thoughts turned fondly toward his Denver bolt-hole. Once he was away from this foul place he would not run. No, they would expect that and expend all their efforts watching the roads out of Denver to find him.

But he would *not* run. He had made provision to hide safely, for months, if need be. He would not run because what he desired was right here. And once the manhunt tapered off . . . Well, *then* he would have his satisfaction.

Finally, he selected a bound volume from a rough shelf hanging precariously over his bed. From within he withdrew several sheets of fine vellum stationery.

As loath as he was to reconnect with his 'roots', his superior mind had sorted the options, selected the best course of action, and stubbornly refused to identify a better one. And the clock was ticking down.

So. He would write a letter, one that was sure to elicit a rapid response and provide him with the alliance and assistance he required.

He began formally: *My dear Madam Chen . . .*

Yes. My dear—yes, *my very dear*—Fang Hua. The set of Morgan's mouth tightened. He would have to be quite careful.

My dear Madam Chen,

I pray this letter finds you well. I have news of the utmost importance to you regarding your son . . .

———

Cal didn't mention his offer of a loan during his next visit, so Esther waited until they were tucked into her bed and had finished their intimacies. The house was closed for the evening. Tom and Donovan would lock the doors as soon as the last client left.

"Cal, I want you to know that I appreciate your offer of a loan," Esther murmured in his ear. "But the girls and I are attached to this house and rather like the business we have built on our own." She paused and then added a little nervously, "Perhaps in a year or two we'll feel differently."

Cal turned on his elbow and smiled at her. Esther suddenly shivered. Something about his smile chilled her. "You are so beautiful, Esther, and I love you dearly, but you don't get it, do you," he drawled softly, tracing the outline of her face.

"Don't . . . don't get what?" Esther asked, her mouth suddenly dry.

He gripped her face, a little too tightly. "You don't understand that this isn't your business any longer, my dear."

"You-you're hurting me," Esther struggled, but Cal's hands were massive, his grip like a vise.

He let go of her at last and got up to dress. "I'll be here tomorrow at three o'clock. Have the girls dressed and waiting for me in the dining room. I will outline the new management policies then. You would do them a favor if you prepared them ahead of time."

"No! You can't do this! I won't let you!" Esther jumped out of bed and ran to the door. "Tom! Donovan!"

Immediately boots pounded on the stairs. Esther hastily threw on a nearby peignoir. Cal just chuckled and buttoned his shirt.

Tom and Donovan burst into Esther's room. Esther, her voice shaking, pointed at Cal and demanded, "Get him out of my room and out of my house! I don't *ever* want him admitted again!"

But neither man moved. They stood silently, waiting, looking to Cal for direction.

"Boys, please give Miss Esther here an introductory lesson. I don't want her face bruised, and I don't want her confined to bed tomorrow. But make it a convincing lesson, will you?"

Esther stared at Cal, aghast. "You . . . I thought you loved me," she stammered, even as Tom and Donovan grabbed her arms.

"But, I do, Esther, I truly do! You are wonderful in so many ways. But if you want to be my woman, you must know your place. I require obedience and loyalty. Tom and Donovan will help you to understand. They've been good employees of mine for quite some time."

Cal tipped his hat to Esther. "Now boys, she's already had one go 'round tonight, so don't wear her out."

The two guards pushed Esther down on the bed and, stifling her screams with a pillow, ripped away her peignoir.

———

Rose awoke in the dark, her heart racing. She told herself it was only a troubling dream. But she had heard a woman screaming and crying for help. More troubling than the woman's shrieks of fear and pain was the undeniable sense that Rose *knew her*.

On her knees beside her bed, Rose sought guidance from the Holy Spirit in her praying. As she opened her mouth to pray, a name tumbled from her lips: "O Lord, I ask for your protection to surround Esther . . ."

Rose stopped, stunned. *Esther!* Yes . . .

Now more determined, Rose turned again to her prayers, convinced that the Lord had awakened her for a purpose.

❧ ❈ ❧

$\mathscr{C}$HAPTER 15

(Journal Entry, October 12, 1909)
Lord, I have shared my dream with Joy, Grant, Breona, Mei-
Xing, Billy, and Marit. Since then we have been praying daily for
Esther, Ava, Molly, and Jess, and we will continue until you bring an
answer.

You know where they are, Lord. You have your eye on them, and
you know the trouble they are in. Whatever evil is happening, we call
on you, Lord, knowing that you hear us and will answer. We call on
you to bring these women out of darkness and into your light. Set
them free, Lord, we ask in Jesus' Name.

———

Word was getting around, and *Michaels' Fine Household*
Furnishings was receiving more customers. After the shop had been
open six weeks, sales reached an acceptable level and remained
fairly constant. However, Joy wondered if another kind of word was
getting around, too. More than once she had witnessed furtive
whispers and covert glances directed toward Sarah or Corrine. A few
days later her concerns were confirmed.

"I should like to be shown your selection of lace tablecloths," the
matronly woman stated loudly to no one in particular. She looked
about the shop haughtily and waited for assistance to come to her.
Her husband, an aging man with an air of bored compliance, lifted
glasses to his eyes and studied a wall painting hanging near them.

Sarah stepped to the woman's side. "Of course. Right this way,
madam." She smiled and gestured toward the rods hung with neatly
folded table linens. At that moment the man turned toward her and
Sarah gasped. She quickly turned away, her hand to her mouth to
cover her shock.

It was too late. He had recognized her—and she him—although
his response was different than hers. A slight, cruel smile tugged at
the corner of his mouth. Standing behind his wife, the wink he threw
Sarah went unseen by that woman.

Sarah composed herself and, ignoring the man, continued toward
the table linens. As Sarah pointed out the various styles and sizes,
the woman scrutinized her, and her mouth turned down in derision.

"Tell me, young lady. Are you one of those women come down from that little town up the mountain? One of those women living in Martha Palmer's house?" The question was loud, clearly spoken for others than just Sarah to hear.

Sarah stood stock-still, unsure of how to answer. Corrine, who had been ringing up a purchase, froze. Joy, who had also overheard the question, tried to excuse herself from her present customer. She was surely not the only one in the shop to overhear the woman's strident voice! Joy's customer turned toward Sarah and the matron, her eyebrow raised.

Finally, Sarah squared her shoulders. "Yes, Mrs. Schumer, I *am* 'one of those women.' Now," she turned stiffly toward the display of table cloths, "what size cloth would interest you today?"

Mrs. Schumer's nose lifted slightly. "Well! I simply did not believe it when I heard it. Employing women of ill repute in what is advertised as a respectable establishment! I wish to see the owner immediately."

Sarah set her lips together and Joy, as she hurried to her aid, could see the stain crawling across Sarah's modest neckline even as white patches appeared on her high cheekbones. Joy composed herself as she reached the matron's side.

"I am Joy Michaels, the owner of this establishment. May I be of assistance, Mrs.—?"

"Mrs. Schumer," Sarah provided, her tone cold.

"Mrs. Schumer, is it? How may I help you today?"

The woman eyed Sarah warily. "I do not believe I introduced myself." She frowned. "I *know* I did not introduce myself." She turned to Joy. "How did this . . . this *woman* know my name?"

Joy was perplexed. "I, well, I'm sure I don't—"

"I know *your* name, Mrs. Schumer," Sarah replied, her face now entirely white with scarcely repressed rage, "because I know your husband, *Mr.* Schumer."

"Well! I am sure you are mistaken," Mrs. Schumer expostulated. "I know all of my husband's acquaintances." The matron raised her finger and wagged it at Sarah. "—and you may well claim to know *him*, but I am certain he does not know *you*!" She ended on a loud note of icy triumph.

Sarah was not cowed. Ignoring Joy's gentle hand pressing on her arm, she retorted, "Oh, I do assure you, Mrs. Schumer, that I am *well* known by Mr. Schumer.

"Of course, I refer to the *Biblical* manner of knowing. After all, I am one of *those* women. Oh, yes. He 'knows' me all right. *Not that I ever had a choice in the matter!*"

She shouted her last sentence. In the stunned silence that followed, Darryl Schumer bent a look of such loathing and rage on Sarah that Joy feared for the girl's safety.

"Sarah!" Joy grasped Sarah's arm firmly. "Sarah, you will excuse yourself. *Now*."

Sarah stared back at the man with equal hatred, her breathing rapid, her chest heaving. Joy gripped Sarah's arm until it hurt and the girl turned, dazed, toward her.

"Sarah. Go to the office. Immediately. Stay there," Joy commanded.

Sarah whirled and stalked away, her face a mask of fury and humiliation. Joy looked about the store. The eyes of her staff and the customers throughout the store were wide and shocked.

Dear Lord, what do I do? Joy implored. All eyes but Grant's were on her. His head was bowed, and Joy knew he was praying.

Joy gathered herself and, turning back to the Schumers, Joy found them staring at each other. Mrs. Schumer's pudgy mouth was open, her eyes wide with shock and disbelief.

Mr. Schumer, the folds of his face set in icy lines, smiled sardonically at his wife. "You are such a fool, Beatrice, a self-righteous busybody and a fool. You always have been." His cutting words were meant only for his wife, but Joy could not help but hear them also.

He bowed slightly to Joy and spoke graciously, a little louder for the audience of customers, "I apologize for this unseemly exhibition, Mrs. Michaels. We have caused you great discomfort today. I assure you it shall not happen again." His eyes belied his words, however, for the look he sent Joy chilled her to the bones.

"Come, Beatrice." Mr. Schumer did not take his wife's arm but turned toward the door and, when he reached it, opened it for his wife.

Mrs. Schumer turned a devastated face to Joy, shame and pain competing for dominance. "I am so sorry," she whispered. She looked away and tried to raise her head as she shuffled toward her husband.

He placed a hand on her elbow to usher her out, but she shuddered, shook it off, and stepped away from him. Outside the shop she straightened her spine, tipped her chin up, and started down the street. Alone.

Mr. Schumer, smiling at Joy again, placed his hat on his head and turned the opposite direction from his wife.

Joy scanned the store. Customers were beginning to whisper. Her staff waited, perhaps for some signal from Joy, she did not know. Suddenly she knew that if she did not address this *head on*, the store—and perhaps the futures of the women at Palmer House, were finished.

She cleared her throat and, in a clear, gentle tone, spoke. "I would like a word with you, our esteemed customers—a moment of your time, if you please. Would you kindly gather around?"

The staff held their breath. The customers looked at each other. Out of the corner of her eye, Joy saw Grant moving toward her. A few women, likely more curious than anything, followed slowly behind him. Soon most of the customers were clustered near Joy. One couple pretended to examine tea services while hovering within earshot.

"Thank you. First, I apologize for the scene you just witnessed. This is not conduct we espouse at *Michaels'*. And I wish to address, forthrightly, the accusations you heard."

Curious eyes bade her to continue. "We have recently relocated from a small mountain community near Denver. During our stay there it came to our attention that young women were being held against their will and forced to live in a manner I will not speak of, but which caused them great distress and degradation." Joy cleared her throat again, the words sticking there, but somehow coming out coherently.

"Those young women, set at liberty by the actions of U.S. marshals, are now attempting to right their lives and make themselves productive and useful in society. These ladies are gracious and genteel. More than that, they are forgiven by God and only wish to live as he would have them live. Yes, some of them are on our staff."

One or two sets of eyes glanced around the store as if hoping to identify who else on the staff had been "one of those women." Joy coughed softly and the eyes returned to her.

"I hope that in your Christian compassion you will applaud and encourage these young women as they attempt to live as God desires. I thank you for your patronage of *Michaels'*. The success of this business means honorable employment for these ladies."

That was all Joy had—she was empty now—but it had been more than she'd realized was in her. She sighed in relief when Grant placed his hand on her shoulder and spoke.

"In appreciation for your gracious understanding and your patronage of *Michaels'*, we will, for the next hour only, offer all of you a ten percent discount on any purchase. Please feel free to make your selections now."

With that he escorted Joy to their office. He looked back and saw the knot of customers rapidly disperse. Billy and Corrine, at Grant's nod, scurried to assist.

Sarah was not in the office.

Joy sank into a chair and found she was trembling. "I cannot believe this has happened," she whispered.

Grant shrugged. "Perhaps it was better to get things into the open, so to speak. If we are going to succeed as a business, we cannot hide that we are also employing girls from the mountain. If Denver's Christian community does not rally to support us, we are finished anyway, no?"

He sat next to Joy. "I do not, however, for a moment, believe we are done before we begin. Rather, this story will be told and retold, passed from one set of lips to another and another. Yes, there will be those who will judge what they know nothing of, but perhaps Mrs. Schumer's experience will caution them. After all . . ." He let his words trail off.

Joy chuckled ruefully. "You mean, *after all*, Mrs. Schumer never in her lifetime believed her husband unfaithful, let alone to frequent brothels?" She sighed. "She received such a shock . . . such a humiliation. I felt almost as badly for her as I did for Sarah."

"She was judging Sarah and doing so without any of the facts." Grant's mouth was firmly set. "When we *who call ourselves Christians* do this, I believe God is honor-bound to set us in our place. Proverbs tells us *pride goeth before destruction, and an haughty spirit before a fall.*"

He shook his head. "Was it pride on her part? I cannot be the judge of that. I only know that God will not allow those of us who *name the name of Jesus* to continue in sinful pride. He will correct us, publicly, if needed."

"I've been wondering how you can remember Scripture when you have forgotten everything else," Joy remarked, so grateful for her husband's wisdom.

"It is a puzzle, I admit. I didn't forget *how* to do things, or things I've read or learned. I only forgot my life and the people in my life—perhaps ten or fifteen years' worth. I do have some vague recollections of my childhood and family, but no names."

Joy was thoughtful. "You said something just now . . ." Her mind was back on Sarah and how their business might be affected by the public scene with the Schumers.

"Hm? What was that?"

"You called them *girls from the mountain*. I rather like that."

"Certainly less degrading than 'former prostitutes'." Grant smiled his endearing half-smile.

"Perhaps that is how we should refer to them from now on. Of course, when the Lord gives us women from Denver, the phrase will no longer apply."

"Denver is surrounded by mountains. I don't see a problem with it. It could be our own little code for the young ladies of Palmer House."

Joy nodded. "I like that. Speaking of the house, I am concerned about Sarah. I wonder if she went there or is walking about on her own. I know she was hurt and angered beyond measure."

"Go. Go home and see if she is there," Grant urged her. "I will close up when it is time."

"Thank you, my love." Joy dropped a kiss on the top of his head.

———

Bao Shin Xang bowed low before his uncle's wife, Fang Hua. The woman, usually as sharp as an adder's tooth—and just as venomous—was visibly distracted. Her complexion was more sallow than usual, her expression . . . stunned.

"I have come, Auntie, as you requested," Bao spoke quietly from his subservient position. He had received a scrawled missive, two words only, delivered by an agitated Chen household servant.

Come now, the unsealed message had read.

Fang Hua did not immediately respond to Bao's greeting. She continued to stare across the room, but at what, Bao could not perceive. As the silence drew on, he slowly unbent and assumed a deferential posture, his hands folded together in front of himself, chin tucked to his chest.

Bao kept his face impassive and smooth, devoid of emotion. He regretted with all his heart the devil's bargain he had entered into with his aunt. *If my bargain was with the Devil,* he thought darkly, *surely he is incarnate in this woman.*

Fang Hua's gaze finally turned on him, although Bao did not believe she actually saw him. Her expression seemed vacant and her eyes roamed as if looking for something. Finally, she fixed on an opened letter lying on the priceless lacquered table near her chair.

My son in prison, in danger of death!

"You will go there for me," she muttered. "You will be my eyes and ears. You will be my hands."

Bao frowned but did not yet speak or move. *What could she mean?*

His aunt, not yet old but well into middle age, came to herself. She straightened in the chair, her thin body taut with self-imposed discipline, her eyes shuttered and cold. She lifted a manicured hand and beckoned him closer.

"You will leave tomorrow," she whispered. Her hand drifted toward the letter and her eyes followed, again losing their focus. She picked up the letter and began to read it, momentarily forgetting Bao, who grew uncomfortable at his nearness to her.

He has seen the girl, Mei-Xing? He must not discover what I have done . . . but if he does?

No one touched Fang Hua without her explicit permission. No one came close enough to touch her without an express purpose. No one stayed near her longer than that purpose demanded. Bao willed himself not to step back and willed himself to remain still, but he began to perspire.

Fang Hua finished with the letter and carefully placed it back on the table. She tapped it repeatedly with one glossy nail, lost in thought.

I must bring him back to me so I can explain! All I have done was for his good. For the good of the family. He will understand. He must *understand.*

She pulled herself from her thoughts and turned a fierce look on Bao. "You will leave tomorrow," she reiterated. "I will write your instructions this evening and have them delivered to you. You will follow them to the letter. Do you understand?"

If Bao had *not* understood, he would never have admitted so, even under pain of death.

"Yes, Auntie. I will follow your instructions perfectly." He watched her again fall into the deep reverie.

I must not fail. Su-Chong must return to me. He must be made to see reason, to remain with his family. My husband can never know . . .

She nodded and gestured for him to step back. "Do not fail me, Bao."

Bao shivered and the unspoken threat instantly dried the sweat trickling down his back. "I will do all you require, Auntie," he answered firmly. When she glanced again at the letter, Bao knew he was dismissed. He bowed low and began backing away.

Near the door, however, he stopped. He asked aloud the question he had been wondering for several minutes. "Where shall I be going, Auntie?" Immediately he cursed himself.

Fang Hua slowly turned to him and she did not speak for a long moment. At last she answered. "You will go to the city called Denver. However, you will not speak of this. To anyone. Is that understood?"

"I am your servant, Auntie," Bao replied, but his bowels clenched. He nodded and left the room, his body cold and his stomach knotted.

A memory of his young friend, Mei-Xing, floated before him. Tiny, gentle Mei-Xing, whose single error was to reject Fang Hua's only son. Mei-Xing was no more than a sweet, innocent kid when *he*, Bao, put her on a train in the night with a ticket to Denver. A ticket that would ensure her a life in hell.

He walked quickly away from the house, but Fang Hua's words ate at him, as did his own conscience. *The Devil incarnate*, he thought once more.

And I am the Devil's servant.

CHAPTER 16

Palmer House was quiet and unexpectedly empty when Joy returned. She made a quick search of the lower floor and then skipped up the staircase to check Sarah's room. She was not there either. Joy recalled then that Emily Van der Pol had invited her mother and the other women to attend lunch at Emily's home.

Concerned about Sarah, Joy sat on the bottom step, chin in hand, and wondering where to look next. That was when she heard the low murmur of voices, floating through the open parlor windows. Quietly she stepped into the parlor. She could see them through the sheer window curtains, seated on the bench in the gazebo.

Sarah's cheek was resting on Mr. Wheatley's thin shoulder, his gnarled old hand resting lightly atop her head. Sarah sniffled and wiped her eyes with what Joy assumed was one of Mr. Wheatley's threadbare hankies.

Joy was eavesdropping and knew in her heart it was wrong, but she wanted so desperately to know if Sarah was all right. She inched farther into the room, nearer the window.

"I don't know what I shall do now," Sarah sobbed. "I have nowhere else to go. Mr. and Mrs. Michaels have been so good to me and I have learned so much, but they cannot possibly have me in their store any longer! It will ruin their business, and I know how much they are depending on the store's income!" She turned her face into Mr. Wheatley's chest and wept fiercely.

Mr. Wheatley whispered something, his papery voice not carrying to Joy.

"Oh, no, I don't think so! How could they? You don't know how many people heard all the terrible things we said." Sarah wiped her nose and drew a ragged breath. "I . . . I behaved so badly, too. Miss Joy must be so disappointed. What will I do now? I have no skills, I cannot sew or cook . . ."

He said something else and Sarah was still for several moments.

"But . . . how would . . . how could I ever . . ." she groaned and shuddered. "Every customer who ever comes into the store will *know*. When I wait on them, they will be thinking, 'That's *her*. She's one of *them*.' How could I ever bear it? And the way they will *look* at me—just like Mr. Schumer did—"

A growl from Mr. Wheatley gently interrupted her.

She replied, "I can't believe you called him that!" and giggled, just before another sob caught in her throat.

He spoke again for a moment.

"Oh! I do know God loves me! . . . That is something I have come to believe with all my heart, but it doesn't change anything, does it? . . . They will still be looking at me as though I were a . . . slut."

Her voice dropped to a whisper on the word 'slut', but Mr. Wheatley's response was strong, angry even, and Joy drew back, a little shocked.

"Now you listen to me, Miss Sarah! Don't you ever be calling yourself such a word again! Do you hear me?"

Sarah drew back too, astonished, and eyes wide.

Mr. Wheatley "hrmphed" and patted her on the shoulder. He lowered his voice again, and what he said next was lost to Joy.

Sarah shook her head slowly. "I am so grateful that you care, dear, dear Mr. Wheatley, but no, I guess I don't believe that. Nothing can change the facts . . . I think Miss Rose and Miss Joy are the most wonderful people in the world, but . . . nothing can erase what I have done, *what I am*."

She rose shakily and got to her feet. "I've heard it said so many times, it must be true. *Once a whore, always a whore*."

———

By that evening, everyone in the house had heard what happened in the store. Sarah merely shrugged her shoulders when Flora gingerly brought it up, and replied, "I am what I am, Flora. If I am to support myself other than as a whore, I may have to leave Denver and find a place where no one knows me. At least I have a little retail experience now."

Joy and Grant met with Sarah privately and assured her that her job was not in jeopardy. Sarah listened coolly, thanked them, and said she would return to work in the morning. She resisted their further attempts to speak of the incident with the Schumers.

Rose and Joy, as they prayed together, sensed something more than just the incident with the Schumers. It was as if a dark tide was turning against their work, and things, often only little things, were beginning to go wrong.

"Lord," Rose prayed earnestly, her head near Joy's as they knelt together to petition heaven, "We are calling on you! We sense that the enemy of our souls is opposing our efforts. Lift us up, Father God, and give us strength to endure and overcome."

The hardest part for Rose, Joy, and Mr. Wheatley was watching Sarah erect walls to keep others out. She believed she was blocking out the pain and shame, but they knew she was enclosing herself *within* those walls and closing herself away from those who loved her.

Her icy façade was affecting the other girls, too. Where before she and Corrine had chatted and giggled on the trolley to and from work, now Sarah kept to herself, barely speaking to Corinne.

Corrine, in turn, felt rejected and became despondent. Joy found her wiping her eyes at the store, and her work began to suffer.

And Tabitha! If that girl had been harboring any "wait-and-see" attitude regarding the spiritual restoration Rose taught in their daily devotions and Pastor Carmichael preached on Sundays, she scoffed openly at it now, her verbal barbs sharper and more frequent.

———

Esther smiled graciously and played her role, but it took all she had to hold herself together. Her dream of having her own house with Ava, Molly, and Jess, making their own choices, and never, ever having to submit to a man's mistreatment again was over. And Cal . . .

Cal acted as though nothing had changed. He came once a week as before and was just as attentive and gentle—as long as Esther did exactly as he required.

Still her perverse heart craved his attentions! She found herself trying so hard to please him, even as a voice deep within warned of the futility of their "relationship."

At Cal's direction, a third guard joined Jack and Donovan during business hours. Besides them, three other men now stood guard at the house during the day, and another two when business hours were over. Cal had made it clear: Esther and the girls were not to leave the house without permission or unaccompanied.

And so we are prisoners once again, Esther moaned within herself. While smiling and mechanically responding to a gentleman caller, Esther played the awful scene in her mind again.

Ava had cursed Cal when he had told them the "new rules of management." One blow of his powerful fist had sent her to the floor. He helped her up and, with his own hand, bathed the blood from her mouth and nose.

"I am so sorry I had to do that, Ava. Can you forgive me?" he soothed her. Ava stared at him, dazed, but also dumbfounded.

"I don't ever want to hurt you, truly I don't." Cal insisted gently. "Please don't cause me to lose my temper." He held a cold cloth to Ava's face and then held her close to his chest as a mother would hold a hurting child.

He looked at each of them in turn. "I will love and care for each of you, but I expect loyalty and obedience in return," he said in a perfectly rational tone. "You must learn to follow my guidance, or I will have to discipline you. I won't enjoy it, but if I must, then I must. Am I making myself clear?"

It made no sense. It was insane! But they were helpless to question or resist him.

Molly and Jess had shot panicked glances at Esther, but Esther would not meet their eyes. She nodded her acquiescence, and Molly and Jess meekly followed suit.

"I have wanted an upscale cathouse for quite some time," Cal continued, still cradling Ava gently. "And you have made a wonderful start here. However, I can tell your resources are thin. Tomorrow I will take you to see a house I recently bought just for you. It is twice this size, and we will decorate it in the finest style."

He turned to Esther. "My darling, you have exquisite taste. You can look forward to several outings with me to select all the furnishings. And please, spare no expense to beautify the house in the best style. I will trust your judgment completely."

He carefully extricated Ava from his embrace. "Dear Ava. You may not be up to working tonight. Shall I have Molly fetch you some ice and help you to bed?"

Without waiting for an answer he stood up. "Now I have business at the *Silver Spurs* that demands my attention. Ladies, will you please be ready Friday at two o'clock? I will come for you and we will view the new house together and make our plans. I expect you to look as lovely and genteel as the day you handed out your calling cards."

He turned back, remembering something. "And that reminds me. We must have new cards printed immediately with our new address."

Esther came back to the present and poured another round of drinks for the men sitting in her parlor.

No, not her parlor. It was Cal's parlor now.

———

"And you cannot tell me where you are going or how long you will be gone?" Ling-Ling's voice was shrill, her words accusatory.

"As I said," Bao answered patiently, "It is business for Madam Chen. It is not to be spoken of. *By anyone.*" He emphasized his last words, hoping his wife of little more than a year would understand the unspoken consequences of imprudent words.

She was pregnant, nearing term, and nervous. Her pregnancy and the anxiety she harbored seemed to have strengthened the character flaws he had believed only minor before they married.

Bao finished his packing, wondering again what task took him to Denver. *Denver.* The name of that city burned like gall in his gut. Every thought of the town and what he had done to Mei-Xing pierced his soul anew.

Bao knew that his Uncle Wei Chen's dealings in Seattle's prostitution trade had provided Fang Hua with connections in Denver. He shuddered again.

Mei-Xing was not, he knew, *in* Denver, but in some small town in the mountains not far away. He shuddered as he recalled Fang Hua's vindictive—no, *diabolical*—plan for the Li's little daughter. A plan to sell her to a brothel where she would be suitably humbled and enslaved to a life of unspeakable perversion.

And he had willingly gone along with Fang Hua's evil plan. He had insinuated himself into Mei-Xing's confidence, had portrayed himself as sympathetic to her situation, and then lied to her about a new life in faraway Colorado.

He had counseled her to leave a note of goodbye that would end her parents' and her family's shame before their good friends, the Chens. He had sent her to Denver to be met, he had assured her, by a childless couple who would receive and embrace her as a daughter.

He had done all this for promotion and prestige, and to gain Fang Hua's favor, so that he could marry Mei-Xing's maid, Ling-Ling. Thinking of the "treasure" he had married, he laughed aloud but without mirth.

"What are you laughing about," Ling-Ling demanded. "I am near to giving birth, and you are leaving me! You show no consideration for me, no respect for my position in our community or as mistress of this house!"

Her voice had ratcheted up several notes and Bao wondered if she was on the edge of one of her now-legendary tantrums. Ling-Ling missed no opportunity to gloat over her stature as his wife while, at the same time, obsessing over any perceived or imaginary slight.

How many times now had he bribed their servants to stay in their employ after they had suffered the lashing of Ling-Ling's tongue?

"You are selfish—you care more for that old hag than you do for your own wife!" Ling-Ling screamed.

Bao rounded on her suddenly and grasped her roughly by the wrist. He pushed her backwards, hard, until she sat on the bed. He leaned over her, pressing his face into hers.

"Your mouth dishonors me," he hissed. "It dishonors me and it dishonors my family. More than that, it endangers us and all we have." He released her with a jerk. "You will not speak to me in this way again, nor will you question where I go or why."

Ling-Ling stared at him in fear, her mouth forming a small "o." Bao folded his arms together and stared back. Finally, he spoke, slowly, deliberately.

"You forget from where you come, Ling-Ling, and of whom you speak." His words sank to a whisper. "Do not forget how Fang Hua repaid Mei-Xing for her insult or forget your part in it."

Ling-Ling did not know what had become of her mistress, Mei-Xing. She had participated in deceiving Mei-Xing's parents—making them believe she had taken her own life—but beyond that Ling-Ling knew only that Mei-Xing had left with Bao, never to be heard from again. Now something akin to terror flickered in her eyes.

Bao finished his packing and closed the case. He left the bedroom without speaking again to his wife.

An hour later a messenger from Fang Hua arrived with a sealed package. Bao was surprised at its weight. As the messenger departed, he spied two bulky figures standing in the shadows.

"Who are you? What is your business?" he demanded.

One of the men answered him in a hard voice, one that brooked no disagreement. "We are to accompany you, Bao Shin Xang. It is all explained." He pointed to the package.

Bao flinched. Likely, if he failed in his mission, those two men had additional instructions.

"A car will come in the morning and take you to the train," the man in the shadows said softly. "Read your instructions well and be ready at the appointed time." With that the two slipped away.

Bao was cold and shaking. There was no way out for him except to succeed. He ordered hot tea and then closeted himself in his office. With the tea steeping on his desk and the door safely locked, he slit open the package.

It was filled with stacks of currency. And gold. That was why it weighed so much! The package also contained a single sealed envelope with no name on the front.

Bao began to sweat. He was not a drinking man, but he suddenly desired the burn of alcohol down his throat and into his chest. He poured a short drink and swallowed it down whole.

The fire made his eyes stream. When they cleared the envelope was still there on his desk, waiting. Waiting to strike at him like the venomous serpent who had written it.

Bao could wait no longer. He slit the envelope and removed a single page written in a clear, spidery hand, the calligraphy characters formed with old-fashioned elegance. He began to read, growing amazed then astounded and alarmed in turn.

You will go to the city called Denver and there discover where a man called Morgan is imprisoned. In the same place you will find my son.

With the moneys I have provided, you will bribe officials to help both of them to escape. Once clear of pursuit, the Morgan man may go his own way. He is of no consequence, but you will bring my son back to me.

You are not to personally approach the men you hire to do this. Your face must never be seen by them. The men I send with you will do your bidding and make every arrangement as you say. They will travel near you but not with you. You will meet with them secretly and only when necessary.

Have a care, Bao, in this that you do. My son may not come willingly. The men I send with you know this and they know his strength and skills. They must ensure he comes to me without harm, but it is you I will hold accountable.

One thing further. Somehow, my son has seen the chòu biǎozi, *the little harlot, who was not worthy of him. He now knows she did not die by her own hand. He must not be allowed to find her again or know I had part in her deception. Take much care with this.*

Bring me my son, Bao. Or do not expect to ever see your own.

Bao shuddered. *I must not fail*, he repeated to himself. *I must not fail.*

Early the following morning a black motorcar deposited Bao at the King Street Station where he boarded a *Great Northern* train headed east and then south to Billings. In Billings he would transfer to the *Chicago, Burlington & Quincy* and travel on to Denver.

The car that dropped him pulled away. Minutes later a second auto stopped at the station. Two men exited the motorcar and boarded the same train, a few cars down from Bao.

CHAPTER 17

With Grant, Joy, and Billy fully engaged in managing the store, Rose found herself overseeing renovations on the house, the carriage house, and the old caretaker's cottage, while Breona supervised the day-to-day household duties. Mr. Wheatley and the girls received their daily assignments from Breona, leaving Rose to deal with (and pay for) carpenters, painters, and roofers.

And Lord knows what else! Rose exclaimed to herself when she received an estimate for repairing the roof. Winter was close on their heels; the roof repairs could not be put off. Neither could last week's bill for firing up the coal furnace, the house's main source of heat.

Rose hadn't been alarmed when she saw the charge for filling the coal bin. Not, that is, until the cheerful man who delivered the coal asked which day of each month she wished to have him *refill* the coal bin.

"We will use the whole bin each month?" Her voice had cracked a little, thinking of the tiny house she and Jan lived in for so many happy years, heated by a single wood-burning stove.

"Well, yes, ma'am," the man replied. "P'raps not this month, but certainly when the cold sets in." He added gently, "This *is* a mighty big house, ma'am."

Rose had nodded and mentally added yet another significant expense to the monthly budget—a budget coming, at present, almost entirely from her own savings. Even when *Michaels' Fine Household Furnishings* began to turn a profit and as additional donations from Emily Van der Pol's women's group came in, most of the house's upkeep would come out of her own pocket.

Until the other girls find work and begin contributing substantially, she mused.

Marit and Gretl were helping with the grocery and butcher bills by peddling their baked goods each day on nearby street corners. Maria, Flora, and Tabitha were taking in laundry and simple mending under Breona and Rose's tutelage. And Nancy was caring for the four energetic children of a recently widowed school teacher, a man so desperate for help that he was willing to overlook Nancy's background on the strength of Emily's reference.

It isn't enough, Lord, not nearly enough.

Rose did not begrudge the drain on her savings. In her heart she had already pledged her worth to this work. But if they used it all, then they must be completely self-sufficient.

Or, rather, lean more deeply on you, Lord, our Provider! she added silently

They had worked so hard, God had answered so many prayers, and they had already battled through many obstacles, but Rose could not deny that she was weary. She thought again of the proposed sewing school and the small café they hoped to open and sighed.

So much to do. So many demands.

"Missus, I hate t' bother you," Mr. Wheatley said meekly. In truth Rose considered him a welcome interruption.

"Yes, Mr. Wheatley?"

He ran gnarled fingers through the grey tufts standing up on his head. "Don't know how t' put this delicately, but . . . well, th' latrines are all backed up."

Rose put a hand over her eyes. *Dear Lord! Please help me—you didn't design me to handle plumbing problems!*

"I'm real sorry, missus," Mr. Wheatley apologized, as though he had caused the problem. "They built this house real fancy with toilets and all, but I can't say as I have much experience with 'em."

"No, no, Mr. Wheatley! You certainly did not cause the plumbing to stop up," Rose remonstrated. And then, perhaps because she needed to laugh rather than cry, she slyly added, "*Or did you?*"

The look of consternation that washed over Mr. Wheatley's face was what Rose needed to draw a low chuckle from her. "I am only teasing, dear Mr. Wheatley. The joy of the Lord is our strength. I am in need of a little joyful strength at the moment!"

With that, he relaxed and grinned. "I know just what you mean, missus. I am certain th' wall of pyracantha on the side of this house holds a personal grudge against me." He pushed a sleeve up to his bony elbow and revealed a thoroughly poked and scratched forearm.

"Goodness! I believe you are right!" Rose said with a little rueful laugh.

Mr. Wheatley re-buttoned his shirt cuff. "Pardon me for my boldness, missus, but I was wondering if I could make a suggestion?"

"Of course, Mr. Wheatley. Please do not apologize," Rose replied.

"Well, it's this way," he said slowly. "When Pastor David and his family and Flinty were down here couple of months ago helping us move in, Flinty, he kinda mentioned that he's awful lonesome up on the mountain, now we've moved away." He shrugged sheepishly. "I've been meaning to mention it, but we've all been working s' hard."

"Thing is," he continued, "Flinty, he knows a powerful lot about such things as plumbing and carpentry and furnaces and so on. Built that lodge himself, he did. He might not be s' strong himself these days, but he could direct us in the right way, if you take my meaning."

Rose nodded thoughtfully, but Mr. Wheatley wasn't quite finished. "I been praying on it for a while, too, 'cause I'm thinking Flinty ought not t' be living alone much longer. Don't think he eats right, for one thing. If he came t' live here, he would earn his keep, I don't doubt that, and it would cheer him to no end t' have folks he loves about him. And I'm thinking Marit might put some meat back on his old bones."

Rose thought on his suggestion. What a relief it would be to have a knowledgeable person to advise her!

"Thank you, Mr. Wheatley. I will discuss your idea with Grant and Joy. I believe we would all love to have Flinty here. Where would he sleep, do you think?"

"Well, that butler's room next to mine has a lot of funny shelves and what-not for silver trays, fancy dishes, and wine bottles, but I don't think Flinty would mind a-tall."

"Oh, Mama! It would be so good to have Flinty here," Joy exclaimed later. "And his advice would be invaluable, especially for you."

Grant, who did not know Flinty well, was willing to respect Joy and Rose's opinion in the matter. "Will he be satisfied with room and board?" he asked. "We certainly cannot pay him."

Rose smiled and thought of Flinty for a moment. "I wouldn't be surprised if he were willing to pay *us* room and board," she finally said. "With his boys grown and gone out into the world, we are as close to family as he has."

"Well, he cannot come soon enough for me!" Grant laughed. He and Billy had spent hours plunging out stopped up toilets. Even after all their efforts, only the commodes on the first floor flushed cleanly.

Reluctantly, but fearful of a disastrous overflow, he had mandated that the second and third floor toilets not be used until the problem was fully resolved. They would wait to have the plumbers in until after Flinty arrived to advise them.

"I am certainly the least liked person in the house at the moment," he added ruefully.

"I must agree," Joy replied, the sarcasm in her voice a reminder of how far the toilets were from their third-floor bedroom.

———

Rose composed a letter and sent it off to Flinty the following day. At dinner that evening she told the household that they had invited Flinty to come live with them.

Breona, Billy, Marit, and Mei-Xing responded enthusiastically. But not everyone reacted as well.

"What? That old man?" Tabitha asked incredulously. "Don't we all have enough to do without having to care for another old geezer?"

Mr. Wheatley looked down at his plate, and color flooded Rose's face as she attempted to control her anger. "Tabitha, Flinty will carry his own weight here just as you do," she replied tightly.

She paused and stared at Tabitha, clearly incensed. "We *need* 'that old geezer' in our home, my dear, as much as he needs us. And perhaps it would do your heart some good to stop and consider where *you* would be if this house were not here for you."

Rose's pointed words hung over a very still table. Finally, Tabitha shrugged. "Fine then. Just so I don't have to clean up after him."

The rest of the meal was uncomfortably quiet, and Rose was still angry when dinner was over. She went immediately to her room and knelt beside her bed.

Lord, she prayed silently. *Please help me. Draw near to me, Lord, and guide my steps and words aright. I am sorry I lost my temper and I forgive Tabitha, Father God. I do! I just don't know how to cope with her selfish outbursts. O Lord, I need you.*

As she often did, Rose looked back on her marriage to Jan and those many happy years in their tiny prairie home for comfort. She had been raised in relative ease and modest wealth and had never worked hard a day in her life, but still, the day she stepped off the train in RiverBend, the prairie had called to her.

It had beckoned for her to let God dig deep into her soul and let him bring her up to higher ground.

Lord, she prayed, *when I arrived in RiverBend, I was as unprepared for the hardships of prairie living as I am now for the new responsibilities you have laid upon my shoulders. Yet I found you in that place, our beloved prairie, and I learned to face and overcome adversity in your strength.*

You have instilled that same strength and faith in my daughter Joy—and now you have given us, Joy and me, many daughters to raise! Help us, O God, to walk faithfully before you. Help us, Lord, to shoulder the work you have given us and to faithfully pass on to our girls the heritage you instilled in us.

Lord, I ask you to break the yoke of bondage that is holding them and our home in its grasp. O God, I am asking in the name of Jesus for you to come with power and set these captives free!

CHAPTER 18

(Journal Entry, November 1, 1909)
Good morning, Lord. Thank you for your new mercy each
morning. I know you will strengthen me this day for all that you
place before me, especially for reaching these young women. You
are my refuge and my fortress! You are my God and I trust in you.

I am reminded today of the mystery of the locked attic. Emily is
coming to visit tomorrow. I will ask her. Surely she will know
something of this house's secrets!

———

Emily Van der Pol came to tea at Palmer House that afternoon.
Rose was grateful for the reprieve from her duties.

"My dear Mrs. Thoresen, I do not like to see you looking so
fatigued," Emily said with a little frown.

Rose smiled. She knew she must appear tired. "I admit that the
responsibility is sometimes more than I can handle. It can be . . .
challenging." She did not mention her growing concerns about the
atmosphere in the house.

"I pray for you daily, Mrs. Thoresen," Emily replied. "This entire
venture is uncharted territory."

Rose passed Emily her tea and hoped to change the topic.
"Emily, when Pastor Jamison visited weeks ago, he said a puzzling
thing. It was when we reached the attic stairs and I said the door was
locked. He replied, and I recall his exact words: *I do understand.*
Perfectly."

She looked at her friend steadily. "Emily, what did he mean?
What is the secret hidden in this house?"

Emily closed her eyes. "Oh dear. I had forgotten that you did not
know." She moistened her lips with another sip of tea. "Where shall
I begin?"

Rose urged gently. "How about at the beginning?"

Chuckling, Emily said, "Always the best place, yes? Well."

She sighed. "Chester and Martha Palmer had only one child, a
daughter, who was the light of their lives. They had quite despaired
of having children, you see, and Martha was, I believe, in her forties
when their baby arrived. Elizabeth-Ann was her name.

"She was a lovely young thing, so sweet and pure. My parents and the Palmers were such good friends, and Bethy-Ann and I were often playmates, although I was older than she."

Emily smiled in remembrance. "We called her Bethy, even after she wasn't a child. As I matured and my social obligations took more of my time, I did not see Bethy-Ann as frequently. Then I was engaged and married.

"Bethy should have come out into society during her sixteenth year, but for some reason the Palmers decided to delay her debut. They did not speak of their reasons to anyone, but slowly some rumors began circulating—a few tales of odd behavior on Bethy's part."

Rose waited, a little frown creasing her forehead.

"I dread to speak of this, I truly do. It breaks my heart," Emily said slowly. "I called on Bethy-Ann one afternoon after my parents had announced my engagement. She was so happy to see me, so *very* happy and effusive that I started to think it a little odd. While we were taking tea, she began to confide in me about some *people* who were bothering her. I asked their names, but she would only call them *those people*.

"I really could not understand what was happening to my little childhood friend. She was sixteen, but seemed to be retreating into childhood rather than maturing.

"I mentioned it to my parents and I will never forget my mother's face. She knew what I did not know, that Bethy-Ann was going mad. The doctors could not cure her. They gave her potions to calm her but those made her nearly catatonic, and Martha forbade their use after a few months' trial.

"I heard that when Bethy-Ann had spates of joy and those around her did not celebrate as she did, she would become angry. When her condition worsened, she even became devious and vindictive, playing terrible pranks on anyone she thought had offended her or, as she saw it, was intent on harming her.

"Martha and Chester built this house and moved in when Bethy-Ann was eight years old, you know. How she loved this house! As she descended into madness, she would roam the halls, morning to evening, more and more a child than an adult, talking with her dolls and playing make-believe.

"Bethy-Ann's behavior became so erratic and her emotions so unpredictable, that Chester and Martha were forced to hire two full-time nurses to watch over her. After three years, the doctors insisted that the Palmers put Bethy-Ann away, but they could not bear to.

"The stress on Chester and Martha was terrible, but Martha kept a level head. She had to, when Chester became ill. Martha realized that Chester could not recover if he were constantly exposed to the stress of Bethy's eroding behavior. So she bought the home she presently lives in and moved the two of them into it. She left Bethy-Ann in the care of her nurses and the house staff, and focused her attention on Chester's recovery."

Emily shuddered. "I heard that Bethy-Ann missed her parents terribly and ran through their rooms and the upstairs halls screaming and crying for them at all hours of the day and night. Eventually—thank the Lord—she calmed and adjusted."

Emily dabbed at her eyes. "I was 29 the last time I visited Bethy-Ann. She did not know me, but we had a lovely little lunch party in the gazebo. Two men, dressed as servants, stayed close by but at a respectful distance while the housekeeper served the lunch. Bethy-Ann had three of her favorite dolls at the table and we talked of nothing but happy nonsense for an hour and a quarter until it was time for me to go."

"As I gathered my things to leave, she declared she did not wish me to, and threw herself into such agitation that the two men standing by had to subdue her. They were gentle but firm; I could see they were accustomed to handling her mad fits, but I could not stand to see it. I fled from this house and never returned. Until Martha gave it to you.

"Bethy-Ann was a prisoner here, but at the same time this house, with its long halls and many rooms, its stairways and turrets, and the wide attic she loved to play in, became her entire world."

Emily gazed at Rose with sadness. "*It was supposed to be safe here.*"

Rose shivered, unable to bear what was coming, yet unable to stop listening. "What . . . what happened to Bethy-Ann?" Rose had to know!

Emily turned and stared into the distance. "She died the next year. I cannot repeat everything I know. I will only tell you this. Someone, some man who had access to her, took advantage of her innocence. Martha never did discover who it was. The terrible wrong only came to light because Bethy-Ann became pregnant."

Rose took a deep breath. Her heart was breaking for the little mad girl.

"She was perhaps four or five months gone, but no one realized she was with child. They only discovered it when she miscarried.

"The poor girl. She could not have known what was happening. She fled, bleeding, to the attic where she felt safest. There, alone, and in what must have been terrible confusion and pain, she lost her baby." Emily fell silent.

It was several long minutes before Emily sighed and looked down. "She was allowed to roam the house freely, as you know, and was often quietly occupied for hours. By the time the staff became concerned and began looking for her, following the drops of blood . . . she had died, curled on the floor of the attic, clutching one of her little dollies in her arms. She was 25 years old, but had never grown up in her mind." Emily wiped away a stray tear.

"Martha had the house shut up. She refused to let anyone tell Chester, whose health was so tenuous. For five years she let him believe Bethy-Ann was alive. He passed away seven years ago never knowing she had gone before him."

Emily smiled wanly. "You know, Martha once said she would never sell this house and would see it burn before someone else lived in it. For many years she struggled to come to terms with losing both Chester and Bethy-Ann. I have to believe that her heart melted when she heard you and Joy speak the needs of these girls, all of them younger than Bethy-Ann when she was taken advantage of."

"Yes," Rose replied thoughtfully. "She said *the Holy Spirit* told her to give us this house."

Emily nodded and clasped her hands in her lap. "My mother urged Martha to either sell the house or tear it down, but Martha said she could neither bear to see someone, some stranger, live where Bethy-Ann had died, nor see it torn down, for the same reason. It was an untouched, unvisited monument to innocence lost."

"So that is why the Lord spoke to Martha to give it to us," Rose said slowly. "It will be used by our girls—and they are no stranger to the violation and pain Bethy-Ann suffered."

Emily nodded in agreement.

"Thank you for telling me this, Emily. Thank you."

CHAPTER 19

(Journal Entry, November 3, 1909)
How my mind has been preoccupied all day with Emily's tale of Bethy-Ann! I believe I understand Mrs. Palmer a little better now, Lord. Thank you for comforting this great woman and giving her grace toward us.

And you have been dealing with me, too. I have drawn back too long from confronting the situation in our home. I suppose it is natural to want to avoid conflict, but the strife and division I have tolerated in the house will bear disastrous fruit if I allow it to persist.

Your chastisement is upon me, Lord—please forgive me. I seek you now and will not resist your guidance. I seek the power of your Holy Spirit to do all that is before me on the morrow. You will not fail, my God: You shall be my shield and buckler.

———

Rose opened her Bible and looked at the faces gathered around the table, each one now dear to her. What she saw was not encouraging. Corinne, Maria, and Gretl were fidgeting, their disinterest apparent. Nancy was sullen and withdrawn. Tabitha and Sarah radiated defiance.

Breona had told Rose that Tabitha and Nancy had quarreled the night before *again*, with Nancy coming out the loser. Tabitha seemed to know instinctively whom she could bully and so would take her frustrations and ill will out on the weaker girls more and more often—Nancy, principally.

This morning Rose sensed that those who had lived at the lodge in Corinth were holding their collective breath. Waiting for her to do *something*. Rose saw that Mei-Xing was quietly watchful. They must all know how tenuous the atmosphere in the house had become and how strained the relationships among the girls were.

Underlying everything was a growing sense of hopelessness—if God did not intervene soon to change the atmosphere in the house, how long could they remain together? How long before some of the girls gave up and began to pull away? Then where would they go and what would become of them if they left?

But it was Sarah who truly worried Rose. Since the altercation in the shop with the Schumers, Sarah had become hard, angry, and defiant, and her natural leadership was influencing the other girls to resent the rules and goals of the house. Rose understood that Sarah's future hung by a fragile thread.

She was saddened and concerned for both Sarah and Tabitha's wellbeing, but they were sowing discord and strife in the house. She could not allow their negative influence to continue, no matter the cost.

Unconsciously she rubbed her face and then, realizing what she was doing, pulled her hand quickly away. She was weary, of that she had no doubt. She had been up much of the night, praying and seeking God for guidance.

"I want to talk to you this morning about hope, particularly hope after a very dark time," Rose began gently. Tabitha rolled her eyes and uttered a little sigh of exasperation under her breath. Rose struggled to keep her temper in check.

"Let's turn in our Bibles to John Chapter 8." She waited as everyone found the chapter in their Bible. Then she noticed that Sarah was not moving.

"Sarah, are you going to open your Bible?" Rose asked calmly.

Sarah stared at her for a moment. Then she shook her head. "No. No, I'm not. This Bible reading may work for you, but it means nothing to me."

Rose saw the astounded looks on Joy and Breona's faces. Grant frowned softly and dropped his head. Rose hoped he was praying.

Mr. Wheatley, sadder than she had seen him for a very long time, sent an imploring look in Sarah's direction. Sarah turned her face from him.

"Sarah, I understand what you are saying. I even understand what you are feeling," Rose responded gently. "What I would ask you to do is this: Listen carefully to what I have to say this morning. If, after we have finished, you still feel the same way, you are free to go."

Sarah stopped short. "What do you mean, 'free to go'?"

"We were very clear before we moved here from Corinth. Everyone who chose to come with us agreed to participate in the house activities, including daily Bible study. If you no longer wish to participate, then you are choosing to go elsewhere."

Redness crept up Sarah's neck and she snapped at Rose, "I should have known you'd throw me out. I suppose you mean to take my job, too!"

"That is the last thing I wish," Rose replied evenly. "I do not wish you to leave and I know Grant and Joy value you as an employee. However, if you choose not to participate, then you are choosing to go. We would miss you very much, but it is your decision."

Joy opened her mouth to say something, but at a look from Rose, she closed it. They had agreed that all things pertaining to the girls' spiritual wellbeing and the conduct of the house were under Rose's guidance. And Joy well knew that undergirding her mama's sweet, steady spirit was a spine of steel. Her authority was not to be challenged.

Now that Sarah had more-or-less publicly defied her, Rose could not allow it to stand. She spoke her next words to all the girls, making eye contact with each one.

Tabitha smirked when Rose's gaze fell upon her. Softly she said, "And I extend the same opportunity to each of you."

Suddenly the room stilled as the import of her words sank in. Tabitha looked around at the others, but Rose, her eyes still fixed on Tabitha, added, "I have neglected to address the serious decline in morale in our home, and I apologize for my inattention. I will remedy that now." When Tabitha realized Rose was speaking directly to her, she flushed angrily.

"Each of you knew the expectations before you accepted our offer to become part of this family. Unfortunately, attitudes and behaviors as of late have deteriorated badly. This must change, and it must change *today*.

"Please do not make a decision at this moment; however, I do ask you to make a decision today, after our study. First, I ask you to listen attentively to what I have to share this morning. Now, will everyone please open their Bibles to John Chapter 8?"

For a few seconds no one moved. Rose waited, staring pointedly at Sarah who seemed to be struggling with herself. Finally, she opened her Bible but kept her eyes downcast, her mouth hard and angry.

"Let's begin in verse 31," Rose instructed. She read aloud,

Then said Jesus to those Jews
which believed on him,
If ye continue in my word,
then are ye my disciples indeed;
And ye shall know the truth,
and the truth shall make you free.

Leaning forward a little and looking earnestly around the table, Rose said, "This house has quite a sad history. Did you know that?"

It was such an abrupt and unexpected segue, that Rose's listeners were taken by surprise.

"You may have heard whispers of what happened here. I, however, know the details. I would like to share them with you, because I think they will help us to understand what Jesus is saying in this passage."

No one fidgeted as Rose slowly told Bethy-Ann Palmer's story. She told of the onset of her madness, explained Martha Palmer's decision to have her cared for in the house where she grew up and was happiest. She described the treachery committed against Bethy-Ann and her heart-breaking, lonely death.

"No one knew she had been betrayed and vilely used by a man trusted to keep her safe," Rose said softly. Around the table faces were sober and some eyes were moist with unshed tears.

"Martha gave us this house to use because she sympathizes with you, with what was done to you. Someone violated *her* child. She was unable to hold Bethy-Ann and comfort her—but she was able to give us this house so that, through this ministry, she could comfort *you.*

"Bethy lived her life as a captive within this house, not because she did something wrong, but because something was wrong inside her. Well, something is wrong inside each of us. We are all held prisoner by the mistakes we have made, the wrongs we have done— *or have been done to us*—and choices that we regret.

"In our minds are voices that continually remind us of what we've done wrong and what that wrong makes us. Those voices rehearse to us, *day in and day out*, every sinful act we have ever committed."

She looked around. "Do you know what I am talking about? Have you heard those accusing voices?" She saw several tiny nods and many grave expressions around the table. Tabitha stared back, a speculative look on her face.

"The Bible tells us, with certainty, that God loves us and sent Jesus to prove that love. But those voices tell us, *No! He cannot possibly love* me! The Bible tells us that Jesus died for our sins and that he forgives our sins. But those voices shout, *Why, you can never be forgiven—you are too* stained, *too* fallen, *too* far gone!

"In Isaiah, the Lord begs us, 'Come, let us reason together; though your sins be as scarlet, they shall be white as snow,' but those voices whisper, *Oh, no!* Your *sins are too scarlet for God to cleanse. After all* you *are a scarlet woman, through and through.*

"In Jeremiah, the Lord says 'For I know the thoughts that *I* think toward you, thoughts of peace, and *not* of evil, to give you in your latter end a *hope*,' but those voices! Oh, how they sneer right back! *Yes,* they whisper, *God may have said that to someone else, but not to you! Because* you *are a whore! Once a whore, always a whore! You will* always *be a whore. You can never be anything* but *a whore!*"

Rose's passionate voice had risen and her breathing was labored. "And we tell ourselves that if we *run away,* run to where no one knows us or knows what we have done, then we will be free—*but that is another lie.* For wherever we go, those voices go with us. We are *trapped* inside with those voices who hate us and who are determined to see us fall.

"Along with those voices in our heads, are people who will point their fingers and cast a judgment that is contrary to what God's word says he has done." She looked right at Sarah. "Sarah, there is nowhere you can run where you can hide from the voices and those kind of people. Nowhere."

Sarah looked away, her eyes filling with tears.

"We are, all of us, *held captive* by the thoughts and judgments we—and others—hold against us. But no one can keep you a captive if you choose instead to be free in Jesus."

Rose touched her Bible. "We read in this passage, *Then Jesus said, 'if you continue in my word, and if you are my disciples indeed*—his followers—*then you will know the truth and the truth will make you free.*' It does not read 'set you free.' It reads, *make* you free.

"I do not wish to be crass, but I see such a spiritual allegory in Bethy-Ann's story. She died, alone and shut away from everyone who could help her. She bled to death from her wounds, both physical and emotional.

"If we allow the trespasses committed against us to hold us captive, we will bleed to death from our wounds, alone and without help. We will have shut out the only One who can heal us, Jesus, the Savior God sent to bleed *for us* so we might be saved.

"Yes, we are all guilty of doing wrong things, bad things, even horrible things. Those may be the *facts* but, when covered by the blood of Jesus, they are no longer the *truth*. The truth is, when Jesus takes up residence in our very being, we are not that old person any longer.

"When we are born again, we truly are what the Bible says . . . *a new creation. Old things have passed away. All things have become new.*

"Jesus calls to us, *Come to me! Come to me all you who are weary . . . weary, worn, and heavy-burdened. Come to me, and I will give you rest for your souls.*

"He calls to us, *Come, lay your burden down, and I will make you free.* And he promises, *He whom the Son sets free is free indeed.* The bravest thing any of us can do is to cast our burden upon the Lord who bore our sin and shame upon the cross.

"Sarah, are you ready to give your heavy burden to Jesus?" Rose walked around the table and knelt by Sarah's chair.

The young woman leaned her head on Rose's shoulder and began to sob. "Yes! Yes . . ."

Joy slid out of her chair and knelt beside it, letting her tears spatter the cushion. She began to pray, and around her she realized, vaguely, that others were praying. Praying and weeping as God had his way.

CHAPTER 20

Dean Morgan drummed his manicured fingertips against his immaculately pressed trousers. He, Su-Chong, and the others had been in this jail now for six months. His attorneys, under his instructions, had impeded trial proceedings as long as possible.

They had incited extradition from other states; then they had fought the motions, using every confounding argument and delaying tactic possible.

In the end, the State of Colorado had refused to yield its rights to him and had pushed for a trial date. His trial was scheduled to begin in early December. Time was running short.

He had written to Fang Hua nearly 30 days ago. *I should have heard from that old witch or her emissary by now*, he scowled.

He'd passed the time in his cell performing complex calculations in his head or reading books he paid guards to bring him. The guards could not keep up with his thirst for knowledge. He had consumed 79 volumes in the past six months: histories and classics writ in Greek and Latin, autobiographies, German and French philosophy, scientific treatises, and modern literature. But he recognized that he was losing his patience.

For the first time, Morgan felt the niggle of a doubt. He did not like the sensation and sneered at his weakness.

With a rattle of keys and the clank of metal against metal, the door to the row opened. Perhaps he would be receiving the new books he had requested. Unmoving, expression composed, Morgan listened to a cart as it was pushed down the row. A letter here; a newspaper for a dime there; cigarettes for two bits—the inmates lining the pockets of the guards.

The cart rolled closer.

As he ambled by, the guard pushing the cart dropped a folded note into Morgan's cell. The man did not pause or turn his head. Morgan waited until the door at the other end clanged shut and the keys jangled in the lock.

He bent over and retrieved the paper. It was small, folded in thirds, folded again cross wise, and sealed. His heart hammered as he slid his nail under the seal and broke it.

Tonight. One o'clock.

Morgan smiled. He placed the note in an ashtray and set it afire, watching it burn, watching the wax seal melt, run, and sputter into nothingness.

At last.

———

Breona poured herself a cup of tea and savored the early morning quiet. She was tired from the months of repairs and renovation, from the tensions and adjustments of having so many under a single roof.

But, at last, life in Denver was beginning to assume a pattern, a rhythm that she could count on. In twenty minutes Gretl would come downstairs to begin breakfast preparations. Miss Rose would not be far behind her.

While Rose sipped her coffee, she and Breona would make a list of the day's tasks. Half an hour after that, everyone in the house would be up preparing for the day. But for now, in these quiet moments, Breona had the kitchen to herself and the utter silence of the pre-dawn to savor.

An hour later the girls had finished their morning ablutions and were getting to their morning chores. Gretl was placing tins of muffins into the gas oven. Flora and Maria were setting the table in the dining room. Nancy was washing up from breakfast preparations. Mei-Xing, Sarah, and Corrine, dressed for their respective jobs, were taking care of their morning chores.

Mr. Wheatley, his hair wild and untamed, was filling the kitchen's wood box and laying fires in the great room to take the chill from the house. As the girls appeared, Breona parsed out little tasks to them. Soon everyone would gather for breakfast and Bible study.

Breona frowned. What was that? The front door slamming noisily? Grant usually went out for the paper about this time. Breona heard running steps slapping across the entryway, down the hallway to the kitchen. Someone in a great hurry.

Breona jumped as Grant, breathless and agitated, tossed a copy of the Denver Post on the kitchen table. "Morgan and his bodyguard have escaped from jail," he blurted, pointing to the headline.

———

(Journal Entry, November 8, 1909)

Dear Lord, I am holding to your promises today. Your word tells us, "With thine eyes thou shalt behold and see the reward of the wicked." Morgan and Su-Chong Chen have escaped from jail, Lord, have escaped from justice. I am confident that it is not permanent—for even if they elude the officers searching so diligently for them, they can never escape you, the God of justice.

We are all a bit shaken, of course. We prayed this morning and read where you commanded, "Let not your hearts be troubled, neither let them be afraid." Each of us has determined to commit this passage to memory and to follow its injunction to not allow our hearts to be troubled or afraid.

Mei-Xing's reaction to the news, however, was different and a little concerning. She will not speak of this man, Su-Chong Chen. How and from where she knows him is beyond us. But I sense that in some way he has a deep hold on her. Lord, please help my dear daughter in the Lord.

———

Bao wiped his face and his stomach churned uneasily. He had done as Fang Hua demanded, but not everything had gone as she had required.

Taking care that they were never seen together, Bao had ordered the two men with him to discreetly probe the jail guards. It had taken more than a week until they found several jail workers amenable to making certain "arrangements" for the right price. Once the day and time had been set, Bao had bought a fast motor car. He had given Fang Hua's men money to buy two speedy cars themselves and hire six able-bodied thugs. They had done so.

When Morgan and Su-Chong exited the jail in the dark of night, two of the hired muscle had met Morgan and four had met Su-Chong. The instant Su-Chong had spotted Morgan, the four thugs had been required to force him into one of the waiting cars. Morgan drove off in the second car.

The two cars were to rendezvous with Fang Hua's two men at a predetermined location. There her men would pay off the two thugs with Morgan, give him some cash and the keys to the car he was in, and watch him drive away.

The men in the second car were under orders to subdue Su-Chong with chloroform. Fang Hua's two men would pay off the four hired thugs and drive an unconscious Su-Chong to the second location where Bao would be waiting. There they would get into Bao's car and abandon the second car used in the escape.

It hadn't worked out like that.

Morgan showed up in the first car. The second car, which should have been right behind them, never arrived. Finally, Fang Hua's two men paid off the hired thugs and, with Morgan in the back seat, drove to the second rendezvous point where Bao waited.

They had lost Su-Chong and brought Morgan to Bao instead! Bao had been furious—furious that they had lost Su-Chong and furious that Morgan had seen his face.

"You may as well accept that the men you sent with Su-Chong are dead," Morgan said, his matter-of-fact manner grating on Bao. "But perhaps I can be of assistance in locating him."

Bao said nothing but glared at Morgan.

"You were going to cut me loose, which suited me fine," Morgan added, "but now I don't want that. Instead I want you to take me to Madam Chen. I will tell her how to find her son. And in return, she will do something for me."

"You will tell me now," Bao stated coldly. He glanced at his two men, and they silently removed guns from their pockets.

"No, I don't think so," Morgan replied, examining his nails. "If you kill me, you will not know where Su-Chong has gone. Fang Hua will be quite displeased."

Left without an alternative, Bao signaled to Fang Hua's men. Bao, Morgan, and the two men climbed into Bao's vehicle and began a five-day drive to Seattle using a predetermined route of lesser-traveled roads and places to safely sleep.

———

Su-Chong Chen abandoned the car a short way from Union Station. The four thugs he left inside the car would not speak, but their bodies would surely tell a tale: The police would believe he had hopped a freight train out of Denver.

That had been his first plan. Ride the train out of town and then drop off somewhere in the mountains and hole up. The police would have no idea where to look for him. But his plan had changed.

Before he left the car, he ripped up one of the men's shirts and tied a thick pad of folded fabric to his outer thigh. One of the dead thugs had been good with a knife. He could not see the cut, but knew it was deep, running diagonally from several inches below his buttock to his hip.

Su-Chong was losing blood. He could not escape the police and this town in his present condition. He needed to get to a place where he could stop the bleeding and heal.

He removed various clothing items from each of the men, shedding his prison wear and dressing quickly. He bundled his blood-stained prison pants in one of the men's shirts. He would dump the bundle a few blocks away where it wouldn't be found. He kept other items of clothing taken from the bodies so that he could vary his look every few blocks.

Su-Chong wended his way through downtown neighborhoods, stealthily moving from shadow to shadow. He changed clothing twice and now wore a long coat and a dark watch cap pulled over his smooth, black hair, his braided queue tucked inside.

To prying eyes he was but one more indistinguishable shadow in the nighttime gloom. The dark of night would cover him for only another hour, but he intended to be safe before the light of another day.

At last he reached a ring of buildings, primarily offices and store fronts. The building in the center of the block, surrounded by four others, was his objective. The windows of the buildings were dark, as they should be.

He looked for and located a loose brick near the rear entrance. He wrestled the brick until it came free from the wall. Within the block's space he found the key, as he had expected to.

Checking again to ensure that he was unobserved, he eased into the doorway and slid the key into the lock. With a satisfying click, the door opened. Su-Chong closed and locked the door behind him.

The man most Denverites knew only as Dean Morgan was nothing if not forward-thinking. Morgan always devised clever contingency plans in the unwelcome event his past should ever catch up with him. Su-Chong was aware of many of them. However, Morgan had hidden *this* place even from him.

Since Su-Chong accompanied Morgan everywhere he went, the mere incident of Morgan going out without him had raised a red flag. On that particular day, Su-Chong had followed Morgan and found he had secured a set of rooms on the top floor of this building.

On a subsequent visit, Su-Chong had observed Morgan hiding a key behind a loosened brick. One night Su-Chong had sneaked out of his room in Morgan's apartment and visited Morgan's secret rooms.

The apartment was small but well-stocked. The cupboards of the tiny kitchen were filled with canned goods and staples. It was obvious that Morgan had prepared the place as a bolt-hole—*a safe house he and only he knew of.*

Except it would be Su-Chong who would use Morgan's rooms to hide from the law. He needed time and a safe place to heal from the skirmish he'd fought with the men his mother had sent.

His mother. Su-Chong frowned and pushed the thought of her from his mind. He had more important issues before him.

He reached the top of the building and crept to the end of the hall. He felt along the ledge above the door. *There.* A piece of the frame had been cleverly chiseled out and then fitted back in place. As he lifted the piece of chiseled wood from the frame, a thin ribbon attached to it came with it. Hanging from the other end of the ribbon was a second key.

Within seconds he was inside.

CHAPTER 21

(Journal Entry, November 10, 1909)

Mrs. Brewster returned our plate in person today, the one we filled with Marit's ginger cookies and sent home with her and Mr. Brewster. She apologized for keeping the plate so long.

"Truthfully, Mrs. Thoresen, I've been remiss. I have wanted to bring it sooner, but . . ." I waited for her to finish her thought, which she finally did, in a great rush.

"Miss DeWitt is terribly wrought up regarding your, er, school. All the neighbors have discussed it and have agreed that, to date, your presence has only been a credit to the neighborhood. Why, just the improvements to the grounds have been a marked advance given the state they have been in for so many years!

"Unfortunately, our wait-and-see decision has rather incensed Miss DeWitt. Since she has not been able to garner the support of the neighborhood, she has taken her cause to other like-minded women. I'm afraid they are bent on seeing your venture discredited."

The poor woman hurried on, quite as though a mad dog was chasing her. "I wanted you to know that she is planning something. I don't know the particulars, but it has to do with the furnishings shop your daughter and her husband have opened."

She leaned toward me and whispered very seriously. "Please do not think Mr. Brewster and I have anything to do with her plans!" I assured her I would not think badly of her and thanked her for her concern.

Lord, we have encountered more difficulties this year than I could have imagined! So, of course, as soon as she left, I wanted to telephone downtown and warn Joy and Grant, but instead I am bringing all these concerns to you!

You already knew all about Miss DeWitt and her schemes, didn't you, Father? I no longer trust in my own strength or abilities. They will not suffice! Rather, I choose to trust and believe you will defend us against Miss DeWitt's accusations, for your word declares that you will defend us.

And so I cast the care of this situation on you. I know you care so very much for us. We also wait in faith for the police to recapture Morgan and Su-Chong.

Lord, we trust you.

———

That evening Rose told Joy and Grant of Mrs. Brewster's visit. They, in turn cautioned Billy, Corrine, and Sarah.

"As you said, Mother Rose, we can do nothing but trust the Lord with this," Grant agreed. "We will pray; however, *we will be watchful as well*, asking the Lord to guide us when the time comes."

Rose watched Sarah fold her hands tightly together. The girl had come a long way in her walk with the Lord since the morning she had truly surrendered to him. Morgan's escape had shaken all of them and elicited many worried questions. Rose had led them to daily confess their trust that God would see justice done.

Your heavenly Father will walk with you through this, dear Sarah! Lean on him, Rose encouraged silently.

———

Pastor Carmichael called upon Palmer House that evening. The household had attended Calvary Temple a few Sundays now, but as yet had not introduced themselves to the pastor. The young man, dressed in ordinary clothing, somewhat worn but presentable, apologized for not being expected.

"I pray you will forgive my unannounced visit," he whispered to Rose. "I do not have a telephone, and Pastor Jamison has given such a glowing account of your work, I could wait no longer to make your acquaintance. On Sundays I am much too occupied to greet newcomers."

"Pastor, you are welcome," Rose assured him. Billy, Marit, and little Will had retired upstairs after dinner, as had Grant and Joy, so only Rose, Mr. Wheatley, and the girls remained to visit with him.

Rose conducted him to the great room rather than the parlor, as he had expressed a wish to meet everyone in the house. Many of the girls were clearly flustered at their unexpected introduction to the preacher, but he soon set them at ease, asking easily about the renovations to the house and their further plans.

"I heartily commend you all," the pastor told them, "and am praying for your continued good work! In fact, I wish to ask more questions, if I may be allowed?"

Just then Breona and Gretl entered the great room with two trays of tea and cakes. As they began to serve, Rose introduced them to the young pastor. Gretl curtsied and handed him a plate with a slice of chocolate cake; Breona came after and settled a cup and saucer beside him.

"It's Miss Byrne, is it?" Pastor Carmichael asked.

"Yis, sir," Breona replied softly.

"I thank you kindly," he added.

Breona colored a tiny bit and said nothing further, but Rose noted that the pastor's eyes followed Breona around the room. Finally, he turned his attention to Rose again.

"Mrs. Thoresen—and all of you, in fact—I believe you have been to Calvary Temple and have seen what God is doing in our services?"

"Yes," Rose replied. "I have come away so blessed and refreshed!"

He nodded. "I am glad indeed. The Lord is moving mightily on the hearts of many. And we have seen several . . . *young ladies* come to the Savior and seek a new life in him."

He cleared his throat. "One of my questions, perhaps a delicate one, is to ask if you are open to receiving new . . . household members?"

Rose nodded, too. Several girls looked to her for her answer. "We are, Pastor."

He sipped his tea thoughtfully. "The Lord has brought five of our congregation out of this way of life. They are doing well, although the transition was difficult and sometimes dangerous. Lately two of the ladies have gone out onto the streets to share what the Lord has done for them—but always accompanied by several strong men charged with protecting them."

He met and held the gaze of several of the girls. "I know how force and brutality were used against many of you. I would never wish you to be in danger of such abuse again and I would, personally, stand between you and any who would ever attempt to harm you."

Turning back to Rose he said, "May I ask you, when we are sharing the Gospel on the street, may we speak of your house as a refuge?"

Rose nodded her acquiescence. "But for safety's sake, we have thought that our location should be withheld until a young woman is ready to make the decision to leave. Perhaps when she is, we could come to the church and meet with her, explaining what is required for her to stay at Palmer House."

"I agree with you, Mrs. Thoresen. I would not wish any of the men who, er, *manage* these ladies to know your location."

Breona gave the conversation half of her attention as she minded the tea things, shuttling between the kitchen and great room to refill the tea pots. But she found herself listening for the pastor's voice.

Loik foine music, 'tis, she thought idly, smiling. Then she blushed a little. Just a very little.

CHAPTER 22

They did not have to wait long for the attack Mrs. Brewster predicted to break. Two mornings later Grant, who had entered from the back door, unlocked the front entrance to *Michaels' Fine Household Furnishings* and turned the "Closed" sign to "Open," ready for another day of business.

He was met by a knot of women clustered on the walk just outside the door. They stared daggers at him through the glass. At their fore was Miss DeWitt.

Grant stepped out of the store. "Good morning, Miss DeWitt. Good morning, ladies." Grant already deduced from the signs they carried why they were there.

One sign read, *Do Not Patronize This Store*. Another, in bold red, declared, *House of Ill-Repute*! Yet another boasted, *Do Not Buy Your Furnishings from Fallen Women*. Instead of responding to Grant's greeting, the women turned up their noses and began walking an oblong circuit the length of the shop, holding their signs high.

They were picketing the store!

"How long will they do this?" Joy asked, worry creasing her brow. It was nearing noon, and not one customer had crossed the lines of women demonstrating in front of their shop. A small crowd had gathered across the street, pointing at the protesters and chattering to themselves. New passersby joined the assembly while others, having watched their fill, continued on their way.

"Surely they must be getting weary," Corrine observed. "They have been walking for three hours now."

"If you watch closely, they take turns taking breaks," Sarah pointed out. "I have counted twelve ladies, but only nine march at a time. Three walk toward the park every fifteen minutes and then return and relieve three others."

"They are well-organized, I'll give them that," Billy answered wryly.

"What are we going to do, Grant?" Joy whispered.

"We are going to pray." He gathered the store staff around him and, within view of the protesters, they held hands and bowed their heads.

At closing time Grant locked the doors and turned over the "Open" sign to "Closed." The protesters smiled broadly and congratulated each other. Not one customer had entered the store all day.

The next day the women and their signs returned. And the day after that. Each morning Grant and Joy gathered their staff and prayed for a quarter of an hour. Then they busied themselves cleaning the store and reorganizing their stock.

On the fourth morning, around 11 o'clock, Martha Palmer's liveried driver pulled up in front of the store and stopped. The elderly woman was impeccably dressed as was her usual manner.

Aided by her companion, Mei-Xing, Mrs. Palmer slowly stepped out of the car and steadied herself with her cane. The group of protesting women considered the formidable old lady warily.

Most knew her by sight. All knew her by reputation.

"Pardon me," Mrs. Palmer said clearly. "You are blocking my way." She began to hobble toward the shop's front door with Mei-Xing following closely behind her.

The women, unsure of what to do, parted for Mrs. Palmer. All but Miss DeWitt. Scowling at the timidity of her followers, she placed herself between Mrs. Palmer and the door.

"Good morning, Mrs. Palmer," she said, twisting her sour face into what might be construed as a smile.

"Good morning. It's Miss DeWitt, isn't it?" Martha Palmer asked, looking up at her.

"Why, yes, it is." Miss DeWitt was somewhat flattered that Mrs. Palmer knew her by name. She smiled again.

"Well, now that we've cleared that up," Martha replied tartly, "would you kindly move out of my way?"

"Pardon me, Mrs. Palmer, but may I draw your attention to our efforts here today? We are protesting this store and its patently dishonest presentation of itself as a respectable establishment."

"You are, are you?" Martha Palmer twisted her head so that she could look Miss DeWitt in the eye. "Well, I am here to support this quite respectable store. Now, for the third time, please give way and allow me to pass."

"I . . . I'm afraid I can't do that, Mrs. Palmer," Miss DeWitt stammered. The conversation was not going as she had anticipated and she flushed, a bit affronted before her fellow protesters.

"Eh? Can't do that?" Mrs. Palmer chuckled. "Miss DeWitt, please allow me to demonstrate how simple it is." She turned slightly. "Miss Li? Your arm, if you please."

Mei-Xing stepped to her side with alacrity and Mrs. Palmer shifted her weight to Mei-Xing's arm. As soon as she was steady, she raised her cane a mere six inches and gave Miss DeWitt a sound rap in the shin.

"Oww!" Miss DeWitt hopped aside in obvious pain.

"As I said," Mrs. Palmer said dryly as she hobbled forward, "quite simple."

Most of Miss DeWitt's compatriots appeared shocked; a few smothered spontaneous smiles, and one could not quite hold back a titter. Mei-Xing opened the door to the shop and Martha Palmer hobbled her way into the store.

"Mrs. Palmer! Good morning—how lovely to see you today!" Joy was sincerely delighted to see the lady and Mei-Xing.

Martha craned her neck and grinned at Joy. "Heard you were experiencing some trouble and thought I would come and have some fun."

Joy's face fell. "Thank you for coming. We have not had a single customer in four days." She looked through the door's glass. Miss DeWitt was scolding her followers and pointing at the door. The women picked up their signs and, as Miss DeWitt gestured, resumed their march up and down the walkway.

One of the demonstrators, however, was arguing with Miss DeWitt. As Joy watched, the woman lost her patience with Miss DeWitt, threw down her sign, and stomped off.

"Look! One of them is leaving!" Joy, Martha Palmer, and Mei-Xing drew near the door's window and watched the woman leave. As they did, Miss DeWitt saw their smiles and turned a bright, angry red. Abruptly, she put her hand on the door's knob and pushed her way into the store.

"Now see here, Martha Palmer! I can*not* believe you actually *struck* me! Why, I could have the police called on you for assault!" Miss DeWitt had pursed her lips together until they resembled an indignant prune.

Martha rounded on her. "And I cannot believe you have committed such egregious defamation of character, Cora DeWitt. I will be in contact with my attorney this very day regarding it."

"Wh-what? You cannot do that!" Miss DeWitt sputtered. "Why, look! There is one of *those women. Right there*!" She pointed a gloved finger at Sarah, who immediately cringed. "The owners promote this, this *place* as an upstanding, reputable establishment, all the while employing *fallen women* as clerks!"

Martha glanced across the store to where the staff was clustered, watching the exchange between the two women. Joy, seething with indignation, could no longer contain herself.

"See here! I will not have you disparage my girls in my own shop!" she cried, advancing on Miss DeWitt. "You will—"

"My dear Mrs. Michaels," Martha interrupted quietly. "Would you please be so gracious as to step back a moment and allow me to handle this?"

Without waiting for Joy's response, she called to Sarah. "Miss Sarah, kindly come here." Corrine and Sarah were standing together and Sarah glanced at Corrine with panic in her eyes.

"Please, my dear." Martha repeated. Sarah straightened herself and walked to the elderly woman. Mei-Xing, off to Mrs. Palmer's side, slanted Sarah a sympathetic look.

Once Sarah was near her, Martha Palmer asked, "Miss DeWitt, is this the young woman to whom you refer?" Sarah managed to stand erect under Miss DeWitt's critical scrutiny.

Miss DeWitt, shocked at having to face one of "those women" began to sputter. "Why, yes, she is! I have seen her at *that house* with my own eyes!"

Martha's eyes glittered and she asked softly, "Miss Sarah, may I ask you a personal question? I only do so because Miss DeWitt is *so* concerned."

"Yes ma'am," Sarah managed, feeling as though her throat was filled with dust.

"Will you please tell Miss DeWitt what Jesus has done for you?"

"I—" Sarah didn't know what to say. Her eyes shot around the room and caught on little Mei-Xing standing behind Mrs. Palmer. The girl's ivory face suddenly curved into a confident smile. She nodded at Sarah.

And then Sarah felt it. That warm, comforting peace! She smiled back at Mei-Xing.

"What are you smiling about?" Miss DeWitt hissed. "Are you making fun of your betters?"

"No, ma'am. I wouldn't do that," Sarah said sincerely. "I was just feeling the peace that Jesus gives me and it . . . made me smile."

"Harrumph!"

"You see, I *was* . . . once one of 'those women'. You know," her voice dropped quite low, "a *prostitute*."

Miss DeWitt drew back a step as Sarah uttered the odious word.

"I never wanted or chose to be one," Sarah shrugged her shoulders. "It was . . . forced on me. Nevertheless, I was one. It blackened my soul as surely as if I *had* chosen it. When the marshals freed us and we came to live with Miss Rose and Mr. and Mrs. Michaels, I didn't have to do such things any longer, but . . . it didn't help. I was still so ashamed."

Sarah sighed. "I thought just as you do—that I would always be one of 'those women'. But then Jesus came to live within me and . . . everything changed. He washed me as clean as a newborn baby. Just as the Bible says, I became a new creation."

She glanced at Mei-Xing, and the girl's eyes were shining with pride. Sarah, still in awe of the truth, looked at Miss DeWitt. "Jesus said, *If the Son therefore shall make you free, ye shall be free indeed.* I am free, Miss DeWitt. Free from my past, free from its chains, even free from the names people sometimes still call me. I no longer need be ashamed."

Miss DeWitt stared at Sarah, her mouth working. Finally, she clamped her lips together into a hard line. "Fiddle-dee-dee! I have never heard such tripe!"

Sarah smiled sadly at her and then looked to Mrs. Palmer. The lady dismissed Sarah with a nod.

Mrs. Palmer vigorously thumped her cane on the floor, and Miss DeWitt jumped. "Miss DeWitt, I have been wondering why you have such a bee in your bonnet over Mr. and Mrs. Michaels' efforts to provide these young women with honest employment. I b'lieve I have figured it out."

She edged closer to Miss DeWitt and crooked her finger at the woman. Flustered and more than a bit disconcerted, Miss DeWitt leaned closer to Martha Palmer's face.

"I know what Clay Redmond did to you all those years ago." Martha whispered, laying one of her bony hands on Miss DeWitt's wrist.

Miss DeWitt jerked as though she had been shot. She attempted to pull away, but Martha Palmer was stronger than she looked, and she gripped Miss DeWitt's wrist tighter.

"I know he threw you over and your parents had to send you away. I know they forced you to give up your baby. I know because that scoundrel Redmond had too much to drink one evening and began to talk about it at the club."

Miss DeWitt's face was bloodless and horrified. Mrs. Palmer pulled her closer.

"I want you to know that my Chester yanked that sorry excuse for a man into a corner and told him in no uncertain terms that if he ever spoke of you again—*to anyone*—he would personally thrash his worthless hide within an inch of his life."

"Ohhh!" Miss DeWitt's eyes were wide in her white face.

"I know you have never gotten over it, Miss DeWitt." Martha craned her neck a bit more, forcing Miss DeWitt to look at her. "It has turned you into a miserable, self-righteous fool. But there is something else I know! I know that Jesus is waiting—*and he is willing*—to take your shame just as he took Sarah's shame. You don't have to hide anymore, Miss DeWitt. You can be happy again." Martha released Miss DeWitt's hand and she stumbled backwards just a little.

Miss DeWitt placed both of her gloved hands over her eyes and gasped out a sob. Then she turned and ran from the store. Her group of protesters gaped after her until Martha Palmer called to them.

"Ladies! This demonstration is over. Please lean your signs against the building." She stood in the doorway, imperious and unflappable. "That's right. Just so. And now I would like to invite you inside to meet Mr. and Mrs. Michaels and their staff."

Somehow Martha Palmer's invitation brooked no refusal. After glancing at each other in consternation, the women filed meekly into the store and Mrs. Palmer undertook the introductions. The ladies met and shook hands with Grant and Joy and each of their employees.

And although they made little conversation during the short exchange, the majority went away genuinely puzzled—and perhaps a trifle relieved—to have encountered only two sweet, conventionally dressed young women rather than the flock of brazen, scantily clad floozies of whom Cora DeWitt had warned them.

After the demonstrators had departed, Martha called Sarah to her. She grasped Sarah's hand and pressed her fingers to her lips. "Well said, child, well said." She smiled, her neck turned sideways. "Jesus has made you beautiful and pure, inside and out. And now, by George, you are *fearless*, too."

One of her wrinkled eyes winked. "Always live a fearless life, my dear. Never be afraid to testify to what God has done—and *never* allow anyone to diminish his great work in you."

Sarah was struck dumb with revelation. *Fearless!* Yes, now she could be fearless, too.

꙳ ✳ ꙳

CHAPTER 23

(Journal Entry, November 15, 1909)

In the past two days we have all heard Joy, Mei-Xing, Sarah, and Corrine tell the tale of Martha Palmer's encounter with Miss DeWitt. Although it was the same event, each teller provided some detail or perspective that the others missed.

We are still marveling, Lord. Thank you for Mrs. Palmer and for her courage. I begin to understand that such courage is birthed in the fire of deep hardship. I thank you particularly for what Mrs. Palmer's courage did for Sarah and for the freedom I see on her face. O Lord, you have done great things and you are greatly to be praised.

Just one more thing, Father. Please heal our plumbing!

———

Fang Hua dismissed her guards and lackeys from the room. Morgan made the observation and wondered at its purpose. Only Bao remained, quietly subservient.

She fears witnesses to our conversation, he thought. He decided to probe. Gently.

"I believe he has gone after her," Morgan said, steepling his fingers and adopting what he hoped was a pensive and caring tone. *And after he has tired of her, I can hope he will come for you*, he added to himself, carefully guarding his face.

"Her? Her? Of whom do you speak?" Fang Hua hissed. She was seated in a tall straight-backed chair beside what he knew to be a rare lacquered table and an equally priceless tea service.

"Why the *Little Plum Blossom*, naturally," Morgan replied, raising his eyebrows.

"You will not speak of her." Fang Hua's tone could freeze men's bones and Morgan shivered even while his mind continued to process new information. Could it be that Fang Hua was nervous?

She left her chair and strode a few steps away. "Why would he seek her? To kill her?"

Interesting. Morgan was quiet for a moment, pursing his lips. On this point he was uncertain—did Su-Chong love the girl still or hate her with equal passion, now that he knew she'd been used by so many men? Su-Chong was rather a mystery.

He decided to be honest. *It was so much easier to convey honesty.*

"I am unsure," he said, hesitating. "When he first recognized her, he was dumbstruck. Why, apparently he believed her to be . . . *dead.*" He let that tidbit dangle, since he knew it was Fang Hua who had told Su-Chong that Mei-Xing had killed herself. Hadn't the *Little Plum Blossom* said as much? He let it dangle because he knew it would hint at the danger Fang Hua herself might be in.

Fang Hua cleared her throat, unsettled. Morgan smiled within himself.

Outside of the room a servant soundlessly approached the door. She knew no one else was allowed in this part of the house at present. With care she placed her ear to the door.

"What is that to me?" Fang Hua replied with feigned nonchalance. "If the girl chose to fake her own death, that is on her head."

Su-Chong and Mei-Xing's words in the Plaza still echoed in Morgan's ears: *They said you were dead. That you killed yourself.*

Your mother told you this? Your mother has always been very clever, Su-Chong. And very vindictive. When I rejected you and then you left, she hated me.

Morgan kept the shock from his face. *She does not know! Fang Hua believes Su-Chong is unaware of her role in Mei-Xing's fate. I must guard this insight carefully and use it to my advantage.*

He tapped his chin. "He may wish to take her away for himself. Or he might seek to . . ." Morgan was thinking aloud, musing on her behalf, "ask her questions."

Fang Hua stilled and deflected Morgan's last words. "You think my son still harbors an affection for this, this whore?" The word grated in her throat.

Morgan shook his head in his very best regret. "I truly cannot say, Madam Chen. But I *can* tell you where the girl is."

The woman turned to him. "Why did you not say so earlier?"

Morgan feigned surprise. "It is why I have come all this way, madam. When Su-Chong overpowered the men you sent to bring him home, I knew right then, *I must tell Madam Chen where her son has gone!*" Well played, he told himself.

"You see," Morgan said with not a hint of guile, "he will be seeking the girl, but I, with my many contacts in Denver, already know where she is.

She studied him. "What is it you want?"

He cocked his head slightly and studied her in return. "I believe it is what we *both* want, madam."

She stared back, challenging him. Finally, she smiled, and Morgan, despite his best efforts, shivered again. "Please do tell me. What is it that we *both* want, my dear *Reggie?*"

Morgan flushed. No one had called him that in more than twenty years. How he hated this woman, possibly more than he hated Joy Michaels! *Well, first things first.*

"We, I believe both you and I, want those responsible for ruining my life and livelihood in Denver, those responsible for imprisoning me and *your son.* The same ones who freed the *Little Plum Blossom* and allowed that unfortunate moment between her and Su-Chong to occur."

"And what people are those?" she asked carefully. "And where might we find them?"

"The first is a woman by the name of Joy Michaels," Morgan said. "Her do-gooder interference brought the law to bear on the house where the *Little Plum Blossom* er, entertained her guests. Then a Pinkerton man named O'Dell who aided in uncovering my enterprises and in arresting Su-Chong. And of course, the *Little Plum Blossom* herself."

"Indeed?" Fang Hua studied him with her hooded, reptilian eyes.

"Oh yes."

"And where might we find these people?" Fang Hua asked, her voice growing soft.

"My sources have given me an address for Joy Michaels. Right in the heart of Denver."

"And the little whore?"

"Oh, this is the easy part. Where you find Joy Michaels, you will find the little whore with her."

"And what do you wish from me, *Reggie?*" she asked her voice even softer, more seductive.

Morgan controlled himself. "I only wish for their demise as you do. I wish nothing more. Except, of course, to leave Seattle and go about my business in peace."

"Indeed." Fang Hua lifted the priceless cup to her lips and sipped. "Very well."

———

Three afternoons later Grant and Joy received a telephone call at the store.

"I shore don' know much 'bout these here telephones," a loud voice on the other end said. "Some feller he'ped me figger it out an' a nice lady sumwheres insid 'a this thing found yer number fer me! I'm at th' train station. Kin ya come an' git me?"

Excited to hear from him, they gave Flinty directions for the trolley that would bring him to the store. Just before closing time, the front door jangled and Flinty shuffled inside, looking about the shop in keen interest. He carried a carpetbag and a stout walking stick.

"This here's a mighty fine 'stablishment!" he grinned. Little Blackie, released from the confines of the office, greeted him with enthusiasm.

After Flinty petted and rubbed the puppy, he looked soberly at Joy. "Yer a sight fer sore eyes, miss, an' tha's a fact." He returned her hug and then pulled back, embarrassed and swiping at his cheeks.

The store staff, with Flinty in tow, took the trolley home and arrived at Palmer House just before dinner as usual. Flinty's good humor was, without a doubt, infectious. A trifle bowlegged, he clomped into the house, set his bag and cane in a corner and immediately began re-introducing himself.

He shook hands and grinned, peppering each person with "Shore am glad y'all 'vited me t' come! Won't be no bother, I promise! Aim t' he'p out and do m' fair share, you'll see!"

Breona was beside herself. "'Tis bakin' an' cookin' all th' day Marit has been!" she prattled happily. For a fact, Marit and Gretl had been cooking up a storm since Joy had called the house to alert them to Flinty's arrival.

"Cain't rightly r'call m' last home-cooked meal!" Flinty licked his lips in anticipation.

Just then he spied Tabitha and grinned at her. "You shore got you sum pretty hair, Red!"

Tabitha froze. "Who told you my name was Red?"

Flinty, paying no notice to her frosty response, grabbed her hand and pumped it vigorously. "M' hair ain't s' red n' more, but used t' be it were as flamin' as yourn."

"This is Tabitha, Flinty," Joy said in his ear.

"Mighty pleased t' meetcha, Miss Tabitha! My, if you ain't a pretty girl! Th' wife an' I, we had us a passel o' boys. Why, iffin I'd had me a girl child, I'm thinkin' she'd look a lot like you!" He beamed at her.

Rose was certain Tabitha would have a sharp retort to Flinty's greeting. And perhaps all of them were a little surprised at her reaction.

"You think so, do you?" A tiny smile pulled at the corner of her mouth.

"Yess'm! Say, d'ya play checkers?" Flinty looked hopefully at her.

Tabitha smiled a little more. "I believe Mr. Wheatley has schooled us fairly well."

Flinty rubbed his hands together in anticipation and grinned again. "Shore is good t' be wi' y'all. Jest what th' doctor ordered, I'm thinkin'!"

Rose was shocked when Tabitha grinned back.

———

Fang Hua closed and rested her eyes. Her plans to bring Su-Chong home had failed. Her husband, Wei Chen, knew that their son had escaped from jail—he read the newspapers after all—but he did not know her part in the escape. It was best that she kept her role in it from him. As she must keep other things from him.

Her husband must not know that Mei-Xing was alive. He must not find out Fang Hua had arranged Mei-Xing's "suicide." He must never discover that his wife had schemed to send Mei-Xing into a life of sexual slavery. Those things must never be known by him.

But what if Su-Chong found Mei-Xing again? Would the girl tell him of Bao's lies and how he had sent her to Denver—not into a loving, new family—but into the horror of forced prostitution? And would Su-Chong trace the scheme back to his mother?

Fang Hua's eyes narrowed. *It was entirely the girl's fault, of course. From the very beginning, her fault!*

Just now she had taken the necessary steps to eliminate the little harlot. Discreet and capable men were already on their way to this Denver city.

They would find and take the girl. No one would ever see her again. It would be as if she truly had killed herself. No one in Seattle would know or believe otherwise.

Then she would not need to eliminate her husband's nephew, Bao, to keep her secrets safe. And his loyalty was assured—that is, if he wished his wife and coming child to remain in good health.

She did not care about the others—this Joy Michaels and the Pinkerton man Morgan wished to be eliminated. They posed no threat to her, only to Morgan.

Fang Hua sneered when she thought of Morgan. *Dear Reggie.* She had allowed him to leave Seattle feeling safe in his going. He would create a new identity for himself in another city and think himself secure in it.

Of course, she was having him followed. If she desired to see him again, it would be quite simple to arrange.

She thought everything through once more and her mouth tightened into a confident smirk. Yes, she had thought of everything.

Once the girl disappeared, so would the danger to herself.

———

O'Dell was in Baltimore. He and local Pinkerton men had rescued an infant boy only the day before.

The boy's nanny and her boyfriend had cooked up the kidnapping and ransom scheme. When the boy disappeared, the nanny had sworn to investigators that she had been attacked and the boy taken while she was unconscious. The investigators had bought it.

When the ransom was paid and the boy was not returned, they summoned the Pinkertons who, in turn, placed a telephone call to the Chicago office demanding that they dispatch O'Dell. By the time he arrived, the boy had been missing six days.

O'Dell re-questioned the nanny. She was beginning to crack from the strain. Apparently, her boyfriend was supposed to have returned the baby boy as soon as the ransom was paid. Then she was to have given two weeks' notice and joined her lover later in Atlantic City.

Instead, the boyfriend had taken the money and left her behind. Worse, he had possibly abandoned or killed the five-month-old infant.

O'Dell, knowing the difference between genuine grief and guilt-induced panic, pressed the woman hard. Finally, she broke.

O'Dell and the local police tracked the boyfriend and the money north to New York. One of his men suffered a gunshot wound to his chest during the takedown, and it had been touch and go for him, but they had gotten the kidnapper and most of the money. The boyfriend confessed to leaving the baby at a convent outside of Philadelphia on his way to New York.

The next morning, in a fine Baltimore hotel paid for by the grateful parents of the recovered baby, O'Dell was enjoying the rare sweetness of a happily concluded case. Leaned far back in an easy chair, his feet up on a coffee table, and surrounded by thick cigar smoke, he had nothing to do but savor the moment.

His partner in recovering the child, a local Pinkerton agent, lounged in a nearby chair catching up on the news. His face was hidden behind a stale copy of the *Baltimore Sun*.

"Say, what was the name o' the mug you collared over near Denver?" Rourke asked.

"Hmm? Morgan. Dean Morgan," O'Dell replied. *Yet another difficult case brought to a successful conclusion*, he reflected contentedly.

"Man-oh-man, O'Dell! Look here! Somebody sprang that guy and his bodyguard from jail." Rourke jumped up and shoved the paper into O'Dell's lap.

O'Dell's feet thumped to the floor. He spread the paper on the table and stared at the story that began on the front-page below the fold and continued on page 4. He read the report—already a week old—three times and then leapt to his feet and began throwing his things into a well-traveled satchel. Ice had settled in his chest.

"Call Parsons right away for me," he barked around the stub of cigar clenched in his teeth. "Tell him I'm on my way. I'll check in with him before going on to Denver."

He finished stuffing his things into the satchel and snapped it closed. "Have him call McParland or whoever McParland has running the Denver office now. Tell them that Joy Michaels and all those with her need protection. I want men watching her and her friends around the clock."

He grabbed the case, snatched up his bowler, and slammed the door behind him. It had already been a week. Were his friends in Denver safe? Was *she* safe? His heart was thundering in his chest.

By the time he arrived in Chicago, Parsons could assure him that the house in Denver where Joy Michaels lived was under continual surveillance. "So is the store she and her husband lease," Parsons added. "Thing is, no one has sighted Morgan or the Chinaman, Su-Chong Chen, anywhere. Common thinking is that they are clean away."

O'Dell slid a cigar out of his pocket and into his mouth. He rolled it around for several minutes before, deep in thought, he replied. "The question is, where would they go? Morgan must still have resources on the outside or how did he pull this off?"

Parsons frowned. "We know Morgan is an assumed name, as was Franklin. Over the past ten years he has lived in many cities, in each place under a new name—each one a complete invention."

"You're right about that," O'Dell replied. "Morgan is an enigma. No one knows who he really is and where he originally came from. I'd give my eye teeth for that information. I'd bet you a box of cigars that he has left a trail of crimes from coast to coast—if we knew where to look.

"And Morgan is not to be underestimated. He is brilliant; his ability to slip on a new identity is one of his strengths. My concern is his narcissistic pride."

"His pride?"

"Yes. I saw something in him that night in the plaza—a genuine disbelief that quickly turned to rage. He could not believe his brilliant plans had been uncovered, and he was enraged that they had been scotched. With his talents, he could quietly find a fresh start somewhere."

"Except?"

"Except his pride has been wounded, his confidence shaken. For this reason, I would not put it past him to seek revenge. That is why I asked you to order guards on Joy Michaels." He took his cigar out of his mouth and tapped the unlit end on the table for emphasis.

He leaned forward. "Who would he know with enough money and influence to bust him out of that jail? It has to be someone with a *great deal* of money and someone who knows who he truly is."

"You have an idea," It wasn't a question. Parsons knew O'Dell and how his mind worked.

"I do. That night, in the plaza, something else happened. One of the girls who lived at the lodge, a little China doll by the name of Mei-Xing, confronted Morgan and his bodyguard, Su-Chong. She likely saved Rose Thoresen's life."

He related the scene to Parsons who listened intently.

"I remember from your report. Very interesting. So?"

"So first off, Mei-Xing Li isn't a poor, uneducated emigrant girl who answered an employment advertisement. She is educated, cultured, and obviously from money. We know she was abducted and taken to Corinth against her will, but she has always been closemouthed about it. She has never offered any details and refuses to talk about her family.

"Secondly, and this is the more curious part, she *knows* Morgan's bodyguard. From what I know of him, Su-Chong Chen is a ruthless killer. I'm pretty sure he poisoned one of the witnesses against Joy Thoresen in her Omaha arson trial and strangled the other."

O'Dell sat back. "This is why it is imperative that a guard be maintained over Miss Li and Mrs. Michaels. If Morgan or Su-Chong seeks retribution, it will be against them."

Parsons nodded. "Agreed. For the time being."

O'Dell looked at the ceiling and wished he could light the moistened cigar he was again rolling around in his mouth. "Thirdly, how does Mei-Xing know this Su-Chong? And not as a mere acquaintance, but know him well enough that seeing her undid him.

"Her words alone caused him to release Mrs. Thoresen. Mei-Xing and this man, Su-Chong Chen, have some sort of history, even though she is little more than a girl."

"And?"

"Morgan's only known associate—*still living* associate—is this Chinaman. That's why I'm wondering just how Mei-Xing knows Morgan's assassin. Why the secrecy on her part? Are they from the same city? And if so, is Morgan also from the same area originally?"

"You want to find out?"

"Yes."

"Where would you start?"

"When Mei-Xing first arrived at the lodge in Corinth, she had been beaten and was badly injured. While she was healing, she let slip to one of the other women at the lodge that she was from around Seattle. We have her name, Mei-Xing Li; we have the Chinaman's name, Su-Chong Chen; and we have a place."

"You want to go to Seattle."

O'Dell nodded. "I want to leave tomorrow. I have two names and a city. If their families can be found, we might find Morgan, too. The *real* Morgan."

"Will you interview Miss Li before you go?"

A shadow passed over O'Dell's face. "No."

Parson wondered about O'Dell's reaction but only demanded, "I want regular reports."

O'Dell jumped to his feet and flipped his derby on to his head. "I'll be in touch.

———

150

If anyone at Palmer House doubted Flinty's contribution to the household, those doubts were erased within days. The little bow-legged man crawled over every inch of the house, the carriage house, and the caretaker's cottage, made copious notes, and sat with Rose for hours advising her.

He scrutinized the plumbers who came to revamp the recalcitrant toilet system. He questioned them until they sent pleading looks in Rose's direction. After they left, he revisited each toilet, making adjustments until the flushing water flowed as easily as a garden spigot.

"Yessir!" he finally admitted. "I'm thinkin' we won't be needin' no fancy plumbers fer a spell!" With that pronouncement, he seemed to deflate and took to a deep arm chair in the great room. For two days he was barely able to drag himself from the chair to the table for meals and then to bed.

"I am so glad he has come to us," Rose told Grant and Joy, "But we must insist that he regulate his energy just as we've advised Mr. Wheatley. It breaks my heart to see how he has exhausted himself for us."

But after a few days rest Flinty was up supervising the final details of converting the carriage house to a little cottage for Billy and Marit. He gleefully reported that they would be able to move into it in a week's time. Grant and Joy would see their quarters ready a month after.

Flinty's arrival brought a light-heartedness that had been lacking for weeks, perhaps months. Meals were now filled with laughter and good-natured teasing as Mr. Wheatley and Flinty vied for checkers partners among the girls. And the girls hung about in the great room in the evenings hugely entertained by the competition of tall tales between the two old men.

Rose took a deep breath of gratitude and reminded herself daily of the many adversities and adversaries now overcome. *We have so much for which to thank you, O Lord, our God! But I do not presume that life ahead is all flowers without thorns. We press on in your strength, Father, and trust you for the future as well as for today.*

$\mathcal{C}$HAPTER 24

(Journal Entry, November 19, 1909)
Good morning, my Lord! This morning I read Isaiah 59:19 in your Word:

> *When the enemy shall come in like a flood,*
> *the Spirit of the Lord*
> *shall lift up a standard against him.*

O Father God! Many floods have washed over us and many voices have lifted against us, yet you have defeated them all. We are weary, Lord, but we are rejoicing in you!

I ask that you bring us now into a time of peace, that we should rest and recover, Lord. How I thank you for the souls you have entrusted to us and the faith they now have in you.

———

"Mei-Xing must have spent the night with Mrs. Palmer," Nancy remarked Saturday morning as they sat down to their breakfast.

"Oh? She did not come home last evening?" Rose responded, distracted by her shopping list and the day's tasks. Thanksgiving was but five days away, and the house would be filled with friends and family for the long weekend.

"No," Flora answered as she buttered a biscuit.

Rose nodded. "Likely Mrs. Palmer's dinner ran late or something unexpected came up. Martha would not have kept her overnight otherwise."

The normal morning chaos ensued as Joy, Grant, Sarah, Corrine, and Billy prepared to leave for the shop and as Breona set the day's chores for the rest of the household.

"Gretl, please be havin' Flora an' Maria cook w' ye t'day. Girls, will ye be makin' breakfas' t'morra by yer ownsel'?"

"Not to worry, Miss Breona," Gretl answered pleasantly. "They are ready for it, I'm thinking!" She smiled at Flora and Maria who were nervous at the prospect of cooking a whole meal for the house on their own. "Let's plan the menu so you can think about it during the day," Gretl suggested.

"Nancy, will ye be helpin' with th' ironin' this morn?"

"Yes, miss." Nancy did not watch the school teacher's children on Saturdays.

Breona always asked rather than ordered. The girls sometimes wondered amongst themselves what would happen if they ever replied, "No, Miss Breona, I would rather not!" Each one agreed that *she* would not be the first one to ever try *that*.

The shop's staff had departed and Rose and Breona were nearly ready to leave for the market when the front doorbell chimed. "I will get it," Rose called cheerfully.

She looked through the peephole and saw the visor of Benton, Martha Palmer's chauffeur. Puzzled, and with a strange foreboding, she unlocked and swung the door wide.

"Good morning, Mrs. Thoresen," he greeted her politely. "Will Miss Li be ready soon?"

A cold hand snaked about Rose shoulders and she felt its fingers travel down her spine to her legs. For a moment she could not answer.

"She . . . she did not stay the night with Mrs. Palmer?" Rose was becoming light-headed.

"Why, no, Mrs. Thoresen." The man looked confused. "I delivered her here just before nine o'clock last evening."

"But-but she-she didn't . . ." Rose's legs gave out and she sat—hard—on the floor.

"Mrs. Thoresen!" The chauffeur knelt beside her and took her hand. "Someone! I require assistance immediately!"

He turned back to Rose and insisted, "But I watched her until she went up the porch steps! I didn't leave until I saw her on the porch! And the guard was there! I saw him! He does not leave until midnight!"

But the day guard, finishing his morning rounds, discovered the night guard in the shrubs on the side of the house, beaten and in serious condition.

Joy and Grant returned home just after the police arrived. The officers asked many questions, and Benton, Rose, Grant, Joy, and the others answered them all. As the morning dragged on, the face of the officer asking most of the questions grew grimmer.

"Dean Morgan and Su-Chong Chen are still at large and, as far as we can tell, they are the only enemies Miss Li has. We assumed that they fled town after their escape. It is possible, though, that they have been hiding within the city."

Breona, as broken as Joy had ever seen her, could not be consoled. Her eyes were red and swollen from weeping. Joy and Rose exchanged a long look. Mei-Xing had already suffered so much . . .

—

(Journal Entry, November 22, 1909)

Mei-Xing has been missing three days, and the police have found no trace of my little daughter in the Lord! They assume that Morgan and Su-Chong Chen have taken her. Could they be wrong, Lord? Are they looking in the wrong places?

O God, my heart is breaking, but you know where she is. She must be so frightened! Please comfort her. Please comfort us!

Lord, only the other evening I asked you for a period of respite. Now I realize that even as I asked this, Mei-Xing was already gone. But you had also given me Isaiah 59:19—I just did not understand why!

O Lord, I am now holding to that promise with all my strength. Holy Spirit, raise up a standard bearer! Send him to us, Lord!

When the enemy shall come in like a flood,
the Spirit of the LORD
shall lift up a standard against him.

—

As he had told Parsons, O'Dell had no intention of stopping in Denver to interview Mei-Xing Li. He was determined to sever all ties with Rose Thoresen and Joy Michaels. As far as he was concerned, he had seen the last of them. Then fate—or someone higher?—had stepped in and reshuffled the cards.

Just as O'Dell was switching trains in Denver, a Pinkerton agent waylaid him and handed him a note. Parsons had heard about Mei-Xing's disappearance. Knowing O'Dell's train was nearing Denver, Parsons had called the Denver office with instructions for an agent to meet O'Dell's train and make sure he received the news.

Rubbing his eyes in worry and weariness, O'Dell hailed a cab. *"Yer a fool, O'Dell,"* he cursed himself. *"A bloody fool."*

Rose heard the bell of the front door but continued to stare at her open Bible on the table in front of her. The cup of tea near Rose's hand was as cold as her heart.

What a blow had been struck them! The entire house seemed frozen, unable to move. Joy and Grant and their staff went to the shop today, but their hearts were grieving. Breona, usually the liveliest soul in the house, moved about mechanically, a stricken look etched upon her face.

Preparations for a Thanksgiving dinner were neglected. No one could bear to think of a festive dinner with Mei-Xing missing.

Mr. Wheatley crept into the dining room. "Missus, you have a visitor," he whispered.

Rose did not acknowledge him. She was lost in thought when another set of footsteps entered the dining room.

"Mrs. Thoresen?"

Rose stirred and finally turned. His bowler in his hand, cigar peeping from his breast pocket, Edmund O'Dell smiled gently at her. Rose could not help it. She launched herself from her chair and into his familiar arms, bursting into tears.

She cried herself out and felt better for it, but could scarcely let go of O'Dell. Eventually he steered her to a sofa and sat beside her, holding her hand while she gave him the details he needed.

Later, O'Dell sat at the dining table surrounded by familiar—and yes, *loved*, blast it all!—faces. He could not deny the affection he held for Rose, Breona, Mr. Wheatley, Flinty, Marit, and little Will. His heart was happy to see them, even though he had set his will to harden himself toward them.

While Breona and Marit plied him with coffee and cake, baby Will, nearly a year old now, perched on his knee. O'Dell mocked himself. *Is this the great O'Dell, dandling a baby on his knee?* he scoffed inwardly. *Who would have dreamed such a thing?*

Will stared soberly at him and then clambered up O'Dell's chest and planted a wet kiss on his lips. Something in O'Dell's heart, long hidden and denied, shuddered and *moved*, and he was undone. He scrambled madly to stuff it back in its place, but could not.

He knew that he would stay on in Denver. He would see Grant and Joy together and would face his pain like a man. He would stay because he *must* search for Mei-Xing rather than go on to Seattle.

Those he loved needed him.

❧ ✻ ❧

CHAPTER 25

December 11, 1909

Ling-Ling's body lay lifeless and cold upon her bed. They had washed and dressed her and removed all evidence of her long labor. Bao stared at her body, staggered at death's finality and unable to accept it.

In the crook of her arm they had laid a small bundle, the child that had perished with her. A son, they told him. The infant's face was covered with the corner of the blanket. Bao could not bring himself to lift the cloth and look upon the tiny face. The child had been weeks overdue, until the doctors, delivering the grave news, told him they could not find a heartbeat.

Ling-Ling had already known. The baby had stopped moving, and she had been hysterical for days, mourning the loss but still carrying the child. Finally, the doctors had recommended Bao seek an herbalist.

The wizened old woman had given Ling-Ling a strong potion to produce a labor. The labor had been agonizingly slow. The baby had been turned the wrong way.

This is my punishment, Bao told himself. *I brought this on Ling-Ling and this innocent child. The guilt is surely* mine *but* they *have paid with their lives for my dishonor and villainy.*

His rambling thoughts turned yet again to his little friend, Mei-Xing. Indeed, she was rarely far from his mind, the familiar and haunting reminder of his evil deeds. He wondered if she still lived or if she daily suffered from the defilement that had been Fang Hua's judgment on her—the sentence *he* had carried out.

I am guilty. My punishment is just, he reflected, *for just as Mei-Xing's suffering and shame is without end, I will carry the weight of my wife and son's deaths into eternity.*

He had another thought, this one strangely comforting. *It is better that my son did not live to bear the shame of my name.*

A sob he had not known was in his throat escaped his mouth. *My son*, he groaned, rocking back and forth in agony.

Ling-Ling's family mourned and wept around him. Her mother threw herself upon the floor next to Ling-Ling's body screaming in grief.

Messengers from the Chens arrived bearing flowers, fruit, and messages of sympathy and support. Two large men took up station outside his home, politely screening mourners as they came to call.

Bao knew why the men were there. Ling-Ling and the baby were dead. Fang Hua could no longer hold his family's safety over his head, wagging her bony finger and breathing thinly veiled threats if he failed to execute her vile wishes.

Righteous fate has freed me from her, he sneered to himself. *With what can she now punish me for failing to bring Su-Chong back to her? My life? My life is but dirt. I am glad her son slipped through her fingers.*

As he pondered his freedom from Fang Hua's clutches, he began to play with an as-yet unformed idea.

———

For three weeks O'Dell had used every resource at his disposal— the police, the Pinkertons, Marshal Pounder's men, the Denver papers, and bribes spread throughout Chinatown and the red light district. No trace of Su-Chong or Mei-Xing surfaced.

He had heard rumors, mere whispers, of strangers arriving in Denver a few weeks back. Dark-haired Asian men, he was told. Men whose hard faces brooked no questions or interference. The Pinkerton agents posted at Palmer House had reported a similar suspicious sighting.

And then nothing.

More frustrated than he could ever remember being over a missing persons case, O'Dell insisted that the guard at Palmer House and *Michaels' Fine Household Furnishings* be maintained. He ground his teeth and drove his sources beyond their tolerances.

"You can't get blood from a turnip, O'Dell," Pounder growled at him. "'Preciate it if you'd ease up a bit on my men. Otherwise I'm gonna have to cut you off."

———

The household of Palmer House gathered together in the great room each evening to pray specifically for Mei-Xing's safety and for O'Dell's efforts to find her. At the end of his own wits and resources, O'Dell began to seriously question whether, perhaps, God was his last resort. *Not that he's helped so far*, he scowled.

After prayer last evening, however, they had celebrated Will's first birthday. Although the little guy was accustomed to being the center of attention much of the time, the cake, candles, singing, and abundance of gifts proved too much. He took refuge in Marit's arms and refused to participate any further.

Everyone laughed but did not pressure the little one-year-old. Occasionally he would peek out to see what was going on before diving into Marit's blouse again. So they cut the cake and enjoyed it with a fruity punch Gretl had made.

O'Dell looked about the room. Even with Mei-Xing's disappearance weighing on them, this group of people—this *family*—took time to truly celebrate a joyous milestone. He found himself wondering if, somewhere, sometime, he would belong to such a family himself.

Don't be going soft, O'Dell, his mind chastened him. *You have a job to do, and you have never failed yet.* O'Dell nodded to himself. He could not—*would not*—fail now.

—

Sarah turned with a smile when she heard the bell on the shop door. An attractive couple entered and looked about with interest.

They were striking together—the man broad and strong, wearing a perfectly cut three-piece suit and derby; the woman, slender and exquisitely gowned. The jet beaded bodice and skirt of her dress tinkled pleasantly. The gentleman was solicitous, cupping the woman's elbow and whispering in her ear.

As the woman turned, she lifted her veil and her midnight blue eyes met Sarah's. For a single second there was stunned recognition on both sides and then—then Sarah saw the soul-wrenching hopelessness written on Esther's face.

With a near imperceptible movement of her head and a glance toward the man, Esther conveyed it all. The man was not solicitous of Esther; he was controlling her.

Sarah turned to the man and, polite mask in place, asked sweetly, "How may I help you today, sir?"

She recognized the scrutiny he gave her for what it was and deduced his thoughts as well. Men like him were always looking for "fresh girls." She kept herself smiling cordially and waited for his response.

"We would like to see your bedroom suites," he replied softly. "Wouldn't we, my dear?"

"Why, yes, Cal," Esther answered quickly. Too quickly, Sarah thought.

"Right this way, sir, madam," Sarah answered, her smile plastered in place.

She led the way through the arched doorway into the bedroom section of the store. On the way they walked by Corrine who started in recognition. Sarah quickly headed her off.

"Corrine," she ordered with a managerial tone she had never used before. "Please see Mrs. Michaels regarding those invoices."

Corrine opened her mouth in confusion, but Sarah cut her off again. "Right away, Corrine."

By this time they had passed the girl who now dimly understood the situation and made her way hastily to the office to inform Joy.

Sarah busied herself displaying every bedroom set in the shop, hoping to somehow separate Esther from the man at her elbow. She was not successful, however, and realized how difficult the situation truly was.

Just then Esther sneezed and sneezed again. "Oh dear! Please forgive me." She reached for the beaded reticule hanging from her wrist. The man released her elbow as Esther required both hands to draw out a hankie.

She turned her back politely and made a small show of sniffling and blowing her nose. The man frowned and moved away in disgust.

Sarah took the opportunity to point out a matching bed frame and chest of drawers in glowing oak. As the man followed Sarah's gestures and stepped away a few feet farther, Esther drew something else from her reticule. Seconds later she stood close by the man admiring the set. He immediately pulled her arm possessively into his.

"Yes, I believe this set will do nicely," Esther breathed, looking up into the man's face with a look of contentment that Sarah knew was forced.

"You heard what the lady said." The man nodded to Sarah and they made their way to the register.

"If you will write the address here, we will have it delivered Thursday." Sarah thought her face would crack from the insincerity of her smile, but the man just took her hand and smiled back, looking deeply into her eyes.

"You are a lovely young woman," he replied, gently stroking her hand with his thumb and gazing at her intimately. "Lovely, indeed." Beside him, Esther reddened and cast her eyes on the floor.

Nausea rose in Sarah's throat. It was all she could do to politely repeat, "Your address, sir?"

The man smiled again and slowly released her hand. "No need. I will send someone to pick it up. Thank you for your excellent service."

"My pleasure," Sarah answered. She waited until the door closed behind Esther and her captor before she sank onto the stool behind the counter. Joy and Corrine were instantly beside her.

"Are you all right, Sarah?" Joy asked. The young woman looked up into Joy's concerned face and crumpled in her arms.

"Thank you," she wept. "Thank you for saving us from that house, from that horror! Thank you, Miss Joy, thank you." She clung to Joy as though she feared being ripped away from the safety and liberty of her new life.

Later, Billy handed Sarah a card. "Found this back in the bedroom furnishings," he said. Sarah, Joy, and Corrine gathered around and studied the words printed on the expensive stock:

Cultured Conversation and Companionship
Monday–Saturday Evenings, Eight O'clock

An address was printed across the bottom of the card. On the back were scrawled two words:

help me

CHAPTER 26

(Journal Entry, December 20, 1909)

We have seen Esther! God himself arranged the meeting and she is, as the Lord revealed in my dream, in serious trouble.

We called Mr. O'Dell as soon as Sarah related the encounter to us and showed him the card she dropped. He took the card and wrote down the address, promising to look into it as soon as possible.

The dear man is discouraged and worn. He has found no sign of Mei-Xing and I know it weighs heavily on him.

O Lord, please strengthen him, I ask in the name of our Savior! Give him a fresh insight into Mei-Xing's disappearance that will encourage him.

———

"Pounder and I sent a man into the house to ascertain the situation," O'Dell related to the household that evening. They were gathered in the great room to hear what he had discovered.

Grant had asked Pastor Carmichael to join them. The young minister sat in the corner behind Rose and observed quietly. Blackie, who was curled as usual beside Joy's chair, thumped his tail as O'Dell spoke.

"Our man "dandied" himself up and lounged about in their parlor drinking watered down bourbon for an evening. He discovered what we needed him to discover."

"Did he see Esther?" Rose asked eagerly.

O'Dell nodded. "Yes. She's the house's madam. She greeted him and set him up with a drink. Offered him a woman, so he asked who was available. She mentioned Jess and two other girls, but we're assuming Ava and Molly are there also."

"What will you do?" Joy whispered her question.

O'Dell didn't look directly at her but replied to the group at large. "It is a large house. Apparently, they have only been in it for a couple of months."

He paused and plucked the ever-present cigar from his breast pocket, rolling it around in his fingers. "The man who was with Esther when she was in the store." O'Dell's voice was flat.

They all waited but he didn't finish his thought. Finally, Grant asked, "Yes? What about him?"

O'Dell ran his hand through his hair, shoved the cigar in his mouth, and pulled it out again. "It's Cal Judd."

Tabitha reacted first. She jumped to her feet in agitation and then slumped back in her chair. Rose was certain she heard the girl use a swear word under her breath.

"His reputation in the market district is fearful," Pastor Carmichael murmured from behind Rose's chair. "I have . . . heard things."

Grant frowned. "Cal Judd? That name sounds familiar."

Joy nodded, downcast. "It is. If I remember correctly, Cal Judd is the owner of the . . . place where you rescued Monika Vogel." She shot a sympathetic look toward Tabitha. "And Tabitha."

All eyes turned to Tabitha. She again looked ready to jump up and run. Flinty took her hand and held it firmly in his.

"Ain't no one gonna come in here 'an' take you, Red," he muttered. "Ya hev m' word." The men in the room, Grant, Billy, Mr. Wheatley, and O'Dell, as one, agreed, and said so.

O'Dell's face darkened. "You all need to understand. If we go forward from here, Judd will become a real problem. We've already stung him once. I took two of his girls but because we all left town right afterwards, he chose to let it slide. This time will be different."

After another long pause, Joy swallowed and asked, "How will it be different?"

O'Dell finally looked at her. "Esther is known to be Cal's woman, his particular property. We take her, the other three, and anyone else who wants to come, and he will certainly *not* let it go. And where would we take the women? Here?"

The danger was instantly obvious. Tabitha shuddered, her face white. "We can't . . . they can't!" she whispered.

O'Dell agreed. "Exactly. If we take them out of there, I will have to take them away from Denver."

Joy interjected, "But what if we *did* bring them here and took adequate precau—"

"*No.*" O'Dell's voice was harsh. "No, they will *not* come here."

Grant stared at O'Dell and a look passed between them. "Mr. O'Dell is right. We cannot bring them here. It would endanger the house and our family. *All* of our family."

Pastor Carmichael made a gesture of agreement that only Grant and O'Dell observed. His face was grave.

Rose, who had been listening with her head bowed, finally spoke again. "What if we sent them to . . . RiverBend?"

Only Joy grasped what Rose was proposing. "You mean send them to Pastor and Mrs. Medford? To Søren and Meg? Brian and Fiona?"

Rose nodded. "No one would dream of looking for them there." There were no objections and O'Dell slowly nodded his approval.

"I will place a telephone call in the morning," Rose said. She looked to O'Dell. "What will happen next?"

"I realize the day after tomorrow is Christmas. A time for celebration and for . . . family." O'Dell swallowed. "And I know how raw Mei-Xing's . . . absence is."

The sweet memories of last year's Christmas at the lodge in Corinth were burned into his heart as surely as if a branding iron had been applied. "But the timing is perfect. Christmas night the guards will be less vigilant, perhaps even lax."

Breona spoke, her words heavy with emotion. "Aye, we'll be makin' sure th' wee 'un is havin' a foine Christmas morn, boot for me," and here her voice cracked, "didna th' babe coom t' set th' captive free? Mus' we na' be aboot his business?"

"Amen," Grant loudly agreed.

"Yes!" a few others replied.

Pastor Carmichael flashed Breona a smile of admiration.

"All right, then." O'Dell set his jaw. "Mrs. Thoresen, those arrangements must be firmly in place tomorrow."

Rose nodded. "They shall be."

———

Explaining to Pastor Medford what they needed was not difficult. Waiting for him to think through the implications of bringing four high-class prostitutes into their tiny farming community and for him to pray about how they would handle the stir took several hours.

When he finally called back he had spoken to Brian and Fiona and two other mature couples in his church. They would take the young women.

"Thank you," Rose breathed to the Lord when the call ended. The arrangements for O'Dell to take them from Denver and hand them off in RiverBend had not been complicated.

No, the difficulties would begin when the inexperienced couples of her former church received the four women.

Joy and I were as naïve as newborns, Lord, when you called us to this ministry. I know you will help Pastor Medford, Vera, and the others. I also know how hard it will be. Please be their strength and courage!

The family at Palmer House observed a sober Christmas Eve and Christmas morning. All the women in the house knew the four girls O'Dell would attempt to rescue that night.

They knew, too, what it was to attempt an escape from such a place. They had experienced or observed in others the consequences of a failed effort. They could not help but place themselves in Esther, Ava, Jess, and Molly's shoes.

———

O'Dell and Pounder sent two of Marshal Pounder's "dandied up" men, Randy and Mike, into Esther's house that evening. Both men were carrying tiny notes for Esther.

They hadn't anticipated Cal Judd being at the house, but there he was, ensconced in the parlor, watching with dangerous, possessive eyes while Esther handled the clients. Neither Randy nor Mike could manage a private moment with her.

The best Randy could do was get himself assigned to Molly. Once they entered her room, he quickly explained who he was and outlined the plan to her. He handed her one of the notes for Esther.

"I-I think I can get her away for a minute," Molly whispered in a shaky voice. "But, but Cal . . . you don't know him! You don't know what he'd do if . . ."

"We know him," Randy assured her grimly. "Six marshals and two Pinkertons will come in the front and back. That's in addition to Mike and me." He showed her the revolver tucked into the back of his pants. "This place has but three guards, right?"

She nodded, fear still showing in her eyes.

"Does Judd carry a gun?"

She nodded again. "It's real showy but small."

Randy nodded. Likely a derringer. "Go. Get Esther away from Cal for a moment. Give her this note. I'll wait here."

At ten minutes past 11 o'clock, the doorbell in Esther's house chimed. The guard, Donovan, peered through a peep hole and saw two likely-looking customers on the porch.

He opened the door and gestured them inside, only to find himself face-to-face with a snub-nosed revolver.

"Make one sound and it will be your last," O'Dell rasped. He pushed Donovan out the door where Pounder's marshals quietly hauled him away.

Two of Pounder's men were to have taken the backdoor guard into custody at the same time. That only left the third guard who would be monitoring the parlor and the staircase.

O'Dell cocked his head toward Tyndell, the marshal with him. "Esther should be along shortly to welcome you. Make it look like you are the only new guest. Position yourself to take out the other—"

Esther was at his elbow then, whispering furiously, "Mr. O'Dell! Cal is in the parlor. He has a gun!"

I should have figured Judd would be here, O'Dell chastised himself. He nodded and shoved her unceremoniously out the door.

He turned to Tyndell. "All right, change of plans. One guard and Cal Judd in the parlor. Let's make it clean and make it quick."

O'Dell and Tyndell heard two men descending the stairs, presumably Randy and Mike. As their footsteps hit the bottom landing, O'Dell and Tyndell moved into action.

Cal Judd did not get to where he was without a suspicious, hyper-vigilant mind. Something was wrong—Esther had not immediately returned with new guests, and he did not hear her voice welcoming them. The entryway was quiet. Too quiet.

When O'Dell and Tyndell jumped into the parlor, Judd was ready. Smoke tore from his gun and Tyndell slumped behind an ornate Victorian settee. O'Dell dove back behind a wall post. The several gentlemen lounging in the parlor shouted and threw themselves on the floor. Confusion reigned.

Randy and Mike sprang from the stairwell and tackled Jack, the third guard, just as he pulled his gun. Randy called out, "O'Dell! We've got this guy!"

That left only Judd.

Randy hollered again. "Judd has a derringer! Sounds like a Remington!"

Two shots, .41 caliber, O'Dell automatically calculated and stared across the room at the wounded marshal. Tyndell was not moving.

O'Dell launched himself from behind the entry wall to the back of the settee near Tyndell. A .41 caliber is slow and O'Dell was fast, but not fast enough. Judd's second shot slammed into O'Dell's left shoulder.

He hit the floor hard and groaned, then turned to Tyndell. The man's eyes fluttered but his chest was wet with blood.

Gingerly O'Dell sat up. His arm ached and felt numb; however, he knew could manage himself for now. And Judd's fancy little popgun should be empty.

O'Dell thought briefly of rushing Judd and shooting him dead. Afterwards he could say that he hadn't been sure, *couldn't be sure*, the man was out of bullets and couldn't take the chance that he wasn't. He cursed himself for having a conscience.

"That's it, Judd!" O'Dell shouted. "You've killed a U.S. marshal and you're out of bullets. You're done for. Throw out that palm pistol and surrender."

The silence dragged on for five minutes. Then a silver, pearl-handled gun arced across the room and landed on a carpet near O'Dell.

"I'm coming out." Judd stood up and O'Dell, keeping his revolver on him, called for Randy and Mike to take him into custody. Judd stared coldly at O'Dell as they fastened the cuffs and dragged him outside. O'Dell followed.

Pounder had the guards, Donovan, Jack, and a third man, lined up against a police wagon. As the marshals led Judd toward the wagon, he spied Esther, standing off to the side, her arms wrapped tightly around her bare shoulders.

Judd called out to her, his voice strident with barely suppressed rage. "Are you part of this, Esther? Did you conspire with this Pinkerton to do this to me?"

Esther, terrified and shaking, did not answer. O'Dell walked over and stood beside Esther. He would have handed her his jacket but the left sleeve was soaked in blood that trickled off his fingers onto the ground.

"I should have aimed better, Pinkerton," Judd called, his words cold with menace.

His eyes returned to Esther, and his tone changed then, his words soft, as if reproaching a child. "Sweet Esther. Disloyal and disobedient—after all I have done for you, given to you, and how I have loved and cared for you. Your error will cost you dearly."

"No, Judd. In fact, I promise you will never see her again," O'Dell replied, placing himself between Judd and Esther.

Judd lunged at O'Dell, but the marshals held him back. "This is the second time you have interfered in my affairs," he roared at O'Dell, his neck and face red, veins distended in anger. "You had best watch your back, Pinkerton! I will come for you, I promise you that."

Not if I see you first, O'Dell answered silently. In his heart he knew that leaving Cal Judd alive was a mistake that would come back to bite him. But on the other hand, so was shooting a man in cold blood. *Blast and damnation!*

Judd hadn't finished ranting yet. "Esther! Listen to me! No matter how far you go or where you hide, I will find you! *And when I find you and I finish with you . . .* little children will run screaming from the sight of your face! No man will ever want you again, *except in the dark.*"

Esther shuddered and hid herself behind O'Dell's broad back. O'Dell just stared nonplussed at Judd as the marshals forced the struggling, cursing man into the back of the police wagon.

He motioned to Esther and they went back into the house. There he found five other women milling about the downstairs, unsure of what to do.

"I am offering you all a chance to change your lives," O'Dell stated tersely. "For those of you willing, tomorrow I will take you aboard a train and to a distant locale."

"Would Cal be able to find us?" Ava asked hesitantly. O'Dell noticed that her nose was changed from the last time he'd seen her, bent to one side, certainly broken.

"I don't believe so," O'Dell replied. "But if you decide to come, it must be now. Tonight you will stay with friends of mine. Pack and take what you need. Leave the rest. You have 30 minutes."

Hesitantly, Esther asked, "Friends of yours?"

"Yours, too. They found your note, Esther," he replied softly, and he saw the glistening moisture that gathered in her eyes.

A half hour later Esther, Ava, Jess, Molly, and two other girls crowded into two cars driven by Pinkertons. O'Dell took a last pull on his cigar. The next few days would be trying at best.

God, if you are there, I'm guessing I need you. O'Dell dropped his half-smoked cigar on the ground and jumped in the waiting car before it sped into the night.

❧ ✳ ❧

CHAPTER 27

(Journal Entry, December 28, 1909)

Father God, you have answered our prayers for Esther, Ava, Jess, and Molly! I stand in awe and amazement, Lord, and thank you.

Your word tells us that you are "able to do exceeding abundantly above all that we ask or think" and you have. Two women in addition to "our" girls arrived at Palmer House Christmas night. They came with a price, though, and I do not forget this.

One of Mr. Pounder's marshals was terribly wounded in their rescue. We do not know yet how he will fare, but we are praying diligently for him. And our dear Mr. O'Dell also suffered a gunshot to his shoulder.

Dr. Murphy came immediately to care for him and pronounced Mr. O'Dell the worst patient he has tended to date. While the wound was not difficult to treat, Mr. O'Dell lost a great deal of blood and the good doctor demanded bed rest.

Our Mr. O'Dell, however, would have nothing of that. He and another Pinkerton man left with the girls the following morning, taking them away from Denver. I will not say where in this entry for fear it may someday be read by those who wish to pursue them.

He did not say, but Mr. O'Dell's eyes told me that he is worried. As he bade me goodbye, he whispered that he cannot return to Denver for a time. He will, he said, go directly to Seattle and attempt to find Mei-Xing's family.

I understand his concern. Cal Judd, a name now infamous in our home, is in jail, but we have already seen that the law is not always able to retain evil men. Still nothing has been found of Dean Morgan or Su-Chong Chen.

If Cal Judd were to be freed from the restraints of the law, to what lengths would he go to reclaim Esther? Mr. O'Dell's worries were unspoken but his eyes told me all. For these reasons, the Pinkertons maintain a guard here and at the shop. We are taking precautions, Lord, but our trust and hope are in you.

—

Bao Xang hovered with indecision across the street from the Li home. What he was considering would have severe, irrevocable consequences. Nevertheless, for the first time in the weeks since Ling-Ling and the baby had died, his heart felt stirred, as though something *right* might come from his wretched, miserable existence. Perhaps Mei-Xing could even be restored to her family.

He shook his head and thought of the more likely consequences of his actions. If he told Mr. Li that Mei-Xing had not killed herself, and that, instead, Fang Hua had arranged for Mei-Xing to be forced into a life of prostitution, would Mr. Li even believe him?

What would Mr. Li do when Bao told of his own part in the deception? He wondered if the man would kill him on the spot.

A suitable response, he mused. *A just end to my dishonorable life.*

If Mr. Li *did* believe Bao, what would he do with the information Bao gave him? He was a wealthy, powerful man, with many loyal employees. He was honest to a fault.

The Chens were also wealthy and powerful, but they did not conduct their businesses honorably. Bao knew well of their gangs of thugs, their cutthroats and "fixers."

If he told Mr. Li, what would the man do? Would there be a bloodbath?

He paced down to the corner, lost in his indecision, and stood staring at nothing.

"Friend, you seem disturbed."

The presence of another man so near him shocked Bao out of his stupor. Wild-eyed, he backed away without thinking and stepped off the curb.

With a cry, the stranger leapt toward him and, grabbing him by the lapels, jerked him back onto the sidewalk. "Have a care! You will be run down!"

To emphasize the man's point, a sleek motor car flashed by, dangerously near the gutter.

"Are you all right?" the man asked solicitously.

Bao nodded and stared about him. He had not realized he was so close to the corner.

"I am Yaochuan Min Liáng," the man, a Chinese perhaps 35 years old, said quietly. He held out his hand and Bao automatically shook it. "You are Bao Shin Xang, are you not?" The man asked his question in Mandarin.

Bao jerked back his hand as though it were afire. "How do you know me?" he demanded.

The man pointed to the Li home. "I am a friend of the Li family. You have been on this sidewalk for several hours. You are a friend of this family. The servants know you and expressed some . . . concern." His expression was gentle, sympathetic. "Mr. and Mrs. Li tell me you recently suffered a great loss."

Bao opened his mouth to speak but nothing came out. He looked toward the Li home, half expecting and dreading that Mei-Xing's parents would be watching from the windows.

The man placed a hand on Bao's arm. "Mr. Xang, I am Mr. and Mrs. Li's minister. Your heart seems greatly burdened. Would you care to talk? I am a good listener," he assured Bao.

"Their minister? But, they are not Christian, are they?" Bao frowned and looked at the man with wary eyes.

"Ah. Yes. They are new to their faith," Minister Liáng told him. "They, too, have lived through a crushing time. Their trials have led them to faith in Christ."

Liáng looked about. "Come, Mr. Xang. Shall we go into that little shop down the street and share a pot of tea? I could use a hot cup."

Bao allowed himself to be ushered along. Perhaps this man could hear what he could not bring himself to say to Mr. and Mrs. Li's face. *Perhaps fate was showing him the way.*

An hour later, hunched over the now-empty pot of tea, Minister Liáng stared at Bao in disbelief. Bao had been on the verge of confessing his burden many times since they sat down, only to avoid confronting his torment by turning the conversation in another direction.

Minister Liáng saw a troubled heart and, puzzled by Bao's behavior, continued to try to draw him out. Oddly, he had finally deduced that whatever was tormenting Bao had not to do with his wife and son's demise, but with the Li family's daughter.

"Bao," he said, earnestly imploring the young man before him, "If you know something about Mei-Xing's death, I urge you to cleanse your conscience. The God of Grace will forgive you, whatever it is!"

"God of Grace?" Bao had never heard this. He turned it over in his mind.

"It *is* about Mei-Xing Li, is it not? This is why you have been standing across the street from the Li home?" Minister Liáng insisted, near to losing his patience.

Bao stared at him and then dropped his head. "I am an evil man, Minister Liáng. It is only fitting that such disaster has come upon me and my family. I . . . I am haunted by Mei-Xing. Soon, I will ensure that justice is meted out on my head as well . . . and, before I am gone, I must speak the truth."

Minister Liáng shivered. "You must tell me then, Bao. Whatever it is. Mr. and Mrs. Li deserve to know the truth."

Bao squeezed his head with both hands as though he could block out his agony. "You don't know what the truth will do! You do not know!"

He spoke loudly and the minister shushed him. Curious faces turned in their direction.

"The truth is important, Bao," Minister Liáng assured him softly.

Bao laughed, sounding crazed as he did. "The truth will mean war, sir! It will lead to death, death, and more death!"

Liáng caught his breath and began to pray. *Oh Lord, you know this man's beleaguered heart. I begin to see that his pain has unhinged him. Father God, have mercy on him right now. Restore his mind and deliver him from the evil that is oppressing him!* For Yaochuan Liáng felt the evil torment under which Bao was laboring.

They were both still for a time, Liáng praying silently, and Bao staring at the table. At last Bao whispered, "She is not dead, you know."

He had spoken so quietly that Liáng was not certain he had heard correctly. "She is not . . . did you say she is not dead?" Certainly he meant his wife, only a few weeks gone now.

Bao nodded. "Yes. I said that. She is not dead."

Yaochuan Min Liáng studied Bao. The younger man seemed calmer, but Liáng had seen mad men appear calm and sane one moment only to descend into babbling lunacy the next.

"I understand she had a difficult childbirth," he temporized, hoping to lead Bao toward reality.

Bao gave a short, harsh laugh. "I do not speak of *my wife*, Minister Liáng."

Liáng's mouth dropped open. "You, you do not?" His head began to spin as Bao's words took on new meaning. Impossible meaning.

Bao's face contorted in anger. "That evil witch hates her. Hates her with all the venom of a serpent. Mei-Xing spurned her son, you see. Fang Hua wanted to punish Mei-Xing, punish her in the most vile, degrading manner she could conceive."

Yaochuan Liáng could not breathe. He knew the Chen family and knew Madam Chen by reputation. What had been whispered to him in confidence by his parishioners had horrified him. "What . . . *what* did Fang Hua do?"

Bao told him. Dry-eyed, he recited the entire tale. Once he began, he could not stop until he had told it all.

Yaochuan Liáng's vision darkened and he felt nauseous. He dropped his head to the table. *This could not be true!* He thought of Mr. and Mrs. Li, so broken by their daughter's suicide, so filled with recrimination. He recalled how their unrelenting guilt had driven them to despair . . . until, urged by a trusted family servant, they had come to him and found forgiveness in Christ.

What would this news do to them? Was it true? Could it be? He shivered. If Fang Hua Chen were involved, it *could* be true.

"How do you know she is still alive?" he whispered to Bao.

The man looked blank for a moment. "I know because Su-Chong has seen her."

Yaochuan Liáng drew back in astonishment. "Su-Chong? Has he been heard from, then?"

Bao nodded slowly. "Men I employed have seen him. In the Denver city of Colorado."

Yaochuan Liáng said nothing, but his eyes asked the question.

"Fang Hua sent me to Denver to break him from jail," Bao replied as though it were an everyday event. "She sent me to bring him back here, but he overpowered and killed the men we hired. He saw her before he was arrested and now he is again looking for her. Looking for Mei-Xing." He related Morgan's conversation with Fang Hua.

The minister sat back. It was too much. Too much to take in, to grasp.

"Will you tell them? Will you tell Mei-Xing's father and mother?" Bao asked. The young man's exhausted eyes begged him.

The dangers were every bit as great as Bao had insisted. But what if what he said was utter nonsense, the ravings of a mad man? And yet his tale seemed all too plausible.

"No," Liáng answered slowly. "It would serve no purpose at present except to horribly distress them . . ." his sentence trailed off. But something had to be done. The web of evil had to be untangled, beginning in the right place.

"No. I will myself go to the town you spoke of," Yaochuan Min Liáng said softly. "This town of Corinth?" The name sickened him, now that he knew of its wickedness. "I will go and, if what you have said is true, I will find Mei-Xing and take her out of that horror."

For the first time in many months, Bao felt a ray of hope. "You will help her?"

Liáng nodded, his face sober. "No one must know, Bao. You must return home and grieve for your family, but speak of *this* to no one. We will trust that the God of Grace will guide me on Mei-Xing's behalf. I will ask him to make a way for me to restore her to her family."

It was the second time Bao had heard Minister Liáng speak of his God of Grace. Was this the Christian god then? *No matter*. He was certain no god could possibly have grace for him.

———

Edmund O'Dell disembarked in King Street Station and took a cab to a modest hotel near the waterfront. He and another Pinkerton agent had seen Esther and the other girls safely to Rose's friends in RiverBend. Then he had immediately set out for Seattle.

His shoulder burned fiercely and he was exhausted. Inwardly he railed at his body's weakness. How many weeks had he spent in Denver searching for Mei-Xing? And had he found any trace of her? Absolutely none. His inability to pick up a trail churned like gall in his gut.

Frustrated, he set his will like iron to press on, ignoring his body's needs. He had no time to waste on an aching shoulder. Discovering Mei-Xing Li and Su-Chong Chen's roots was his best hope now.

In a moment of weakness, Mei-Xing had told Breona she was from Seattle. Mei-Xing and Su-Chong had a history. Therefore, presumably, Su-Chong was from Seattle. Su-Chong and Morgan had a history. Perhaps Morgan was also from Seattle. The keys to finding all three of them *had* to be somewhere in Seattle.

He refused to think on how large Seattle was and how little he had to go on. He would start by searching for families with Mei-Xing's last name, Li. He didn't fool himself about that possibility. Seattle and the surrounding area would likely be home to hundreds of families with the Li name.

However, something else tugged at the back of his mind, something that Mei-Xing and Su-Chong had said to each other that eventful night in the plaza. *Something important* to his search.

He frowned and rubbed a hand across his bleary eyes. As soon as he checked in he would sit down and write out everything he could recall of their confrontation in Corinth. He would start with when Su-Chong grabbed Mrs. Thoresen by the throat and Mei-Xing stepped in front of him . . .

What was it that they said?

CHAPTER 28

(Journal Entry, January 11, 1910)

Dear Lord, even with the rescue of Esther and the other girls, I confess that I have never experienced a more difficult entrance to a New Year. We miss Mei-Xing daily.

I miss her, O Lord. She is as much my daughter as Joy is and, if I did not know with all my heart that you have her in your care, I would lose my courage. Her continued absence has been hard on Breona too. She loves Mei-Xing as a sister and is but a shadow of herself lately.

And the house feels even emptier this evening. Flinty left to Corinth this morning to collect some of his belongings. He will return within a few days.

The girls quietly watched him eat breakfast and then fussed over him as he readied for the train. I might go so far as to say that Tabitha was downright possessive of him, if only for a moment, insisting on verifying that he had his coat, hat, gloves, scarf, and extra socks!

She still does not trust herself to others easily, but she has no such barrier with Flinty. We all can see the love between them, even if Tabitha cannot openly express it.

Our Mr. O'Dell has now gone on to Seattle to search for Mei-Xing's family. He, too, carries the weight of Mei-Xing's disappearance heavily. Father, you know where Mei-Xing is. We believe you are upholding her with your strong arm. Please lead our Mr. O'Dell by your Spirit, and bring Mei-Xing home to us, Lord!

I am reminded of the woman Jesus told his disciples about who sought justice from a judge. She would not leave the judge in peace until she received the just ruling she asked for. Jesus told us we should, in the same manner, ask and continue asking you for what we need.

And so, Lord, we ask you to move on Mei-Xing's behalf to deliver her and bring her home. We will not stop, Lord. We will not tire, and we will not give up. Lord, our hope is in you.

Flinty stepped off the train in Corinth and shuffled toward his shop and his attached house. It wasn't home anymore, though. Nope. After many years of solitude, he had again found a home, a real home, filled with laughter and vitality, purpose and love.

He chuckled as he thought of each one at Palmer House. And that Tabitha! *Yessir!* He loved that little firecracker like a daughter.

He unlocked the shop and looked around. He had decided to crate up his tools and bring down the few household goods he felt were needed at the house. He would sell any tools Palmer House couldn't use and give the money to Miss Rose. Something told him that lady was carrying more load than she ought.

He would only stay two nights in Corinth. Mebbe Pastor Kalbørg or Domingo would help him haul the crates to the siding. Then he would catch the midmorning train.

Yep. And mebbe someone would buy his shop and little house, too. He stood at a window and stared at where the lodge had stood, just nine months ago.

He'd lived much of his adult life in that house. Built it from scratch. Raised his boys there. Said goodbye to his sweetheart there. Had moved out and away from all the memories clamorin' at him in that empty place.

Then, all these years later, outta the blue, the house'd come alive again, and so had he. His eyes misted a bit. *Lord, bless them folks at Palmer House fer takin' in an old man like me an' lettin' me be part o' a fam'ly agin.* Then he straightened himself out and set to work.

———

Mei-Xing walked the length of her prison, automatically counting off the steps and turning to retrace them. The room was small and its furnishings sparse: A bed, a chamber pot, a small table and chair, two side-by-side windows, a door.

The door was solid wood, hinged from the outside. The walls were lath and plaster over brick. *The windows were bricked in.*

She stopped pacing and found herself at the end of her bed. She pulled it away from the wall. Studied the eleven groups of scratches, each group containing four vertical and one diagonal line slashed through the vertical ones. Fifty-five days . . . more or less.

What was happening outside these walls? Were they still looking for her or had they given up? No, she would not allow herself to think that way. But so much had happened, so much that could not be undone. She let her mind wander back to that night . . .

Like most evenings since the guards had been posted, she had greeted the Pinkerton man as she climbed the steps to the front door of Palmer House. He had been standing post on the porch, within the shadows, as usual.

But when Mei-Xing opened her bag to retrieve the door key, the man had grabbed her from behind. Pressed something wet and sickly smelling to her face and held it there. She struggled with all her might but then *she heard Su-Chong's voice softly insisting that she not fight him.*

When she awoke, she was in this room.

As she slowly came to herself, she became violently sick to her stomach. Two jars of water had been left on the table, so after emptying her stomach into the chamber pot, Mei-Xing dampened a corner of her shawl and wiped her mouth and face.

She drank most of the water in one of the jars. That seemed to help settle her stomach and clear away the drug-induced cobwebs. As her mind cleared, she walked around the faintly lit room.

She tried to open the door. Locked!

Looked under the door. Darkness!

A dim electric bulb hung from the high ceiling. Her only light.

Went to the windows. Solid bricks!

What could she do but wait? So she waited. Waited and prayed for peace while frantic thoughts clawed through her head.

What if he never came back? What if he did come back? What would he want of her? Why had he taken her? Why was she here? What if he left her in this room to starve?

She eyed the water in the remaining jar, trembling, fighting against imagined horrors and rising panic. As hard as she fought, her thoughts ran wild and tumbled out of control.

She began to gasp, to choke. A buzzing in her head grew louder. The room was closing in! It was out of air! She shuddered as her lungs struggled to find oxygen and her eyesight dimmed. She fell to the floor, blessedly unconscious.

—

The narrow gauge train pulled into the little town of Corinth in the late afternoon. Yaochuan Min Liáng disembarked and took stock of his surroundings. The ground was crusty with old snow, and the waning sunlight warned that the current temperature, just above freezing, would be dropping soon.

His first order of business was to find a place to spend the night. No passengers boarded the train in Corinth. In fact, the siding seemed little used of late. He looked about, wondering in which way the little town lay.

Not far from the siding he spotted a small cabin tucked back in the trees. He could see someone puttering near a cold forge. Liáng hoisted his satchel and made his way to what he deduced was a smithy.

"Good afternoon," he called.

A grizzled man with graying red hair looked up. "Afternoon," he called back. He looked Liáng over, clearly puzzled. "Y' lost, mister?"

Liáng laughed. "I well may be. I want to walk into Corinth and I need a room for the night. Could you help me with either of those items?"

"Sure 'nuff. Got but one place t' stay these days." He grinned. "Hope ya like yer bedbugs plenty an' loud!" He laughed and slapped his thigh. Liáng must have blanched, for the old man offered his hand and added, "Name's Flinty. Don't mind me, now."

"Yaochuan Min Liáng," he replied shaking the man's hand in return.

"Tha's a mouthful, fer sure!" The old gent's humor was infectious. Liáng grinned back.

"It is, indeed. Please call me Yao."

"Yow, eh? Well, Yow, iff'n yer headed int' town, ya jest go on down that road. Coupla' hundred feet, you'll start seein' a few houses, then you'll come right up on the place. 'Taint big an' th' boardin' house is past th' plaza an' turn right."

The old man shook his head and pointed. "Iff'n y'd been here a year back, why ya coulda stayed at th' Corinth Mountain Lodge, right over yonder."

Liáng peered through the twilight but saw nothing.

"Sorry, son. Burned down las' April. Sure were a sad night."

"Have you lived in Corinth long?" Suddenly Liáng felt hopeful that he may have found someone who could tell him some of the things he'd traveled here to find out.

"Yep. Came in with th' silver strike. Bin here ivir since. Raised a passel o' boys, but they growed an' moved on. Th' wife passed ten years back."

"I'm sorry to hear that," Liáng said, meaning it.

"I thank ya. Say," the gent said, perking up. "Ya hungry? Got a nice stew, jest simmerin' on th' back o' th' stove. I rolled out some mighty fine biscuits t' go with! Truth b' told, I wouldn't mind th' comp'ny."

"Would I have any difficulty finding the boarding house and getting a room after dark?" Liáng could not help but notice that the light was fading rapidly.

"Ya look like a honest man. If'n ya don't mind a thin mattress, got me an extry bed over yonder." Flinty pointed with his chin toward a narrow cot. "No bedbugs, neither!" He laughed and asked. "Say, ya play checkers?"

Flinty's manner was infectious. Liáng grinned and nodded.

"Well then! Set yerself down."

Over dinner Flinty said, "'Twas providence ya found me here t'day."

"Oh?"

"Don' live here n'more, y'know. Jest came up ta clear out th' place a bit." He gestured at several boxes and crates under the smithy's eaves.

"Planned ta take th' train this mornin' 'cept Pastor an' Mrs. Kalbørg, why they hed me fer supper las' night an' midweek church after. Done slep' in an' 'cided t' kech th' train t'morrer. Ain't as young as I was oncet."

Yaochuan Min Liáng's almond eyes crinkled appreciatively. "Are you a Christian man, then, Flinty?"

"Yessir. Bin lovin' m' Lord fer more'n 25 years now."

"I am a Christian also, my friend," Minister Liáng responded warmly. "Perhaps your pastor would meet with me? I am looking for someone and would value his help."

"Why shore he would! Iffn ya don't mind m' askin', who might ya be lookin' fer?"

Liáng hesitated and studied his plate for a moment. "It is a delicate situation, but I feel I can trust you, Flinty, so I will confide in you."

"As you have lived here a long while," here he paused again, "are you familiar with any houses of, of soiled doves in Corinth?"

Flinty turned from jovial host to hard-eyed stranger in a heartbeat. He looked Liáng over again and replied carefully. "Mister, ya said ya was a Christian. Kin ya tell me what a house of o' ill repute holds fer ya?"

Minister Liáng nodded. "I understand your reaction, Mr. Flynn. I assure you, I am not looking for . . . for my own, uh, purposes." At that point he blushed and Flinty's eyes softened and turned curious.

"I am, however, looking for a young lady, a very young lady whom, I was told, was taken into such a, ah, house against her will."

He held his hands out in appeal to Flinty. "I hope you will believe me—I would not frequent such a place. Rather, I was hoping to find this young lady and restore her to her family. You see, I am her parents' pastor."

Liáng stared at the old man who was beginning to wipe his eyes. "But, friend, I see I have moved you somehow . . ."

Flinty's face creased in a small smile. "The Lor' shore do work in mysterious ways, don' he? Like I were sayin', I shoulda bin gone on this mornin's train, but guess he a-wanted you an' me t' meet up an' all."

He wiped his eyes again. "See, them houses o' evil 'r all shut down, they are, an' I kin tell ya all 'bout how it happened. 'Twas surely God what done it."

He studied the Asian man for another moment, a possibility slowly dawning on him. "Say, what's th' name o' the young lady ya lookin' fer?"

Liáng sighed and took a chance. "Her name is Mei-Xing Li."

But Flinty was already nodding his head before the words were out of his mouth. "Mister Liáng, I know Miss Mei-Xing. I know her real well." A rain of tears fell as he told Yaochuan Min Liáng everything he knew about Mei-Xing.

❧ ✽ ❧

CHAPTER 29

As she came to, Mei-Xing had felt the floor's iciness in her bones. She opened her eyes, struggling to understand what she was looking at.

She was lying on the floor near the bed, staring at its underside. A familiar strap dangled between the bed and the wall. The strap of her reticule.

Mei-Xing pulled herself to her knees. She had to lay her head against the bed until the dizziness and nausea subsided. Across the bed a bit of her bag peeped at her—it had slid between the bed and wall. She grasped at it and slowly pulled the bag to her.

Hand trembling, she loosened the drawstring. *It was there.*

Her fingers trembling, she pulled out the small book, clasping it to her breast. It had been a gift from Rose and Joy. Much of her time with Mrs. Palmer was spent in relative inactivity, so one day Mei-Xing had designed and sewn a lovely cover for the book out of a scrap of blue, watered silk. She had edged it in lace.

Her New Testament and Psalms.

She held it with desperate eagerness. *Thank you, Lord!*

Hours later she heard the key rattle in the door. It opened and Su-Chong stood there. Neither of them spoke. Mei-Xing, sitting on the edge of the bed, did not move except to slowly smooth her skirt, covering the testament in its folds.

Su-Chong wordlessly retrieved a tray from behind him. Mei-Xing could not see into the room behind him. It, too, was dimly lit. She could not tell if it was day or night.

He placed the tray on the table and removed the two empty jars. Then, with a pronounced limp, he backed out and relocked the door. He had not said a word.

Mei-Xing still did not move, but when she smelled the yeasty scent of warm bread, everything within her rumbled in response. With her eye on the door, she slid the testament under her mattress and cautiously approached the table.

The tray contained two jars of fresh water, a bowl of soup, and several dinner rolls. Mei-Xing's mouth watered. She lifted one of the rolls to her nose and inhaled the smell of it, the warmth of it. Then she sat and devoured the food.

After a while the light in her room went out so she lay down on the bed, anxious and trembling. What if he came into the room while she was sleeping? She breathed a short prayer and, in spite of her worry, slept.

She started and woke in the dark. The door was opening and she could see him outlined in the faint light behind him. She held completely still, pretending to sleep.

He removed the tray and then the chamber pot, locking the door behind him. A few minutes later he returned, laid something on the chair, and replaced the empty pot, sliding it under the bed.

Mei-Xing knew he was standing near her, watching her, so she remained still, breathing softly. Finally, he turned and left, again locking the door behind him. She sighed in relief and eventually fell back asleep.

When Mei-Xing awoke, the light was on. A tray with oatmeal and coffee waited for her on the table. She gulped the bitter coffee gratefully and wiped the sleep from her eyes.

Then she saw the neat stack of clothing setting on the chair. A towel. A wash cloth. Soap. Two simple, shapeless dresses, much too large for her. She flushed when she found items of personal clothing. And then shivered.

How long did he mean for her to remain in this room?

She had been taken at night. She awoke from the drugged sleep during, presumably, the day. Much later he brought dinner. Then the light went out and she slept. When she woke the light was on and breakfast awaited her.

Picking up the spoon from her breakfast, Mei-Xing looked for something to scratch on. She pulled her bed away from the wall and, where the mattress covered the wall, she scratched two short, vertical lines.

She occasionally heard him moving about the rooms on the other side of the door. When he brought food and water neither of them spoke.

On what was perhaps the fourth day, Su-Chong opened the door and stood staring at her, saying nothing. He looked thinner than she remembered him. Then Mei-Xing noticed his feverish cheeks and glazed eyes.

For the first time, he spoke. "I need your help."

Mei-Xing licked her lips and swallowed. She was afraid to answer.

"I need your help," he said again. He turned and limped away, leaving the door agape.

Quickly, Mei-Xing ran to the open door. A short hallway opened immediately into a sitting room. She saw a sink and small gas stove on the other side of the sitting room and three windows on the wall to the right. The windows were bricked in just as in her room!

She assumed she would find a door on the left side of the sitting room and her heart began to hammer—but then Su-Chong stepped out of a room at the opposite end of the hall.

He stared at her. She stared back. In his hands he held towels and a large basin. He walked toward her, and she retreated into her prison.

Limping, he followed her into the room and set the things on the table. Then he locked the door from the inside. The key hung from a chain. He put the chain over his head and the dangling key inside his shirt. With some difficulty, he began to remove his trousers.

Mei-Xing was terrified—until she noticed him grimacing in pain. Cautiously, she watched as he removed a soiled bandage from his upper thigh. Even from across the room she could see how inflamed the wound was.

"I need your help," he said for the third time.

She slowly drew near. What she saw made her gag. The wound should have been stitched but had not been. It gaped open, six inches or so of it, across the muscle and around the back of the thigh, angry and festering.

She, as well as the others at Palmer House, had read and reread the newspaper accounts of Morgan and Su-Chong's escape and disappearance. Accounts of four men found in a car near Union Station, four men who had suffered violent deaths.

He must have been cut during his escape.

Eyes glazed but intent, Su-Chong stared at her. Something of the young man he had been, the boy she had known, glimmered for a brief moment.

Finally, Mei-Xing swallowed and whispered. "I will need needle and thread. Alcohol."

He nodded toward the basin. Mei-Xing, trembling, reached for it and found what she needed in it.

Mei-Xing bowed her head as she remembered. That moment had changed things between them. She could not think on the weeks after that without shuddering in shame.

Oh God! What have I done?

CHAPTER 30

(Journal Entry, January 14, 1910)

We have received a note from Mr. O'Dell. He has taken rooms in Seattle and is now looking for Mei-Xing's family. It has now been eight weeks since her disappearance. Oh, if only she had confided a little more in Breona or Joy. If only we had pressed her a bit to tell us of her past, her family!

Emily tells me that Martha Palmer has taken Mei-Xing's loss very badly. She does not go out or receive visitors. Lord, please comfort us by your Spirit. You promised to never leave us comfortless.

———

Yaochuan Min Liáng hung back to study the large house on the corner. He noted the distinct air of disrepair about the place, but also the visible efforts recently undertaken to improve it.

The grounds showed evidence of sharply trimmed back shrubbery. The tall, wrought iron fence surrounding the grounds was newly painted. The house, of a magnificent design, was set far back from the street, sheltered by tall Ponderosa pines and shrubs that softened the look of neglect. Liáng turned resolutely and followed Flinty up the house's walkway.

Flinty nodded at a man standing on the front porch. The guard Flinty had told him of? Flinty removed a key and opened the locked front door. Liáng followed him into a large entryway and then through a set of closed doors on the right into the house's great room.

A slender woman, her ash blonde hair caught up in a braided knot at her neck was working at a desk in a corner of the room. She looked up and smiled when she saw Flinty.

"My dear friend!" She left the desk to come and greet him. The woman, perhaps in her sixties, took his hands and gave him a soft kiss on his cheek. And then saw Liáng in the doorway behind him.

Flinty nodded at Liáng. "Miss Rose, this here's Mr. Liáng. Mr. Liáng, this here's Mrs. Thoresen, what I tole ya 'bout."

Flinty's eyes were alight with hope. "Met Mr. Liáng here up in Corinth, I did. Ya won't b'lieve who he's a-lookin' fer."

Liáng stepped fully into the room and extended his hand to Rose. "Madam. I am Minister Yaochuan Min Liáng. My church is in Seattle." He smiled, his manner placid. "I am honored to be pastor to Mr. and Mrs. Jinhai Li."

Rose gripped his hand. "Seattle! Mr. and Mrs. Li. Do they . . . have a daughter?"

Liáng, still smiling softly, bowed in assent. "Yes, Mrs. Thoresen. Her name was Mei-Xing Li."

"Was? Her name *was*?" Rose's eyes filled.

"Ah! I am so clumsy and insensitive! Please, may we sit down?" Liáng apologized, compassion showing on his face.

Rose was trembling as Liáng handed her into one of the great room chairs and took another near her. Flinty stood by Rose's chair, waiting to hear Liáng tell his story again.

"My dear lady," he said gently, "Sadly, I used a wrong word. Mr. Flynn has told me that, until several weeks ago, Mei-Xing was living happily in this house. Is this so?"

"Yes," Rose replied. "Are we speaking of the same young woman? Just sixteen years old? A tiny, beautiful girl?"

Liáng sighed in relief. "I believe we must be. Please let me show you and tell you what I know."

At Rose's anxious "Yes, please do," Liáng removed a newspaper clipping from his coat's breast pocket. He unfolded it and handed it to Rose.

Rose took the clipping from his hand and stared into a grainy photo of her beloved Mei-Xing. The image, not recent, was of a child on the cusp of womanhood. Beside it was her obituary.

"But, but I don't understand," Rose muttered. Her shocked face told Liáng what he needed to know.

"So this *is* the Mei-Xing you know?" he had to ask.

"Yes! Yes, it is her! Please tell me what this means!" Rose demanded.

Minister Liáng bowed his head. "I can tell you. I didn't believe it when it was told to me. Did not wish to believe it. I came here to prove it an unspeakably evil falsehood, but now I must face the truth."

"It is a story of two families," he began.

—

Edmund O'Dell reread what he had scrawled the night before. He had written down every detail he could recall of the confrontation between Mei-Xing and Su-Chong on that infamous night in Corinth last year. And then he had fallen asleep with his face on the paper.

He wiped the sleep from his eyes and read it again. They had hurled the words at each other while Su-Chong Chen held Rose Thoresen by the throat. Su-Chong threatened to end Rose's life if the U.S. marshals and Pinkerton agents did not allow him and Dean Morgan to escape their custody. O'Dell could remember, could clearly hear, every word from that night being spoken and yet . . .

He growled in frustration. Some *piece* of what they had said eluded him. *And a blamed important piece*, he remonstrated with himself. *I need coffee*. He heard a thump as something hit the bottom of his hotel door. O'Dell hoped it was his requested copy of the *Seattle Daily Times*.

He retrieved the paper and began reading it from front to back. He reached the society section and studied the announcements and black and white photographs.

Would Mei-Xing's family have moved in these circles? It was obvious to those who knew her that she came from wealth and had been carefully educated and brought up. However, she was Chinese. Would Seattle society mingle with and acknowledge the Chinese elite?

O'Dell finished the society pages and moved on. When he reached the obituaries he perused each one, looking in particular for Chinese names, finding some, but not the name Li or Chen. He finished and turned the page.

And stopped. That "thing," that forgotten tidbit, tugged at his memory again. He slowly turned back to the obituaries although his eyes were focused elsewhere, his mind on that night . . .

They said you were dead.

He sucked in his breath. Su-Chong Chen had said that!

Mei-Xing's voice floated in his memory. *She hated me.*

Who? Who hated you, Mei-Xing? O'Dell ground his fists into his forehead trying to recall the elusive conversation.

Nothing more came. O'Dell stepped out onto the room's veranda. He could smell the tang of salt water from the nearby wharves. Could hear gulls circling overhead crying to each other.

Placing a cigar to his lips, his mind raced to process the new tidbits of information his incomplete memories had provided. He automatically lit the cigar's end and sucked repeatedly it to make it draw.

As sparse as those bits of memory might be, he could reasonably conclude two important facts from them. One . . . Mei-Xing was believed dead.

He glanced inside his room at the crumpled newspaper. The obituaries. If she were believed dead then—

O'Dell nodded to himself. He would visit the *Times*, search the obituaries, find those persons at the paper who could help him find what he looked for.

And two . . . *she hated me.*

Hated me. Someone hated Mei-Xing. Hated her enough to arrange her "death" and consign her instead to a life of living hell?

O'Dell's expression darkened and a hot fury sparked within him. He didn't know how long he stood there lost in his dark thoughts. He only knew that when he shook himself into action and brought the forgotten cigar to his lips, it was broken, crushed within his clenched fist.

CHAPTER 31

Heat radiated from the red swelling of Su-Chong's leg. He lay on his side on the edge of her bed. Mei-Xing had cleaned the infection from the wound as best she could, her stomach revolting as it drained its poisons.

Although he flinched, Su-Chong had made no sound when she poured the alcohol over the wound. She caught the alcohol and what flowed from his leg in the basin then repeated the process until, finally, she could see the edges of the wound more clearly.

Her hands trembled as she threaded the needle. She took a small dish, poured alcohol in it, and placed the threaded needle in the alcohol. As she stared at where she must pull the edges of the wound together, her whole body began to shake uncontrollably.

"I can't do it," she whispered through chattering teeth.

Su-Chong grasped her wrist. She tried to pull away, but he held her firmly.

"Look at me," he commanded.

Unwillingly, Mei-Xing did. Su-Chong's eyes may have been glassy with fever, but his voice was adamant.

"You must do this, Mei-Xing. I have seen your embroidery and needlepoint, remember? You excel at needlework. Think of this as only simple mending. Nothing more."

He gripped her wrist so tightly that Mei-Xing gasped in pain. Still he held her wrist and his eyes commanded her compliance.

Wild thoughts pummeled her mind as he stared at her. *What if he dies? What if he dies outside this locked door? Who would know? How long would it be before anyone found him? Found me?*

His grip on her wrist did not lessen. Reluctantly, she realized, *O God, please help me! I must do this.*

Finally, she nodded and he released her. For a moment she wavered, unsteady on her feet. Then she gathered herself and pulled the needle and thread from the dish of alcohol. She knelt beside the bed and took a deep breath. And began.

He stayed within her room that day, sleeping fitfully on her bed. In her heart Mei-Xing was glad. If he were to die in her room, at least she would be able to take the key and escape!

However, after several hours of sleep he awakened and, although feverish and weak, forced himself to rise and leave, locking the door behind him. When he returned she saw he had stacked jars of water—enough for a week at least—on the floor just outside the door.

He leaned heavily against the door frame and motioned to her. She brought the jars, two at a time, into the room. Then he left again.

He returned a bit later and pointed to a tray on the floor piled with food: crackers, cheese, canned fruit and soups. She understood. She dragged the heavy tray into the room, but he left once more. This time he returned with a pillow and a stack of blankets.

After locking the door and tucking the key within his shirt, he collapsed on her bed and fell into a restless sleep. As his fever increased, Mei-Xing huddled on the floor, watching, waiting, listening to his groans. Once he called for water and aspirin and Mei-Xing gave them to him.

She had no real sense of time because the light was always on. When she grew hungry, she ate. When her eyes would stay open no longer, she made a bed on the floor and slept. When she awoke, she cleaned and re-bandaged his wound, watching their supplies carefully.

Twice more he called for water and aspirin and she gave them to him. After what Mei-Xing guessed was three days, he began to improve. The fever broke and he sweated profusely.

Mei-Xing bathed his face with a damp rag. The wound, although puckered and dreadful looking, drained clear fluids.

He would live.

On the fifth day he left the room, limping and unsteady. Mei-Xing looked about her. The room and bed linens stank. Only a bit of food and water remained.

When she heard him return a few hours later, she was relieved. He had bathed and changed his clothes.

He gestured to her. "Come out here."

Mei-Xing froze, unsure of his direction to her. He gestured again. "I have clean clothes for you, but you should bathe first."

He was right about that. Mei-Xing had not bathed in going on two weeks now. But he was asking her to leave the room? She was suddenly afraid.

She walked slowly into the little sitting room she had glimpsed once before. A hip bath sat by the sink, filled with clean, hot water. Su-Chong's rank-smelling clothes lay in a pile off to the side. Clean clothes for her lay stacked nearby.

"I couldn't carry the tub into your room and bring the water, too," Su-Chong murmured. He was weak, Mei-Xing could see. He had lost more weight.

He placed a cushioned chair against the door of the small apartment, the effort clearly taxing him. "This door is locked," he said wearily. "No one else is in the building right now. I will sit here while you bathe." He gestured weakly. "The door in the hallway. A commode."

He sank into the chair and she soon heard deep, regular breathing. He was asleep, his head resting on the back of the chair.

The water in the bath steamed, and Mei-Xing tested it with her hand. With a glance to where Su-Chong slept, she quickly threw off her filthy clothes, tossing them into the same heap as his.

She sank into the steaming water until it covered her completely. She had never felt a pleasure as exquisite.

———

O'Dell found the sprawling *Seattle Daily Times* building and asked to see the archives. After showing his Pinkerton credentials and receiving permission from the managing editor, a receptionist led him down damp stairs and a dimly lit hall to the vault.

Casually, O'Dell asked, "If I were to need some assistance, perhaps from a long-time employee, whom would you recommend?"

The receptionist, a too-blonde blonde with frizzed tresses, studied him for a minute, her hand on her hip. "Ya might try Hank," she finally offered and started back the way they'd come.

"Hank, huh?" O'Dell called after her. "Where do I find Hank?"

"Here," a voice spoke from behind him. O'Dell saw a middle-aged man wearing an ink-stained vest over his shirt.

"Hank, I'm O'Dell. Can I buy you a cup of coffee?" O'Dell asked.

Hank, as it turned out, managed the vault and archives. "I was a crack reporter until I broke m' hip," he explained. "Since I can't chase stories anymore, they offered me this job down here."

Without giving too much away, he hoped, O'Dell told him what he was looking for.

"Sure, I remember that girl. Quite a sad story," Hank mused.

"Can you help me find the obituary?" O'Dell hid his excitement, but it was difficult. Finally, he was catching a break!

In addition to the obituary Hank found two issues that reported Mei-Xing's disappearance and then the finding of a suicide note and the location where she was presumed to have jumped to her death.

"Never found a body, though," Hank told him. "The tides below the bluff she jumped from are pretty nasty. And they never could figure how she got there. Was pretty far from her home."

O'Dell scanned the details of the articles: *Daughter of Mr. and Mrs. Jinhai Li. Suicide note discovered. Believed drowned. Tragic romantic association.*

His eyes returned to the last sentences:

Miss Li's death by her own hand is said to be attributed to a tragic romantic association. According to close acquaintances who do not wish to be identified, Miss Li had been engaged to be married last year to Mr. Su-Chong Chen, the son of Mr. and Mrs. Wei Lin Chen, long-time family friends of the Li family. Miss Li had unexpectedly broken off the engagement resulting in strained relations between her family and that of her fiancé.

Su-Chong Chen! *He had found the connection at last.* O'Dell quickly read the rest of the article and then carefully copied both of them word for word.

—

Mei-Xing roused herself from her reverie. She again studied the scratches representing her time in this place. She carefully added the first line of a new group. Her accounting would not be entirely accurate. She had lost track while Su-Chong battled his fever. But it was close enough.

She pushed the bed against the wall. Sat down. Wrapped herself in the bed's blanket.

The room had no heat but what worked its way up from below. During the day her room was a little warmer; in the evenings she had to wear all the clothing Su-Chong had provided for her and wrap herself in blankets.

Occasionally, when a winter storm was blasting Denver, Mei-Xing could hear its wailing through the thick walls and bricked over windows. Although Mei-Xing did not know where she was, she had the sense that this room was not on a ground floor.

She walked across the room and back again, picking up the threads of her thoughts.

It had taken several more days for Su-Chong to regain his strength. While he rested she washed their clothing and the linens, hanging them about the rooms wherever she could. She wore one of the too-large dresses he had left for her because she had nothing else. At least it was clean.

She prepared canned foods she found in the tiny kitchen, worrying when she saw the stock diminishing. Then the flour ran out and they ate the last of the stale crackers in the cupboard.

That night, he had led her back into the little bedroom. Later he had turned off the light and she had slept. But something had wakened her in the night. The creak of the apartment door. Su-Chong opening and closing cupboards.

The next morning he unlocked her door and gestured for her to come out. "Please fix us something to eat." He was fatigued and limping again.

Mei-Xing almost said there was nothing to fix but then she remembered the noises in the night. When she opened the cupboards they had been refilled—not fully, but with enough to last a few days. Her mouth watered when she found fresh bread, fruit, and cheese.

"Where did you get these things?" she asked. She felt no immediate fear of him after the amount of time they had been together.

He stared at her.

Mei-Xing remembered the noises. "Have you also become a thief in the night?" she demanded.

His face flamed but still he said nothing.

So. That answered her question.

"How long will you keep me here?" Mei-Xing demanded again, tears clogging her voice. "How long will I be your prisoner?"

Again, he did not immediately answer. When he finally did, her blood ran cold.

"I am sorry." His words were spoken softly. "I am sorry I had to take you, but I had no one else to turn to." He sighed. "I cannot let you go, Mei-Xing. Not without endangering myself."

He gestured to a tin of bacon sitting near the small gas burners. "Please."

Mechanically, Mei-Xing turned to preparing a meal for them. He sat at the table and waited for her. When she placed his food in front of him he gestured to the other chair.

"Please eat with me."

"I-I would prefer not to," Mei-Xing replied, not meeting his eyes. "I will take my food into my . . . room."

"No. You will sit with me." It was not a request.

Reluctantly, Mei-Xing placed her food on the table. Su-Chong did not pick up his fork until she seated herself. Then he ate ravenously. When he finished he watched as she picked at her food.

"Will you tell me what happened?" His question stunned Mei-Xing. What she heard *unspoken* in his question stunned her more. Compassion. Pain.

"I cannot," she whispered.

He was silent. Finally, he replied, "I understand."

He did not ask again. The days dragged by and settled into a routine marked by shared meals and few words.

Every night he would lock her in her room. When supplies ran low, Mei-Xing would arise in the morning to find more food in the kitchen. During the day they would both read, Mei-Xing her little testament and Psalms, Su-Chong from the volumes that lined the shelves in the sitting room.

Often Mei-Xing would look up from her reading to find his eyes on her. She read many things on his face. Loneliness. Regret. And longing.

The open longing nearly destroyed her composure. How she had loved him!

As they sat at the meager dinner she had prepared one evening he asked her again. "Will you not tell me what happened?"

This time Mei-Xing hesitated. In her heart she heard a soft warning. *Do not open this door*, the voice whispered. She hesitated. Finally, she nudged the warning aside . . . and the story she had never spoken of—to anyone—began to trickle from her lips:

Breaking her engagement to him. The anger and disbelief of her parents and other family members. Su-Chong's abandonment of home and family. Fang Hua's public vilification and ostracism. The continuing shame and strain.

Su-Chong's eyes narrowed as she told of his cousin Bao's friendship, his compassion and understanding shoulder.

The ticket and the late-night train. The long ride to Denver.

Mei-Xing knew she should stop. That voice within her was warning her. She thought she could tell the tale without feeling much emotion, but she was wrong.

She was reliving the horror all over again: *Not the loving adoptive family she expected to find. Instead, Darrow, his meaty hand easily spanning her arm, clamping across her mouth, dragging her. Corinth. The house. Roxanne Cleary. Drinking what they forced on her. The man they gave her to and . . .*

Mei-Xing stopped, her mouth open on unspoken words. Her eyes were wide reliving the terror and shame.

And then Su-Chong's arms were around her and he was holding her, rocking her, whispering comforting words into her ear, across her neck, along her jaw, into her mouth.

His lips moved upon hers until she responded. The warning voice in her heart grew softer and more distant as she allowed Su-Chong's solace to altogether drown it out.

CHAPTER 32

It took several days to investigate Mei-Xing and Su-Chong's families. Armed with business and home addresses, O'Dell hired a driver to take him to the posh residential area where Mr. and Mrs. Li lived. O'Dell was always careful. He had the driver drop him several blocks from his destination.

He walked half a mile and found the Li's home. He studied it then wandered the neighborhood, striking up casual conversations, occasionally pretending he was in need of directions.

He would admire the architecture and gardens of the houses, usually finding opportunity to insert innocent questions about long-time neighborhood families. Of the Li home itself he saw nothing that would speak to anything other than a law-abiding, well-to-do family.

The next day he dressed as though he were looking for manual labor and walked to the wharves. He found the Li warehouses and asked Li employees if they knew of available work. He casually asked how it was to work for the Li family. Universally people spoke well of Jinhai Li: He was a fair man to work for and did not dabble in illegal activities.

O'Dell had a driver drop him a distance from the Chen home. From there he walked. What he observed immediately set off alarms in his head. He proceeded cautiously.

The Li house fronted an expensive avenue in the middle of a stylish, open neighborhood. Unlike the Li family, the Chen home was built on a solitary road, surrounded by a tall wall, and maintained like a fortress. Iron gates blocked the entrance.

O'Dell burrowed into wild undergrowth across the road where he could watch the comings and goings of the Chen estate. He spent an entire day peering through shadowed foliage, watching and waiting.

He made notes on every motor car and its license plate. He counted guards and watched their movements. He wrote down delivery trucks and their frequency.

Wei Lin Chen owned restaurants, import shops, and a chain of laundries. The next day O'Dell had a cab drop him downtown. A Chen restaurant and import shop were within walking distance. He strolled and he watched, eating lunch and making small purchases to keep up appearances.

196

The following two days he changed locations and repeated his activities. He noted the same young boys running errands from place to place and once thought someone was watching him. Just in case, he stepped into a Chen competitor's import shop and bought a sack of trifles that the girls in Palmer House would enjoy—carved fans, jade ear bobs, silk scarves, ivory hair combs.

At the end of three days O'Dell was convinced. If the Chen's were not deeply invested in crime and vice, he'd eat his hat. He took dinner in a downtown restaurant intending to return to his hotel before the late afternoon grew any darker.

As he approached a taxi stand two men passed him, one on either side. He realized the danger too late.

———

O'Dell's jaw felt unhinged and his pulse pounded in his head with the frequency and volume of a jackhammer. Every part of his body ached. He could not open his eyes. He was piled in a heap somewhere, but had no idea where.

Through the crusted blood in his nose he smelled something unfamiliar—incense of some kind. Without intending to, he groaned. He heard footsteps and strong hands jerked him to his feet. O'Dell's stomach lurched at the sudden motion and he retched, emptying its contents on the floor.

He heard a stream of high-pitched invective and his captors stiffened. They dragged O'Dell aside and dumped him again. Two sets of feet scurried to clean the mess he'd made.

Then, amid hurled curses from across the room, someone stomped on his hand. He felt the bones shatter before two sets of boots began kicking him viciously in his ribs, his face, his hips, his back. All O'Dell could think as he again lost consciousness was that the voice he'd heard screaming was a woman's, and she had not spoken in English.

Fang Hua fingered the notebook found on the unconscious man. He used some sort of shorthand, and that in itself disturbed her. He had been seen too many days near too many of their businesses to be merely a white man shopping in China town.

As she paged through the entries she noticed sets of numbers. She studied them. What? Her own motor car's plate number! He *had* been spying. But for whom? And why?

She frowned and looked into his wallet. Money only. Nothing to provide his name. Suspicious. Only the little book with its secrets. She did not like it.

Could Reggie be right? Could Su-Chong have sent this man to seek opportunities to strike at her? No. Even if the unthinkable were so, would he use this *guĭlăo*–this white man? No. Would he not come himself? She shuddered.

"Take him down to the waterfront where foolish white men should know better than to go. Beat him more and leave him in the cold to die. It will look like robbery." *The police have many of those to deal with. It will not seem uncommon*, she assured herself.

But she did not like it.

—

(Journal Entry, February 3, 1910)

Minister Liáng returned to Seattle this past week. There was nothing more he could do here in Denver, but in Seattle he could join with our dear Mr. O'Dell and share the information we now have regarding Mei-Xing's family.

The story he tells us is incredible and heartbreaking. Minister Liáng says that even now, this man, Bao, who played such a large role in the evil done to Mei-Xing, waits for Mr. Liáng's return, hoping to beg Mei-Xing's forgiveness.

Minister Liáng wanted to be able to bring Mei-Xing home. It will be a great blow to Bao.

Father, I lift up Bao to you. Your Son forgave even those who crucified him. As hard as it is, we must forgive Bao and show him to your throne of grace. Lord, have mercy on this man, we ask!

Minister Liáng will not tell Mei-Xing's parents what he knows. Not until she is safely found. We believe you will restore her to us, Lord, and then to her family! We hold to our trust in you.

I sent a letter to Mr. O'Dell introducing Minister Liáng and gave Mr. Liáng Mr. O'Dell's hotel. Minister Liáng will find Mr. O'Dell as soon as he returns to Seattle.

We did ask Mr. O'Dell to telephone us at his earliest convenience. The letter went out ten days ago. I confess that I grow concerned. Mr. O'Dell should have called by this time.

—

Yaochuan Min Liáng left the hotel confused and concerned. Yes, Mr. O'Dell was registered; however, he had not been seen for several days and the maids reported that his room had not been used in that same time.

Standing outside under the hotel's awning, Liáng prayed. *O Lord, this man has perhaps become prey to the Dragon. Your people have been praying for him, O God. I am, therefore, confessing my confidence in his deliverance! Show me, O Most High.*

You, who see everything, please show me . . .

As he prayed, he walked, shutting out the sights and sounds of the busy wharves. Should he visit the police? Should he make a trunk call to Denver?

Without conscious thought, he walked away from the waterfront and toward Chinatown. He scarcely noticed as the cries of gulls and shouts of workers on the piers gave way to the rumble of wagons, motor cars, and clanging trolleys.

He was surprised to see he had reached 5th Street. He stopped. He was facing a sign pointing north: *First Providence Hospital*. He turned and soon his steps quickened.

Liáng knew the Sisters of Providence who had founded the hospital; he was acquainted with the sister administrator. He hurried. *Lord, have you shown me?* Liáng breathed in awed thanksgiving.

The nursing sister who escorted him had permanent creases between her eyes. Sister Mary James had nursed Seattle's indigent and affluent for more than 30 years. The worry lines deepened when she showed Liáng to the bedside of an unidentified man.

Minister Liáng gasped with dread when he looked down.

With his characteristic enthusiasm, Flinty had described the Pinkerton man to Liáng. "Dapper, that 'un is!" he'd laughed. "Black hair, al'ays combed back jest so an' wears a fancy hat, one o' them derby kind. An' I niver seed 'im w'out a fine cigar."

Flinty's pronunciation of "cigar" came out "see-gar." Thinking on his colorful new friend lifted the corner of Liáng's mouth. Then he looked closely at the man lying helpless in the bed. His face was swollen, bloodied, and bruised beyond identification. Black hair was his only distinguishing feature.

Even your dear friends would not recognize you, my friend, whomever you are, he worried.

"He was found by workers at the waterfront," the sister whispered. "The police brought him here four days ago. We believe he was out in the cold all night. We found no wallet but did find a hotel key. Tucked into the side of his shoe."

In his shoe? That piqued Liáng's curiosity. "May I see it?"

While Liáng examined the key, the sister checked the man's pulse and spread an ointment across his cracked lips. He moaned, and she spooned water into his mouth.

"We held little hope he would make it through the first day," she added. "But we prayed, and he has surprised us all." From the side, her white wimple hid her face but not the compassion in her voice.

"May I see his clothes and other belongings?" Liáng hoped for something, some sign.

She handed him a large paper sack and watched him as he took out each article. Trousers, shirt, waistcoat, all bloodied and torn. Socks, muddied shoes. At the bottom of the sack something rustled. He turned the sack over and the crushed remains of a cigar fell onto the table.

Ah!

Liáng looked at the man again. As gently as possible he took one of the man's hands into his own.

"Friend," he whispered into to the man's ear. "If you can hear me and your name is Edmund O'Dell, will you squeeze my hand?"

He waited. And then he felt a tremor in the fingers he held and a gentle pressure. And the man groaned.

"Again, please," Liáng breathed into O'Dell's ear. He took care that his whispered words were not heard by Sister Mary James. "If you are Edmund O'Dell, squeeze my hand."

A few seconds later he felt the man's finger close on his. And hold on.

Liáng leaned near O'Dell's ear again and spoke slowly. "Mr. O'Dell, your friends in Denver have sent me to find you. Mrs. Thoresen. Mr. and Mrs. Michaels. Flinty! You are safe here. I will take care of everything for you while you recover. Do you understand me?"

This time the man uttered a garbled "yes" followed by a groan of pain. He tried to open his eyes.

Liáng whispered again, "Do not try to move just now, Mr. O'Dell. I will let your friends know I have found you."

"This is him," Liáng informed the sister. "His name is, uh, Jones. Timothy Jones."

Dear Lord, forgive my deceit, but I wish this man to live, not die. "When can he be discharged?"

"Not soon. His injuries will take time to heal. He will need care even when he leaves."

Minister Liáng nodded. "Thank you. Here is my card. I will make the arrangements for when he is able to be released."

He looked again at the hospital bed and realized the man was still gripping his hand. "Do not worry, my friend," Liáng spoke aloud. "I will return soon."

CHAPTER 33

(Journal Entry, February 7, 1910)

We received the most distressing news from Minister Liáng. Mr. O'Dell is seriously injured in the hospital. He believes Mr. O'Dell was either robbed or his investigation put him in the way of harm. We do not know which.

We gathered the household immediately to pray for him. Minister Liáng is watching over him as he recovers and will keep us informed.

Tonight I confess I longed for Jan's strong arms to hold and comfort me! So many trials are upon us, and I just wanted to run from them, run into Jan's embrace and hear him say "Nei, Rose; I have you."

Lord, we are pressed out of measure, above strength. We cannot trust in ourselves and so we trust in you, Lord, the God which raiseth the dead.

———

February dragged on, miserably wet, slushy, and cold. Spirits flagged under the distressing news and grey, overcast skies.

Heating the house became such a financial strain that Rose, Grant, and Joy made the unpopular decision to tamp down the coal furnace until it was barely burning. This economy plus judicious use of the many fireplaces kept the household from freezing. But just.

Everyone gathered in the great room in the evenings where its two fireplaces blazed continually. By shutting off the room from the entryway and dining room, they kept in the warmth generated by the two fires.

"Missus, I wish you'd take a look at Flinty," Mr. Wheatley said to Rose one evening. She saw the concern underlying his request and hurried to check on their friend.

The butler quarters near the back of the house were relatively dry and not too cold, but Flinty was huddled in his bed under many blankets, shivering violently. Rose laid a hand on his forehead and was alarmed at how hot it felt.

"Will you fetch Breona, please?" she asked Mr. Wheatley. Without a word, he left her.

Rose sat on the edge of the bed. "Dear Flinty, how are you feeling?"

"Bin better, I reckon," he wheezed. Then he coughed and grimaced. Rose could hear the tightness of his chest in both his cough and his labored breathing.

Breona hurried into the room, felt Flinty's forehead, and listened to his breathing. He coughed several time while she watched him, groaning in pain each time.

Out in the hall, Breona whirled to face Rose. "Miss Rose, ye mus' be keepin' Billy, Marit, an' Will from th' house." Her tone conveyed fear.

Rose grasped her meaning. "Certainly. I-I will send Mr. Wheatley to tell them immediately."

Breona's fierce response startled Rose. "Nay! He canna go t' them!" Her brows drew together sharply. "If 'tis bein' catchin' . . ." She left her sentence unfinished.

Rose shivered. Flinty likely had only a bad cold, but if it *were* something more, Mr. Wheatley was already exposed—as were she and Breona.

Breona was right. They must ban Billy, Marit, and little Will from the house as a precaution. Breona led the way to the kitchen where she and Rose scrubbed their hands with hot water and strong soap.

By Friday, sniffing, sneezing, and coughing were heard throughout the house. Maria, who shared a room with Tabitha, coughed incessantly until her chest and throat were inflamed. Nancy and Flora, who shared a room, took to bed with fevers.

They sent word to Nancy's employer, the school teacher, saying she could not come to watch the children. The young woman shivered under the piled on blankets and fretted about the children she cared for and whether they would become ill.

Mr. Wheatley kept the fireplaces in the sick rooms alight until, as Breona had feared, he, too, came down with an aching fever and was confined to his bed as was Flinty.

"'Tis th' grippe," Breona muttered darkly as she filled hot water bottles. They called Doctor Murphy, who confirmed her diagnosis, calling it a harsh "seasonal influenza."

"Influenza is not commonly dangerous but can be concerning in the very young and the elderly," the doctor cautioned. "I don't like how Mr. Flynn is faring. We may need to move him to a hospital where he can receive around-the-clock care."

"No." Tabitha, who had listened to the exchange from a few feet away, shook her head firmly. "I will care for him. I want to do it," she insisted to Rose. "I *can* do it. Breona has more than enough on her plate. And *you* cannot do it! You must be careful also."

Rose frowned at Tabitha's tactless reference to her age . . . and then realized with a start that she would be turning 63 in a few short months. She then tried to suggest that it was, perhaps, *indelicate* for an unmarried woman to care for two men.

"It's not as though I'm a blushing virgin!" Tabitha rejoined tartly. Rose was the one to blush then and, finally, admit to Tabitha's logic. Reluctantly, she turned all care of the two old gents over to Tabitha.

Within a day Tabitha was running the sick rooms upstairs as well as down. Rose wondered how Tabitha might treat Nancy, given their history of quarreling, but Tabitha surprised them all. She consulted with the doctor on the patients' needs, drew up a schedule, and invested herself completely in the care of "her" patients.

Rose remarked to Breona that it was the most content they had seen Tabitha. Breona lifted her eyebrows but nodded in silent agreement.

Joy and Grant were in a quandary regarding the store. They quickly recognized that if any of the store's staff gave Billy the flu while he was at work, their quarantine at home would be in vain. They ordered him to remain at home with Marit and Will. He would have to content himself with running errands for Palmer House and adding to the renovations within their cottage.

———

O'Dell listened as the sister recited a long list of injuries to him: severe concussion, perforated ear drum, broken jaw, two lost teeth, broken nose, broken collarbone, dislocated shoulder, *recent gunshot wound to the same shoulder*—the nun frowned at him, the two lines between her eyes deepening, before concluding—three broken ribs, bruised kidneys, cracked hip and pelvis, fractured right hand.

O'Dell felt broken indeed. The pain was excruciating, his mind a tangle of confusion and uncertainty. He stared at the hospital walls. Knew he'd never been as helpless as he was now and had been for more days and sleepless nights than he could count.

Gradually he began to recognize the man who came every-other day to check on him. After a week he could even remember his name: *Something long and impossible-to pronounce followed by "Liáng."* A Chinaman. That puzzled him.

So did the fact that the nursing sisters addressed their patient as *Mr. Jones.* O'Dell was too exhausted to correct them, and each time the Chinaman visited, he repeated that he would be safer if no one knew his real name.

Slowly, he was able to retain other things Liáng told him: He was a minister. He knew O'Dell's friends in Denver. The police had brought him, O'Dell, to this hospital in Seattle because he had been beaten. He had nearly died.

He had nearly died . . .

During the long, pain-racked hours of the night he turned that over in his mind, looking at it, feeling the legitimacy of its claim in his battered body.

What if he *had* died? What then?

The ward he lay in had twelve beds, eleven other men in various stages of illness or recovery. The nights were often filled with groans of pain and sometimes, hardest to bear, the muffled weeping of grown men.

He listened as families came and went during visiting hours. Overheard wives murmuring to their husbands and children struggling to be on their best behavior. No one other than Liáng came to see him, of course.

In the night he was assaulted by anxieties and, surprisingly, regret. He regretted that he had placed his work above all else. He regretted that he had no wife, no home, no family.

On the little table by his bed sat a lone pot of hothouse geraniums, their spicy scent comforting him. *Our dear Mr. Jones, We are praying for you daily! Come home to us soon. Rose Thoresen,* the card read.

Rose. Grant. Joy. Breona. Billy. Marit. Baby Will. Mei-Xing. Mr. Wheatley. Flinty. The closest thing to family he had in this world.

He regretted that he wouldn't be able to "come home" to them. They were part of God's family. He was not. He understood that. Arnie Thoresen had explained it that last evening before the lodge burned.

God's family. He had paid scant attention to the daily Bible studies Rose and Joy led during his stay at Corinth Mountain Lodge.

Even so, *somehow*, whole passages and intact discussions seemed to have stuck somewhere inside him.

Of their own volition they replayed in his head during the long, wakeful nights. He heard them so often he likely could have preached them himself.

Some phrases even seemed to play along with the rhythmic throb of his aching, mending bones:

Throb. Throb-a. Throb. *Then. Jesus. Said.*
Throb. Throb-a. Throb. *Come. Unto. Me.*
Come unto me.
Come unto me.

———

Before many more days passed, Sarah, Corrine, and Joy had also come down with high fevers, coughs, and congestion. Grant manned the store alone as best he could until, midweek, he felt the aching of a fever rack him.

With head pounding and hands pulsing in pain, he scribbled a note that read, "Closed due to illness" and pasted it in the front window. Then he locked up, walked up the street, and stood in the biting wind, hunched over and shivering with ague, until the trolley came.

By the end of the week, only Tabitha, Breona, and Gretl remained untouched by the flu. Tabitha, tireless and determined, ordered the care of those confined to bed with the precision of a general commanding an army.

Gretl spent her days brewing mugs of tea and honey, simmering nourishing broths, and concocting soft puddings, all designed to sooth aching chests and raw throats. Billy and Marit did the marketing and ran errands, leaving supplies on the back porch.

Tabitha and Breona ran upstairs and down placing poultices on congested chests, supplying steaming basins to which a tincture of camphor had been added, administering aspirins and drops of vitamins, bathing fevered bodies, and changing and washing linens and bed clothes.

Even Breona conformed to Tabitha's schedule and dictates. She was too exhausted to do otherwise. Besides, she had witnessed Tabitha roundly scolding *Miss Rose* and sending her to bed! Breona would never admit it, but she was a *tiny* bit afraid of this new, self-assured Tabitha.

———

The sisters finally allowed O'Dell to be discharged into Liáng's care, but not before Liáng had carefully thought through the situation. He was determined to keep O'Dell's identity secret.

In the Chinese community, secrecy was often difficult. Businesses and empires were owned and operated by the family. Good marriages and family connections meant opportunities, favors, and advancement, and so family loyalty was stressed from birth.

The Chen family, wealthy, powerful, and controlling many businesses, had listening ears everywhere. One never knew if neighbor, acquaintance, friend, parishioner, or household help had loyalties to such a family. Liáng trusted only a handful of close Christian friends upon whose discretion he could completely rely.

When Liáng visited O'Dell, he mentioned to his housekeeper that he was visiting an old mate from school who was ill. Liáng had gone to Bible school in Los Angeles. If prying ears were listening, they only heard mundane details of his acquaintance's condition and eventual discharge. Nothing of note or value.

Liáng had made several discreet telephone calls to the Chicago Pinkerton office and spoken to a man named Parsons who claimed to be O'Dell's boss. "Whatever costs are involved, I will stand for," Parson's tinny voice shouted down the line. He wired monies to Liáng and sent his address, demanding, "I want weekly reports on his condition."

While Liáng continued with his regular pastoral duties, his trusted friends located and rented a small bungalow far into the outskirts of the city. The sisters engaged a full-time nurse for him and arranged O'Dell's transportation. Now all was ready.

Liáng waited for O'Dell to be settled at the secret house before he left his church office. He drove the well-worn motor car his congregation gave him the use of for paying calls. When he arrived, the nurse let him in.

O'Dell was sitting up in a chair, freshly shaved, but obviously fatigued from the efforts of the day. His broken hand was slung close to his body. A cane rested against the chair.

"My friend," Liáng greeted him with real pleasure. "I cannot tell you how happy I am to see you out of the hospital and out of bed."

O'Dell grinned. And then grimaced. "Soon as my fine nurse puts a cigar in my hand, it will be a perfect day."

His nurse, a no-nonsense woman perhaps in her mid-thirties, grinned back and then caught herself and frowned. "We have a great deal of work ahead of us, Mr. Jones—walking, strengthening your muscles, rebuilding your stamina. Smoking will inhibit your bones knitting properly and delay your rehabilitation."

Liáng and O'Dell exchanged a look. Even the nurse would not know O'Dell's real name.

"Miss Greenbow, if you don't mind, I'd like to speak privately with my, ah, minister," O'Dell replied, still trying out a cocky grin on her.

She turned away smiling in spite of herself. "Shall I make you both some lunch?"

She left the room and O'Dell looked at Liáng. "We have a lot to talk about." His jaw still hurt abominably if he opened his mouth too wide, so he had gotten into the habit of talking through his teeth. "You didn't happen to bring some cigars with you, did you?"

Liáng shook his head but affably added, "If you'd said, 'say, d'ya play checkers?' I could help you out, Mr. er, *Jones*."

"Ha! You have met our Mr. Flynn."

Liáng settled himself in the other chair in the small living room. "Yes. When I got off the train in Corinth to look for Mei-Xing Li."

At O'Dell's shocked expression, Liáng added, "I believe I arrived in Corinth about the same time you arrived in Seattle. We have been, shall I say, working at cross purposes?"

He studied the Pinkerton agent. A lesser man might have died from the beating he'd sustained. Or perhaps it was truly only God's grace that he was still alive.

He saw the questions in O'Dell's eyes begin to bubble over. "Why don't I talk for a while and you stop me when you have questions."

O'Dell studied him a minute and then nodded.

"I told this same story to your friends at Palmer House," Liáng said, gazing out the window. "It is a story of two families . . ."

———

Gradually fevers dissipated, appetites returned, and wan faces appeared at Palmer House's breakfast table one by one. Coughs lingered, and Tabitha was firm that Billy, Marit, and Will were not to be admitted to the big house until all coughs and fevers were gone—after which every square inch of the house would be thoroughly scrubbed and disinfected.

"Young lady, you have done as well as any trained nurse could have done! I give you great credit for that," Doctor Murphy praised when he came to check on the progress of the patients. "With nurses in short supply at present, you have been a god-send to your friends."

Tabitha flushed under his praise.

"And you may well have saved Mr. Flynn's life," he confided. "He is no longer robust, and such an illness is often a death knell."

Life at Palmer House began to resume its usual rhythm and order. Although Tabitha never succumbed to the influenza, she had worn herself thin. For the first night in many, she did not feel the need to make the rounds of sick rooms. She slept soundly and was amazed and embarrassed to find the day half gone when she finally woke.

"How could you let me sleep so long!" she hissed at Breona in the kitchen.

"Aye, an' 'tis servin' ye well, Miss Tabitha," Breona grinned. The two women stared at each other a few silent moments, understanding and new respect flowing between them.

After a flurry of cleaning, the outcasts were again allowed in the big house. Billy, Marit, and Will joined Joy and Grant and the inhabitants of the big house at the breakfast table. Two long weeks had passed. Rose opened her Bible and smiled around the table with love and appreciation. Fourteen pairs of eyes smiled back.

"The great blessing of family is never so dear or more appreciated as it is after such a trial," she said quietly. Heads nodded, and more than a few voices whispered "amen."

They had weathered the storm together and come out on the other side unified. Finally, the dream of Palmer House was becoming a reality.

CHAPTER 34

(Journal Entry, February 26, 1910)

Our dear Flinty is still weak, but he is in such good spirits and cheers the entire house. He is spending much of his recovery in the comfort of his favorite old chair in the great room.

How the girls of the house pamper and fuss over him! They are always fetching blankets and books and tea, keeping the fire built up, and generally spoiling the old gent.

He nods off frequently, but between naps he can be found grinning and thanking his gentle nurses with a hearty, "The Lor' bless ya, miss!" and "Yessir! Yer jes' what th' doctor ordered!" How precious is the sound of laughter and tall tales heard so often these days!

I must say, dear Lord, that Tabitha is a changed woman. She, too, spends many hours perched on Flinty's ottoman, listening raptly to his stories. I cannot explain it, Lord, but she has softened and, in a deep way, has fully opened her heart to our convalescing gent.

Indeed, through this fortnight of illness and hardship Tabitha has bloomed. She has even forged other relationships that, I confess, are quite amazing. The most notable is a friendship with Breona.

I see these two very different women smiling and agreeing with each other and then I know, Father, you have done great things!

———

Mei-Xing sat at the little table with her New Testament. She had retired to her room alone to 'take a rest.' Rather than lie down, she pulled the little book from her purse and stared at it.

She had not opened it for days, perhaps weeks. Instead, she and Su-Chong had lived in a make-believe world where only the two of them existed.

But they could not stay here in this fantasy forever. Su-Chong was again healthy and whole. The forced inactivity was not to his liking. And he could not steal their food and supplies forever.

She sensed his unrest and noted the dark mood when it settled on him. In those moments she heard a still, small voice calling to her.

How was she to respond to that voice after what she had done? She laid her head atop the little book and wept in shame and sorrow.

———

"How are you today, my friend?" Minister Liáng greeted O'Dell.

O'Dell was bundled against the misting rain, walking steadily about the enclosed garden behind the bungalow. His splinted right hand hung in a sling about his neck; his gloved left hand gripped his cane with determination.

"Fighting boredom on two fronts," O'Dell replied tersely. "Miss Greenbow insists on a strict regimen of exercise and fresh air. *Tiresome*. The remainder of my time is spent sitting, reading, and thinking. *Maddening*! I need to be *out there*, investigating Mei-Xing and Su-Chong's families so that we can find Mei-Xing."

Unvoiced but written across the lines on his face was fear. Fear that Mei-Xing was already beyond his help.

Liáng nodded. "I understand. Perhaps I can provide more information today. I have held back some things, not wishing to add to your frustration, knowing that you were unable to act on anything. And today I bring a bit more news."

O'Dell jerked his head toward the house. "Let's go in."

"I have told you about Wei Chen's nephew, Bao, and his role in sending Mei-Xing to Denver," Liáng said as he shook the rain off his coat and took his seat.

O'Dell's eyes narrowed. He had never seen this man Bao, but he despised him nonetheless.

Liáng looked cautiously at O'Dell. "What I haven't told you is that much of my information comes directly *from* Bao."

If possible, O'Dell's eyes grew harder.

"You see, I meet with Bao every week."

"Why?" O'Dell's voice grated on the single word.

Liáng studied the man opposite him for several minutes. "Do you believe in forgiveness, Mr. O'Dell?"

"Not for men like him."

"I see." Liáng nodded thoughtfully. "Do you believe in regret?"

O'Dell opened his mouth and then closed it and said nothing.

"Have you never regretted something you have done? Tried to undo it?"

"Some things cannot be fixed," O'Dell snapped.

"I agree. That is why," he said softly, "all of us need a savior."

At O'Dell's snort of derision, Liáng changed the subject. "But that topic is, perhaps, for another day. Today I wish to tell you news that Bao gave me this morning."

"You *trust* him?"

"I find that I do. As you know, Fang Hua Chen sent Bao to Denver to arrange for Morgan and Su-Chong's escape and to bring Su-Chong back to his mother. Fang Hua made it clear to Bao that he must not fail. Nevertheless, Su-Chong escaped from Bao's men. Bao was prudent to fear for his life and that of his wife and the child she carried."

"Too bad."

"It *is* too bad," Liáng replied, his voice dropping, "but both his wife and his child died in childbirth in December." He looked steadily at O'Dell who finally had to look away.

"Bao believed their deaths were just punishment for the evil he helped perpetrate on Mei-Xing. He felt that to make complete atonement for his shame, he should tell her parents what he—what he and Fang Hua Chen—had done. After he did that, he intended to kill himself. More justice, you see."

O'Dell said nothing but watched and listened, a frown on his brow.

"The servants saw him standing across the street from the Li's home. I was visiting Mr. and Mrs. Li. I should mention that they are members of my church."

He let that sink in for a moment. "I went out to speak to Bao and found he was crazed with grief and guilt. He told me everything that day."

Liáng glanced up at O'Dell. "Well, you must understand that I could not believe it! I thought he was mad!"

He shook his head, remembering. "But the more he talked, the stronger was the ring of truth upon his words. He wished me to tell Mr. and Mrs. Li, but I convinced him that to confess all to Mei-Xing's parents would be cruel and unwise at this time. Instead, I would go to this place he spoke of, this Corinth in Colorado and, if God gave me favor, I would bring Mei-Xing home."

"Why would you not tell her parents?"

"Would you have me tell a father and mother that their daughter is alive when I have no proof? Worse, that she has been defiled and debased? I could not be so heartless a man."

Liáng raised his eyebrows. "And you perhaps do not grasp the dynamics of the situation. These are two powerful families, Mr. O'Dell, accustomed to meting out justice on their own terms. They have men who have sworn allegiance to them. One might call them armies, you understand."

He sighed deeply. "What do you suppose will happen the day Jinhai Li confronts Wei Lin Chen with the truth of his daughter's disappearance? What if Mei-Xing herself were to return from the dead and testify to what was done to her?"

O'Dell shook his head slowly and then quietly muttered, "War."

Liáng nodded in agreement. "Yes. And there is more. Mr. and Mrs. Li were broken after they believed Mei-Xing died by her own hand. Broken and filled with guilt. In their pain and brokenness, they sought for peace of some kind. One of their household told them of Jesus and sent them to speak to me. They gave their lives to the Savior, Mr. O'Dell. They belong to him now."

O'Dell heard what Liáng was saying, but he couldn't get past the first sentence. *Broken. They were broken.* He pushed at the words but they would not go. They whispered in the back and corners of his mind even as O'Dell struggled to hear and grasp all Liáng said.

"What I mean to tell you today are two things, my friend. The first is that Jinhai Li would not go to war against the Chens. He is an honorable man but he is also a changed man. However, that does not mean that Wei Chen could allow such an accusation to stand. His 'honor' would not permit it. Do you follow me?"

O'Dell did. "It would be a bloodbath," he whispered.

"Very possibly."

O'Dell swept a hand across his eyes. "And the other thing?"

Liáng roused himself. "Yes, the other thing. I said before, *what if Mei-Xing were to testify to what was done to her*? Bao believes that Wei Chen does not know of his wife's actions. Fang Hua is a powerful and wealthy figure in her own right. Nevertheless, the family is all important. Her disgrace and dishonor would be Wei Chen's disgrace and dishonor. She would never permit this."

"Why does this Bao think Wei Chen is ignorant of his wife's actions?" O'Dell demanded.

"Because Fang Hua secretly—without Wei Chen's knowledge—sent men to Denver to seek out and destroy Mei-Xing."

At O'Dell's sharp intake of breath his ribs jangled with pain. He felt his heart crush; he could not breathe. "*They* took her." He choked on the words. "Fang Hua's men!"

Liáng shot O'Dell a shrewd look "Ah. Then why does Bao report that Fang Hua is furious beyond measure? He reports that, after weeks of searching for her, the men have returned from Denver empty-handed."

The vise on O'Dell's heart loosened. With difficulty he stood up and began pacing, breathing again. "So they did *not* take her."

"It would seem so."

"What about Morgan?"

Liáng shook his head emphatically. "Bao knows that Fang Hua allowed him to go his way."

"Who does that leave?"

"Only Su-Chong," Liáng replied.

$\mathcal{C}$HAPTER 35

(Journal Entry, March 10, 1910)

Emily's friend, Viola Lind, has taken our Gretl under her wing. She is determined to help Gretl prepare for and secure a position as cook for a good family. To that end, Gretl is to write out three full weeks of menus.

Of course, all of us in the house have ideas and we all wish to see our favorite dishes included. We have placed a chalk board in the kitchen. Everyone is free to write their suggestions on the board. Gretl will add the dishes of her choosing to her menus.

This has proven to be great fun! On any given day the most eclectic list of entrees, side dishes, garnishes, and desserts can be found on this little board. It is quite amazing, actually, to see the variety. Marit is helping Gretl by writing out the recipes to her Swedish specialties.

When Viola has approved the final menus, we will take them to a printer to be set in elegant type and have a number of copies printed. Viola will present the menus to her friends and acquaintances until a prospective employer asks to interview Gretl.

Lord, please bless Viola for helping this young woman to achieve her dream!

———

While the health of most everyone in the house continued to improve, a few setbacks did surprise them. Maria and Flora's coughs and sniffles returned for several days as did Flinty's. That same week Grant and Joy experienced a return of fever and kept to their bed two days.

And after all had recovered and the doctor again declared the house free of influenza, Breona unexpectedly spiked a high fever accompanied by sneezing and coughing. Tabitha sent her to her room and called Doctor Murphy's office once more.

She kept the fireplace in Breona's bedroom burning and attempted to nurse her, but found her patient quite uncooperative. The truth was that a sick Breona exhibited a foul temper to everyone.

"I don't believe I have known Breona to even complain of a cold in the year and a half I have known her," Joy remarked when Tabitha, in a huff, reported Breona's bad behavior to her and to Rose. "And I have never seen her abed during the day!"

"She is too stubborn to admit to being sick," Tabitha fumed. Only her threats that Breona could endanger little Will kept the grumpy but ill woman moored to her room.

Thankfully, Breona's illness was short-lived. After a few days she joined Flinty in the great room to convalesce. She spent one day idling in a chair near a warm fire before, shrugging off all cautions, she declared herself "fit as a fiddle" and resumed her duties.

———

Mei-Xing avoided sleeping or laying in her bed, the site of her many sins. She lay on the floor of her room, begging God for forgiveness. She confessed to ignoring the warnings of the Holy Spirit and choosing her own desires instead. But although she had repented of her sins, her heart still felt like lead in her breast.

As she withdrew from Su-Chong, he had changed toward her, too. It was as though, as the fever of their lovemaking had cooled, they had both stepped back to look at each other, and had not liked what they saw.

Lately when he had gone in the night to steal food he had also stolen alcohol. The next day he would drink steadily and descend into a dark and foul mood. Then he would watch her.

Mei-Xing kept as still and as quiet as she could during those days. Most nights she slept alone, but other nights . . . he came in the dark and forced himself on her. She endured the act as she had in Corinth, drawing in on herself, wandering far away in her mind.

Only it was different than in Corinth. There she had been taken and forced against her will; here she had allowed it to begin. She was as much at fault as he.

O God! Do you see me? I am filled with shame and grief. Please . . .

———

That morning Gretl and Flora delivered breakfast to the table and rang the small bell used to announce meals. When it was time to eat, Mr. Wheatley and Flinty had not yet arrived at table.

Rose looked up. Mr. Wheatley stood in the dining room doorway. Tears streamed down his face.

"Flinty," he sobbed, placing a gnarled hand on his head in anguish. Tabitha leapt to her feet, knocking over her chair . . .

They found Flinty lying on his side, curled under his blankets, a hand tucked under his pillow. His mouth curved in a slight, peaceful smile.

Tabitha knelt by the bed and touched his cold face, caressed his fading red hair. "Oh, my dear old friend! I thought we had saved you!" she cried, breaking down completely. She remained there, sobbing, until Rose and Breona gently pulled her away from Flinty's side.

"Heart failure," the doctor murmured after examining Flinty. "I believe his old heart just quit."

Tabitha was in agony. "But he was doing so well! I . . . I thought he had recovered from the flu!" She wept in Rose's arms but could not be consoled. "What did I do wrong? I thought he was going to be fine! I should have taken better care of him!"

"Now see here, Miss Tabitha!" Doctor Murphy spoke sharply. "Mr. Flynn did not die from the influenza or from anything lacking in his care. His heart was old and tired. I'm sure the flu weakened him, but his heart had simply run its course."

He cleared his throat. "Now, young lady, if you are going to be a nurse, you must understand that you will sometimes lose patients. You must prepare yourself ahead of time to be strong and professional. I expect you to mourn the loss of your friend, but I will also expect you to adopt the calm attitude of which I speak."

Tabitha lifted a wet face from Rose's shoulder.

The doctor fumbled in his pocket and retrieved a small pamphlet. "I brought this for you," he directed, handing the folded paper to her. "God has given you a calling. I believe you should prayerfully consider his direction."

Tabitha stared at the wording on the pamphlet: *Training School for Nurses, University Hospital, Boulder, Colorado.*

—

Friends arrived from Corinth to pay their respects to Flinty, including the Kalbørgs, Sheriff Wyndom, his nephew Luke, and Domingo Juarez. A large wreath arrived from Arnie and Anna Thoresen.

As for those who lived at Palmer House, they thanked God with many tears for the time Flinty had spent with them and laid him to rest with care. Grant delivered the eulogy; Pastor Carmichael spoke fitting words over Flinty's grave and prayed for them all.

At dinner following the service, Joy murmured, "We thought we were saving Flinty from loneliness in Corinth, but how lonely this table feels without him!"

Tabitha broke down and sobbed, "I can't forget how I objected to his coming, how selfish and hard-hearted I was! Oh, I shall miss him so . . . Please forgive me!"

Breona leaned over and pulled Tabitha to her shoulder. "Whist? Naught t' f'rgive, Miss Tabitha."

CHAPTER 36

(Journal Entry, March 30, 1910)

Peace has descended on Palmer House, Lord, but it is a somber
one. We are learning to live without another we love so dearly. Last
evening Grant read comforting words to us from 1 Thessalonians:

> But I would not have you to be ignorant, brethren,
> concerning them which are asleep,
> that ye sorrow not,
> even as others which have no hope.
> For if we believe that Jesus died and rose again,
> even so them also which sleep in Jesus
> will God bring with him.
> For this we say unto you by the word of the Lord,
> that we which are alive and remain
> unto the coming of the Lord
> shall not prevent them which are asleep.
> For the Lord himself
> shall descend from heaven with a shout,
> with the voice of the archangel,
> and with the trump of God:
> and the dead in Christ shall rise first:
> Then we which are alive and remain
> shall be caught up together
> with them in the clouds, to meet the Lord in the air:
> and so shall we ever be with the Lord.

Dear Maria did not quite understand that "them which are
asleep" refers to those who have died and left this life, but Grant
explained it so beautifully. He said, "When we die, our bodies fall
asleep, to rest and wait for the return of Jesus. When he awakens us,
our bodies will be restored, not to their fragile former state, but to
one that is incorruptible and eternal."

How you fed and strengthened us with the Bread of Life in that
moment, Lord! We have so much hope for eternity.

———

"I need your help," Bao whispered to Liáng.

They had been meeting secretly in small cafés and out-of-the way tea houses for weeks. They talked. Liáng read to Bao from his Bible. Bao asked questions about the Christian God, and Liáng did his best to answer them. Each time they parted, Liáng prayed for Bao.

Today the look of grief and shame Bao usually wore was overwritten by one of panic. "What has happened?" Liáng demanded.

Bao looked about the café nervously. "Madam Chen. She has asked me to come to her house today." He glanced at his watch. "In less than two hours."

"Do you know why?" Liáng became as concerned as Bao.

"You know that she is obsessed with finding and destroying Mei-Xing. A live Mei-Xing is Fang Hua's greatest threat. Two days ago she suggested that *I* should take men and go back to Denver to seek her out."

"What did you say to her?"

"I have never before answered her so, so . . . defiantly. I said, how can you ask me, a grieving father and widower, to leave my family's graves so soon? She was, I believe, astounded at my, my brash behavior, as was I." He shivered.

"What did she say then?"

"She just stared at me, but I could see her scheming, calculating mind at work. Finally, she dismissed me. I-I am not sure why."

Liáng studied Bao and saw what Fang Hua must have seen: A young man whose clothes hung upon his body; his lank, unwashed hair, and eyes sunken from lack of sleep.

"Why do you think she calls you back today?"

Bao stared absently at his tea. "You know my wife . . . Ling-Ling . . . was a maid in the Li home?"

Liáng nodded. Bao had confessed that Ling-Ling was part of his payment for helping Fang Hua debase Mei-Xing.

"She was so pretty." Bao's voice dropped away, and Liáng wondered briefly if his young friend was losing hold of his senses. He reached across the table and grasped Bao's wrist.

Bao looked down at Liáng's hand on his wrist and then into Liáng's face. "Hear me. Ling-Ling's father's older sister had a son. His widow works in the kitchen in the Chen home. She has been with the Chen family for more than twenty years.

"Her eldest daughter—a second cousin to Ling-Ling—is a servant in the house also. She, she overheard Fang Hua tell one of her men . . ."

He stared with anxious eyes into Liáng's face. "You must see that I am also a threat to Fang Hua. I was not as long as my wife and child bound me to her evil plans. But now . . . The girl told her mother who passed the message until it reached me."

Liáng nodded, prodding him to finish.

"Fang Hua now has reason to mistrust my loyalty. If I refuse to do her bidding today, they have been told to . . ." He tore his watch from his pocket and looked again. "An hour and a quarter." He was trembling.

"I cannot go to Fang Hua. I cannot, I *will not* do this vile thing she wishes of me. I cannot even pretend I will. Minister Liáng, if you can help me, I no longer wish to die . . . not before, not before I make this right—" He covered his mouth and could speak no further.

Liáng gripped his wrist tighter. "I can hide you, Bao, for a time. Is that what you wish?"

Bao nodded, his hand still across his mouth, eyes skittering anxiously around the room.

———

"How many?" Su-Chong demanded one night, his brows furrowed.

"H-how many what?" she'd stuttered, fearful of his question. He had been drinking steadily all day. Mei-Xing knew what drink could do to an already unstable man.

"How many men have you given yourself to?" he repeated coldly. The disdain dripping from his curled lips chilled her.

She watched him, finding again in his eyes and manner all the reasons she had broken their engagement: His indulgent upbringing; the explosive, unpredictable anger; his mother's ruthlessness. *The incipient madness.*

I have so deceived myself, she mourned.

"I have only ever *given* myself to one man. *You,* Su-Chong Chen," she whispered. "Against my will, however, I was taken by many men. You know this already. I have told you how this was done to me. You know who ordered it."

He had studied her, his eyes hardening toward her. "I have defiled myself with you."

His hatred solidified. "My mother was right. You cannot be trusted," he added categorically.

From that moment on, he had again locked her in the little room.

———

As Liáng pointed his motor car toward the bungalow where O'Dell was recuperating, he shook his head and fervently prayed. He did not look forward to what he must do today.

He arrived and, after greeting O'Dell and Miss Greenbow, asked to speak with the nurse privately. They adjourned to the tiny kitchen.

"My dear lady," he began tentatively. "I have some unfortunate news."

"What is it?" she asked, surprised.

"I am afraid that your service to us is at an end. I must let you go." Liáng disliked himself intensely at that moment.

"What! Who will care for Mr. Jones? Certainly he is mending, but he still requires some nursing care. Have I done anything wrong—"

Liáng held up his hand, interrupting her. "Miss Greenbow, your care has been exceptional. I will write you a fine recommendation. But our, ah, circumstances have changed. I'm afraid I must let you go. Today. Now, in fact."

He removed an envelope from his pocket and handed it to her. "You will find that I have added an additional week's salary. I apologize for the abrupt end of your time with us. I should have liked to have given you proper notice."

She slowly took the envelope. "Well, if you are sure then . . . I . . . it will take me a few minutes to pack."

"May I help you gather your things?" Liáng had never felt quite such a heel. As they passed into the living room where O'Dell sat, Liáng laid his forefinger across his lips.

O'Dell looked from Liáng to a stunned Miss Greenbow and back. He pressed his lips together as she gathered her knitting and a book she had been reading and retired to her room. O'Dell and Liáng could hear her opening and closing drawers.

"What in blazes is going on?" O'Dell whispered, eyes narrowed.

"After she leaves, if you please," Liáng replied.

Twenty minutes later, Miss Greenbow donned her coat and hat. "I am leaving, Mr. Jones," she said weakly. "I do hope you will continue to do the exercises as I've shown you. I—" She twisted the strap of her handbag. "I wish you all the best."

O'Dell carefully got to his feet and offered her his hand. "Miss Greenbow, it is I who am indebted to you." A look, something of perhaps both surprise and disappointment, passed between them.

Liáng and O'Dell watched her carry her little suitcase to the end of the street and turn the corner. She would catch the trolley along there within the hour.

When she was gone, O'Dell rounded on Liáng. "Now tell me! What is going on?"

Liáng mutely shook his head and went out the back door. O'Dell heard him opening the gate to the yard. A minute later he had backed into the yard and closed the gate behind his little motor car. O'Dell heard the trunk of the auto close and the murmur of Liáng's voice.

The back door opened and Liáng entered followed by someone. They walked into the little sitting room, Liáng leading a young man with haunted eyes.

"Mr. O'Dell," Liáng said softly. "This is Bao Shin Xang."

———

Fang Hua listened with growing frustration and rage to her man's report. "He cannot have just vanished! Watch the trains. Keep eyes on his house at all times. Someone knows where he is."

If she was worried at Bao's disappearance, she did not allow it to show. "Bao has shown himself to be disloyal to his family. When he is found, you will make him disappear."

She continued to think. "I also wish someone to watch for him near my husband at all times. This is of great importance. You will not allow him access to Wei Lin Chen."

Pulling herself erect, she waved a hand in dismissal. "Go. Do as I have directed. Find him."

The young servant girl crept away from the closed door and continued about her duties.

CHAPTER 37

O'Dell glared at Bao Xang. "What is *he* doing here?"

Liáng answered simply, "He refuses to hunt down Mei-Xing as Fang Hua demands. Now she will hunt *him*. This was the only safe place I could think of."

Bao endured O'Dell's withering glare without resistance. O'Dell took in the young man's blank and spiritless manner, but he felt no pity.

"Is this why you dismissed Miss Greenbow?"

Liáng inclined his head.

O'Dell cursed under his breath. "I'll pack my bags."

"No, Mr. O'Dell, you should not do that," Liáng remonstrated.

"Look, Liáng, I appreciate all you have done for me, but I won't stay in the same house as this, this murderer." He hobbled toward his room.

"Do you wish to find Mei-Xing?" Liáng called after him.

O'Dell turned. "That," he snarled, "is a *stupid* question."

"Bao is your best chance of finding her," Liáng replied. "He knows Su-Chong, has known him all his life. To date I have only been able to give you second-hand information, but I am not a trained investigator. Perhaps *you* should interview him."

O'Dell slammed the door behind him and leaned against it shaking with anger. And exhaustion. He knew he was not yet fit to travel. Just twice around the enclosed yard set his hip to throbbing. The more he exerted himself, the harder he breathed. That was when pain would shoot through his lungs, ribs, and shoulder again. *Like right now.*

Then the pounding of his half-healed jaw overrode everything else, and O'Dell realized he was grinding his teeth together. He uttered a string of choice swear words.

Liáng showed Bao to the room just vacated by Miss Greenbow. Bao did not look around. He sat down on the bed and nodded without seeing.

Liáng sighed and retraced his steps to the back door. Stepping outside he breathed deeply and began to pray. *Lord, here I am, in water far over my head, and I don't know what to do now.*

He checked his pocket note book. Two appointments later this afternoon. He could not cancel them without good reason.

Stepping back inside the house he checked the food supply in the kitchen. Someone would need to shop for Bao. He would have to cook for himself. Liáng wondered if Bao knew anything of what went into preparing a meal. Or if he was in any state to care.

O Lord!

O'Dell unclenched his teeth and gently waggled his jaw to release the tension in it. His head pounded. His hip ached. He needed to sit down.

He sat gingerly on his bed and rubbed the muscles along his hip. Against the antipathy he held toward Bao, he was thinking about what Liáng had said. Could Bao hold the key to Mei-Xing's recovery?

He sat there for twenty minutes, thinking, before he heard his stomach grumbling. *Miss Greenbow had fed him well.* He snarled again as his stomach growled for its lunch.

———

Joy was staring from the window of one of the third floor towers when Rose found her. The street fronting Palmer House was not as busy as a downtown thoroughfare, but was bustling nonetheless. Carts laden with goods on their way to market slowly clanked by. The occasional motorcar passed the slower traffic with an audacious honk.

"Spring is on its way, but I miss the mountains," Joy confessed. Of all they had lost when the lodge in Corinth burned, the wonder of its views had been among the most difficult to bear.

"Is that all of what troubles you, Joy?" Rose inquired softly.

"No," Joy admitted, but did not immediately add to that single syllable. She continued to stare unseeing at the light traffic passing the house. Rose waited beside her.

"Is it Grant?"

Joy fidgeted uneasily. "We are so happy, Mama, even if so many of his memories are still lost," Joy began, "but . . ."

"But?"

Joy sighed. "I can't put my finger on it."

"Is he still the Grant you married?" Rose offered.

"Oh, yes. Yes, he is! Even though I have to remind him of so many things. Even though he has lost the use of his arm. When he looks at me, he is every bit the man I married. Godly. Caring. Happy. Strong. So gentle and sweet."

"What is it, Joy?" Rose probed. "What is bothering you?"

Joy faced her mother, anxiety on her face. "Since his bout with the influenza he is still not quite well, Mama. Instead of growing healthier and becoming clearer in his mind these last weeks—I don't know, but he is often away in his thoughts, a worried look on his face, and I have to bring him back. He seems . . . distracted, and I am concerned."

Rose drew a sharp breath. "Have you spoken to him of your concerns?"

"Yes, I *have* asked how he feels. He smiles and tells me he is fine," she stared out the window again, "so why do I feel he is withholding something from me?"

She sighed. "I have not wanted to, I don't know, nag him, I suppose, but I see changes, subtle changes. Yesterday we had to run to catch our trolley. We always laugh when we make it just in time but . . ." Joy fiddled with a button on her blouse.

"What, Joy?"

Joy sighed again. "Instead of laughing about it, he was out of breath."

She turned to Rose. "Mama, we ran less than half a block. I know it is indecorous to run in public, but it was the last trolley of the day, so we ran. And *he was out of breath!* He was not comfortable again for several blocks, Mama."

She looked steadily at Rose. "That is not like him, Mama. And he was so tired last night that he went to bed right after dinner."

"Perhaps it is time he saw a doctor," Rose suggested.

———

Liáng was about to knock on O'Dell's door and offer him a ride to the train station when the door opened and O'Dell hobbled out and collapsed in his chair.

"I'm hungry," he said in a grumpy tone.

Liáng nodded. "I am not much of a hand in the kitchen."

"Was it necessary to let Miss Greenbow go? Couldn't you make up a name for *him*?" O'Dell pointed haphazardly behind him in the direction of the other bedroom.

Liáng opened his mouth in surprise and then closed it. "You are staying then?"

O'Dell stared at Liáng. He had to will himself not to clench his teeth again. "I want to find Mei-Xing. If that . . . miserable excuse for a man has any information, I want it."

"I know you despise me," the voice came from behind them. Bao stood in the doorway of the bedroom. "I do not blame you—I despise myself."

He slowly walked into the sitting room. "Mr. O'Dell, please allow me to help you. I-I will do whatever you ask of me, but please allow me to help you find Mei-Xing."

O'Dell studied Bao again, looking him up and down. If ever he had seen a beaten man, Bao was one.

"Liáng, I want two things."

"Name them," Liáng responded. "I will get them."

"Well, first get Miss Greenbow back. She's likely still waiting around the corner for her trolley."

"Wha—" Liáng frowned. "We could not possibly hide what we are doing here from her," he answered slowly. "Fang Hua does not know *you* are alive, but she will be actively searching for Bao! Miss Greenbow could inadvertently give something away. Is it right to put her in danger?"

"Go get her. You don't know her; I do. I will tell her exactly what we are doing here. She will keep our secrets."

"What makes you think this?" Liáng demanded.

O'Dell's laugh was touched with irony. "Because she's one of *you*."

"Us? What do you mean?"

"*She's a Christian.* Been preaching at me for weeks. Now go get her before her trolley arrives."

Liáng finally agreed and leapt to his feet. "Oh. What is the second thing you require, Mr. O'Dell?"

O'Dell bared his teeth in wolfish delight. "A box of cigars, Liáng. And not cheap ones either."

Liáng slowly smiled back. "It goes against my better judgment, but you will have them."

As Liáng's motor car pulled away O'Dell stared at Bao who just stared back.

"Miss Greenbow will need her room back," O'Dell snarled. "You can sleep on the floor for all I care."

Bao nodded and cast down his eyes. "Whatever you wish, Mr. O'Dell."

O'Dell continued to watch Bao, formulating the questions he would put to the man.

As Liáng rounded the corner, he heard the clang of an approaching trolley. He spotted the nurse sitting on the bench, her eyes on the book opened in her lap. She heard the trolley's bell, too, and began to gather her things.

"Miss Greenbow!" Liáng swung his car around into the other lane so that he was facing the direction he'd come from. He leaned out the window. "Miss Greenbow. We have, ah, reconsidered. Would you please come with me back to the house?"

She glared suspiciously at Liáng whose usually neatly combed hair was blowing in the breeze.

"You said you no longer needed me." The trolley pulled up to the stop, blocking her from view.

He backed up and she moved a few steps his way. "I sincerely apologize. Mr. O'Dell has a, um, proposition to put to you."

The trolley bell clanged and she glanced to the driver who was impatiently waiting. She walked to the trolley door and a moment later the driver pulled away. Miss Greenbow was still standing next to the stop, looking at Liáng as though he had lost his mind.

Liáng swung around again, pulling up to the curb. He got out and walked around to open the door.

With one more quizzical look, Miss Greenbow slid into the seat. Liáng lifted her suitcase into the small rear seat and got behind the wheel.

While Bao and Liáng waited in the back yard, O'Dell had a long conversation with Miss Greenbow. When he had finished her eyes were wide.

"You are not joking, are you," she murmured. It was a statement, not a question.

"I assure you, I am not," O'Dell answered. Liáng had retrieved O'Dell's baggage from the hotel while he was in the hospital and had brought it to him when he was released. He handed the nurse his Pinkerton credentials. "My real name is O'Dell. Edmund O'Dell."

She held his credentials and read them thoroughly before handing them back. Her auburn hair, glinting with a few strands of grey, had been hastily shoved under her hat and just as hastily uncovered when she walked back into the house. O'Dell could see she was tired.

He cleared his throat. "I have been on this case for more than a year. Unfortunately, like the mythological Medusa, we remove one head only, seemingly, to find another."

She glanced nervously toward the back door. "You say there is a man with Mr. Liáng who will also be staying here? And he is the one who . . ." she swallowed.

"He is nothing to fear, Miss Greenbow," O'Dell assured her. "You have put up with me for all these weeks and, in comparison, you will find him to be quite tame. However, we—he and I—have a great deal of work to do, work that you cannot but help be privy to."

He gave her a half smile. "And so I must ask you, are you able to keep our secrets, knowing that very dangerous men are likely looking for us? I would never knowingly place you in harm's way, but we are trying desperately to save our young friend."

Miss Greenbow shook her head, still a bit overwhelmed. "I wondered how you had gotten yourself so badly beaten just by way of a mugging. I guess I understand now."

She finally agreed. "Yes. I will do it. But . . ."

"But?"

"But I will keep the extra week's pay Mr. Liáng gave me. I deserve it, the awful way you both treated me today."

"Of course." O'Dell saw then that they had wounded her. "I'm sorry," he said softly.

She swallowed and nodded. "I accept your apology."

O'Dell slowly stood up. "Good. Now, could you possibly rustle up some lunch?"

$\mathcal{C}$HAPTER 38

(Journal Entry, April 6, 1910)

Father, it has now been nearly twelve months since the lodge burned, nearly a year since you used the marshals and Pinkertons to free our girls from the houses in Corinth. Almost a year since Grant returned to us.

Our lives—and the lives of our girls—have changed forever, Lord, because of these events. Slowly, ever so slowly, we are gaining ground here in Denver. We thank you, Lord, for the progress we see.

Gretl has secured a position in Littleton! It is wonderful for her, but will be hard on us to lose her. Viola Lind assures us that the family Gretl goes to is well thought of. She will earn a good living, and we hope she will come home to us at Christmas.

Tabitha is making application to the nursing school in Boulder. Doctor Murphy has written a glowing letter of recommendation. Tabitha shines with hope, Lord. I am convinced she will make an exceptional nurse.

And Pastor Carmichael reports that women in our church—women, like our girls, who have found you, Lord—have been ministering on the streets of the red light district. We may soon welcome new refugees to Palmer House.

Lord, Joy remains insistent that we should open a sewing school. Is this what you desire? I ask this because we have found no one to lead us in this direction. It is beyond my skills, dear Lord. You know how rudimentary my sewing abilities are! I trust you, but you must provide if this is the direction you wish us to go.

———

She spent hours on the floor of her room crying out to God. If not for her little book, she surely would have gone mad. The door to Mei-Xing's room suddenly slammed opened.

A drunken Su-Chong stood in the doorway. "Why are you lying on the floor?" he demanded. Mei-Xing quickly got up. He had not visited her bed in a month. She picked at the dress that fit her so ill, grateful that it veiled her body's curves.

Su-Chong watched her with an intensity that terrified her. It seemed the only way he looked at her now. He stared at her as though trying to decide how to dispose of her. "What is that book you are hiding from me?"

"I-I am not hiding anything," she said weakly. *Lord! Please don't let him take your word from me!*

He ripped the book from her hand. "What is this nonsense? You are no *Christian*."

He smiled at her then, a poisonous smile so much like Fang Hua's that Mei-Xing nearly fainted. "Let me tell you something, Mei-Xing, something you must take to heart. You are a whore. I have enjoyed your body whenever I wished, because you are nothing *but* a whore. You tried to trick me, but I discerned the truth about you. You are a whore. You will always be a whore. You can never be anything but a whore!"

He tore the book in two down its spine and tossed it on the floor. Mei-Xing eyed the pieces hungrily and he spotted her desire.

"Oh, no. No, I won't leave you even this deceitful garbage for comfort. You deserve no mercy for your lies and perfidy." He picked up the two halves of the book and carried them with him through the door.

She remained frozen in place as he locked the door behind him. She could hear his words resounding in her ears. Hateful, hopeless words.

Words that were, somehow, strangely familiar. She strained to recall hearing those same words in another place and another time . . . spoken by someone who had loved her so deeply.

"Those voices! They sneer at you, *you are a whore. You will always be a whore. Once a whore, always a whore! You can never be anything* but *a whore!*"

Mama Rose! Mei-Xing sank into a heap on the floor, squeezing her eyes closed and shutting out everything but the sound of Rose's voice, speaking truth to her broken heart.

"Yes, we are all guilty of doing wrong things, bad things, even horrible things. Those may be the *facts* but, when covered by the blood of Jesus, they are no longer the *truth*.

"Choose instead to follow the voice of Jesus, *the voice of truth.* He calls to us, *Come to me all you who are weary . . . weary, worn, and heavy-burdened. Come to me, and I will give you rest for your souls.*"

Oh, Jesus, yes!

Yes.

———

For a long week, O'Dell pressed Bao, and he was merciless. No detail Bao spoke was insignificant. O'Dell made Bao tell all he knew of Su-Chong and rehearse every conversation he'd had with Fang Hua. He took copious notes and then had Bao repeat it all again.

For a while Miss Greenbow stayed in the tiny kitchen trying not to listen or at least pretending not to. After a day or so she sat in the living room watching and listening to the interplay between the two men, one harsh and pressing, the other broken and compliant.

As the days passed and no helpful information emerged, O'Dell became more frustrated. He began to berate Bao.

As this continued, Miss Greenbow chewed her bottom lip, unhappy with O'Dell's contempt, concerned about Bao's lifeless responses. At last she could keep quiet no more.

"Mr. O'Dell?"

With an impatient gesture, O'Dell turned.

"You are a bully, Mr. O'Dell. You are bullying him. I-I do not like to see it."

He glared at her. "This is not your concern, Miss Greenbow."

Miss Greenbow pressed her lips together. "You will catch more flies with sugar than with vinegar, Mr. O'Dell."

"Again, this is not your concern, Miss Greenbow, O'Dell snapped. "Kindly keep out."

Her eyes flashed. "You are so intent on *punishing* him, you would miss the information you seek even if it hit you square on the head."

She jumped to her feet. "And it is not *your* job to punish him." With that, Miss Greenbow flounced into the kitchen.

O'Dell listened as she banged cupboard doors and pots and pans. His mouth gaped. Demure Miss Greenbow was throwing a tantrum!

Then he caught himself. *Is that what I am doing? Throwing a tantrum?* Her words convicted him. *And is that what I'm I trying to do? Punish Bao?*

He looked at Bao and, for the first time in days, really saw the man. If possible, he had lost more weight. Although Bao was supposed to sleep on the sofa at night, O'Dell knew he spent much of the long nights in the back yard staring into the dark skies. His eyes appeared hollow, burned out.

At that moment Bao glanced up and O'Dell caught a glimpse into his hopeless soul. He flushed and stood up, irritated. *This wasn't about Bao; it was about justice for Mei-Xing!*

But he didn't like the feeling that lurked just below the surface, the sense that he'd lost Miss Greenbow's good opinion. *A bully? She'd called him a bully!* He stomped through the kitchen, ignoring her, and out the back door. He needed to clear his head.

O'Dell lost track of how long he'd stayed outside. The weather was cool, but spring was on the air. He could smell the perfume of lilacs from some yard nearby. Scotch broom cascaded over the back fence in a wild, yellow blanket. Tulips, nearly spent, wagged in a gentle breeze.

I've lost my objectivity, he grudgingly admitted. For a long while he watched rain falling in the distance, the mist of the downpour tugging and pulling the clouds toward the ground.

He let himself back into the house. Bao and Miss Greenbow were seated at the little kitchen table. She had fixed him lunch and was coaxing him to eat it. What she said next stunned O'Dell.

"Now, when this Mr. Morgan was talking to Madam Chen, I think I remember you saying that she called him some sort of nick name. What was it she called him again?"

Bao chewed on a bite of sandwich and thought hard. "I think she called him . . . *Reggie?*"

"Yes, that's what it was! What do you suppose that means?"

O'Dell inched closer. Bao, with his back to O'Dell, did not notice him, but Miss Greenbow, facing him, gave him a tiny, solemn shake of her head. O'Dell stopped where he was, afraid to breathe.

"I-I think I've heard it before," Bao said, unsure of himself. "Because Morgan used to live in Seattle, you know. Grew up here."

Miss Greenbow was tempted to pursue that line of information but resisted. "Reggie. Do you think it is short for something else? Reginald, perhaps?"

Bao rested his forehead on the heel of his hand. "Not Reginald."

Miss Greenbow glanced at O'Dell and then back to Bao. "No? Not Reginald?"

He stopped chewing. "Regis. They called him Reggie, short for Regis."

She licked her lips. "Regis. Not a very common name, is it? Has a nice ring, though. Um, Regis . . . what? Do you recall a last name?"

Bao ignored her. "They called him Reggie. I remember my father and uncle laughing about it. Not because it was so terribly funny, but because . . . because *he hated* it. I don't know why, but it made him very angry, and his anger amused Wei Lin Chen."

Miss Greenbow looked to O'Dell for help.

O'Dell asked, as quietly as he could, "Regis. Can you remember his last name?"

Bao started and turned fearfully toward O'Dell. He lowered his eyes and shook his head.

He's clammed up. Great job, O'Dell!

"That sandwich looks great, Miss Greenbow. Ah, any chance I could get one?"

She left her chair and began to pull out the sandwich makings. He slid into the chair opposite Bao and tried to figure out how to begin again with him.

"Bao, you haven't told us much about your family, your parents, brothers, sisters." O'Dell made sure his voice was light, conversational. He waited, not giving in to the urge to badger him as he'd done previously.

When Bao still remained silent, O'Dell asked quietly, "You mentioned that your father knew Reggie. Is he still around?"

Bao shook his head. "No."

"Do you have any relatives who would recall Reggie?"

Bao thought. "I . . . yes; but only on Uncle Wei Lin's side."

O'Dell frowned. "If only we could only talk to someone who would remember. You see," he leaned confidentially toward Bao, "we have searched property records in Denver under every alias of Morgan's that we know, which is the problem. We don't think we know them all.

"If Su-Chong is still hiding in Denver, it must be in a place that was prepared ahead of time—stocked with food and other necessities. What is called a bolt-hole.

"In Omaha, Morgan went by the name of Franklin. Franklin owned dozens of properties. One of them was prepared as I've described—but was owned under the name of *Dean Morgan*. I guess I'm wondering . . ."

He didn't finish his sentence and, after a few moments, Bao dared look at him. "What are you wondering, Mr. O'Dell?"

O'Dell saw Bao, this time not as a piece of filth to be wiped off his feet, but as a man. "I am wondering if Morgan has a bolt-hole in Denver under a name we don't yet know. If he does, I'm betting Su-Chong knows of it and is hiding there. And if he *is* hiding there, perhaps he has Mei-Xing with him. I guess that makes Regis' last name pretty important."

The kitchen was utterly quiet except for the ticking of the clock on the wall. Still O'Dell waited.

Tentatively Bao whispered, "My wife's name was Ling-Ling."

O'Dell was confused but nodded, pushing down his irritation. "I understand she passed away recently."

Miss Greenbow stared at him. He could feel her eyes boring into him, challenging him, willing him, to not *bully* an already mortally wounded human being.

"I'm sorry for your loss," O'Dell added.

Bao's eyes became moist. "Yes. She and a baby son."

O'Dell would not look at Miss Greenbow. "I am truly sorry, Bao."

Bao shuddered. "The cook in the Chen home is related to Ling-Ling. Her daughter is also a servant in the house. They were the ones who warned me of Fang Hua."

"You think they would remember Reggie?"

He shrugged. "One of them may."

O'Dell looked at Miss Greenbow then. "We need Liáng."

"What do you want me to do?"

"Will you walk to the grocer's and use his telephone? If you have to leave a message, just say that Mr. Jones has taken a turn and hopes Minister Liáng will visit soon."

She was already pulling on her gloves and hat. "I'll be back shortly."

CHAPTER 39

Rose rubbed her eyes and refocused her thoughts. The new year was almost a third gone, the house still had so many needs, and managing it required her attention to so many details!

Joy and Grant still felt that it was the right time to push ahead to found a sewing school. Rose knew they felt it time for all of them to shake off the listlessness that Mei-Xing's disappearance and Flinty's passing had engendered.

But a sewing school and business? It had taken years of plodding under the patient tutelage of her friend Vera Medford back in RiverBend for Rose to become even a modest seamstress!

For a moment she questioned her expanding role in their endeavors. Her heart was in ministering to the young women in the house—teaching them how to remake their lives and find peace with God. She had not bargained on all these other, more practical details.

Joy was far better at these things than she was. But Grant and Joy were fully immersed in running the store. Rose groaned inwardly. She needed a cup of tea. And her Bible.

She took her cup and saucer and returned to her desk and the many details demanding her attention. While the tea was steeping, she thumbed through her Bible and began to read Psalm 37. She stopped at verses 4 and 5 and smiled. Oh, yes!

Delight thyself also in the LORD:
and he shall give thee the desires of thine heart.
Commit thy way unto the LORD;
trust also in him; and he shall bring it to pass.

She fed on those words and prayed over the many needs of the house. She was sipping her tea and gathering her energy when the front doorbell sounded.

The doorbell rang again, and Rose sighed. Breona, Marit, Mr. Wheatley, and the girls were likely at the market. Grant and Joy were due home from the shop in a while.

She pushed herself to her feet wondering again how they could begin a sewing school let alone a sewing business. And yet the rest of the girls—and those who would be coming after them—must have employment. They could not sit idle. They needed to be working toward their future independence.

"Lord," she whispered as she trod toward the door, "Let every plan of ours begin and end with you. If a sewing business is not your plan, we will look elsewhere for your hand. If it is not your timing, we will wait on you until it is."

She glanced through the peephole. Rose saw a fashionably dressed woman facing away from the door, looking with interest at the yard and the porch that wrapped itself around the front of the house. A mass of tight, glossy-black curls peeked out from under a wide, beautiful hat.

What a gorgeous hat! Rose thought. Everything about this woman bespoke elegance and the finest style.

Rose glanced down at her dress and then touched her hair self-consciously. Her dress was simple and of good quality, but downright primitive compared to the visitor on the porch!

The bell rang again and Rose pulled herself together, quickly unlocking and swinging wide the door. The woman, now facing her, smiled pleasantly. Her glowing skin was the color of warm, creamed coffee.

"Is this the residence of Miss Thoresen? Miss Joy Thoresen?"

"Yes it is, but she is away at present. I am her mother, Mrs. Thoresen. May I be of help?"

The woman smiled again. "Mrs. Van der Pol speaks very highly of you, Mrs. Thoresen. But I apologize. May I introduce myself?"

She offered Rose her card. The stiff ivory paper had a gold border around the engraved words *Miss Victoria Washington*.

"How may I be of service to you, Miss Washington?" Rose asked, her curiosity aroused.

"I have only arrived in Denver, just last evening," the young woman replied, "and I am staying with Mrs. Van der Pol for the present. However, I came back to Denver to offer my services."

Before Rose could respond, she heard the front gate open and the sounds of Grant and Joy's voices coming up the walk. The woman also heard and turned eagerly toward them.

Joy stopped when she saw their visitor. Something was so familiar about her . . .

"Tory?"

"Yes, miss!"

"Oh, my goodness!" Joy rushed to embrace her. "Oh, my dear, but I am so happy to see you!" She pulled back and gazed in Tory's face. "You look so well, so *lovely*!"

Tory blushed, her cheeks reddening prettily under Joy's praise. "I am equally happy to see you, miss."

"Forgive me," Joy said, "I would like you to meet my husband, Grant Michaels."

Grant offered Tory his left hand and she graciously took it, confused both by the arm hanging lifelessly by his side and by the introduction.

"But . . . I mean, I thought—" she pulled herself up short and managed, "A pleasure to meet you," while trying hard to mask her puzzlement.

"Yes, I see we have confounded you," Joy laughed. "My husband died nearly three years ago—and yet here he stands. Perhaps we can go inside and explain. But first, have you met my mother?"

Joy turned to Rose. "Mama, this is Tory. She is one of the first girls we helped to escape from Corinth!"

"Tory! Mei-Xing spoke often of you," Rose responded warmly.

"There is no word of Mei-Xing?" Tory's eyes saddened. "Mrs. Van der Pol sent the news to me months ago and I have prayed . . ." She stopped and cleared her throat.

Rose took her by the arm and led her inside. "No, nothing to date, but we still hope. We have placed our trust in the Lord."

They moved into the parlor and seated themselves. Tory gracefully arranged her skirts and crossed her ankles demurely. Joy sat close beside her.

For more than an hour, Joy, Rose, and Grant explained all that had happened in the fifteen months since that bitterly cold January when Tory and her friend Helen had arrived at the lodge in the dark hours of the night. Tory listened intently, her brow creasing in fear and sorrow as they told of Banner and his men burning the lodge and taking Joy prisoner.

Her worry turned to triumph as they described the U.S. marshals and Pinkerton agents descending on Corinth and arresting Morgan, Banner, and his gang of thugs, finally breaking their hold on the girls in Corinth's two infamous houses.

"I would have loved to have seen it all," she whispered, breathing hard. "I would have loved to have seen Banner and Darrow and Roxanne taken away in handcuffs." She dashed away a few tears. "I would have given anything for Helen to have seen it."

Joy touched Tory's hand gently. "I'm so sorry about Helen, Tory."

Tory nodded. "Thank you. Thank you for everything you did for us, Miss Joy. *For everything.* Mrs. Van der Pol sent us to the Misses Wright—Miss Eloise and Miss Eugenia Wright—in Philadelphia, and they have been so good, so kind to us. They, they cared for Helen until the end. She had the finest doctors, but they all said . . . they said they could do nothing for her."

She was quiet for a moment, lost in her thoughts. "Miss Eugenia spent the most time with Helen. She sang to her. Sang for hours." Now tears trickled down Tory's face. "She sang the most beautiful hymns to her. Then she would describe heaven to Helen, how beautiful it would be, and how much Jesus loved her and how he would be waiting for her." Tory choked and had to stop speaking.

"It's all right, Tory," Joy soothed her.

"I want to tell you, Miss Joy." She looked from Rose to Grant and back to Joy. "I want to tell you what happened."

Grant handed Tory a clean handkerchief and she dabbed her eyes. "Thank you. I want you all to know." She took a deep breath, composing herself. "Helen was so weak and in so much pain, but she asked Miss Eugenia how Jesus could possibly be waiting for her, after, after all the awful things she had done."

Here Tory bowed her head and spoke as though remembering each word of the conversation. "Miss Eugenia told her, 'Child, Jesus has been waiting for you all your life. If you will go to him right now and ask his forgiveness, he will certainly receive you.' Well, Helen prayed right then—and oh! I saw it! I saw it, Miss Joy! I saw the forgiveness wash over her and the grief leave her poor, thin face! She became young and lovely again, even though the disease had wasted her so. It was the most wondrous thing I ever saw."

Tory wiped a stray tear with Grant's handkerchief. "Helen died three days later, yet in those three days she was so happy, so peaceful. When Miss Eugenia would sing to her, Helen would smile and she was beautiful."

Grant cleared his throat, clearly moved, but Joy and Rose were weeping unabashedly.

"Thank you, dear Lord," Rose murmured. Joy nodded in agreement, unable to speak for the awe of that moment.

"I gave my heart to Jesus when Helen passed," Tory added, sniffling through her tears. "And I am determined to serve him however he leads me. The Misses Wright apprenticed me to Monsieur LeBlanc, and I have been working for him for more than a year."

Joy looked up sharply. "M. LeBlanc is well known, even in Europe, for his designs."

"Yes, miss. I began in the workroom, but when I showed him some of my sketches, he assigned two seamstresses to me to make two of my designs." She ducked her head modestly. "The dresses were well received, and M. LeBlanc moved me permanently to my own design table with my own seamstresses."

Joy and Grant murmured their compliments and congratulations, but Rose's heart began to beat a little more quickly.

"Many months back I received a letter from Mrs. Van der Pol about this house, the girls you have living here, and some of your plans," Tory continued. "I have been praying for you and wishing I might help in some way. Of course, since I am apprenticed to M. LeBlanc for five years I could not come to help, although I felt the desire to do so very much."

"But one day just two weeks ago, M. LeBlanc called me into his office." Tory paused. "He had received a visit from the Misses Wright."

She looked earnestly at the small group gathered around her. "M. LeBlanc is a good man, a man who loves the Lord. He knew who I was—what I had been—when he took me on, but he had compassion on me.

"We all agreed that it was best for his business to keep my past in confidence, but . . ." here her voice trailed off, "my designs were beginning to bring me recognition, and we were both somewhat concerned that eventually my past would come out.

"When I received the letter from Mrs. Van der Pol, the Misses Wright explained to M. LeBlanc that I was needed in Denver. They expressed their confidence that the Lord would make a way. And he has.

"M. LeBlanc has released me from my apprenticeship. He and the Misses Wright have decided to anonymously establish me in my own shop here in Denver. M. LeBlanc is sending a large selection of fabrics and notions and several machines here.

"The Misses Wright have provided funds to rent space for the first year. They will remain silent partners in my endeavor, and I will share the profits with them. All I need is a suitable building to begin."

Instinctively, she turned to Rose. "Mrs. Thoresen, that is why I am here. I want to train your girls to design and sew."

"Merciful heavens above!" Rose exclaimed.

Joy gaped. "Mama!"

———

Minister Liáng looked over his shoulder—again.

I would not make a very good investigator, he fretted. He checked his pocket—again—for the note Bao had written. It wasn't signed, and the contents were terse: *Tell this man what he asks.*

Liáng pushed farther back into the shadows, waiting for the woman who cooked for the Chens to return to her home. *The cook in the Chen home is related to Ling-Ling*, Bao had said.

He heard shuffling steps approaching and froze. The steps came closer and Liáng saw the woman, probably in her early fifties, approach the door of the little house.

"Madam Wong." Liáng spoke softly.

The woman jumped and peered into the shadows fearfully. "Who is there?"

"A friend of Bao. May I speak with you?"

She shivered and looked about her, much the same way Liáng had done a moment before. "Quickly." She opened the door and they disappeared inside.

She locked the door behind them and ushered him into her kitchen, closing the door behind her and pulling down the shade on the single window. Only then did she light the lamp on the table nearby.

"Who are you?" She examined Liáng's face. "I do not know you."

"No, nor I you. Our mutual, ah, friend sent me."

"He is in great peril," she hissed. "My daughter has overheard Fang Hua give orders. If they find him . . ."

Liáng nodded. "We suspected as much. I am sorry to involve you, but I have come on an important errand, important enough to risk his safety and ours."

He handed her the note; she read it quickly. "What do you want?"

"May we sit?"

Reluctantly, she agreed. Liáng studied the woman. Her face was lined from years of hard work, but he sensed a good heart in her.

"A few months ago a man who calls himself Morgan came back to Seattle after a long absence. Do you know the man of whom I speak?" He looked steadily at the woman, hoping she could sense his heart, too.

She slowly inclined her head. "Yes."

Liáng hadn't realized he'd been holding his breath until he let it go. "This man, Morgan, grew up in Seattle?"

She nodded again.

"Do you remember when he was young and they called him *Reggie*?"

She chuckled once, silently and without mirth. "Yes."

So close, Lord! So close!

"His real name was Regis, no? Do you remember his last name?"

This time she frowned and thought for a moment. "No; I didn't know him as Regis. I only remember 'Reggie.' He was an arrogant white boy, full of himself, but I do not know a last name."

Liáng deflated. He stared at the table, wondering what to do next. *What would O'Dell do? What would he ask this lady?*

"I believe he has an uncle still living. He raised him, his sister's son."

Liáng's mouth dropped open. "Where . . . how do I find him?"

Madam Wong took the note Bao had sent her and scribbled something on the back. "You will find him here."

Liáng grabbed the scrap of paper and read it. *Freddie Fetch. Bogg's.* "What is this 'Bogg's'?"

She snorted. "The lowest sort of bar on the wharves for the lowest sort of people. You be careful. It is not for Chinese."

She put her hand on his arm. "And that man Freddie is not to be trusted." She made a small gesture, her finger drawn across her throat. Liáng swallowed. He understood. Perfectly.

He nodded. "Thank you."

"You had better go. Tell B—" she stopped herself. "Tell our friend we hope for the best for him."

When Liáng arrived back at the bungalow, he found O'Dell, Bao, and Miss Greenbow waiting up. He quickly conveyed his conversation with Bao's distant cousin-in-law and showed them the scribbled words.

"Freddie Fetch," O'Dell repeated. "Would that make Morgan's name Regis Fetch?"

"Not likely. He was Freddie's sister's son." Liáng hesitated. "This 'Bogg's' is a white man's bar. She warned of the place, said Freddie could not be trusted, warned me not to go there."

O'Dell nodded. "Then I guess I will have to."

Miss Greenbow opened her mouth to object. At a look from O'Dell she closed it.

❧ ✸ ❧

CHAPTER 40

(Journal Entry, April 22, 1910)

Two very notable events have occurred here at Palmer House, and I thank you for both of them, dear Lord. First, Tory has come with the backing of her wealthy patrons to establish a design and sewing house. O Lord, your provision is always so much more than we expect!

The second is the addition of a new girl. Her name is Jenny. She is a funny little thing, just as plain and sweet as a prairie girl from back home. I already love her.

Joy and I described our expectations to her and, I confess, Jenny's eyes became as large as saucers. "Lor', Miss Rose! I've never had no religion!" she said. Joy and I chuckled and Joy, always so practical, told Jenny, "We hope you never 'get religion,' Jenny. We just hope you will come to know God and his Son Jesus."

In closing, Joy has convinced Grant to see Doctor Murphy. They have an appointment this week. We trust you, Lord. In all things, we trust you.

———

O'Dell stared at himself in a mirror. He hadn't had a proper haircut since he'd arrived in Seattle. His black hair crept over his ears and down his neck. He hadn't shaved or bathed since Liáng returned with the words *Freddie Fetch. Bogg's.* Now his face sprouted two days' worth of thick, black whiskers.

Liáng had brought the clothing O'Dell asked for, purchased from the Sisters of Providence's second-hand store. He also brought information, garnered from the nuns, of the notorious bar, *Bogg's.*

"The sisters don't go in the bar, but they know—and are known in—the area. It's notorious for cutthroats, thieves, and homeless drunkards. Only the opium dens are said to be more dangerous. The sisters distribute sandwiches, coffee, and blankets to those they find on the streets and in the alleys. They often find men who have been set upon."

"And this is the place Freddie Fetch frequents." O'Dell thought about that. "Morgan is brilliant and fastidious; quite the contrast, I should think."

He donned the worn trousers, shirt, pea coat, and midnight-blue watch cap. "Do I fit the part?"

"Too neat and clean," Miss Greenbow answered. Her mouth was pinched, and O'Dell could feel the worry radiating from her.

He took off the coat, grabbed a sharp knife from the kitchen, and sawed a ragged hole around a pocket flap. With a few nicks he removed a button, popped the stitches around a shoulder, and pulled on the sleeve.

"Better?"

She nodded. "Still too clean."

O'Dell hobbled into the back yard and dragged the coat across the steps and yard, grinding in dirt and grass stains. He was breathless when he finished. Miss Greenbow appeared at his side with a mug of coffee. She dumped it across the breast and one sleeve.

"Let that soak in a bit, then wipe some of it off."

Bao and Liáng watched silently, concern etched on their faces.

An hour later it was dark. Liáng would drive O'Dell into town and drop him near the wharves. With a well-chewed cigar butt in his mouth, O'Dell finally looked the part. He nodded and opened the door.

"Not yet," Miss Greenbow said softly. "We must pray."

For once, O'Dell thought prayer was a good idea. They huddled together in the sitting room, O'Dell and Bao awkward and unsure. Liáng simply laid his hand upon O'Dell's shoulder and prayed. When he finished, Miss Greenbow added her petition:

"Father in heaven, I am asking for your ministering angels to follow Mr. O'Dell everywhere he goes this night. We ask that they watch over him and safeguard his steps, Lord, and we ask that you lead Mr. O'Dell to the information we need to find Mei-Xing."

She paused, her voice rough with emotion. "You are the Most High God—and with you, Lord, nothing is impossible."

And with you, Lord, nothing is impossible. O'Dell trembled at the power those few words had over him.

With you, Lord, nothing is impossible.

—

"Well now, let's take a listen, shall we?" Doctor Murphy smiled professionally and placed a stethoscope on Grant's chest. He listened for a few moments then moved the instrument and listened again.

Joy watched him carefully and, although it was barely perceptible, she saw his brows twitch and draw together ever-so-briefly. He listened to Grant's lungs as he drew deep breaths. Then he listened to Grant's heart again.

Noncommittally, he said, "Mr. Michaels, my office is on the second floor of this building, which has two stories above us. I would like you to walk to the first floor and then run the flights to the top floor and then run back to me. Are you able to do that?"

"Yes, Doctor." But Joy saw Grant glance away. Even as he excused himself, he would not meet Joy's eyes. Her breath caught and she turned to the physician.

The doctor studied her in return. "Do not alarm yourself, Mrs. Michaels. It may be nothing."

They waited for Grant. When the doctor looked at his pocket watch the second time, Joy jumped to her feet and sprinted from his office. She stared down the stairwell and saw nothing.

Taking the stairs two at a time, she ran up to the third floor. There, on the landing, his head between his legs, sat Grant. He was breathing hard. His face was white, tinged in blue.

"Oh, my darling!" Joy exclaimed. "Why did you not tell the doctor you could not do it? Why do harm to yourself?"

Grant shook his head. He still could not answer. It was minutes before his color began to return and Joy heard other steps in the stairwell. The doctor, his nurse with him, soon reached them. With their help Grant returned to the doctor's office.

"I am sorry I asked this exercise of you, Mr. Michaels. You made out that you are fine, but you have not been forthcoming, eh?" The doctor, his face solemn, forced Grant to admit to the truth.

"Ever since the influenza, I have felt weak. I had hoped that with time and proper rest, I would recover," he confessed. "But rather than improving, I am more winded and easily fatigued each day."

Joy felt as though she had been punched in her stomach. She gripped Grant's arm and held it tightly. "Why didn't you tell me?" she whispered.

His chin dropped to his chest. "I'm sorry. I-I did not want to worry you. Again."

The doctor nodded, watching them. Pursing his lips he said, "I would like you to see a colleague of mine, a specialist."

"Certainly, if you feel it necessary," Grant replied uneasily. "What kind of specialist?"

"A cardiologist," the doctor replied. He wrote the specialist's information on a card and handed it to Grant.

"I will call for an appointment," Grant said weakly, taking the card.

"No need. My nurse has already called. He will see you in 30 minutes."

Joy's head began to spin. This could not be happening! *Lord Jesus! Please help us!*

Dr. Peabody listened to Grant's heart and lungs in the same manner the other physician had and questioned Grant about his symptoms. Finally, he sat back in his chair.

"I have an idea of what is going on," he began, "But I would like my associate to confer with me. Do you have any objections to my asking him to join us?"

A few minutes later, Dr. Peabody's young assistant joined them. He, too, listened. And frowned. The look he exchanged with Dr. Peabody pierced Joy's heart. After a short whispered consultation, Dr. Peabody's associate excused himself.

"Mr. and Mrs. Michaels, I'm afraid I have some difficult news."

After dinner the household gathered in the great room to hear what Grant and Joy had to tell them. "I have been feeling more and more tired as of late," Grant began calmly. "Today Joy and I saw several doctors."

He looked around at the shocked expressions on the dear faces around them. How he hated to pain them further!

Joy held his arm as if afraid to let go. It was the pinched expression on her face that hurt him the most. Her mother, who already knew what he was about to say, sat calmly with her head bowed.

"The doctors say that in most cases, the effects of influenza are temporary," Grant continued slowly. "However, in a very few cases, the virus may attack the heart. The symptoms are increasing fatigue and chest palpitations."

He looked down. "They tell me that the left side of my heart is damaged, likely by the virus. This is why I have been so tired."

He remained silent until Tabitha exploded, demanding what everyone else was afraid to ask. "But what does that mean?"

Grant remained silent several more minutes. Beside him, Joy's soundless tears dropped onto their joined hands.

"There is nothing they can do to reverse the damage," he said quietly. "It means my heart is failing."

That night when they climbed into bed, Grant and Joy reached for each other. They said nothing, but held on to each other. Joy sought and found Grant's lips, kissing them desperately. He responded with a fierceness that stunned her and enflamed them both until the intensity of their passion took them both to that place of release.

CHAPTER 41

Mei-Xing awakened abruptly. The door to the apartment had just slammed shut. Su-Chong was stumbling about the sitting room. Had he been drinking again? He had not forced himself on her for weeks—would he do so this night?

She sat up, trembling, but no longer in fear. *O God, I will be afraid no longer. Whatever comes, I choose to be free . . . in you.*

She listened, following his movements to the little washroom and then into the other bedroom, hearing cupboards and drawers opening and slamming, contents being tossed against the wall. *What is he doing?*

He is coming.

The light above her head came on and Su-Chong fumbled to fit the key into the lock. Objects clattered to the floor on his side of the door and still he struggled to unlock the door.

Mei-Xing steeled herself. *If he is that drunk . . .*

The door swung open. He sagged against it, breathing heavily. "Come. Here."

Mei-Xing crept to the door, saw the large basin lying beside Su-Chong's feet, towels, bandages, scissors, and alcohol scattered near it. Then she saw the blood. So much blood.

Su-Chong grabbed the neck of her nightdress. His hand dripped blood, splattering her face and gown. Mei-Xing shrieked and tried to pull away, but he only pulled her closer. And laughed.

He is hysterical, insane, Mei-Xing's mind shouted.

"Once again, Mei-Xing, you will help me." He laughed again, more quietly. "I seem to have dropped some things."

Grabbing the skirt of her shift, he nodded to the items strewn at his feet. "Pick them up." Mei-Xing obeyed, piling the items into the basin.

"Set them on the table. Then help me to sit."

She did as he demanded. When she was ready to move him, he grasped the neck of her nightdress again and closed the door behind them. He handed her the key. "Lock it."

Mei-Xing fumbled with the key, feeling his grip on her gown tighten, pulling her to him. When the lock clicked over, Su-Chong gestured. "Put it over my head."

Mei-Xing lifted the chain over his head, watched her freedom dangle about his neck, so close but still so far away.

When he was seated, she tried to help him remove his shirt, but it was too painful and difficult. "Cut it off," he ordered through gritted teeth.

A few moments later she stared at the damage with dread. A bullet had penetrated Su-Chong's chest below his left collarbone. They both stared at the ragged entrance wound. It was draining blood heavily.

"So," he whispered.

He knows I will never be able to get it out! Mei-Xing automatically grabbed a clean hand towel, folded it twice, and pressed it against the bleeding hole. He flinched. "Hold this tightly," she said softly.

She opened a bottle of alcohol and prepared some heavy gauze pads. Holding the bottle over the wound she looked Su-Chong in the face. "This will hurt."

He nodded. Mei-Xing quickly peeled back the folded towel, holding it below the wound, and poured the alcohol. Su-Chong gasped and cried out. Just as quickly she pressed the towel back into place. The blood had already soaked through.

They stared at each other. Finally, she whispered, "I . . . I could get help for you."

As he looked away for a long moment Mei-Xing prayed, *O God, I am calling on you*!

When Su-Chong turned his eyes back to her, she knew what his answer would be.

"No, Mei-Xing." He shook his head slowly. "Do what you can to stop the bleeding."

Not "remove the bullet," not "fix me up." Only "do what you can." Resigned words uttered with deadly finality.

She licked her lips and looked over the supplies. She folded the other clean towel and wadded two small gauze pads tightly. When she was ready, she pulled off the drenched towel and packed a wadded pad into the hole. Over it she placed another, holding it as firmly as she could.

On top of the pads she placed the clean, folded towel and held all in place with the heel of her hand, leaning her weight on it. With great difficulty she maintained the pressure while wrapping long bandages about Su-Chong's neck and muscular chest. She used her teeth to tighten the final knots.

"You must lie down and, and keep pressure on it," Mei-Xing murmured. She gestured to her bed.

Through her ministrations, Su-Chong had said nothing. He had stared straight ahead at the wall. Still staring, he spoke, and Mei-Xing could scarcely hear him. "No. I will go to my own bed."

"But, but you must not move about and, and I will have to change the bandages when they soak through," Mei-Xing protested.

He placed his hand on her shoulder. "Help me up." He stumbled to the door. "Unlock it for me."

Slowly, Mei-Xing did as he asked. He pushed the door open. She tried to press past him, but he blocked her, pushed her back. Blood was already seeping from the towel, dripping onto the floor. "Give me the key."

"No, Su-Chong! No!" Mei-Xing was crying now, begging him. "Please, do not leave me in here!"

Her voice rose to a keening cry as the door closed and he fumbled determinedly to re-lock it. She leaned against the barrier between them, calling out in anguish as Su-Chong dragged himself into his room.

Eventually she calmed and took stock. Two jars sat on the table. One was full, the other half empty. Trembling, her hands and nightgown sticky with Su-Chong's blood, Mei-Xing crumpled to the floor.

O Jesus, I need you . . .

———

As Liáng drove through the darkness, O'Dell sipped on a bottle of cheap wine. He shuddered. "Nasty stuff." He spit a mouthful into his hand and rubbed it in his hair, dabbed more on his coat.

They didn't talk. Liáng let him off down a particularly dark alleyway after giving O'Dell the directions the sister at the thrift store had provided him.

"God go with you," he said, his voice raw.

O'Dell nodded and got out. Liáng drove off, and O'Dell sauntered over to the alley wall, leaning against it, letting his eyes adjust, steeling himself for the walk ahead. He rubbed his back against the rank-smelling bricks.

"Just for good measure, my dear Miss Greenbow," he whispered.

He wandered toward the bar, taking his time, stopping to swill a little of the wine. A dark figure detached itself from the shadows and approached him. O'Dell stiffened.

"Give a brother a taste, man?"

O'Dell handed over the bottle. A filthy hand reached for it eagerly, lifting the lip of the bottle to a grizzled face.

"Than's, man. Say, you got any spare change?"

O'Dell knew better than to show money. "Sorry."

"Tha's all righ'." He disappeared into the shadows again.

O'Dell kept meandering through the streets, some stinking of rotting garbage, all moist with mold and decay. He knew he was near the water when the tang of salt and flotsam overpowered the other smells.

Bogg's was tacked onto the side of a decaying warehouse abutting a listing dock. In the dim light O'Dell picked out knots of longshoremen, some obviously fallen on hard times, standing about or sitting with their backs against the warehouse. He ignored them and sauntered toward the bar.

Inside, he made his way to an open seat about half-way down the bar. "Gimme a beer," he muttered, slapping down a nickel. He stared down at the bar, looking neither left nor right, letting his ears acclimate. When his beer arrived, he gulped at it, and set it sloshing back on the counter.

He ignored the men around him. He knew he was being scrutinized, but he focused only on the mug he gripped with both hands.

"'Nuther," he muttered when he'd downed the last of the first one. This one he nursed slowly. Still he kept his eyes and nose pointed down, minding his own business. Listening.

He slowly finished his beer and laid out another nickel. A fresh beer landed on the bar and the nickel disappeared.

The men around him had resumed their whispered conversations. O'Dell wondered how many beers he would have to drink before he could look around for Freddie Fetch.

He shifted on the stool, belched loudly, and pushed off from the bar. His head swum and he grabbed the counter.

"Steady, mate." The man next to him growled, not turning.

"Right," O'Dell said to himself. He belched again and stole a glance deeper into the room.

Down at the end of the bar he spotted an old man studying him with thirsty, conniving eyes. O'Dell lurched in that direction. His painful hip aided in exaggerating his state of inebriation. He'd seen an empty seat next to the old guy.

When he reached the seat, he more or less fell onto it. Then he signaled the bartender and laid out a dime on the bar.

"Buy an old man a beer, mister?"

O'Dell slowly looked up. "Sure. Why not." He signaled the bartender again and pointed at the old man. Two beers, the foaming heads dripping from the mugs, slid their way.

"Cheers," the old man said, grinning. O'Dell did not miss the way the old man was sizing him up.

"Likewise," O'Dell answered. They drank in silence until the old man wiped his mouth.

"Name's Freddie. Yours?"

O'Dell nearly choked. He wiped his mouth slowly. "Jones."

"Buy 'nother round?" Freddie wasn't shy.

"Depends."

"Oh? On what?" The cunning look was more pronounced.

Because of the beer, O'Dell's judgment was not as sharp as it should have been, but he figured it would only worsen as the evening dragged on. He took the plunge. "You have a nephew named Reggie?"

"Whadda you want t' know fer?"

O'Dell heard anger in the old man's words, and gambled that Freddie would be happy to rat on Reggie. "I might have a bone to pick with him."

Freddie studied O'Dell for a long minute.

"Worthless piece o'—" He cursed his nephew in colorful language that even O'Dell had never heard before.

"No love lost between you, I take it."

For the next ten minutes Freddie, plied with two more beers, told O'Dell everything he'd ever need or want to know about Reggie—everything but his last name.

"M' sister Maggie got 'erself knocked up. Th' skunk niver married 'er. Well, I give 'er an' 'er son a place t' live, roof over they's head after 'is ol' man run out on 'em," Freddie snarled. "But was 'e ever grateful? Not that 'un. Actin' like 'e was above everybody."

He nodded at O'Dell. "Oh, yes! Smarter an' better, 'e was! Always with 'is nose in a derned book an' correctin' 'is elders. Oh, 'e hated it when 'is ma called 'im *Reggie* like sh' did when 'e's a tot."

Freddie's snicker was downright malicious. "Hated it bad when we called 'im tha', 'e did. An' tha's why we did it."

All I need is his last name. O'Dell struggled to contain his temper.

"Near t' got 'imself kilt when 'e took up with them Chinese." Freddie sniggered. "Woulda served 'im too right. They don't tolerate no high-an'-mighty guff."

"You don't want to mess with them," O'Dell agreed.

"Nosirree, Bob," Freddie cackled.

"Heard Reggie left town again," O'Dell managed to say casually.

"Tha's what I heered, too."

O'Dell had reached the end of his patience. "Well, I need to go, Freddie. Thanks for the conversation."

"I thank ya fer th' brews," Freddie smiled.

"Say, what was Reggie's last name again? It's on the tip of my tongue," It was O'Dell's best shot.

"Saint John," Freddie spat. "*Reggie bloomin' Saint John.* Like 'e's anythin' near a saint!"

"That's right." O'Dell dropped two quarters in front of the old man. "Save some for tomorrow, Freddie." He slid off his stool and steadied himself and his aching hip.

"Yer a good man, Jones," Freddie replied. His eyes narrowed. Behind O'Dell's back, Freddie's chin jerked in his direction. Three men slowly unfolded from a booth.

O'Dell stumbled toward the front of the bar and out the door, relieved to be breathing the cool air, rank as it was, rather than the foul, sweltering fog of the bar.

He'd swallowed five beers in the course of the evening, and they'd caught up to him, but only his brain felt numb: His hip ached incessantly and his stiff shoulder throbbed. Sharp twinges reminded him that his hand was still mending.

He straightened and began to amble away from the docks. He was to meet Liáng at a predetermined intersection. *Reggie bloomin' Saint John.*

He'd leave for Denver as soon as he could make the arrangements. Send ahead and have Pounder's men search for property records under the name of *Regis St. John*.

He was a block from the bar when two men stepped out of the shadows several yards ahead of him. Their expressions were hard, merciless. He heard a third set of feet shuffle behind him and off to the right.

"I don't want any trouble," he said quietly.

"Shouldn't ask so many questions if you don't want trouble." The man off to O'Dell's right cracked his knuckles.

"Empty your pockets now. By the way, Freddie thanks you for the beers."

O'Dell remembered the words Liáng had used to describe Bogg's: *The lowest sort of bar on the wharves for the lowest sort of people.* He dumped a handful of coins onto the street and then turned his trouser pockets inside out, letting the men see them.

O'Dell knew it was only prelude. The men slowly advanced on him, one of them brandishing a length of pipe.

His body broke into a cold sweat, and the weeks of agony crashed through his mind—he had no defense, no reserves left. He could save himself no longer.

O God, I can't do this again! Help me—save me!

CHAPTER 42

The room grew hot, the air stale. On the other side of the brick-filled windows Mei-Xing knew there would be a sweet, refreshing breeze. She leaned against the cool bricks, but could find not a wisp of fresh air to relieve her.

She had not heard Su-Chong move for two days. In her heart she knew . . . he was dead.

The last jar on the table, a quarter full, mocked her. She had carefully rationed the water, but the room was so warm and she was so thirsty. The little water remaining would soon be gone. There would be no more.

"Lord, no one knows I am here but you," she whispered. "No one will find me until it is too late. I do not care so much for myself, but—"

Come to me all you who are weary, worn, and heavy-burdened. Come to me, and I will give you rest for your souls.

She bowed her head and prayed. "You have given me such peace and rest, Jesus. I am so glad I have you. I will die in this room, but I will die with a free soul . . . and then I will truly see you, touch you! I love you so."

A sob caught in her dry throat. "Lord, please help me not to be afraid to die this way . . ."

———

The thugs charged O'Dell, landing blows on his head, shoulders, and sides. Lights exploded behind his eyes.

And then nothing.

He was on his knees, wiping fresh blood from his nose, his temple. His attackers were backing up, backing away. Their eyes were focused somewhere behind O'Dell.

"There you are, Mr. Jones."

O'Dell thought he recognized the voice. He could not yet get up.

"We've been looking for you—it is time to leave and you promised to help us load our carts into the truck."

The thugs melted into the shadows. O'Dell tried to get to his feet and failed. Strong arms came to his aid.

Through a bloody haze he saw a white wimple dance before his eyes and a silver cross float below it. Within the headdress two worry lines deepened.

"We should go," she said firmly. Another set of arms helped her guide O'Dell to a hand cart. They dropped him into the cart and, together, the two sisters pushed the cart with him in it, to where, O'Dell did not know.

Eventually they stopped next to a rusty truck. Strong hands again helped O'Dell to his feet. He finally looked the sister in the face.

"I've only seen you in all white," he muttered incoherently.

Five nuns scurried around him, loading the hand carts into the truck. He only had eyes for the sixth as she steadied him. Her habit, like the other sisters, was all black with the exception of the stiff, rounded, white headdress. Under cover of night their black habits were invisible, so only their heads, faces, hands, and the large crosses dangling from their necks were readily evident.

"I come down here once or twice a month," Sister Mary James answered, wiping the blood from his eyes, "to work among the poor. It helps me keep my heart and priorities right. When I do, I exchange my white nursing habit for a regular one so I don't stand out."

O'Dell's mind still echoed the words, *O God, I can't do this again! Help me—save me!*

"But how did you find me?" he whispered.

"We were passing out blankets and simply saw you from a distance as you came toward us. I recognized you . . . even in your, um, getup."

O God! Help me! Save me!

"But why did they run?"

"Those men? They leave us strictly alone. Even *they* know who we are and who protects us." She helped O'Dell into the cab of the truck. The nuns, with the exception of the driver and Sister Mary James, climbed into the back with the hand carts.

"Has anyone ever called you an angel?" O'Dell wondered aloud. "She prayed for angels to keep me safe."

"Did she?" Sister Mary James knew he was rambling in shock. "The Bible says angels are God's ministering spirits, sent to watch over those who inherit salvation." O'Dell heard the peaceful smile in her voice.

Miss Greenbow's prayer and his own frantic cry for help were indelibly branded into his soul. *Father in heaven, I am asking for your ministering angels . . . that they watch over him and safeguard his steps . . .*

O God, I can't do this again! Help me! Save me!
You are the Most High God—and with you, Lord, nothing is
impossible.

———

Edmund O'Dell breathed in the sights and sounds of Denver
as he pressed through the crush of people on the platform. His
face bore fresh bruises and a neat line of stitches across an
eyebrow. He carried a cane, but used it mostly when walking up
and down steps.

O'Dell had telephoned the Denver Pinkerton office the morning
after he'd learned Morgan's real, full name. Pinkerton men, aided by
Pounder's marshals, were, at this moment, again combing through
Denver County property files.

O'Dell had insisted that they hurry. It was tedious work since the
files were organized by property number and legal description, not
by date or owner, but O'Dell had felt compelled to push them.

Over the long distance call, Jackson, the new head of the Denver
office, reported that Cal Judd had been tried, convicted, and
sentenced to a year in prison. Everyone involved in the trial, perhaps
excepting Judd, had been astounded at the light sentence.

The defense had pressed prosecution witnesses on these points:
Yes, Marshal Tyndell was recovering; yes, Esther and the other girls
had been voluntarily practicing their, er, trade before meeting Judd;
no, the marshal had not obtained a warrant before raiding the
brothel.

Only the fact that *Judd had fired first* saved the trial.
Nevertheless, money had more than likely changed hands, and
Judd's one-year sentence was nearly half served. Such was "justice"
in Denver.

O'Dell chuckled aloud at the irony. It was a good thing Judd was
still behind bars, because it would be a while before O'Dell would
be fit for another fight.

His last exchanges with Liáng, Bao, and Miss Greenbow back in
Seattle stayed uppermost in his thoughts. He and Liáng had talked
long into that night and they had prayed together before O'Dell fell
into an exhausted sleep.

Before he left Seattle late the next day, O'Dell had asked Bao to forgive him. The man had shaken his head and muttered, "There is nothing to forgive." O'Dell knew how the young man's own guilt weighed him down. Bao was seeking . . . as was he.

Miss Greenbow had searched his face and asked him if he would be returning to Seattle. Asked if he would write to her.

O'Dell thought about the folded paper tucked into his breast pocket. *Darla Greenbow*. Her name was *Darla*. He understood what writing to her would imply.

Perhaps it was time to stop living in regret.

CHAPTER 43

O'Dell dropped his bag at the hotel and immediately took a cab to Pounder's office. He didn't know why, but he sensed that urgency was needed.

"I'm sorry, O'Dell." Pounder truly did sound sorry. "We have found no trace of a Regis St. John or Saint John on any Denver County property record."

O'Dell was stunned. He had arrived in Denver with such confidence and hope! Now he had nothing—no other plan, no other lead. *Nothing.*

The fear that he had failed Mei-Xing, always lurking in the back of his mind, pounced. He could not escape its crushing weight.

O God, help me! Save me!

When had that plea become his daily bread? And yet . . . he took a cleansing breath as fear retreated and peace descended on him.

You are the Most High God! With you, nothing is impossible. He shook his head. He was quickly becoming dependent on those words. He laid his hand over his eyes, absorbing Pounder's information, letting the peace guard his mind. Still, he still felt that sense of urgency propelling him.

"Marshal?" O'Dell scarcely took notice as a stranger stood in the doorway of Pounder's office.

"Chief Groves. What brings you here?" The head U.S. marshal and the Denver police chief shook hands.

"I was in the neighborhood. Wanted to be sociable." Groves was accompanied by a uniformed policeman who kept back a respectful distance.

Groves was new as chief. The honest Denver citizenry was again attempting to combat corruption in the police ranks and city government. They'd elected Groves, a cop with an unimpeachable reputation, to help clean out the department. Pounder did not envy Groves his difficult job.

Groves noticed O'Dell and put out his hand. "Chief Groves."

"O'Dell. Edmund O'Dell," he automatically replied, rising stiffly and taking the chief's hand.

"Pinkerton, right?" Groves eyed O'Dell's slow response and battered face speculatively. "I've heard good things about you."

He turned back to Pounder. "Wanted to pass on some information to you, just in case your men are out and about and see something suspicious. It's a city problem, but, well, we'd welcome your look-out."

Pounder responded congenially. "Be our pleasure, Chief." He recognized that the new chief was trying to promote a cordial relationship between the two law entities.

"We've had a series of break-ins of a most curious nature over the last half year."

"Oh?"

"They occur on a fairly regular basis, every five to seven days. The burglars target stores and homes but don't take the usually burgled property, like jewelry or money. When the owners report the break-ins, they often cannot say what is missing, only that a window is broken, a door jimmied. A few have reported food stuffs taken and one reported the theft of clothing. Lately, alcohol has been stolen along with food."

"What kind of clothing?" O'Dell snapped out of his stupor.

Groves thought about it. "Women's clothing, some dresses and such. But that was back in November."

"November?"

Groves consulted the uniformed officer with him. "Booker. Was the clothing reported missing in November?"

The officer shifted on his feet. "Yessir. Women's dresses and personal items."

O'Dell's heart began to hammer. "Are these break-ins scattered throughout the city or localized?"

Groves looked to Pounder who nodded his go-ahead. "Actually, all within a mile radius of this area—" he strode to a city map "right here." His finger scribed a circle near the center of town.

O'Dell stared at Groves. "Dean Morgan and Su-Chong Chen escaped the county jail in November. They have not been recaptured. I have good reason to believe that Morgan is clean away from Denver, but his bodyguard, Su-Chong Chen, may still be here. Holed up."

"After seven months?" Groves looked skeptical.

O'Dell glanced from Groves to Pounder and back. "Mei-Xing Li disappeared in November. *November 20.* We now know she was once engaged to Su-Chong Chen."

Groves frowned, his mind working quickly. "What I hadn't mentioned yet is that a little more than a week ago a man named Curtis Shupe reported that he winged an intruder. He described the man as small but light on his feet, very fit. Black hair."

O'Dell nodded emphatically. "That is a good description of Su-Chong Chen. Does the owner know how badly he was wounded?"

"No, but he left a good trail of blood. We got dogs out the next day, but by then it was pouring rain. We lost the trail. Just bad luck."

Pounder looked at Groves and O'Dell then drew with his finger on the city map. "So somewhere within this circle."

O'Dell didn't know where the command came from, only that he gave it a voice. "Hurry. We must hurry."

Two marshals and two Pinkerton men accompanied O'Dell to the county courthouse. O'Dell carried the rolled-up city map from Pounder's wall under his arm. He'd demanded and received the undivided assistance of the county clerk.

"We'll do it differently this time," O'Dell stated flatly. He'd rolled out the map on a table and weighted its edges with books. "We only want to see the records for this area," he pointed to a chalked circle on the map.

"What name this time?" The two marshals and two Pinkerton men had already searched the county records twice, the first time for every known alias of Shelby Franklin/Dean Morgan; the second time for Regis St. John.

O'Dell leaned over the map, intent on the area within the circle. "Read the owners of each property aloud."

He raised his face from the map to the four men and the clerk. "I'll know it when I hear it." His look defied the others to say differently.

The marshals and Pinkerton agents exchanged dubious looks but, at the clerk's direction, began pulling the records that conformed to the circled area. After a few minutes, one of the marshals began reading names.

"Bigalow, Eugenia B."

"Porter, Afron M."

"McGuffin, Edna Mae."

"Cromwell, George Carson."

O'Dell focused on each name, willing himself to stay alert and fully engaged.

"Sayer, David L."

"Sayer, Martha G."

"Pearsall, Bonna Beulow."

"Garrett, Delanie W."

The names droned on. O'Dell began to whisper under his breath, *O God, help us. Please help Mei-Xing. Don't let us be too late.*

"Van Buren, Robert L."

"Van Buren, Peter M."

"Goldblum, Hymie Joseph."

An hour passed. The fear began to push and nag at O'Dell. He refused to listen to it.

"Pringle, James C."

"Fetch, Margaret L."

"Yeardly, Carroll G."

"What? Stop." O'Dell awkwardly got up. "Read the last one again."

"Yeardly, Carroll G."

"No!" he shouted. "The one before that!"

The marshal scrabbled with the papers. "Fetch, Margaret L."

"Fetch." O'Dell grabbed the record from the marshal. "Margaret Fetch."

Maggie Fetch.

"This is it."

Marshals and Denver policemen surrounded the brick building. At Pounder and Groves' direction, the men kept themselves hidden from the building's many windows.

Pounder shared new information with O'Dell. "This building is managed by an attorney. He collects the rents and pays all the utilities. And has never met the owner."

O'Dell, the butt of a cigar clamped between his teeth, studied the building. He walked his eyes from window to window, up the four stories. Nothing.

He and Pounder worked their way around to another side, keeping well out of sight, O'Dell sweeping his eyes over the windows—

He nudged Pounder. "Fourth floor, left."

Pounder squinted, saw what O'Dell had. "Those windows bricked in?"

"That's what I see."

Pounder glanced at O'Dell. "That floor is supposedly vacant."

"I'll bet you a box of cigars it isn't."

"That," Pounder answered, "is a bet I won't take."

They circled back to Groves and his men and Pounder reported, "Top floor, northeast corner. Windows are bricked in."

"Two sets of stairs, sir," one of Groves' men reported. "On opposite corners of the building." Quickly Groves separated his men into two groups.

"I want to go first," O'Dell suddenly insisted. "It will take me a while to get up four flights. Let me go first and reconnoiter." He laughed harshly, pointing to his cane. "One man gimping up the stairs will allay suspicion."

Groves studied O'Dell. "I give you five minutes to get up the stairs. Wait for us at the top. Got it?"

O'Dell tipped his head. "Thank you." He tossed his derby to a uniformed man. "Hold on to that for me."

By the time O'Dell reached the last flight, he hip ached abominably, but he had seen nothing of Su-Chong, nothing suspicious. Far below he heard the faint shuffling of many feet beginning their rush up the stairs.

O'Dell pressed forward, reaching the fourth floor and easing his head around the corner. The hall was unlit. Quiet. He left his cane at the top of the stairs and moved cautiously until he reached the door he believed to belong to the bricked-in windows.

Creeping up to the door, he placed his ear against it and listened. He heard nothing. In fact, the silence was ominous.

Revolver drawn, he waited to the side of the door. If Su-Chong heard the approaching policemen and opened the door, O'Dell was ready for him.

Within seconds uniformed officers appeared carrying a two-man battering ram. The door splintered open and policemen, guns at the ready, swarmed into the room. O'Dell followed and stopped.

The stench of death filled the apartment. Dried blood spattered the floor. O'Dell drew a handkerchief and covered his mouth; some of the less-seasoned officers gagged and retreated into the hall.

O'Dell's blood turned to ice in his veins even as his heart cried out, *Oh God! With you nothing is impossible! Nothing!*

"Mr. O'Dell!" Groves' sergeant called him from beyond the sitting room.

On wooden legs, O'Dell followed the sound of his voice. The smell of death grew stronger. Then he was standing next to a bed, looking down at the blackened body of Su-Chong Chen.

"Sir! We have a locked door!"

O'Dell wheeled about, nearly falling as his hip clenched. Someone was battering the lock on the door just down the short hall. O'Dell shouldered men aside to reach the doorway.

The room was warm, almost unbearably so. A tiny, prone figure lay on the floor. O'Dell shoved aside another officer and dropped to the floor beside her, lifting her up in his arms.

"Mei-Xing!"

Her eyes were closed and sunken; her cracked lips were barely open, and he could sense no breath in her. But her skin, while cool, was not cold.

"Water! Get me water!" he shouted.

Pounder himself took the glass a young officer brought and grabbed a piece of gauze lying on the nearby table. O'Dell dipped the gauze and wiped it across Mei-Xing's lips, squeezing drops between them. He squeezed more and then wiped the gauze across her eyes, her face.

He saturated the gauze and squeezed more water into her mouth. "Come on! Mei-Xing! Swallow! Swallow the blasted water!"

Her eyes fluttered. He dribbled more water into her mouth, willing her to swallow the live-giving liquid.

And then she did.

ℭHAPTER 44

May 6, 1910

The city of Denver had received days of unusually warm spring weather, but Denverites knew better than to trust in fickle spring. In Palmer House, they saw the ominous thunderheads building in the distance, felt the storm's approach, and ran throughout the house to close and latch windows.

Breona stared out her bedroom window, eyeing flashes of lightning as the storm marched toward them. As the clouds built, the daylight grew dull and dim.

She sighed. Almost a year ago she had run up the front steps of this house, filled with hope and energy. Today she found herself asking if she could bear to stay at Palmer House. She had lost so much.

She shook herself sternly. *Ye have a home here, Breona Byrne, a family. Ye have those as is lovin' and carin' fer ye.* And she loved them so much in return! Rose, Joy, Grant, Marit, Billy, Little Will, Mr. Wheatley, the girls . . .

For the first time in her life, she loved and was loved so much. She just hadn't known that in such love dwell both joys and sorrows. She was learning how deeply those sorrows could wound.

Ye canna be mournin' forever what is goon, she told herself. But one look at the tidy little bed on the other side of the room from hers, and the ache for her friend Mei-Xing returned. Would they ever know what had become of her?

It wasn't like Breona to stand about idly—it just wasn't in her nature. So she chided herself. *'Tis bein' th' coomin' storm*, was the weak excuse she offered, but she knew it was her heavy heart that weighed down her hands and feet.

She decided to watch the play of lightning just a few more minutes. And then, *no more excuses.*

A motorcar stopped down the street. A man wearing a bowler slowly emerged and turned to help another passenger out. Through the trees, Breona caught a glimpse of a slight, dark-haired woman. Her over-large dress billowed about her as the storm edged closer.

The man, carefully supporting the woman, walked her along the edge of the street until they paused not far from the gate to Palmer House. They appeared to be talking, or at least the man was.

He removed his hat and bent toward her in a solicitous manner while the woman leaned on his arm.

Breona watched them idly for a moment and then her gaze shifted as the wind bowed the tops of the Ponderosa pines clustered out in the yard. It was high time she got back to her work.

She hesitated and glanced back. The woman, really just a young girl, stood staring at the front door of the house, while the man ran a hand through his dark hair, something of frustration in his gesture, something familiar . . .

Breona opened her window and leaned out, the curtains blowing wildly about her. The movement caught the eye of the woman standing far below at the gate. She gazed up and into Breona's face; the girl's hand slowly lifted to acknowledge her.

Breona began to tremble. The girl's hand dropped to her side. She bowed her head and turned away. Breona could see the man remonstrating with the woman as she brushed off his arm and slowly began making her way toward the parked car.

"Nay," Breona whispered. "Nay, dinna ye go . . ."

She slammed the window shut and flew down the stairs into the entry hall, her leather-soled shoes slapping and clattering on the steps and on the parquet floor. She fumbled with the locked door, threw it open wide, and ran across the porch and down the stairs.

Rose, at work in the great room, leapt to her feet. Wind howled through the front door and into the house. "What is it?" she cried anxiously.

Breona could not see the woman anymore! "Wait! Wait! Mei-Xing!" she called into the roaring wind.

She screamed again, "Mei-Xing! Mei-Xing!" as she was running to the gate. Swinging it wide and heedless of traffic, she ran out into the street, ran past the man . . . *O'Dell?*

She disregarded him and ran on. Thunder boomed over them. There. She was not far away, not moving quickly. Breona hastened to her. It *was* Mei-Xing. It was her friend! Her sister! She was . . .

"Mei-Xing!"

Mei-Xing weaved unsteadily on her feet, the wind pulling at her. "Breona." The single word was flat, emotionless. Her lips were cracked and crusted, her face pinched, drawn.

Breona placed an arm about her to steady her. She leaned close to her ear. "Aye, m' sweet lass." She turned Mei-Xing about and began to slowly lead her back toward the house.

"I can't . . ." Mei-Xing protested weakly. But she had no strength to resist.

"Aye, ye can. 'Tis home ye air!"

Rose and Marit saw them from the gate. They began to weep. As Breona and Mei-Xing drew near, Marit gasped and Rose gripped her arm. "Shush now," she whispered.

Mei-Xing saw Rose and her face crumpled. Then she was in Rose's arms, sobbing, and Rose was holding her with all the love she had in her heart.

"You are safe, little one. You are home. We will never let go of you," Rose whispered again and again. Breona and Marit simply wrapped their arms about both Rose and Mei-Xing, holding them close.

Over them the storm broke. Lightning and thunder cracked and sizzled. It did not move them.

O'Dell stood aside, his face turned away, trying to school the tide of emotions sweeping him away. Rain fell, pounding the ground, and drops streamed their way down his face. He automatically pulled a cigar from his breast pocket and, as he brought it up to his mouth, surreptitiously swiped the moisture away.

It took O'Dell a few minutes to navigate the steps up the front porch. He was tired and sore, having used his injured hip more in the last two days than the last two months.

Finally, he stepped inside the front door of Palmer House, but held himself back, peering into the great room from the entryway, an awkward voyeur to Mei-Xing's homecoming.

Or he *tried* to hold himself back. Mr. Wheatley spied him and hustled over to pump his hand and pull him into the room. Before long, Breona, Marit, and Rose took turns embracing and tearfully thanking him for bringing Mei-Xing home.

As they greeted him they stared askance at the swollen bruises across his face and the tidy row of stitches above his eye. Noted the cane and his stiff leg.

"Looks like you tangled with a mountain cat," Mr. Wheatley suggested with raised brows.

"I lost," O'Dell replied, trying to laugh it off, but he knew already that these people saw through his deflection. They would wait, some patiently, others not so patiently, for him to speak of his injuries. This happy moment was not that time.

O'Dell backed unobtrusively into a corner near the door and leaned against the wall. He looked about him and saw one or two girls he did not know. They stared at him with wide eyes. He nodded a silent greeting.

Billy had answered Breona's telephone call to the shop. When Joy finally understood the garbled words Billy kept shouting, she locked the doors and threw the closed sign over.

O'Dell was still standing awkwardly apart from the others when Billy, Sarah, Corrine, and Joy ran into the house. O'Dell turned stiffly at their entrance, leaning on his cane. The expression on their faces became concerned when they saw him.

"It will be all right," O'Dell shrugged. "I will mend. It is over now, and Mei-Xing is home."

He shook hands with them in turn and studied Joy for a moment. Then Billy, Sarah, and Corrine left to greet Mei-Xing, leaving Joy and O'Dell alone in the corner of the room.

O'Dell glanced around, anxious to change the subject. "Where is Grant? And Flinty? I haven't seen them yet."

Joy shuddered and looked down. "We had . . . a difficult winter," she murmured.

O'Dell looked sharply at her then. He had not heard any news. "Is everything all right?"

Her eyes shifted away. "The influenza." She swallowed. "We lost Flinty."

O'Dell reeled. "Flinty? Flinty!"

Suddenly he had to find a chair and sit. He lowered himself stiffly into one of the great room's several overstuffed chairs.

Joy sat across from him, saw his pained disbelief. She added softly, "You know Flinty was ailing when he came to live with us. He came to us so we could watch over him. He . . . he weathered the flu when it struck, but, but, afterwards his heart just gave out."

O'Dell sat for several moments without speaking. *Flinty gone!* Finally, he whispered, "I am sorry, Joy, so sorry. I know all of you will miss Flinty. I surely will."

He raised his head. "And Grant? Where is he?"

Joy answered more slowly. "He, too, was hit hard by the influenza and . . . has not yet fully recovered. He tires easily, so, so when we came home, he went to rest in our cottage."

She is holding something back, O'Dell thought, but he would not press her. "Can I do anything to help?"

She shook her head. "Thank you, no. He has a good doctor."

Just then Marit appeared. "Miss Joy, Mei-Xing vould like to speak to you and Miss Rose privately. Vill you come?"

Joy nodded and turned back to O'Dell. He reached across and took her hand and held it in both of his.

"Joy, I will pray that Grant recovers soon. Nothing is impossible with God." He pressed her hand gently before letting it go.

Joy's eyes swept up to his in surprise. For a long moment they shared a look. *Something has happened*, Joy realized in astonishment. *Something has changed.*

She swallowed. "What will you do now? Where will you go?"

"Not a good idea for me to be near Denver when Cal Judd finishes his sentence in a few months." He laughed and thought for a moment. "I think I will be going back to Seattle."

CHAPTER 45

They sequestered themselves in the small parlor. Joy and Mei-Xing sat next to each other, Joy holding Mei-Xing's hands. Rose pulled her chair close and seated herself across from them.

What was obvious to all had not yet been spoken of: Tiny Mei-Xing was quite large with child. No one had asked, no one had yet alluded to it.

"I must make a confession to you," Mei-Xing said, looking from Rose to Joy soberly. "I have never fully confided in anyone, have never trusted anyone completely, but now. . . . It is important that I hold nothing back."

Rose nodded. Joy squeezed her hands gently.

"I loved Su-Chong from the time I was a little girl," Mei-Xing whispered, "and he said he loved me. Our families were very close and hoped we would marry. It was what both of us wanted, also." Rose handed Mei-Xing her hanky and Mei-Xing wiped her eyes.

"I would have been so happy to marry Su-Chong!" she quietly sobbed. "But I discovered by accident that his family was very corrupt—they sold drugs and did with young Chinese girls the very thing Morgan and Banner did with us! Worse, Su-Chong worked for his father in all these evil businesses.

"Oh, how my heart broke when I knew he was not the honorable man I had believed him to be! I could not marry him then, but I was afraid to tell my father why. I knew it would crush him. He and Wei Lin Chen, Su-Chong's father, had been friends for many years.

"So I simply told Su-Chong I would not marry him. No one understood, and my father was so disappointed, my mother so very angry with me. She would not even look at me any longer.

"I decided then that I *must* tell my father why I had refused Su-Chong—but Wei Chen's family warned me . . ." she broke down again. "They, they *threatened* my father's life! Oh, Miss Rose, what was I to do?

"After I refused Su-Chong, he begged me many times to change my mind. When I would not, he became angry, almost violent. In a rage, he left Seattle. I think I knew then that something was not right with him. He is an only child, you see. His mother had indulged and spoiled him. He was not accustomed to being denied anything he wished for.

"No one knew where Su-Chong had gone. For more than a year no one heard from him. All during that year, Su-Chong's mother, Fang Hua, blamed me."

Here Mei-Xing shuddered. "Fang Hua is a spiteful woman. She began to publicly scorn and humiliate me—I became such a great shame to my family that I could no longer be seen in public with them." She bowed her head and sobs racked her body until Rose and Joy became alarmed.

"Mei-Xing, Mei-Xing, you must stop." Rose stroked her head and her back. "Please, little one. For the baby. You must not harm the baby."

"Ohhhh, *the baby*!" Mei-Xing was nearly hysterical now. "Oh, what will I do?"

"Shhh, shhh," Rose soothed. "Come now. You are trying to make a clean breast of everything. We do not judge you, Mei-Xing. We will hear you out, and God will provide the answers."

After a few minutes Mei-Xing was able to take up her story again. "Su-Chong has a cousin, Bao. His mother was Wei Chen's sister. Bao told me he understood how lonely I must have felt, how hopeless." Mei-Xing's eyes focused far away, and Rose and Joy could tell she was remembering.

"He told me of a wonderful, childless Chinese couple here in Denver. They wanted a daughter, he told me. They would take me in and treat me as their own, he said. My leaving would remove the continual shame from my parents, and I would have a new life. He bought me a ticket and after dark he took me to the station."

The skin down Joy's arms prickled. She looked at her mother; they had heard the same horrible tale from Minister Liáng.

Mei-Xing stared and her voice took on a mechanical tone. "Instead of a loving couple, *Darrow* met me when the train reached Denver. You know . . . what happened."

She turned to Joy, dazed. "It was Fang Hua's doing. When Su-Chong returned home, she told him I was dead, but she was behind Bao's deceit. She hated me that much, you see.

"When, when you took me in, you showed me real love and taught me forgiveness. I forgave Bao and Fang Hua . . . and Jesus forgave me! Oh, Miss Rose, Miss Joy, I was so content here with you.

"You see, like Su-Chong, I, too, was raised in a privileged home—waited on, pampered, educated. I never lifted a finger in my life until you taught me the satisfaction of working hard with my hands and the joy of real family bonds. I learned to cook and to clean and to take care of others because I loved them.

"Then one night I came home from Mrs. Palmer's, and Su-Chong was waiting for me on the front porch. I don't remember what he did to me, but I awoke in a bedroom. The windows in the room were bricked up! I could hear nothing from the outside. When I tried to open the door, it was locked. After a while, Su-Chong opened it."

She told Rose and Joy how Su-Chong had been wounded, how she had nursed him until he recovered, how he had asked to know how she had ended up in Corinth. How she had first refused but had finally given in and told him how she had been tricked and forced into slavery. How he had then held her gently and comforted her . . .

Rose and Joy glanced at each other, their thoughts running along the same lines.

"I know," Mei-Xing said sadly. "I know what you are thinking and you are right. I should never have spoken to him of such intimate things. I think—no, *I know*—that the Lord was warning me, but I . . . ignored his warnings, again and again."

Her voice dropped. "I have had to come to terms with how deceitful my heart can be. I confess now that I told Su-Chong those things because I desired his love and comfort so badly."

She sighed and wiped tears from her eyes. "He held me and kissed me and for one single moment I let myself remember what it was like before I knew who he really was, before I broke our engagement—just one single moment! Then we, we just, just . . . You know what we did."

Joy started to say something, but Mei-Xing said softly, "Please. I must finish."

She straightened resolutely. "Once we began, I was powerless to stop it. But after a few weeks, I could tell Su-Chong was becoming restless. He wanted to leave, but if he released me, I would be a threat to him.

"I could tell he was thinking of just . . . leaving me to die locked in that room. For some reason, he could not bring himself to do so.

"Oh, I knew I had sinned! I called on the Lord and confessed my sins to him. Yet for a long while it seemed as though he was far away and did not answer. I felt such guilt and shame."

Her voice sank to a whisper. "And I began to suspect that I was with child."

"All along Su-Chong had gone out in the night to steal food for us. Then he began drinking. When he drank up all the alcohol in the apartment, he began stealing that, too.

"He would drink every day. When he drank he brooded and became angry and, and, I think, more irrational. I tried to stay quiet and out of Su-Chong's way as his drinking increased. As much as he would allow, I would stay in my room.

"Other times when he drank he would look at me and I knew that look. I knew what he was thinking. He would come into my room at night and—"

The girl began to cry again. "He grew to hate me, but still forced himself on me again and again. Even though he came to my bed many times in the next weeks, he despised me. He called me a whore—he said if a hundred men had used me, he was defiling himself with me—but then he would take me again.

"It was when he said I was a whore—that I would always be a whore!—that I remembered, Miss Rose! I remembered what you said that morning when you told us about Bethy Ann. And then—at last!—Jesus spoke to me! *Come unto me*, he said! *Come unto me, you who are weary and heavy burdened.*

Mei-Xing bowed her head and wept, so weak she had not even the strength to cover her face. "I surrendered my guilt. I was not afraid to die then."

"But now, Mei-Xing?" Joy asked in a hushed voice.

"Now what shall I do?" Her anguish pierced Joy's heart. "I did not die, and now I must live! I am not afraid for myself, but I will have a child and I am not married. My child will have no father and my shame will follow *him* all his life . . ."

Joy shook her head slowly. "There is no shame in you, Mei-Xing. You know that Jesus has already forgiven you. You said so yourself."

"But the baby . . ."

"You are not alone in this world, Mei-Xing," Rose replied. "You will have your baby here, and you will not raise him or her alone."

"No. Not alone," Joy quietly agreed, a tiny smile tugging at the corner of her mouth.

Something in Joy's tone caused Rose to turn. Just then a commotion in the entry way interrupted them.

"Where is she? Move out of my way, now. I *will* see her!"

Mei-Xing, Joy, and Rose looked at each other. Mei-Xing, her eyes wide with dread, whispered, "Mrs. Palmer!"

The door flew open. Breona scurried aside to allow Martha Palmer entrance. The little woman, out of breath, hobbled in as quickly as she could manage.

Rose and Joy stood up, Rose happily greeting her. "Mrs. Palmer!" Mei-Xing slowly rose to her feet, swaying unsteadily.

"Where is the dear girl? I—" Martha Palmer ignored Joy and Rose and reached for Mei-Xing. "Oh, my dear! Oh, thank ye, Lord!" she said breathlessly, grasping Mei-Xing's hand to steady herself.

Martha Palmer lifted her face to study Mei-Xing. She took in the sunken eyes and cracked, peeling lips.

"Are you all right, missy?" her voice was low and gentle, warm and healing.

Mei-Xing, tears standing in her eyes, could not look at the old woman. "Yes, ma'am. I believe I will be. Thank you."

Martha Palmer could not miss Mei-Xing's averted gaze. She frowned. Then she glanced down . . . and froze. She said nothing for a long moment.

Slowly she lifted her fragile, gnarled hand from Mei-Xing's. She gently placed it on Mei-Xing's swollen belly.

"Yes, you will be all right," she said firmly. "Both of you will be all right. I promise."

———

(Journal Entry, May 6, 1910)

Lord, Palmer House was aglow in celebration today as our lost lamb, Mei-Xing, came home! That she brings her unborn child with her is a surprise and challenge none of us expected. Even so, we will welcome this child, Lord, and willingly provide the love and support Mei-Xing and her baby need.

Father, you have proven yourself faithful in so many ways. You tell us that your thoughts toward us are of peace and not of evil, that when we call on you, you will hearken. Your word and your faithfulness give me such great hopes for the future!

We still have much to do for you, Lord. Yes, I know that as we press forward we will encounter obstacles and challenges. Nevertheless, our trust and our strength are in you.

By your grace we will not falter.

The End

$\mathcal{P}$OSTSCRIPT

October 1910

He didn't know how Fang Hua's thugs had found him. Morgan had established himself with a new identity in faraway Sacramento, and yet it had not been far enough! Fang Hua's men had found and delivered him to her, in one piece. More or less.

And now Dean Morgan, *Regis St. John*, lately known as Paul Westford, calculated his odds and did not find them to his liking. He really had but one card left up his sleeve, and to reveal it here, now, was to leave him with nothing in reserve.

On the other hand, the information would certainly do him no good if he were *dead*.

"Madam Chen," he opened, bowing low before the woman's chair. "I have important news for you."

She eyed him as a snake eyes a doomed mouse before it strikes.

"You can have no news that will be of significance to me," she hissed. With a flick of her hand, the four men in the room were on him. Two of them pushed him to his knees; another moved behind him and pulled his head back. He heard the 'snick' of a knife leaving its scabbard.

"What of your son?" he choked the words out. "What of your lineage?"

She leapt to her feet, shrieking, "*I have no son*! Because of you *he is dead*! Because of you, my husband's line will die with him!"

Fear vied with rage on Fang Hua's face. She feared what Wei Lin Chen would do if he ever discovered her connection with Su-Chong's dishonor and death. Her husband might still be able to father children, but *she* was too old to bear him another son! Would he divorce her and take a young wife, one who could give him many children?

She snarled at Morgan, "My husband's line may die with him, but I say that *you* will die first. And I will pleasure myself with the sounds of your agony!"

She began to curse him in Mandarin and did not hear what he yelled back, but Morgan was certain the men holding him down did. They shifted nervously. He continued to talk, knowing that if he kept repeating himself the old witch would eventually stop ranting long enough to hear him.

She did finally stop, swaying unsteadily on her feet, wiping spittle from her mouth. Morgan kept repeating himself, waiting for his words to sink in.

He saw the very moment when what he'd said penetrated the fog of her rage.

"Wha . . . what did you say?"

Morgan was silent, watching for the crazed light to leave her eyes. She strode over and squatted in front of him.

"What did you say?" she insisted, her words ragged, harsh.

The man behind him released his hold and Morgan took a careful, cleansing breath, cautiously watching her. "I said, there is a child. You have a grandson."

Morgan had no idea whether the child was a male or a female. His informants had only told him that the *Little Plum Blossom* had been five or six months gone when she had been returned her to the bosom of her friends in Denver. Surely she would have had the child by now.

He watched Fang Hua's eyes dilate and saw a light spark in them. She slowly stood up.

"So. The little whore gave him a child . . ." she walked back to her chair and sank into it. He swallowed as she fixed him with her cold, mad eyes.

"You will tell me where to find my grandson."

$\mathscr{S}$OILED $\mathscr{D}$OVE $\mathscr{P}$LEA

Gentlemen of the jury: You heard with what cold cruelty the prosecution referred to the sins of this woman, as if her condition were of her own preference. The evidence has painted you a picture of her life and surroundings. Do you think that they were embraced of her own choosing? Do you think that she willingly embraced a life so revolting and horrible? Ah, no! Gentlemen, one of our own sex was the author of her ruin, more to blame than she.

Then let us judge her gently. What could be more pathetic than the spectacle she presents? An immortal soul in ruin! Where the star of purity once glittered on her girlish brow, burning shame has set its seal and forever. And only a moment ago, they reproached her for the depths to which she had sunk, the company she kept, the life she led. Now, what else is left her? Where can she go and her sin not pursue her? Gentlemen, the very promises of God are denied her. He said: "Come unto me all ye that labor and are heavy laden and I will give you rest." She has indeed labored, and is heavily laden, but if, at this instant she were to kneel before us all and confess to her Redeemer and beseech His tender mercies, where is the church that would receive her? And even if they accepted her, when she passed the portals to worship and to claim her rest, scorn and mockery would greet her; those she met would gather around them their spirits the more closely to avoid the pollution of her touch. And would you tell me a single employment where she can realize "Give us our daily bread?"

Our sex wrecked her once pure life. Her own sex shrink from her as they would the pestilence. Society has reared its relentless walls against her, and only in the friendly shelter of the grave can her betrayed and broken heart ever find the Redeemer's promised rest.

They told you of her assumed names, as fleeting as the shadows on the walls, of her sins, her habits, but they never told you of her sorrows, and who shall tell what her heart, sinful though it may be, now feels? When the remembered voices of mother and sisters, whom she must see no more on this earth, fall again like music on her erring soul, and she prays God that she could only return, and must not—no—not in this life, for the seducer has destroyed the soul.

You know the story of the prodigal son, but he was a son. He was one of us, like her destroyers; but for the prodigal daughter there is no return. Were she with her wasted form and bleeding feet to drag herself back to home, she, the fallen and the lost, which would be her welcome? Oh, consider this when you come to decide her guilt, for she is before us and we must judge her. They (the prosecution) sneer and scoff at her. One should respect her grief, and I tell you that there reigns over her penitent and chastened spirit a desolation now that none, no, none but the Searcher of all hearts can ever know.

None of us are utterly evil, and I remember that when the Saffron Scourge swept over the city of Memphis in 1878, a courtesan there opened wide the doors of her gilded palace of sin to admit the sufferers, and when the scythe of the Reaper swung fast and pitiless, she was angelic in her ministering. Death called her in the midst of her mercies, and she went to join those she tried to save. She, like those the Lord forgave, was a sinner, and yet I believe that in the days of reckoning her judgment will be lighter than those who would prosecute and seek to drive off the earth such poor unfortunates as her whom you are to judge.

They wish to fine this woman and make her leave. They wish to wring from the wages of her shame the price of this meditated injustice; to take from her the little money she might have—and God knows, gentlemen, it came hard enough. The old Jewish law told you that the price of a dog, nor the bite of such as she, should come not within the house of the Lord, and I say unto you that our justice, fitly symbolized by this woman's form, does not ask that you add to the woes of this unhappy one, one only asks at your hands the pitiful privilege of being left alone.

The Master, while on Earth, while He spake in wrath and rebuke to the kings and rulers, never reproached one of these. One he forgave. Another he acquitted. You remember both—and now looking upon this friendless outcast, if any of you can say to her, 'I am holier than thou' in the respect which she is charged with sinning, who is he? The Jews who brought the woman before the Savior have been held up to execution for two thousand years. I always respected them. A man who will yield to the reproaches of his conscience as they did has the element of good in him, but the modern hypocrite has no such compunctions. If the prosecutors of the woman whom you are trying had brought her before the Savior, they would have accepted His challenge and each one gathered a rock and stoned her, in the twinkling of an eye. No, Gentlemen, do as your Master did twice under the same circumstances that surround you. Tell her to go in peace.

Source: http://en.wikipedia.org/wiki/Soiled_Dove_Plea. Public Domain.

ABOUT THE AUTHOR

Vikki Kestell's passion for people and their stories is evident in her readers' affection for her characters and unusual plotlines. Two often-repeated sentiments are, "I feel like I know these people" and "I'm right there, in the book, experiencing what the characters experience."

Vikki holds a Ph.D. in Organizational Learning and Instructional Technologies. She left a career of twenty-plus years in government, academia, and corporate life to pursue writing full time. "Writing is the best job ever," she admits, "and the most demanding."

Also an accomplished speaker and teacher, Vikki and her husband Conrad Smith make their home in Albuquerque, New Mexico.

To keep abreast of new book releases, sign up for her newsletter on her website at **http://www.vikkikestell.com/** or connect with her on Facebook at **http://www.facebook.com/TheWritingOfVikkiKestell**.

Made in the USA
Columbia, SC
25 April 2017